Nada the Lily

H. Rider Haggard

ÆGYPAN PRESS

Nada the Lily
A publication of
ÆGYPAN PRESS

www.aegypan.com

Nada the Lily

DEDICATION

SOMPSEU:

For I will call you by the name that for fifty years has been honored by every tribe between Zambesi and Cape Agulbas, — I greet you!

Sompseu, my father, I have written a book that tells of men and matters of which you know the most of any who still look upon the light; therefore, I set your name within that book and, such as it is, I offer it to you.

If you knew not Chaka, you and he have seen the same suns shine, you knew his brother Panda and his captains, and perhaps even that very Mopo who tells this tale, his servant, who slew him with the Princes. You have seen the circle of the witch-doctors and the unconquerable Zulu *impis* rushing to war; you have crowned their kings and shared their counsels, and with your son's blood you have expiated a statesman's error and a general's fault.

Sompseu, a song has been sung in my ears of how first you mastered this people of the Zulu. Is it not true, my father, that for long hours you sat silent and alone, while three thousand warriors shouted for your life? And when they grew weary, did you not stand and say, pointing towards the ocean: "Kill me if you wish, men of Cetywayo, but I tell you that for every drop of my blood a hundred avengers shall rise from yonder sea!"

Then, so it was told me, the regiments turned staring towards the Black Water, as though the day of Ulundi had already come and they saw the white slayers creeping across the plains.

Thus, Sompseu, your name became great among the people of the Zulu, as already it was great among many another tribe, and their nobles did you homage, and they gave you the Bayéte, the royal salute, declaring by the mouth of their Council that in you dwelt the spirit of Chaka.

Many years have gone by since then, and now you are old, my father. It is many years even since I was a boy, and followed you when you went up among the Boers and took their country for the Queen.

Why did you do this, my father? I will answer, who know the truth. You did it because, had it not been done, the Zulus would have stamped out the Boers. Were not Cetywayo's *impis* gathered against the land, and was it not because it became the Queen's land that at your word he sent them murmuring to their kraals?* To save bloodshed you annexed the country beyond the Vaal. Perhaps it had been better to leave it, since "Death chooses for himself," and after all there was killing — of our own people, and with the killing, shame. But in those days we did not guess what we should live to see, and of Majuba we thought only as a little hill!

Enemies have borne false witness against you on this matter, Sompseu, you who never erred except through over kindness. Yet what does that avail? When you have "gone beyond" it will be forgotten, since the sting of ingratitude passes and lies must wither like the winter veldt. Only your name will not be forgotten; as it was heard in life so it shall be heard in story, and I pray that, however humbly, mine may pass down with it. Chance has taken me by another path, and I must leave the ways of action that I love and bury myself in books, but the old days and friends are in my mind, nor while I have memory shall I forget them and you.

Therefore, though it be for the last time, from far across the seas I speak to you, and lifting my hand I give your "Sibonga"† and that royal salute, to which, now that its kings are gone and the "People of Heaven" are no more a nation, with Her Majesty you are alone entitled: —

Bayéte! Baba, Nkosi ya makosi!
Ngonyama! Indhlovu ai pendulwa!
Wen' o wa vela wasi pata!
Wen' o wa hlul' izizwe zonke za patwa nguive!
Wa geina nge la Mabun' o wa ba hlul' u yedwa!
Umsizi we zintandane e ziblupekayo!
Si ya kuleka Baba!
Bayéte, T' Sompseu!‡

---

* "I thank my father Sompseu for his message. I am glad that he has sent it, because the Dutch have tired me out, and I intended to fight them once and once only, and to drive them over the Vaal. Kabana, you see my *impis* are gathered. It was to fight the Dutch I called them together; now I send them back to their homes." — Message from Cetywayo to Sir. T. Shepstone, April, 1877.

† Titles of praise.

‡ Bayéte, Father, Chief of Chiefs!
Lion! Elephant that is not turned!
You who nursed us from of old!
You who overshadowed all peoples and took charge of them,

and farewell!

H. Rider Haggard

To Sir Theophilus Shepstone, K.C.M.G., Natal. 13 September, 1891

And ended by mastering the Boers with your single strength!
Help of the fatherless when in trouble!
Salutation to you, Father!
Bayéte, O Sompseu!

Preface

*T*he writer of this romance has been encouraged to his task by a purpose somewhat beyond that of setting out a wild tale of savage life. When he was yet a lad, — now some seventeen years ago, — fortune took him to South Africa. There he was thrown in with men who, for thirty or forty years, had been intimately acquainted with the Zulu people, with their history, their heroes, and their customs. From these he heard many tales and traditions, some of which, perhaps, are rarely told nowadays, and in time to come may cease to be told altogether. Then the Zulus were still a nation; now that nation has been destroyed, and the chief aim of its white rulers is to root out the warlike spirit for which it was remarkable, and to replace it by a spirit of peaceful progress. The Zulu military organization, perhaps the most wonderful that the world has seen, is already a thing of the past; it perished at Ulundi. It was Chaka who invented that organization, building it up from the smallest beginnings. When he appeared at the commencement of this century, it was as the ruler of a single small tribe; when he fell, in the year 1828, beneath the assegais of his brothers, Umhlangana and Dingaan, and of his servant, Mopo or Umbopo, as he is called also, all southeastern Africa was at his feet, and in his march to power he had slaughtered more than a million human beings. An attempt has been made in these pages to set out the true character of this colossal genius and most evil man, — a Napoleon and a Tiberiius in one, — and also that of his brother and successor, Dingaan, so no more need be said of them here. The author's aim, moreover, has been to convey, in a narrative form, some idea of the remarkable spirit which animated these kings and their subjects, and to make accessible, in a popular shape, incidents of history which are now, for the most part, only to be found in a few scarce works of reference, rarely consulted, except by students. It will be obvious that such a task has presented difficulties, since he who undertakes it must for a time forget his civilization, and think with the mind and speak with the voice of a Zulu of the old regime. All the horrors perpetrated by the Zulu tyrants cannot be published in this polite age of melanite and torpedoes; their details have, therefore, been suppressed. Still much remains, and those who think it wrong that massacre and fighting should be written of, — except by special correspondents, — or that the sufferings of mankind beneath one of the world's most cruel tyrannies should form the groundwork of romance, may be invited to leave this book unread. Most, indeed nearly all, of the historical incidents here recorded are substantially true. Thus, it is said that Chaka did actually kill his mother, Unandi, for the reason given, and destroy an entire tribe in the Tatiyana cleft, and that he prophesied of the coming of the white man after receiving his death wounds. Of the incident of the Missionary and the furnace of logs, it is impossible to speak so certainly. It came to the writer from the lips of an old traveler in "the Zulu"; but he cannot discover any confirmation of it. Still, these kings undoubtedly put their soldiers to many tests of equal severity. Umbopo, or Mopo, as he is named in this tale, actually lived. After he had stabbed Chaka, he rose to great eminence. Then he disappears from the scene, but it is not accurately known whether he also went "the way of the assegai," or perhaps, as is here suggested, came to live near Stanger under the name of Zweete. The fate of the two lovers at the mouth of the cave is a true Zulu tale, which has been considerably varied to suit the purposes of this romance. The late Mr. Leslie, who died in 1874, tells it in his book "Among the Zulus and Amatongas." "I heard a story the other day," he says, "which, if the power of writing fiction were possessed by me, I might have worked up into a first-class sensational novel." It is the story that has been woven into the plot of this book. To him also the writer is indebted for the artifice by which Umslopogaas obtained admission to the Swazi stronghold; it was told to Mr. Leslie by the Zulu who performed the feat and thereby won a wife. Also the writer's thanks are due to his friends, Mr. F. B. Fynney,* late Zulu border agent, for much information given to him in bygone years by word of mouth, and more recently through his pamphlet "Zululand and the Zulus," and to Mr. John Bird, formerly treasurer to the Government of Natal, whose compilation, "The Annals of Natal," is invaluable to all who would study the early history of that colony and of Zululand.

As for the wilder and more romantic incidents of this story, such as the hunting of Umslopogaas and Galazi with the wolves, or rather with the hyenas, — for there are no true wolves in Zululand, — the author can only say that they seem to him of a sort that might well have been mythically connected with the names of those heroes. Similar beliefs and traditions are common in the records of primitive peoples. The

---

* I grieve to state that I must now say the late Mr. F. B. Fynney.

club "Watcher of the Fords," or, to give its Zulu name, U-nothlola-maz-ibuko, is an historical weapon, chronicled by Bishop Callaway. It was once owned by a certain Undhlebekazizwa. He was an arbitrary person, for "no matter what was discussed in our village, he would bring it to a conclusion with a stick." But he made a good end; for when the Zulu soldiers attacked him, he killed no less than twenty of them with the Watcher, and the spears stuck in him "as thick as reeds in a morass." This man's strength was so great that he could kill a leopard "like a fly," with his hands only, much as Umslopogaas slew the traitor in this story.

Perhaps it may be allowable to add a few words about the Zulu mysticism, magic, and superstition, to which there is some allusion in this romance. It has been little if at all exaggerated. Thus the writer well remembers hearing a legend how the Guardian Spirit of the Ama-Zulu was seen riding down the storm. Here is what Mr. Fynney says of her in the pamphlet to which reference has been made: "The natives have a spirit which they call Nomkubulwana, or the Inkosazana-ye-Zulu (the Princess of Heaven). She is said to be robed in white, and to take the form of a young maiden, in fact an angel. She is said to appear to some chosen person, to whom she imparts some revelation; but, whatever that revelation may be, it is kept a profound secret from outsiders. I remember that, just before the Zulu war, Nomkubulwana appeared, revealing something or other which had a great effect throughout the land, and I know that the Zulus were quite impressed that some calamity was about to befall them. One of the ominous signs was that fire is said to have descended from heaven, and ignited the grass over the graves of the former kings of Zululand. . . . On another occasion Nomkubulwana appeared to someone in Zululand, the result of that visit being, that the native women buried their young children up to their heads in sand, deserting them for the time being, going away weeping, but returning at nightfall to unearth the little ones again."

For this divine personage there is, therefore, authority, and the same may be said of most of the supernatural matters spoken of in these pages. The exact spiritual position held in the Zulu mind by the Umkulunkulu, — the Old — Old, — the Great — Great, — the Lord of Heavens, — is a more vexed question, and for its proper consideration the reader must be referred to Bishop Callaway's work, the "Religious System of the Amazulu." Briefly, Umkulunkulu's character seems to vary from the idea of an ancestral spirit, or the spirit of an ancestor, to that of a god. In the case of an able and highly intelligent person like the Mopo of this story, the ideal would probably not be a low one; therefore he is made to speak of Umkulunkulu as the Great Spirit, or God.

It only remains to the writer to express his regret that this story is not more varied in its hue. It would have been desirable to introduce some gayer and more happy incidents. But it has not been possible. It is believed that the picture given of the times is a faithful one, though it may be open to correction in some of its details. At the least, the aged man who tells the tale of his wrongs and vengeance could not be expected to treat his subject in an optimistic or even in a cheerful vein.

Introduction

Some years since — it was during the winter before the Zulu War — a White Man was traveling through Natal. His name does not matter, for he plays no part in this story. With him were two wagons laden with goods, which he was transporting to Pretoria. The weather was cold and there was little or no grass for the oxen, which made the journey difficult; but he had been tempted to it by the high rates of transport that prevailed at that season of the year, which would remunerate him for any probable loss he might suffer in cattle. So he pushed along on his journey, and all went well until he had passed the little town of Stanger, once the site of Duguza, the kraal of Chaka, the first Zulu king and the uncle of Cetywayo. The night after he left Stanger the air turned bitterly cold, heavy grey clouds filled the sky, and hid the light of the stars.

"Now if I were not in Natal, I should say that there was a heavy fall of snow coming," said the White Man to himself. "I have often seen the sky look like that in Scotland before snow." Then he reflected that there had been no deep snow in Natal for years, and, having drunk a "tot" of squareface and smoked his pipe, he went to bed beneath the after-tent of his larger wagon.

During the night he was awakened by a sense of bitter cold and the low moaning of the oxen that were tied to the trek-tow, every ox in its place. He thrust his head through the curtain of the tent and looked out. The earth was white with snow, and the air was full of it, swept along by a cutting wind.

Now he sprang up, huddling on his clothes and as he did so calling to the Kaffirs who slept beneath the wagons. Presently they awoke from the stupor which already was beginning to overcome them, and crept out, shivering with cold and wrapped from head to foot in blankets.

"Quick! you boys," he said to them in Zulu; "quick! Would you see the cattle die of the snow and wind? Loose the oxen from the trek-tows and drive them in between the wagons; they will give them some shelter." And lighting a lantern he sprang out into the snow.

At last it was done — no easy task, for the numbed hands of the Kaffirs could scarcely loosen the frozen reims. The wagons were outspanned side by side with a space between them, and into this space the mob of thirty-six oxen was driven and there secured by reims tied crosswise from the front and hind wheels of the wagons. Then the White Man crept back to his bed, and the shivering natives, fortified with gin, or square-face, as it is called locally, took refuge on the second wagon, drawing a tent-sail over them.

For awhile there was silence, save for the moaning of the huddled and restless cattle.

"If the snow goes on I shall lose my oxen," he said to himself; "they can never bear this cold."

Hardly had the words passed his lips when the wagon shook; there was a sound of breaking reims and trampling hoofs. Once more he looked out. The oxen had "skrecked" in a mob. There they were, running away into the night and the snow, seeking to find shelter from the cold. In a minute they had vanished utterly. There was nothing to be done, except wait for the morning.

At last it came, revealing a landscape blind with snow. Such search as could be made told them nothing. The oxen had gone, and their spoor was obliterated by the fresh-fallen flakes. The White Man called a council of his Kaffir servants. "What was to be done?" he asked.

One said this thing, one that, but all agreed that they must wait to act until the snow melted.

"Or till we freeze, you whose mothers were fools!" said the White Man, who was in the worst of tempers, for had he not lost four hundred pounds' worth of oxen?

Then a Zulu spoke, who hitherto had remained silent. He was the driver of the first wagon.

"My father," he said to the White Man, "this is my word. The oxen are lost in the snow. No man knows whither they have gone, or whether they live or are now but hides and bones. Yet at the kraal yonder," and he pointed to some huts about two miles away on the hillside, "lives a witch doctor named Zweete. He is old — very old — but he has wisdom, and he can tell you where the oxen are if any man may, my father."

"Stuff!" answered the White Man. "Still, as the kraal cannot be colder than this wagon, we will go and ask Zweete. Bring a bottle of squareface and some snuff with you for presents."

An hour later he stood in the hut of Zweete. Before him was a very ancient man, a mere bag of bones, with sightless eyes, and one hand — his left — white and shriveled.

"What do you seek of Zweete, my white father?" asked the old man in a thin voice. "You do not believe in me and my wisdom; why should I help you? Yet I will do it, though it is against your law, and you do wrong to ask me, — yes, to show you that there is truth in us Zulu doctors, I will help you. My father, I know what you seek. You seek to know where your oxen have run for shelter from the cold! Is it not so?"

"It is so, Doctor," answered the White Man. "You have long ears."

"Yes, my white father, I have long ears, though they say that I grow deaf. I have keen eyes also, and yet I cannot see your face. Let me hearken! Let me look!"

For awhile he was silent, rocking himself to and fro, then he spoke: "You have a farm, White Man, down near Pine Town, is it not? Ah! I thought so — and an hour's ride from your farm lives a Boer with four fingers only on his right hand. There is a kloof on the Boer's farm where mimosa trees grow. There, in the kloof, you shall find your oxen — yes, five days' journey from here you will find them all. I say all, my father, except three only — the big black Africander ox, the little red Zulu ox with one horn, and the speckled ox. You shall not find these, for they have died in the snow. Send, and you will find the others. No, no! I ask no fee! I do not work wonders for reward. Why should I? I am rich."

Now the White Man scoffed. But in the end, so great is the power of superstition, he sent. And here it may be stated that on the eleventh day of his sojourn at the kraal of Zweete, those whom he sent returned with the oxen, except the three only. After that he scoffed no more. Those eleven days he spent in a hut of the old man's kraal, and every afternoon he came and talked with him, sitting far into the night.

On the third day he asked Zweete how it was that his left hand was white and shriveled, and who were Umslopogaas and Nada, of whom he had let fall some words. Then the old man told him the tale that is set out here. Day by day he told some of it till it was finished. It is not all written in these pages, for portions may have been forgotten, or put aside as irrelevant. Neither has it been possible for the writer of it to render the full force of the Zulu idiom nor to convey a picture of the teller. For, in truth, he acted rather than told his story. Was the death of a warrior in question, he stabbed with his stick, showing how the blow fell and where; did the story grow sorrowful, he groaned, or even wept. Moreover, he had many voices, one for each of the actors in his tale. This man, ancient and withered, seemed to live again in the far past. It was the past that spoke to his listener, telling of deeds long forgotten, of deeds that are no more known.

Yet as he best may, the White Man has set down the substance of the story of Zweete in the spirit in which Zweete told it. And because the history of Nada the Lily and of those with whom her life was intertwined moved him strangely, and in many ways, he has done more, he has printed it that others may judge of it.

And now his part is played. Let him who was named Zweete, but who had another name, take up the story.

Chapter I

THE BOY CHAKA PROPHESIES

You ask me, my father, to tell you the tale of the youth of Umslopogaas, holder of the iron Chieftainess, the axe Groan-maker, who was named Bulalio the Slaughterer, and of his love for Nada, the most beautiful of Zulu women. It is long; but you are here for many nights, and, if I live to tell it, it shall be told. Strengthen your heart, my father, for I have much to say that is sorrowful, and even now, when I think of Nada the tears creep through the horn that shuts out my old eyes from light.

Do you know who I am, my father? You do not know. You think that I am an old, old witch-doctor named Zweete. So men have thought for many years, but that is not my name. Few have known it, for I have kept it locked in my breast, lest, thought I live now under the law of the White Man, and the Great Queen is my chieftainess, an assegai still might find this heart did any know my name.

Look at this hand, my father — no, not that which is withered with fire; look on this right hand of mine. You see it, though I who am blind cannot. But still, within me, I see it as it was once. Aye! I see it red and strong — red with the blood of two kings. Listen, my father; bend your ear to me and listen. I am Mopo — ah! I felt you start; you start as the regiment of the Bees started when Mopo walked before their ranks, and from the assegai in his hand the blood of Chaka* dropped slowly to the earth. I am Mopo who slew Chaka the king. I killed him with Dingaan and Umhlangana the princes; but the wound was mine that his life crept out of, and but for me he would never have been slain. I killed him with the princes, but Dingaan, I and one other slew alone.

---

* The Zulu Napoleon, one of the greatest geniuses and most wicked men who ever lived. He was killed in the year 1828, having slaughtered more than a million human beings. — EDITOR

What do you say? "Dingaan died by the Tongola."

Yes, yes, he died, but not there; he died on the Ghost Mountain; he lies in the breast of the old Stone Witch who sits aloft forever waiting for the world to perish. But I also was on the Ghost Mountain. In those days my feet still could travel fast, and vengeance would not let me sleep. I traveled by day, and by night I found him. I and another, we killed him — ah! ah!

Why do I tell you this? What has it to do with the loves of Umslopogaas and Nada the Lily? I will tell you. I stabbed Chaka for the sake of my sister, Baleka, the mother of Umslopogaas, and because he had murdered my wives and children. I and Umslopogaas slew Dingaan for the sake of Nada, who was my daughter.

There are great names in the story, my father. Yes, many have heard the names: when the *Impis* roared them out as they charged in battle, I have felt the mountains shake and seen the waters quiver in their sound. But where are they now? Silence has them, and the white men write them down in books. I opened the gates of distance for the holders of the names. They passed through and they are gone beyond. I cut the strings that tied them to the world. They fell off. Ha! ha! They fell off! Perhaps they are falling still, perhaps they creep about their desolate kraals in the skins of snakes. I wish I knew the snakes that I might crush them with my heel. Yonder, beneath us, at the burying place of kings, there is a hole. In that hole lies the bones of Chaka, the king who died for Baleka. Far away in Zululand there is a cleft upon the Ghost Mountain. At the foot of that cleft lie the bones of Dingaan, the king who died for Nada. It was far to fall and he was heavy; those bones of his are broken into little pieces. I went to see them when the vultures and the jackals had done their work. And then I laughed three times and came here to die.

All that is long ago, and I have not died; though I wish to die and follow the road that Nada trod. Perhaps I have lived to tell you this tale, my father, that you may repeat it to the white men if you will. How old am I? Nay, I do not know. Very, very old. Had Chaka lived he would have been as old as I.* None are living whom I knew when I was a boy. I am so old that I must hasten. The grass withers, and the winter comes. Yes, while I speak the winter nips my heart. Well, I am ready to sleep in the cold, and perhaps I shall awake again in the spring.

Before the Zulus were a people — for I will begin at the beginning — I was born of the Langeni tribe. We were not a large tribe; afterwards,

---

* This would have made him nearly a hundred years old, an age rarely attained by a native. The writer remembers talking to an aged Zulu woman, however, who told him that she was married when Chaka was king. — EDITOR

all our able-bodied men numbered one full regiment in Chaka's army, perhaps there were between two and three thousand of them, but they were brave. Now they are all dead, and their women and children with them, — that people is no more. It is gone like last month's moon; how it went I will tell you by-and-bye.

Our tribe lived in a beautiful open country; the Boers, whom we call the Amaboona, are there now, they tell me. My father, Makedama, was chief of the tribe, and his kraal was built on the crest of a hill, but I was not the son of his head wife. One evening, when I was still little, standing as high as a man's elbow only, I went out with my mother below the cattle kraal to see the cows driven in. My mother was very fond of these cows, and there was one with a white face that would follow her about. She carried my little sister Baleka riding on her hip; Baleka was a baby then. We walked till we met the lads driving in the cows. My mother called the white-faced cow and gave it mealie leaves which she had brought with her. Then the boys went on with the cattle, but the white-faced cow stopped by my mother. She said that she would bring it to the kraal when she came home. My mother sat down on the grass and nursed her baby, while I played round her, and the cow grazed. Presently we saw a woman walking towards us across the plain. She walked like one who is tired. On her back was a bundle of mats, and she led by the hand a boy of about my own age, but bigger and stronger than I was. We waited a long while, till at last the woman came up to us and sank down on the veldt, for she was very weary. We saw by the way her hair was dressed that she was not of our tribe.

"Greeting to you!" said the woman.

"Good-morrow!" answered my mother. "What do you seek?"

"Food, and a hut to sleep in," said the woman. "I have traveled far."

"How are you named? — and what is your people?" asked my mother.

"My name is Unandi: I am the wife of Senzangacona, of the Zulu tribe," said the stranger.

Now there had been war between our people and the Zulu people, and Senzangacona had killed some of our warriors and taken many of our cattle. So, when my mother heard the speech of Unandi she sprang up in anger.

"You dare to come here and ask me for food and shelter, wife of a dog of a Zulu!" she cried; "begone, or I will call the girls to whip you out of our country."

The woman, who was very handsome, waited till my mother had finished her angry words; then she looked up and spoke slowly, "There is a cow by you with milk dropping from its udder; will you not even give me and my boy a gourd of milk?" And she took a gourd from her bundle and held it towards us.

"I will not," said my mother.

"We are thirsty with long travel; will you not, then, give us a cup of water? We have found none for many hours."

"I will not, wife of a dog; go and seek water for yourself."

The woman's eyes filled with tears, but the boy folded his arms on his breast and scowled. He was a very handsome boy, with bright black eyes, but when he scowled his eyes were like the sky before a thunderstorm.

"Mother," he said, "we are not wanted here anymore than we were wanted yonder," and he nodded towards the country where the Zulu people lived. "Let us be going to Dingiswayo; the Umtetwa people will protect us."

"Yes, let us be going, my son," answered Unandi; "but the path is long, we are weary and shall fall by the way."

I heard, and something pulled at my heart; I was sorry for the woman and her boy, they looked so tired. Then, without saying anything to my mother, I snatched the gourd and ran with it to a little donga that was hard by, for I knew that there was a spring. Presently I came back with the gourd full of water. My mother wanted to catch me, for she was very angry, but I ran past her and gave the gourd to the boy. Then my mother ceased trying to interfere, only she beat the woman with her tongue all the while, saying that evil had come to our kraals from her husband, and she felt in her heart that more evil would come upon us from her son. Her Ehlose* told her so. Ah! my father, her Ehlose told her true. If the woman Unandi and her child had died that day on the veldt, the gardens of my people would not now be a wilderness, and their bones would not lie in the great gully that is near U'Cetywayo's kraal.

While my mother talked I and the cow with the white face stood still and watched, and the baby Baleka cried aloud. The boy, Unandi's son, having taken the gourd, did not offer the water to his mother. He drank two-thirds of it himself; I think that he would have drunk it all had not his thirst been slaked; but when he had done he gave what was left to his mother, and she finished it. Then he took the gourd again, and came forward, holding it in one hand; in the other he carried a short stick.

"What is your name, boy?" he said to me as a big rich man speaks to one who is little and poor.

"Mopo is my name," I answered.

"And what is the name of your people?"

I told him the name of my tribe, the Langeni tribe.

---

* Guardian spirit. — EDITOR

"Very well, Mopo; now I will tell you my name. My name is Chaka, son of Senzangacona, and my people are called the Amazulu. And I will tell you something more. I am little today, and my people are a small people. But I shall grow big, so big that my head will be lost in the clouds; you will look up and you shall not see it. My face will blind you; it will be bright like the sun; and my people will grow great with me; they shall eat up the whole world. And when I am big and my people are big, and we have stamped the earth flat as far as men can travel, then I will remember your tribe — the tribe of the Langeni, who would not give me and my mother a cup of milk when we were weary. You see this gourd; for every drop it can hold the blood of a man shall flow — the blood of one of your men. But because you gave me the water I will spare you, Mopo, and you only, and make you great under me. You shall grow fat in my shadow. You alone I will never harm, however you sin against me; this I swear. But for that woman," and he pointed to my mother, "let her make haste and die, so that I do not need to teach her what a long time death can take to come. I have spoken." And he ground his teeth and shook his stick towards us.

My mother stood silent awhile. Then she gasped out: "The little liar! He speaks like a man, does he? The calf lows like a bull. I will teach him another note — the brat of an evil prophet!" And putting down Baleka, she ran at the boy.

Chaka stood quite still till she was near; then suddenly he lifted the stick in his hand, and hit her so hard on the head that she fell down. After that he laughed, turned, and went away with his mother Unandi.

These, my father, were the first words I heard Chaka speak, and they were words of prophecy, and they came true. The last words I heard him speak were words of prophecy also, and I think that they will come true. Even now they are coming true. In the one he told how the Zulu people should rise. And say, have they not risen? In the other he told how they should fall; and they did fall. Do not the white men gather themselves together even now against U'Cetywayo, as vultures gather round a dying ox? The Zulus are not what they were to stand against them. Yes, yes, they will come true, and mine is the song of a people that is doomed.

But of these other words I will speak in their place.

I went to my mother. Presently she raised herself from the ground and sat up with her hands over her face. The blood from the wound the stick had made ran down her face on to her breast, and I wiped it away with grass. She sat for a long while thus, while the child cried, the cow lowed to be milked, and I wiped up the blood with the grass. At last she took her hands away and spoke to me.

"Mopo, my son," she said, "I have dreamed a dream. I dreamed that I saw the boy Chaka who struck me: he was grown like a giant. He stalked across the mountains and the veldt, his eyes blazed like the lightning, and in his hand he shook a little assegai that was red with blood. He caught up people after people in his hands and tore them, he stamped their kraals flat with his feet. Before him was the green of summer, behind him the land was black as when the fires have eaten the grass. I saw our people, Mopo; they were many and fat, their hearts laughed, the men were brave, the girls were fair; I counted their children by the hundreds. I saw them again, Mopo. They were bones, white bones, thousands of bones tumbled together in a rocky place, and he, Chaka, stood over the bones and laughed till the earth shook. Then, Mopo, in my dream, I saw you grown a man. You alone were left of our people. You crept up behind the giant Chaka, and with you came others, great men of a royal look. You stabbed him with a little spear, and he fell down and grew small again; he fell down and cursed you. But you cried in his ear a name — the name of Baleka, your sister — and he died. Let us go home, Mopo, let us go home; the darkness falls."

So we rose and went home. But I held my peace, for I was afraid, very much afraid.

Chapter II
MOPO IS IN TROUBLE

Now, I must tell how my mother did what the boy Chaka had told her, and died quickly. For where his stick had struck her on the forehead there came a sore that would not be healed, and in the sore grew an abscess, and the abscess ate inwards till it came to the brain. Then my mother fell down and died, and I cried very much, for I loved her, and it was dreadful to see her cold and stiff, with not a word to say however loudly I called to her. Well, they buried my mother, and she was soon forgotten. I only remembered her, nobody else did — not even Baleka, for she was too little — and as for my father he took another young wife and was content. After that I was unhappy, for my brothers did not love me, because I was much cleverer than they, and had greater skill with the assegai, and was swifter in running; so they poisoned the mind of my father against me and he treated me badly. But Baleka and I loved each other, for we were both lonely, and she clung to me like a creeper to the only tree in a plain, and though I was young, I learned this: that to be wise is to be strong, for though he who holds the assegai kills, yet he whose mind directs the battle is greater than he who kills. Now I saw that the witch-finders and the medicine-men were feared in the land, and that everybody looked up to them, so that, even when they had only a stick in their hands, ten men armed with spears would fly before them. Therefore I determined that I should be a witch-doctor, for they alone can kill those whom they hate with a word. So I learned the arts of the medicine-men. I made sacrifices, I fasted in the veldt alone, I did all those things of which you have heard, and I learned much; for there is wisdom in our magic as well as lies — and you know it, my father, else you had not come here to ask me about your lost oxen.

So things went on till I was twenty years of age — a man full grown. By now I had mastered all I could learn by myself, so I joined myself on to the chief medicine-man of our tribe, who was named Noma. He was old, had one eye only, and was very clever. Of him I learned some tricks and more wisdom, but at last he grew jealous of me and set a trap to catch me. As it chanced, a rich man of a neighboring tribe had lost some cattle, and came with gifts to Noma praying him to smell them out. Noma tried and could not find them; his vision failed him. Then the headman grew angry and demanded back his gifts; but Noma would not give up that which he once had held, and hot words passed. The headman said that he would kill Noma; Noma said that he would bewitch the headman.

"Peace," I said, for I feared that blood would be shed. "Peace, and let me see if my snake will tell me where the cattle are."

"You are nothing but a boy," answered the headman. "Can a boy have wisdom?"

"That shall soon be known," I said, taking the bones in my hand.*

"Leave the bones alone!" screamed Noma. "We will ask nothing more of our snakes for the good of this son of a dog."

---

* The Kafir witch-doctors use the knuckle-bones of animals in their magic rites, throwing them something as we throw dice. — Editor

"He shall throw the bones," answered the headman. "If you try to stop him, I will let sunshine through you with my assegai." And he lifted his spear.

Then I made haste to begin; I threw the bones. The headman sat on the ground before me and answered my questions. You know of these matters, my father — how sometimes the witch-doctor has knowledge of where the lost things are, for our ears are long, and sometimes his Ehlose tells him, as but the other day it told me of your oxen. Well, in this case, my snake stood up. I knew nothing of the man's cattle, but my Spirit was with me and soon I saw them all, and told them to him one by one, their color, their age — everything. I told him, too, where they were, and how one of them had fallen into a stream and lay there on its back drowned, with its forefoot caught in a forked root. As my Ehlose told me so I told the headman.

Now, the man was pleased, and said that if my sight was good, and he found the cattle, the gifts should be taken from Noma and given to me; and he asked the people who were sitting round, and there were many, if this was not just. "Yes, yes," they said, it was just, and they would see that it was done. But Noma sat still and looked at me evilly. He knew that I had made a true divination, and he was very angry. It was a big matter: the herd of cattle were many, and, if they were found where I had said, then all men would think me the greater wizard. Now it was late, and the moon had not yet risen, therefore the headman said that he would sleep that night in our kraal, and at the first light would go with me to the spot where I said the cattle were. After that he went away.

I too went into my hut and lay down to sleep. Suddenly I awoke, feeling a weight upon my breast. I tried to start up, but something cold pricked my throat. I fell back again and looked. The door of the hut was open, the moon lay low on the sky like a ball of fire far away. I could see it through the door, and its light crept into the hut. It fell upon the face of Noma the witch-doctor. He was seated across me, glaring at me with his one eye, and in his hand was a knife. It was that which I had felt prick my throat.

"You whelp whom I have bred up to tear me!" he hissed into my ear, "you dared to divine where I failed, did you? Very well, now I will show you how I serve such puppies. First, I will pierce through the root of your tongue, so that you cannot squeal, then I will cut you to pieces slowly, bit by bit, and in the morning I will tell the people that the spirits did it because you lied. Next, I will take off your arms and legs. Yes, yes, I will make you like a stick! Then I will" — and he began driving in the knife under my chin.

"Mercy, my uncle," I said, for I was frightened and the knife hurt. "Have mercy, and I will do whatever you wish!"

"Will you do this?" he asked, still pricking me with the knife. "Will you get up, go to find the dog's cattle and drive them to a certain place, and hide them there?" And he named a secret valley that was known to very few. "If you do that, I will spare you and give you three of the cows. If you refuse or play my false, then, by my father's spirit, I will find a way to kill you!"

"Certainly I will do it, my uncle," I answered. "Why did you not trust me before? Had I known that you wanted to keep the cattle, I would never have smelt them out. I only did so fearing lest you should lose the presents."

"You are not so wicked as I thought," he growled. "Get up, then, and do my bidding. You can be back here two hours after dawn."

So I got up, thinking all the while whether I should try to spring on him. But I was without arms, and he had the knife; also if, by chance, I prevailed and killed him, it would have been thought that I had murdered him, and I should have tasted the assegai. So I made another plan. I would go and find the cattle in the valley where I had smelt them out, but I would not bring them to the secret hiding place. No; I would drive them straight to the kraal, and denounce Noma before the chief, my father, and all the people. But I was young in those days, and did not know the heart of Noma. He had not been a witch-doctor till he grew old for nothing. Oh! he was evil! — he was cunning as a jackal, and fierce like a lion. . He had planted me by him like a tree, but he meant to keep me clipped like a bush. Now I had grown tall and overshadowed him; therefore he would root me up.

I went to the corner of my hut, Noma watching me all the while, and took a kerrie and my small shield. Then I started through the moonlight. Till I was past the kraal I glided along quietly as a shadow. After that, I began to run, singing to myself as I went, to frighten away the ghosts, my father.

For an hour I traveled swiftly over the plain, till I came to the hillside where the bush began. Here it was very dark under the shade of the trees, and I sang louder than ever. At last I found the little buffalo path I sought, and turned along it. Presently I came to an open place, where the moonlight crept in between the trees. I knelt down and looked. Yes! my snake had not lied to me; there was the spoor of the cattle. Then I went on gladly till I reached a dell through which the water ran softly, sometimes whispering and sometimes talking out loud. Here the trail of the cattle was broad: they had broken down the ferns with their feet and trampled the grass. Presently I came to a pool. I knew it — it was the pool my snake had shown me. And there at the edge of the pool floated the drowned ox, its foot caught in a forked root. All was just as I had seen it in my heart.

I stepped forward and looked round. My eye caught something; it was the faint grey light of the dawn glinted on the cattle's horns. As I looked, one of them snorted, rose and shook the dew from his hide. He seemed big as an elephant in the mist and twilight.

Then I collected them all — there were seventeen — and drove them before me down the narrow path back towards the kraal. Now the daylight came quickly, and the sun had been up an hour when I reached the spot where I must turn if I wished to hide the cattle in the secret place, as Noma had bid me. But I would not do this. No, I would go on to the kraal with them, and tell all men that Noma was a thief. Still, I sat down and rested awhile, for I was tired. As I sat, I heard a noise, and looked up. There, over the slope of the rise, came a crowd of men, and leading them was Noma, and by his side the headman who owned the cattle. I rose and stood still, wondering; but as I stood, they ran towards me shouting and waving sticks and spears.

"There he is!" screamed Noma. "There he is! — the clever boy whom I have brought up to bring shame on me. What did I tell you? Did I not tell you that he was a thief? Yes — yes! I know your tricks, Mopo, my child! See! he is stealing the cattle! He knew where they were all the time, and now he is taking them away to hide them. They would be useful to buy a wife with, would they not, my clever boy?" And he made a rush at me, with his stick lifted, and after him came the headman, grunting with rage.

I understood now, my father. My heart went mad in me, everything began to swim round, a red cloth seemed to lift itself up and down before my eyes. I have always seen it thus when I was forced to fight. I screamed out one word only, "Liar!" and ran to meet him. On came Noma. He struck at me with his stick, but I caught the blow upon my little shield, and hit back. Wow! I did hit! The skull of Noma met my kerrie, and down he fell dead at my feet. I yelled again, and rushed on at the headman. He threw an assegai, but it missed me, and next second I hit him too. He got up his shield, but I knocked it down upon his head, and over he rolled senseless. Whether he lived or died I do not know, my father; but his head being of the thickest, I think it likely that he lived. Then, while the people stood astonished, I turned and fled like the wind. They turned too, and ran after me, throwing spears at me and trying to cut me off. But none of them could catch me — no, not one. I went like the wind; I went like a buck when the dogs wake it from sleep; and presently the sound of their chase grew fainter and fainter, till at last I was out of sight and alone.

Chapter III

MOPO VENTURES HOME

I threw myself down on the grass and panted till my breath came back; then I went and hid in a patch of reeds down by a swamp. All day long I lay there thinking. What was I to do? Now I was a jackal without a hole. If I went back to my people, certainly they would kill me, whom they thought a thief. My blood would be given for Noma's, and that I did not wish, though my heart was sad. Then there came into my mind the thought of Chaka, the boy to whom I had given the cup of water long ago. I had heard of him: his name was known in the land; already the air was big with it; the very trees and grass spoke it. The words he had said and the vision that my mother had seen were beginning to come true. By the help of the Umtetwas he had taken the place of his father Senzangacona; he had driven out the tribe of the Amaquabe; now he made war on Zweete, chief of the Endwande, and he had sworn that he would stamp the Endwande flat, so that nobody could find them anymore. Now I remembered how this Chaka promised that he would make me great, and that I should grow fat in his shadow; and I thought to myself that I would arise and go to him. Perhaps he would kill me; well, what did it matter? Certainly I should be killed if I stayed here. Yes, I would go. But now my heart pulled another way. There was but one whom I loved in the world — it was my sister Baleka. My father had betrothed her to the chief of a neighboring tribe, but I knew that this marriage was against her wish. Perhaps my sister would run away with me if I could get near her to tell her that I was going. I would try — yes, I would try.

I waited till the darkness came down, then I rose from my bed of weeds and crept like a jackal towards the kraal. In the mealie gardens I stopped awhile, for I was very hungry, and filled myself with the half-ripe mealies. Then I went on till I came to the kraal. Some of my people were seated outside of a hut, talking together over a fire. I crept near, silently as a snake, and hid behind a little bush. I knew that they could not see me outside the ring of the firelight, and I wanted to hear what they said. As I guessed, they were talking of me and called me many names. They said that I should bring ill-luck on the tribe by having killed so great a witch-doctor as Noma; also that the people of the headman would demand payment for the assault on him. I learned, moreover, that my father had ordered out all the men of the tribe to hunt for me on the morrow and to kill me wherever they found me. "Ah!" I thought, "you may hunt, but you will bring nothing home to the pot." Just then a dog that was lying by the fire got up and began to sniff the air. I could not see what dog it was — indeed, I had forgotten all about the dogs when I drew near the kraal; that is what comes of want of experience, my father. The dog sniffed and sniffed, then he began to growl, looking always my way, and I grew afraid.

"What is the dog growling at?" said one man to another. "Go and see." But the other man was taking snuff and did not like to move. "Let the dog go and see for himself," he answered, sneezing, "what is the good of keeping a dog if you have to catch the thief?"

"Go on, then," said the first man to the dog. And he ran forward, barking. Then I saw him: it was my own dog, Koos, a very good dog. Presently, as I lay not knowing what to do, he smelt my smell, stopped barking, and running round the bush he found me and began to lick my face. "Be quiet, Koos!" I whispered to him. And he lay down by my side.

"Where has that dog gone now?" said the first man. "Is he bewitched, that he stops barking suddenly and does not come back?"

"We will see," said the other, rising, a spear in his hand.

Now once more I was terribly afraid, for I thought that they would catch me, or I must run for my life again. But as I sprang up to run, a big black snake glided between the men and went off towards the huts. They jumped aside in a great fright, then all of them turned to follow the snake, saying that this was what the dog was barking at. That was my good Ehlose, my father, which without any doubt took the shape of a snake to save my life.

When they had gone I crept off the other way, and Koos followed me. At first I thought that I would kill him, lest he should betray me; but when I called to him to knock him on the head with my kerrie, he sat down upon the ground wagging his tail, and seemed to smile in my face, and I could not do it. So I thought that I would take my chance, and we went on together. This was my purpose: first to creep into my own hut and get my assegais and a skin blanket, then to gain speech with Baleka. My hut, I thought, would be empty, for nobody sleeps there except myself, and the huts of Noma were some paces away to the right. I came to the reed fence that surrounded the huts. Nobody was to be seen at the gate, which was not shut with thorns as usual. It was my duty to close it, and I had not been there to do so. Then, bidding the dog lie down outside, I stepped through boldly, reached the door of my hut, and listened. It was empty; there was not even a breath to be heard. So I crept in and began to search for my assegais, my water-gourd, and my wood pillow, which was so nicely carved that I did not like to leave it. Soon I found them. Then I felt about for my skin rug, and as I did so my hand touched something cold. I started, and felt again. It was a man's face — the face of a dead man, of Noma, whom I had killed and who had been laid in my hut to await burial. Oh! then I was frightened, for Noma dead and in the dark was worse than Noma alive. I made ready to fly, when suddenly I heard the voices of women talking outside the door of the hut. I knew the voices; they were those of Noma's two wives, and one of them said she was coming in to watch by her husband's body. Now I was in a trap indeed, for before I could do anything I saw the light go out of a hole in the hut, and knew by the sound of a fat woman puffing as she bent herself up that Noma's first wife was coming through it. Presently she was in, and, squatting by the side of the corpse in such a fashion that I could not get to the door, she began to make lamentations and to cal down curses on me. Ah! she did not know that I was listening. I too squatted by Noma's head, and grew quick-witted in my fear. Now that the woman was there I was not so much afraid of the dead man, and I remembered, too, that he had been a great cheat; so I thought I would make him cheat for the last time. I placed my hands beneath his shoulders and pushed him up so that he sat upon the ground. The woman heard the noise and made a sound in her throat.

"Will you not be quiet, you old hag?" I said in Noma's voice. "Can you not let me be at peace, even now when I am dead?"

She heard, and, falling backwards in fear, drew in her breath to shriek aloud.

"What! will you also dare to shriek?" I said again in Noma's voice; "then I must teach you silence." And I tumbled him over on to the top of her.

Then her senses left her, and whether she ever found them again I do not know. At least she grew quiet for that time. For me, I snatched up the rug — afterwards I found it was Noma's best *kaross*, made by Basutos of chosen cat-skins, and worth three oxen — and I fled, followed by Koos.

Now the kraal of the chief, my father, Makedama, was two hundred paces away, and I must go thither, for there Baleka slept. Also I dared not enter by the gate, because a man was always on guard there. So I cut my way through the reed fence with my assegai and crept to the hut where Baleka was with some of her half-sisters. I knew on which side of the hut it was her custom to lie, and where her head would be. So I lay down on my side and gently, very gently, began to bore a hole in the grass covering of the hut. It took a long while, for the thatch was thick, but at last I was nearly through it. Then I stopped, for it came into my mind that Baleka might have changed her place, and that I might wake the wrong girl. I almost gave it over, thinking that I would fly alone, when suddenly I heard a girl wake and begin to cry on the other side of the thatch. "Ah," I thought, "that is Baleka, who weeps for her brother!" So I put my lips where the thatch was thinnest and whispered: —

"Baleka, my sister! Baleka, do not weep! I, Mopo, am here. Say not a word, but rise. Come out of the hut, bringing your skin blanket."

Now Baleka was very clever: she did not shriek, as most girls would have done. No; she understood, and, after waiting awhile, she rose and crept from the hut, her blanket in her hand.

"Why are you here, Mopo?" she whispered, as we met. "Surely you will be killed!"

"Hush!" I said. And then I told her of the plan which I had made. "Will you come with me?" I said, when I had done, "or will you creep back into the hut and bid me farewell?"

She thought awhile, then she said, "No, my brother, I will come, for I love you alone among our people, though I believe that this will be the end of it — that you will lead me to my death."

I did not think much of her words at the time, but afterwards they came back to me. So we slipped away together, followed by the dog Koos, and soon we were running over the veldt with our faces set towards the country of the Zulu tribe.

Chapter IV

THE FLIGHT OF MOPO AND BALEKA

*A*ll the rest of that night we journeyed, till even the dog was tired. Then we hid in a mealie field for the day, as we were afraid of being seen. Towards the afternoon we heard voices, and, looking through the stems of the mealies, we saw a party of my father's men pass searching for us. They went on to a neighboring kraal to ask if we had been seen, and after that we saw them no more for awhile. At night we traveled again; but, as fate would have it, we were met by an old woman, who looked oddly at us but said nothing. After that we pushed on day and night, for we knew that the old woman would tell the pursuers if she met them; and so indeed it came about. On the third evening we reached some mealie gardens, and saw that they had been trampled down. Among the broken mealies we found the body of a very old man, as full of assegai wounds as a porcupine with quills. We wondered at this, and went on a little way. Then we saw that the kraal to which the gardens belonged was burned down. We crept up to it, and — ah! it was a sad sight for us to see! Afterwards we became used to such sights. All about us lay the bodies of dead people, scores of them — old men, young men, women, children, little babies at the breast — there they lay among the burned huts, pierced with assegai wounds. Red was the earth with their blood, and red they looked in the red light of the setting sun. It was as though all the land had been smeared with the bloody hand of the Great Spirit, of the Umkulunkulu. Baleka saw it and began to cry; she was weary, poor girl, and we had found little to eat, only grass and green corn.

"An enemy has been here," I said, and as I spoke I thought that I heard a groan from the other side of a broken reed hedge. I went and looked. There lay a young woman: she was badly wounded, but still alive, my father. A little way from her lay a man dead, and before him several other men of another tribe: he had died fighting. In front of the woman were the bodies of three children; another, a little one, lay on her body. I looked at the woman, and, as I looked, she groaned again, opened her eyes and saw me, and that I had a spear in my hand.

"Kill me quickly!" she said. "Have you not tortured me enough?"

I said that I was a stranger and did not want to kill her.

"Then bring me water," she said; "there is a spring there behind the kraal."

I called to Baleka to come to the woman, and went with my gourd to the spring. There were bodies in it, but I dragged them out, and when the water had cleared a little I filled the gourd and brought it back to the woman. She drank deep, and her strength came back a little — the water gave her life.

"How did you come to this?" I asked.

"It was an *impi* of Chaka, Chief of the Zulus, that ate us up," she answered. "They burst upon as at dawn this morning while we were asleep in our huts. Yes, I woke up to hear the sound of killing. I was sleeping by my husband, with him who lies there, and the children. We all ran out. My husband had a spear and shield. He was a brave man. See! he died bravely: he killed three of the Zulu devils before he himself was dead. Then they caught me, and killed my children, and stabbed me till they thought that I was dead. Afterwards, they went away. I don't know why they came, but I think it was because our chief would not send men to help Chaka against Zweete."

She stopped, gave a great cry, and died.

My sister wept at the sight, and I too was stirred by it. "Ah!" I thought to myself, "the Great Spirit must be evil. If he is not evil such things would not happen." That is how I thought then, my father; now I think differently. I know that we had not found out the path of the Great Spirit, that is all. I was a chicken in those days, my father; afterwards I got used to such sights. They did not stir me anymore, not one whit. But then in the days of Chaka the rivers ran blood — yes, we had to look at the water to see if it was clean before we drank. People learned how to die then and not make a noise about it. What does it matter? They would have been dead now anyway. It does not matter; nothing matters, except being born. That is a mistake, my father.

We stopped at the kraal that night, but we could not sleep, for we heard the Itongo, the ghosts of the dead people, moving about and calling to each other. It was natural that they should do so; men were looking for their wives, and mothers for their children. But we were afraid that they might be angry with us for being there, so we clung together and trembled in each other's arms. Koos also trembled, and from time to time he howled loudly. But they did not seem to see us, and towards morning their cries grew fainter.

When the first light came we rose and picked our way through the dead down to the plain. Now we had an easy road to follow to Chaka's kraal, for there was the spoor of the *impi* and of the cattle which they had stolen, and sometimes we came to the body of a warrior who had been killed because his wounds prevented him from marching farther. But now I was doubtful whether it was wise for us to go to Chaka, for after what we had seen I grew afraid lest he should kill us. Still, we had nowhere to turn, so I said that we would walk along till something happened. Now we grew faint with hunger and weariness, and Baleka said that we had better sit down and die, for then there would be no more trouble. So we sat down by a spring. But I did not wish to die yet, thought Baleka was right, and it would have been well to do so. As we sat, the dog Koos went to a bush that was near, and presently I heard him spring at something and the sound of struggling. I ran to the bush — he had caught hold of a duiker buck, as big as himself, that was asleep in it. Then I drove my spear into the buck and shouted for joy, for here was food. When the buck was dead I skinned him, and we took bits of the flesh, washed them in the water, and ate them, for we had no fire to cook them with. It is not nice to eat uncooked flesh, but we were so hungry that we did not mind, and the good refreshed us. When we had eaten what we could, we rose and washed ourselves at the spring; but, as we washed, Baleka looked up and gave a cry of fear. For there, on the crest of the hill, about ten spear-throws away, was a party of six armed men, people of my own tribe — children of my father Makedama — who still pursued us to take us or kill us. They saw us — they raised a shout, and began to run. We too sprang up and ran — ran like bucks, for fear had touched our feet.

Now the land lay thus. Before us the ground was open and sloped down to the banks of the White Umfolozi, which twisted through the plain like a great and shining snake. On the other side the ground rose again, and we did not know what was beyond, but we thought that in this direction lay the kraal of Chaka. We ran for the river — where else were we to run? And after us came the warriors. They gained on us; they were strong, and they were angry because they had come so far. Run as we would, still they gained. Now we neared the banks of the river; it was full and wide. Above us the waters ran angrily, breaking into swirls of white where they passed over sunken rocks; below was a rapid, in which none might live; between the two a deep pool, where the water was quiet but the stream strong.

"Ah! my brother, what shall we do?" gasped Baleka.

"There is this to choose," I answered; "perish on the spears of our people or try the river."

"Easier to die by water than on iron," she answered.

"Good!" I said. "Now may our snakes look towards us and the spirits of our fathers be with us! At the least we can swim." And I led her to the head of the pool. We threw away our blankets — everything except an assegai, which I held in my teeth — and we plunged in, wading as far as we could. Now we were up to our breasts; now we had lost the earth and were swimming towards the middle of the river, the dog Koos leading the way.

Then it was that the soldiers appeared upon the bank. "Ah! little people," one cried, "you swim, do you? Well, you will drown; and if you do not drown we know a ford, and we will catch you and kill you — yes! if we must run over the edge of the world after you we will catch you." And he hurled an assegai after us, which fell between us like a flash of light.

While he spoke we swam hard, and now we were in the current. It swept us downwards, but still we made way, for we could swim well. It was just this: if we could reach the bank before we were swept into the rapids we were safe; if not, then — good-night! Now we were near the other side, but, alas! we were also near the lip of the foaming water. We strained, we struggled. Baleka was a brave girl, and she swam bravely; but the water pushed her down below me, and I could do nothing to help her. I got my foot upon the rock and looked round. There she was, and eight paces from her the broken water boiled. I could not go back. I was too weak, and it seemed that she must perish. But the dog Koos saw. He swam towards her, barking, then turned round, heading for the shore. She grasped him by the tail with her right hand. Then he put out his strength — he was very strong. She took struck out with her feet and left hand, and slowly — very slowly — drew near. Then I stretched out the handle of my assegai towards her. She caught it with her left hand. Already her feet were over the brink of the rapids, but I pulled and Koos pulled, and we brought her safe into the shadows, and from the shallows to the bank, and there she fell gasping.

Now when the soldiers on the other bank saw that we had crossed, they shouted threats at us, then ran away down the bank.

"Arise, Baleka!" I said: "they have gone to see a ford."

"Ah, let me die!" she answered.

But I forced her to rise, and after awhile she got her breath again, and we walked on as fast as we could up the long rise. For two hours we walked, or more, till at last we came to the crest of the rise, and there, far away, we saw a large kraal.

"Keep heart," I said. "See, there is the kraal of Chaka."

"Yes, brother," she answered, "but what waits us there? Death is behind us and before us — we are in the middle of death."

Presently we came to a path that ran to the kraal from the ford of the Umfolozi. It was by it that the *Impi* had traveled. We followed the path till at last we were but half an hour's journey from the kraal. Then we looked back, and lo! there behind us were the pursuers — five of them — one had drowned in crossing the river.

Again we ran, but now we were weak, and they gained upon us. Then once more I thought of the dog. He was fierce and would tear anyone on whom I set him. I called him and told him what to do, though I knew that it would be his death. He understood, and flew towards the soldiers growling, his hair standing up on his spine. They tried to kill him with spears and kerries, but he jumped round them, biting at them, and kept them back. At last a man hit him, and he sprang up and seized the man by the throat. There he clung, man and dog rolling over and over together, till the end of it was that they both died. Ah! he was a dog! We do not see such dogs nowadays. His father was a Boer hound, the first that came into the country. That dog once killed a leopard all by himself. Well, this was the end of Koos!

Meanwhile, we had been running. Now we were but three hundred paces from the gate of the kraal, and there was something going on inside it; that we could see from the noise and the dust. The four soldiers, leaving the dead dog and the dying man, came after us swiftly. I saw that they must catch us before we reached the gate, for now Baleka could go but slowly. Then a thought came into my head. I had brought her here, I would save her life if I could. Should she reach the kraal without me, Chaka would not kill a girl who was so young and fair.

"Run on, Baleka! run on!" I said, dropping behind. Now she was almost blind with weariness and terror, and, not seeing my purpose, staggered towards the gate of the kraal. But I sat down on the veldt to get my breath again, for I was about to fight four men till I was killed. My heart beat and the blood drummed in my ears, but when they drew near and I rose — the assegai in my hand — once more the red cloth seemed to go up and down before my eyes, and all fear left me.

The men were running, two and two, with the length of a spear throw between them. But of the first pair one was five or six paces in front of the other. This man shouted out loud and charged me, shield and spear up. Now I had no shield — nothing but the assegai; but I was crafty and he was overbold. On he came. I stood waiting for him till he drew back the spear to stab me. Then suddenly I dropped to my knees and thrust upward with all my strength, beneath the rim of his shield, and he also thrust, but over me, his spear only cutting the flesh of my shoulder — see! here is its scar; yes, to this day. And my assegai? Ah! it went home; it ran through and through his middle. He rolled over and over on the plain. The dust hid him; only I was now weaponless, for the haft of my spear — it was but a light throwing assegai — broke in two, leaving nothing but a little bit of stick in my hand. And the other one was upon me. Then in the darkness I saw a light. I fell on to my hands and knees and flung myself over sideways. My body struck the legs of the man who was about to stab me, lifting his feet from beneath him. Down he came heavily. Before he had touched the ground I was off it. His spear had fallen from his hand. I stooped, seized it, and as he rose I stabbed him through the back. It was all done in the shake of a leaf, my father; in the shake of a leaf he also was dead. Then I ran, for I had no stomach for the other two; my valor was gone.

About a hundred paces from me Baleka was staggering along with her arms out like one who has drunk too much beer. By the time I caught her she was some forty paces from the gate of the kraal. But then her strength left her altogether. Yes! there she fell senseless, and I stood by her. And there, too, I should have been killed, had not this chanced, since the other two men, having stayed one instant by their dead fellows, came on against me mad with rage. For at that moment the gate of the kraal opened, and through it ran a party of soldiers dragging a prisoner by the arms. After them walked a great man, who wore a leopard skin on his shoulders, and was laughing, and with him were five or six ringed councilors, and after them again came a company of warriors.

The soldiers saw that killing was going on, and ran up just as the slayers reached us.

"Who are you?" they cried, "who day to kill at the gate of the Elephant's kraal? Here the Elephant kills alone."

"We are of the children of Makedama," they answered, "and we follow these evildoers who have done wickedness and murder in our kraal. See! but now two of us are dead at their hands, and others lie dead along the road. Suffer that we slay them."

"Ask that of the Elephant," said the soldiers; "ask too that he suffer you should not be slain."

Just then the tall chief saw blood and heard words. He stalked up; and he was a great man to look at, though still quite young in years. For he was taller by a head than any round him, and his chest was big as the chests of two; his face was fierce and beautiful, and when he grew angry his eye flashed like a smitten brand.

"Who are these that dare to stir up dust at the gates of my kraal?" he asked, frowning.

"O Chaka, O Elephant!" answered the captain of the soldiers, bending himself double before him, "the men say that these are evildoers and that they pursue them to kill them."

"Good!" he answered. "Let them slay the evildoers."

"O great chief! thanks be to thee, great chief!" said those men of my people who sought to kill us.

"I hear you," he answered, then spoke once more to the captain. "And when they have slain the evildoers, let themselves be blinded and turned loose to seek their way home, because they have dared to lift a spear within the Zulu gates. Now praise on, my children!" And he laughed, while the soldiers murmured, *"Ou!* he is wise, he is great, his justice is bright and terrible like the sun!"

But the two men of my people cried out in fear, for they did not seek such justice as this.

"Cut out their tongues also," said Chaka. "What? shall the land of the Zulus suffer such a noise? Never! lest the cattle miscarry. To it, ye black ones! There lies the girl. She is asleep and helpless. Kill her! What? you hesitate? Nay, then, if you will have time for thought, I give it. Take these men, smear them with honey, and pin them over ant-heaps; by tomorrow's sun they will know their own minds. But first kill these two hunted jackals," and he pointed to Baleka and myself. "They seem tired and doubtless they long for sleep."

Then for the first time I spoke, for the soldiers drew near to slay us.

"O Chaka," I cried, "I am Mopo, and this is my sister Baleka."

I stopped, and a great shout of laughter went up from all who stood round.

"Very well, Mopo and thy sister Baleka," said Chaka, grimly. "Good-morning to you, Mopo and Baleka — also, good-night!"

"O Chaka," I broke in, "I am Mopo, son of Makedama of the Langeni tribe. It was I who gave thee a gourd of water many years ago, when we were both little. Then thou badest me come to thee when thou hadst grown great, vowing that thou wouldst protect me and never do me harm. So I have come, bringing my sister with me; and now, I pray thee, do not eat up the words of long ago."

As I spoke, Chaka's face changed, and he listened earnestly, as a man who holds his hand behind his ear. "Those are no liars," he said. "Welcome, Mopo! Thou shalt be a dog in my hut, and feed from my hand. But of thy sister I said nothing. Why, then, should she not be slain when I swore vengeance against all thy tribe, save thee alone?"

"Because she is too fair to slay, O Chief!" I answered, boldly; "also because I love her, and ask her life as a boon!"

"Turn the girl over," said Chaka. And they did so, showing her face.

"Again thou speakest no lie, son of Makedama," said the chief. "I grant thee the boon. She also shall lie in my hut, and be of the number of my 'sisters.' Now tell me thy tale, speaking only the truth."

So I sat down and told him all. Nor did he grow weary of listening. But, when I had done, he said but one thing — that he would that the dog Koos had not been killed; since, if he had still been alive, he would have set him on the hut of my father Makedama, and made him chief over the Langeni.

Then he spoke to the captain of the soldiers. "I take back my words," he said. "Let not these men of the Langeni be mutilated. One shall die and the other shall go free. Here," and he pointed to the man whom we had seen led out of the kraal-gate, "here, Mopo, we have a man who has proved himself a coward. Yesterday a kraal of wizards yonder was eaten up by my order — perhaps you two saw it as you traveled. This man and three others attacked a soldier of that kraal who defended his wife and children. The man fought well — he slew three of my people. Then this dog was afraid to meet him face to face. He killed him with a throwing assegai, and afterwards he stabbed the woman. That is nothing; but he should have fought the husband hand to hand. Now I will do him honor. He shall fight to the death with one of these pigs from thy sty," and he pointed with his spear to the men of my father's kraal, "and the one who survives shall be run down as they tried to run you down. I will send back the other pig to the sty with a message. Choose, children of Makedama, which of you will live."

Now the two men of my tribe were brothers, and loved one another, and each of them was willing to die that the other might go free. Therefore, both of them stepped forward, saying that they would fight the Zulu.

"What, is there honor among pigs?" said Chaka. "Then I will settle it. See this assegai? I throw it into the air; if the blade falls uppermost the tall man shall go free; if the shaft falls uppermost, then life is to the short one, so!" And he sent the little spear whirling round and round in the air. Every eye watched it as it wheeled and fell. The haft struck the ground first.

"Come hither, thou," said Chaka to the tall brother. "Hasten back to the kraal of Makedama, and say to him, Thus says Chaka, the Lion of the Zulu-ka-Malandela, 'Years ago thy tribe refused me milk. Today the dog of thy son Mopo howls upon the roof of thy hut.' Begone!"*

The man turned, shook his brother by the hand, and went, bearing the words of evil omen.

---

* Among the Zulus it is a very bad omen for a dog to climb the roof of a hut. The saying conveyed a threat to be appreciated by every Zulu. — EDITOR

Then Chaka called to the Zulu and the last of those who had followed us to kill us, bidding them fight. So, when they had praised the prince they fought fiercely, and the end of it was that the man of my people conquered the Zulu. But as soon as he had found his breath again he was set to run for his life, and after him ran five chosen men.

Still, it came about that he outran them, doubling like a hare, and got away safely. Nor was Chaka angry at this; for I think that he bade the men who hunted him to make speed slowly. There was only one good thing in the cruel heart of Chaka, that he would always save the life of a brave man if he could do so without making his word nothing. And for my part, I was glad to think that the man of my people had conquered him who murdered the children of the dying woman that we found at the kraal beyond the river.

Chapter V

MOPO BECOMES THE KING'S DOCTOR

*T*hese, then, my father, were the events that ended in the coming of me, Mopo, and of my sister Baleka to the kraal of Chaka, the Lion of the Zulu. Now you may ask why have I kept you so long with this tale, which is as are other tales of our people. But that shall be seen, for from these matters, as a tree from a seed, grew the birth of Umslopogaas Bulalio, Umslopogaas the Slaughterer, and Nada the Beautiful, of whose love my story has to tell. For Nada was my daughter, and Umslopogaas, though few knew it, was none other than the son of Chaka, born of my sister Baleka.

Now when Baleka recovered from the weariness of our flight, and had her beauty again, Chaka took her to wife, numbering her among his women, whom he named his "sisters." And me Chaka took to be one of his doctors, of his *izinyanga* of medicine, and he was so well pleased with my medicine that in the end I became his head doctor. Now this was a great post, in which, during the course of years, I grew fat in cattle and in wives; but also it was one of much danger. For when I rose strong and well in the morning, I could never know but that at night I should sleep stiff and red. Many were the doctors whom Chaka slew; doctored they never so well, they were killed at last. For a day would surely come when the king felt ill in his body or heavy in his mind, and then to the assegai or the torment with the wizard who had doctored him! Yet I escaped, because of the power of my medicine, and also because of that oath which Chaka had sworn to me as a child. So it came about that where the king went there I went with him. I slept near his hut, I sat behind him at council, in the battle I was ever at his side.

Ah! the battle! the battle! In those days we knew how to fight, my father! In those days the vultures would follow our *impis* by thousands, the hyenas would steal along our path in packs, and none went empty away. Never may I forget the first fight I stood in at the side of Chaka. It was just after the king had built his great kraal on the south bank of the Umhlatuze. Then it was that the chief Zwide attacked his rival Chaka for the third time and Chaka moved out to meet him with ten full regiments,* now for the first time armed with the short stabbing-spear.

The ground lay this: On a long, low hill in front of our *impi* were massed the regiments of Zwide; there were seventeen of them; the earth was black with their number; their plumes filled the air like snow. We, too, were on a hill, and between us lay a valley down which there ran a little stream. All night our fires shone out across the valley; all night the songs of soldiers echoed down the hills. Then the grey dawning came, the oxen lowed to the light, the regiments arose from their bed of spears; they sprang up and shook the dew from hair and shield — yes! they arose! the glad to die! The *impi* assumed its array regiment by regiment. There was the breast of spears, there were the horns of spears, they were numberless as the stars, and like the stars they shone. The morning breeze came up and fanned them, their plumes bent in the breeze; like a plain of seeding grass they bent, the plumes of the soldiers ripe for the assegai. Up over the shoulder of the hill came the sun of Slaughter; it glowed red upon the red shields, red grew the place of killing; the white plumes of the chiefs were dipped in the blood of heaven. They knew it; they saw the omen of death, and, ah! they laughed in the joy of the waking of battle. What was death? Was it not well to die on the spear? What was death? Was it not well to die for the king? Death was the arms of Victory. Victory would be their bride that night, and oh! her breast is fair.

---

* About 30,000 men. — Editor

Hark! the war-song, the Ingomo, the music of which has the power to drive men mad, rose far away to the left, and was thrown along from regiment to regiment — a rolling ball of sound —

We are the king's kine, bred to be butchered,
    You, too, are one of us!
We are the Zulu, children of the Lion,
    What! did you tremble?

Suddenly Chaka was seen stalking through the ranks, followed by his captains, his *indunas*, and by me. He walked along like a great buck; death was in his eyes, and like a buck he sniffed the air, scenting the air of slaughter. He lifted his assegai, and a silence fell; only the sound of chanting still rolled along the hills.

"Where are the children of Zwide?" he shouted, and his voice was like the voice of a bull.

"Yonder, father," answered the regiments. And every spear pointed across the valley.

"They do not come," he shouted again. "Shall we then sit here till we grow old?"

"No, father," they answered. "Begin! begin!"

"Let the Umkandhlu regiment come forward!" he shouted a third time, and as he spoke the black shields of the Umkandhlu leaped from the ranks of the *impi*.

"Go, my children!" cried Chaka. "There is the foe. Go and return no more!"

"We hear you, father!" they answered with one voice, and moved down the slope like a countless herd of game with horns of steel.

Now they crossed the stream, and now Zwide awoke. A murmur went through his companies; lines of light played above his spears.

Ou! they are coming! *Ou!* they have met! Hearken to the thunder of the shields! Hearken to the song of battle!

To and fro they swing. The Umkandhlu gives way — it flies! They pour back across the stream — half of them; the rest are dead. A howl of rage goes up from the host, only Chaka smiles.

"Open up! open up!" he cries. "Make room for the Umkandhlu *girls!*" And with hanging heads they pass us.

Now he whispers a word to the *indunas*. The *indunas* run; they whisper to Menziwa the general and to the captains; then two regiments rush down the hill, two more run to the right, and yet another two to the left. But Chaka stays on the hill with the three that are left. Again comes the roar of the meeting shields. Ah! these are men: they fight, they do not run. Regiment after regiment pours upon them, but still they stand. They fall by hundreds and by thousands, but no man shows his back, and on each man there lie two dead. Wow! my father, of those two regiments not one escaped. They were but boys, but they were the children of Chaka. Menziwa was buried beneath the heaps of his warriors. Now there are no such men.

They are all dead and quiet. Chaka still holds his hand! He looks to the north and to the south. See! spears are shining among the trees. Now the horns of our host close upon the flanks of the foe. They slay and are slain, but the men of Zwide are many and brave, and the battle turns against us.

Then again Chaka speaks a word. The captains hear, the soldiers stretch out their necks to listen.

It has come at last. "Charge! Children of the Zulu!"

There is a roar, a thunder of feet, a flashing of spears, a bending of plumes, and, like a river that has burned its banks, like storm-clouds before the gale, we sweep down upon friend and foe. They form up to meet us; the stream is passed; our wounded rise upon their haunches and wave us on. We trample them down. What matter? They can fight no more. Then we meet Zwide rushing to greet us, as bull meets bull. *Ou!* my father, I know no more. Everything grows red. That fight! that fight! We swept them away. When it was done there was nothing to be seen, but the hillside was black and red. Few fled; few were left to fly. We passed over them like fire; we ate them up. Presently we paused, looking for the foe. All were dead. The host of Zwide was no more. Then we mustered. Ten regiments had looked upon the morning sun; three regiments saw the sun sink; the rest had gone where no suns shine.

Such were our battles in the days of Chaka!

You ask of the Umkandhlu regiment which fled. I will tell you. When we reached our kraal once more, Chaka summoned that regiment and mustered it. He spoke to them gently, gently. He thanked them for their service. He said it was natural that "girls" should faint at the sight of blood and turn to seek their kraals. Yet he had bid them come back no more and they had come back! What then was there now left for him to do? And he covered his face with his blanket. Then the soldiers killed them all, nearly two thousand of them — killed them with taunts and jeers.

That is how we dealt with cowards in those days, my father. After that, one Zulu was a match for five of any other tribe. If ten came against him, still he did not turn his back. "Fight and fall, but fly not," that was our watchword. Never again while Chaka lived did a conquered force pass the gates of the king's kraal.

That fight was but one war out of many. With every moon a fresh *impi* started to wash its spears, and came back few and thin, but with victory and countless cattle. Tribe after tribe went down before us. Those of them who escaped the assegai were enrolled into fresh regiments, and thus, though men died by thousands every month, yet the army grew. Soon there were no other chiefs left. Umsuduka fell, and after him Mancengeza. Umzilikazi was driven north; Matiwane was stamped flat. Then we poured into this land of Natal. When we entered, its people could not be numbered. When we left, here and there a man might be found in a hole in the earth — that was all. Men, women, and children, we wiped them out; the land was clean of them. Next came the turn of U'Faku, chief of the Amapondos. Ah! where is U'faku now?

And so it went on and on, till even the Zulus were weary of war and the sharpest assegais grew blunt.

Chapter VI

THE BIRTH OF UMSLOPOGAAS

*T*his was the rule of the life of Chaka, that he would have no children, though he had many wives. Every child born to him by his "sisters" was put away at once.

"What, Mopo," he said to me, "shall I rear up children to put me to the assegai when they grow great? They call me tyrant. Say, how do those chiefs die whom men name tyrants? They die at the hands of those whom they have bred. Nay, Mopo, I will rule for my life, and when I join the spirits of my fathers let the strongest take my power and my place!"

Now it chanced that shortly after Chaka had spoken thus, my sister Baleka, the king's wife, fell in labor; and on that same day my wife Macropha was brought to bed of twins, and this but eight days after my second wife, Anadi, had given birth to a son. You ask, my father, how

I came to be married, seeing that Chaka forbade marriage to all his soldiers till they were in middle life and had put the man's ring upon their heads. It was a boon he granted me as *inyanga* of medicine, saying it was well that a doctor should know the sicknesses of women and learn how to cure their evil tempers. As though, my father, that were possible!

When the king heard that Baleka was sick he did not kill her outright, because he loved her a little, but he sent for me, commanding me to attend her, and when the child was born to cause its body to be brought to him, according to custom, so that he might be sure that it was dead. I bent to the earth before him, and went to do his bidding with a heavy heart, for was not Baleka my sister? and would not her child be of my own blood? Still, it must be so, for Chaka's whisper was as the shout of other kings, and, if we dared to disobey, then our lives and the lives of all in our kraals would answer for it. Better that an infant should die than that we should become food for jackals. Presently I came to the Emposeni, the place of the king's wives, and declared the king's word to the soldiers on guard. They lowered their assegais and let me pass, and I entered the hut of Baleka. In it were others of the king's wives, but when they saw me they rose and went away, for it was not lawful that they should stay where I was. Thus I was left alone with my sister.

For awhile she lay silent, and I did not speak, though I saw by the heaving of her breast that she was weeping.

"Hush, little one!" I said at length; "your sorrow will soon be done."

"Nay," she answered, lifting her head, "it will be but begun. Oh, cruel man! I know the reason of your coming. You come to murder the babe that shall be born of me."

"It is the king's word, woman."

"It is the king's word, and what is the king's word? Have I, then, naught to say in this matter?"

"It is the king's child, woman."

"It is the king's child, and it is not also my child? Must my babe be dragged from my breast and be strangled, and by you, Mopo? Have I not loved you, Mopo? Did I not flee with you from our people and the vengeance of our father? Do you know that not two moons gone the king was wroth with you because he fell sick, and would have caused you to be slain had I not pleaded for you and called his oath to mind? And thus you pay me: you come to kill my child, my first-born child!"

"It is the king's word, woman," I answered sternly; but my heart was split in two within me.

Then Baleka said no more, but, turning her face to the wall of the hut, she wept and groaned bitterly.

Now, as she wept I heard a stir without the hut, and the light in the doorway was darkened. A woman entered alone. I looked round to see who it was, then fell upon the ground in salutation, for before me was Unandi, mother of the king, who was named "Mother of the Heavens," that same lady to whom my mother had refused the milk.

"Hail, Mother of the Heavens!" I said.

"Greeting, Mopo," she answered. "Say, why does Baleka weep? Is it because the sorrow of women is upon her?"

"Ask of her, great chieftainess," I said.

Then Baleka spoke: "I weep, mother of a king, because this man, who is my brother, has come from him who is my lord and they son, to murder that which shall be born of me. O thou whose breasts have given suck, plead for me! Thy son was not slain at birth."

"Perhaps it were well if he had been so slain, Baleka," said Unandi; "then had many another man lived to look upon the sun who is now dead."

"At the least, as an infant he was good and gentle, and thou mightest love him, Mother of the Zulu."

"Never, Baleka! As a babe he bit my breast and tore my hair; as the man is so was the babe."

"Yet may his child be otherwise, Mother of the Heavens! Think, thou hast no grandson to comfort thee in thy age. Wilt thou, then, see all thy stock wither? The king, our lord, lives in war. He too may die, and what then?"

"Then the root of Senzangacona is still green. Has the king no brothers?"

"They are not of they flesh, mother. What? thou dost not hearken! Then as a woman to woman I plead with thee. Save my child or slay me with my child!"

Now the heart of Unandi grew gentle, and she was moved to tears.

"How may this be done, Mopo?" she said. "The king must see the dead infant, and if he suspect, and even reeds have ears, you know the heart of Chaka and where we shall lie tomorrow."

"Are there then no other newborn babes in Zululand?" said Baleka, sitting up and speaking in a whisper like the hiss of a snake. "Listen, Mopo! Is not your wife also in labor? Now hear me, Mother of the Heavens, and, my brother, hear me also. Do not think to play with me in this matter. I will save my child or you twain will perish with it. For I will tell the king that you came to me, the two of you, and whispered plots into my ear — plots to save the child and kill the king. Now choose, and swiftly!"

She sank bank, there was silence, and we looked one upon another. Then Unandi spoke.

"Give me your hand, Mopo, and swear that you will be faithful to me in this secret, as I swear to you. A day may come when this child who has not seen the light rules as king in Zululand, and then in reward you shall be the greatest of the people, the king's voice, whisperer in the king's ear. But if you break your oath, then beware, for I shall not die alone!"

"I swear, Mother of the Heavens," I answered.

"It is well, son of Makedama."

"It is well, my brother," said Baleka. "Now go and do that which must be done swiftly, for my sorrow is upon me. Go, knowing that if you fail I will be pitiless, for I will bring you to your death, yes, even if my own death is the price!"

So I went. "Whither to you go?" asked the guard at the gate.

"I go to bring my medicines, men of the king," I answered.

So I said; but, oh! my heart was heavy, and this was my plan — to fly far from Zululand. I could not, and I dared not do this thing. What? should I kill my own child that its life might be given for the life of the babe of Baleka? And should I lift up my will against the will of the king, saving the child to look upon the sun which he had doomed to darkness? Nay, I would fly, leaving all, and seek out some far tribe where I might begin to live again. Here I could not live; here in the shadow of Chaka was nothing but death.

I reached my own huts, there to find that my wife Macropha was delivered of twins. I sent away all in the hut except my other wife, Anadi, she who eight days gone had born me a son. The second of the twins was born; it was a boy, born dead. The first was a girl, she who lived to be Nada the Beautiful, Nada the Lily. Then a thought came into my heart. Here was a path to run on.

"Give me the boy," I said to Anadi. "He is not dead. Give him to me that I may take him outside the kraal and wake him to life by my medicine."

"It is of no use — the child is dead," said Anadi.

"Give him to me, woman!" I said fiercely. And she gave me the body.

Then I took him and wrapped him up in my bundle of medicines, and outside of all I rolled a mat of plaited grass.

"Suffer none to enter the hut till I return," I said; "and speak no word of the child that seems to be dead. If you allow any to enter, or if you speak a word, then my medicine will not work and the babe will be dead indeed."

So I went, leaving the women wondering, for it is not our custom to save both when twins are born; but I ran swiftly to the gates of the Emposeni.

"I bring the medicines, men of the king!" I said to the guards.

"Pass in," they answered.

I passed through the gates and into the hut of Baleka. Unandi was alone in the hut with my sister.

"The child is born," said the mother of the king. "Look at him, Mopo, son of Makedama!"

I looked. He was a great child with large black eyes like the eyes of Chaka the king; and Unandi, too, looked at me. "Where is it?" she whispered.

I loosed the mat and drew the dead child from the medicines, glancing round fearfully as I did so.

"Give me the living babe," I whispered back.

They gave it to me and I took of a drug that I knew and rubbed it on the tongue of the child. Now this drug has the power to make the tongue it touches dumb for awhile. Then I wrapped up the child in my medicines and again bound the mat about the bundle. But round the throat of the still-born babe I tied a string of fiber as though I had strangled it, and wrapped it loosely in a piece of matting.

Now for the first time I spoke to Baleka: "Woman," I said, "and thou also, Mother of the Heavens, I have done your wish, but know that before all is finished this deed shall bring about the death of many. Be secret as the grave, for the grave yawns for you both."

I went again, bearing the mat containing the dead child in my right hand. But the bundle of medicines that held the living one I fastened across my shoulders. I passed out of the Emposeni, and, as I went, I held up the bundle in my right hand to the guards, showing them that which was in it, but saying nothing.

"It is good," they said, nodding.

But now ill-fortune found me, for just outside the Emposeni I met three of the king's messengers.

"Greeting, son of Makedama!" they said. "The king summons you to the Intunkulu" — that is the royal house, my father.

"Good!" I answered. "I will come now; but first I would run to my own place to see how it goes with Macropha, my wife. Here is that which the king seeks," and I showed them the dead child. "Take it to him if you will."

"That is not the king's command, Mopo," they answered. "His word is that you should stand before him at once."

Now my heart turned to water in my breast. Kings have many ears. Could he have heard? And how dared I go before the Lion bearing his living child hidden on my back? Yet to waver was to be lost, to show fear was to be lost, to disobey was to be lost.

"Good! I come," I answered. And we walked to the gate of the Intunkulu.

It was sundown. Chaka was sitting in the little courtyard in front of his hut. I went down on my knees before him and gave the royal salute, Bayéte, and so I stayed.

"Rise, son of Makedama!" he said.

"I cannot rise, Lion of the Zulu," I answered, "I cannot rise, having royal blood on my hands, till the king has pardoned me."

"Where is it?" he asked.

I pointed to the mat in my hand.

"Let me look at it."

Then I undid the mat, and he looked on the child, and laughed aloud.

"He might have been a king," he said, as he bade a councilor take it away. "Mopo, thou hast slain one who might have been a king. Art thou not afraid?"

"No, Black One," I answered, "the child is killed by order of one who is a king."

"Sit down, and let us talk," said Chaka, for his mood was idle. "Tomorrow thou shalt have five oxen for this deed; thou shalt choose them from the royal herd."

"The king is good; he sees that my belt is drawn tight; he satisfies my hunger. Will the king suffer that I go? My wife is in labor and I would visit her."

"Nay, stay awhile; say how it is with Baleka, my sister and thine?"

"It is well."

"Did she weep when you took the babe from her?"

"Nay, she wept not. She said, 'My lord's will is my will.'"

"Good! Had she wept she had been slain also. Who was with her?"

"The Mother of the Heavens."

The brow of Chaka darkened. "Unandi, my mother, what did she there? My myself I swear, though she is my mother — if I thought" — and he ceased.

Thee was a silence, then he spoke again. "Say, what is in that mat?" and he pointed with his little assegai at the bundle on my shoulders.

"Medicine, king."

"Thou dost carry enough to doctor an *impi*. Undo the mat and let me look at it."

Now, my father, I tell you that the marrow melted in my bones with terror, for if I undid the mat I feared he must see the child and then —
"

"It is *tagati*, it is bewitched, O king. It is not wise to look on medicine."

"Open!" he answered angrily. "What? may I not look at that which I am forced to swallow — I, who am the first of doctors?"

"Death is the king's medicine," I answered, lifting the bundle, and laying it as far from him in the shadow of the fence as I dared. Then I bent over it, slowly undoing the *rimpis* with which it was tied, while the sweat of terror ran down by face blinding me like tears. What would I do if he saw the child? What if the child awoke and cried? I would snatch the assegai from his hand and stab him! Yes, I would kill the king and then kill myself! Now the mat was unrolled. Inside were the brown leaves and roots of medicine; beneath them was the senseless bade wrapped in dead moss.

"Ugly stuff," said the king, taking snuff. "Now see, Mopo, what a good aim I have! This for thy medicine!" And he lifted his assegai to throw it through the bundle. But as he threw, my snake put it into the king's heart to sneeze, and thus it came to pass that the assegai only pierced the outer leaves of the medicine, and did not touch the child.

"May the heavens bless the king!" I said, according to custom.

"Thanks to thee, Mopo, it is a good omen," he answered. "And now, begone! Take my advice: kill thy children, as I kill mine, lest they live to worry thee. The whelps of lions are best drowned."

I did up the bundle fast — fast, though my hands trembled. Oh! what if the child should wake and cry. It was done; I rose and saluted the king. Then I doubled myself up and passed from before him. Scarcely was I outside the gates of the Intunkulu when the infant began to squeak in the bundle. If it had been one minute before!

"What," said a soldier, as I passed, "have you got a puppy hidden under your *moocha*,* Mopo?"

I made no answer, but hurried on till I came to my huts. I entered; there were my two wives alone.

"I have recovered the child, women," I said, as I undid the bundle.

Anadi took him and looked at him.

"The boy seems bigger than he was," she said.

"The breath of life has come into him and puffed him out," I answered.

"His eyes are not as his eyes were," she said again. "Now they are big and black, like the eyes of the king."

---

* Girdle composed of skin and tails of oxen. — Editor

"My spirit looked upon his eyes and made them beautiful," I answered.

"This child has a birthmark on his thigh," she said a third time. "That which I gave you had no mark."

"I laid my medicine there," I answered.

"It is not the same child," she said sullenly. "It is a changeling who will lay ill-luck at our doors."

Then I rose up in my rage and cursed her heavily, for I saw that if she was not stopped this woman's tongue would bring us all to ruin.

"Peace, witch!" I cried. "How dare you to speak thus from a lying heart? Do you wish to draw down a curse upon our roof? Would you make us all food for the king's spear? Say such words again, and you shall sit within the circle — the Ingomboco shall know you for a witch!"

So I stormed on, threatening to bring her to death, till at length she grew fearful, and fell at my feet praying for mercy and forgiveness. But I was much afraid because of this woman's tongue, and not without reason.

Chapter VII

UMSLOPOGAAS ANSWERS THE KING

*N*ow the years went on, and this matter slept. Nothing more was heard of it, but still it only slept; and, my father, I feared greatly for the hour when it should awake. For the secret was known by two women — Unandi, Mother of the Heavens, and Baleka, my sister, wife of the king; and by two more — Macropha and Anadi, my wives — it was guessed at. How, then, should it remain a secret forever? Moreover, it came about that Unandi and Baleka could not restrain their fondness for this child who was called my son and named Umslopogaas, but who was the son of Chaka, the king, and of the Baleka, and the grandson of Unandi. So it happened that very often one or the other of them would come into my hut, making pretence to visit my wives, and take the boy upon her lap and fondle it. In vain did I pray them to forbear. Love pulled at their heart-strings more heavily than my words, and still they came. This was the end of it — that Chaka saw the child sitting on the knee of Unandi, his mother.

"What does my mother with that brat of thine, Mopo?" he asked of me. "Cannot she kiss me, if she will find a child to kiss?" And he laughed like a wolf.

I said that I did not know, and the matter passed over for awhile. But after that Chaka caused his mother to be watched. Now the boy Umslopogaas grew great and strong; there was no such lad of his years for a day's journey round. But from a babe he was somewhat surly, of few words, and like his father, Chaka, afraid of nothing. In all the world there were but two people whom he loved — these were I, Mopo, who was called his father, and Nada, she who was said to be his twin sister.

Now it must be told of Nada that as the boy Umslopogaas was the strongest and bravest of children, so the girl Nada was the gentlest and most fair. Of a truth, my father, I believe that her blood was not all Zulu, though this I cannot say for certain. At the least, her eyes were softer and larger than those of our people, her hair longer and less tightly curled, and her skin was lighter — more of the color of pure copper. These things she had from her mother, Macropha; though she was fairer than Macropha — fairer, indeed, than any woman of my people whom I have seen. Her mother, Macropha, my wife, was of Swazi blood, and was brought to the king's kraal with other captives after a raid, and given to me as a wife by the king. It was said that she was the daughter of a Swazi headman of the tribe of the Halakazi, and that she was born of his wife is true, but whether he was her father I do not know; for I have heard from the lips of Macropha herself, that before she was born there was a white man staying at her father's kraal. He was a Portuguese from the coast, a handsome man, and skilled in the working of iron. This white man loved the mother of my wife, Macropha, and some held that Macropha was his daughter, and not that of the Swazi headman. At least I know this, that before my wife's birth the Swazi killed the white man. But none can tell the truth of these matters, and I only speak of them because the beauty of Nada was rather as is the beauty of the white people than of ours, and this might well happen if her grandfather chanced to be a white man.

Now Umslopogaas and Nada were always together. Together they ate, together they slept and wandered; they thought one thought and spoke

with one tongue. *Ou!* it was pretty to see them! Twice while they were
still children did Umslopogaas save the life of Nada.

The first time it came about thus. The two children had wandered
far from the kraal, seeking certain berries that little ones love. On they
wandered and on, singing as they went, till at length they found the
berries, and ate heartily. Then it was near sundown, and when they had
eaten they fell asleep. In the night they woke to find a great wind blowing
and a cold rain falling on them, for it was the beginning of winter, when
fruits are ripe.

"Up, Nada!" said Umslopogaas, "we must seek the kraal or the cold
will kill us."

So Nada rose, frightened, and hand in hand they stumbled through
the darkness. But in the wind and the night they lost their path, and
when at length the dawn came they were in a forest that was strange to
them. They rested awhile, and finding berries ate them, then walked
again. All that day they wandered, till at last the night came down, and
they plucked branches of trees and piled the branches over them for
warmth, and they were so weary that they fell asleep in each other's arms.
At dawn they rose, but now they were very tired and berries were few,
sot hat by midday they were spent. Then they lay down on the side of
a steep hill, and Nada laid her head upon the breast of Umslopogaas.

"Here let us die, my brother," she said.

But even then the boy had a great spirit, and he answered, "Time to
die, sister, when Death chooses us. See, now! Do you rest here, and I will
climb the hill and look across the forest."

So he left her and climbed the hill, and on its side he found many
berries and a root that is good for food, and filled himself with them.
At length he came to the crest of the hill and looked out across the sea
of green. Lo! there, far away to the east, he saw a line of white that lay
like smoke against the black surface of a cliff, and knew it for the
waterfall beyond the royal town. Then he came down the hill, shouting
for joy and bearing roots and berries in his hand. But when he reached
the spot where Nada was, he found that her senses had left her through
hunger, cold, and weariness. She lay upon the ground like one asleep,
and over her stood a jackal that fled as he drew nigh. Now it would
seem that there but two shoots to the stick of Umslopogaas. One was
to save himself, and the other to lie down and die by Nada. Yet he found
a third, for, undoing the strips of his *moocha*, he made ropes of them,
and with the ropes he bound Nada on his back and started for the king's
kraal. He could never have reached it, for the way was long, yet at evening
some messengers running through the forest came upon a naked lad
with a girl bound to his back and a staff in his hand, who staggered

along slowly with starting eyes and foam upon his lips. He could not speak, he was so weary, and the ropes had cut through the skin of his shoulders; yet one of the messengers knew him for Umslopogaas, the son of Mopo, and they bore him to the kraal. They would have left the girl Nada, thinking her dead, but he pointed to her breast, and, feeling it, they found that her heart still beat, so they brought her also; and the end of it was that both recovered and loved each other more than ever before.

Now after this, I, Mopo, bade Umslopogaas stay at home within the kraal, and not lead his sister to the wilds. But the boy loved roaming like a fox, and where he went there Nada followed. So it came about that one day they slipped from the kraal when the gates were open, and sought out a certain deep glen which had an evil name, for it was said that spirits haunted it and put those to death who entered there. Whether this was true I do not know, but I know that in the glen dwelt a certain woman of the woods, who had her habitation in a cave and lived upon what she could kill or steal or dig up with her hands. Now this woman was mad. For it had chanced that her husband had been "smelt out" by the witch-doctors as a worker of magic against the king, and slain. Then Chaka, according to custom, dispatched the slayers to eat up his kraal, and they came to the kraal and killed his people. Last of all they killed his children, three young girls, and would have assegaied their mother, when suddenly a spirit entered into her at the sight, and she went mad, so that they let her go, being afraid to touch her afterwards. So she fled and took up her abode in the haunted glen; and this was the nature of her madness, that whenever she saw children, and more especially girl children, a longing came upon her to kill them as her own had been killed. This, indeed, she did often, for when the moon was full and her madness at its highest, she would travel far to find children, snatching them away from the kraals like a hyena. Still, none would touch her because of the spirit in her, not even those whose children she had murdered.

So Umslopogaas and Nada came to the glen where the child-slayer lived, and sat down by a pool of water not far from the mouth of her cave, weaving flowers into a garland. Presently Umslopogaas left Nada, to search for rock lilies which she loved. As he went he called back to her, and his voice awoke the woman who was sleeping in her cave, for she came out by night only, like a jackal. Then the woman stepped forth, smelling blood and having a spear in her hand. Presently she saw Nada seated upon the grass weaving flowers, and crept towards her to kill her. Now as she came — so the child told me — suddenly a cold wind seemed to breathe upon Nada, and fear took hold of her, though she did not see the woman who would murder her. She let fall the flowers, and looked before her into the pool, and there, mirrored in the pool, she saw the greedy face of the child-slayer, who crept down upon her from above, her hair hanging about her brow and her eyes shining like the eyes of a lion.

Then with a cry Nada sprang up and fled along the path which Umslopogaas had taken, and after her leapt and ran the mad woman. Umslopogaas heard her cry. He turned and rushed back over the brow of the hill, and, lo! there before him was the murderess. Already she had grasped Nada by the hair, already her spear was lifted to pierce her. Umslopogaas had no spear, he had nothing but a little stick without a knob; yet with it he rushed at the mad woman and struck her so smartly on the arm that she let go of the girl and turned on him with a yell. Then, lifting her spear, she struck at him, but he leapt aside. Again she struck; but he sprang into the air, and the spear passed beneath him. A third time the woman struck, and, though he fell to earth to avoid the blow, yet the assegai pierced his shoulder. But the weight of his body as he fell twisted it from her hand, and before she could grasp him he was up, and beyond her reach, the spear still fast in his shoulder.

Then the woman turned, screaming with rage and madness, and ran at Nada to kill her with her hands. But Umslopogaas set his teeth, and, drawing the spear from his wound, charged her, shouting. She lifted a great stone and hurled it at him — so hard that it flew into fragments against another stone which it struck; yet he charged on, and smote at her so truly that he drove the spear through her, and she fell down dead. After that Nada bound up his wound, which was deep, and with much pain he reached the king's kraal and told me this story.

Now there were some who cried that the boy must be put to death, because he had killed one possessed with a spirit. But I said no, he should not be touched. He had killed the woman in defense of his own life and the life of his sister; and everyone had a right to slay in self-defense, except as against the king or those who did the king's bidding. Moreover, I said, if the woman had a spirit, it was an evil one, for no good spirit would ask the lives of children, but rather those of cattle, for it is against our custom to sacrifice human beings to the Amatonga even in war, though the Basuta dogs do so. Still, the tumult grew, for the witch-doctors were set upon the boy's death, saying that evil would come of it if he was allowed to live, having killed one inspired, and at last the matter came to the ears of the king. Then Chaka summoned me and the boy before him, and he also summoned the witch-doctors.

First, the witch-doctors set out their case, demanding the death of Umslopogaas. Chaka asked them what would happen if the boy was not killed. They answered that the spirit of the dead woman would lead him to bring evil on the royal house. Chaka asked if he would bring evil on him, the king. They in turn asked the spirits, and answered no, not on him, but on one of the royal house who should be after him. Chaka said that he cared nothing what happened to those who came after him, or whether good or evil befell them. Then he spoke to Umslopogaas, who looked him boldly in the face, as an equal looks at an equal.

"Boy," he said, "what hast thou to say as to why thou shouldst not be killed as these men demand?"

"This, Black One," answered Umslopogaas; "that I stabbed the woman in defense of my own life."

"That is nothing," said Chaka. "If I, the king, wished to kill thee, mightest thou therefore kill me or those whom I sent? The Itongo in the woman was a Spirit King and ordered her to kill thee; thou shouldst then have let thyself be killed. Hast thou no other reason?"

"This, Elephant," answered Umslopogaas; "the woman would have murdered my sister, whom I love better than my life."

"That is nothing," said Chaka. "If I ordered thee to be killed for any cause, should I not also order all within thy gates to be killed with thee? May not, then, a Spirit King do likewise? If thou hast nothing more to say thou must die."

Now I grew afraid, for I feared lest Chaka should slay him who was called my son because of the word of the doctors. But the boy Umslopogaas looked up and answered boldly, not as one who pleads for his life, but as one who demands a right: —

"I have this to say, Eater-up of Enemies, and if it is not enough, let us stop talking, and let me be killed. Thou, O king, didst command that this woman should be slain. Those whom thou didst send to destroy her spared her, because they thought her mad. I have carried out the commandment of the king; I have slain her, mad or sane, whom the king commanded should be killed, and I have earned not death, but a reward."

"Well said, Umslopogaas!" answered Chaka. "Let ten head of cattle be given to this boy with the heart of a man; his father shall guard them for him. Art thou satisfied now, Umslopogaas?"

"I take that which is due to me, and I thank the king because he need not pay unless he will," Umslopogaas answered.

Chaka stared awhile, began to grow angry, then burst out laughing.

"Why, this calf is such another one as was dropped long ago in the kraal of Senzangacona!" he said. "As I was, so is this boy. Go on, lad, in that path, and thou mayst find those who shall cry the royal salute of Bayéte to thee at the end of it. Only keep out of my way, for two of a kind might not agree. Now begone!"

So we went out, but as we passed them I saw the doctors muttering together, for they were ill-pleased and foreboded evil. Also they were jealous of me, and wished to smite me through the heart of him who was called my son.

Chapter VIII
THE GREAT INGOMBOCO

*A*fter this there was quiet until the Feast of the First-fruits was ended. But few people were killed at these feast, though there was a great Ingomboco, or witch-hunt, and many were smelt out by the witch-doctors as working magic against the king. Now things had come to this pass in Zululand — that the whole people cowered before the witch-doctors. No man might sleep safe, for none knew but that on the morrow he would be touched by the wand of an Isanusi, as we name a finder of witches, and led away to his death. For awhile Chaka said nothing, and so long as the doctors smelt out those only whom he wished to get rid of — and they were many — he was well pleased. But when they began to work for their own ends, and to do those to death whom he did not desire to kill, he grew angry. Yet the custom of the land was that he whom the witch-doctor touched must die, he and all his house; therefore the king was in a cleft stick, for he scarcely dared to save even those whom he loved. One night I came to doctor him, for he was sick in his mind. On that very day there had been an Ingomboco, and five of the bravest captains of the army had been smelt out by the Abangoma, the witch-finders, together with many others. All had been destroyed, and men had been sent to kill the wives and children of the dead. Now Chaka was very angry at this slaying, and opened his heart to me.

"The witch-doctors rule in Zululand, and not I, Mopo, son of Makedama," he said to me. "Where, then, is it to end? Shall I myself be smelt out and slain? These Isanusis are too strong for me; they lie upon the land like the shadow of night. Tell me, how may I be free of them?"

"Those who walk the Bridge of Spears, O king, fall off into Nowhere," I answered darkly; "even witch-doctors cannot keep a footing on that bridge. Has not a witch-doctor a heart that can cease to beat? Has he not blood that can be made to flow?"

Chaka looked at me strangely. "Thou art a bold man who darest to speak thus to me, Mopo," he said. "Dost thou not know that it is sacrilege to touch an Isanusi?"

"I speak that which is in the king's mind," I answered. "Hearken, O king! It is indeed sacrilege to touch a true Isanusi, but what if the Isanusi be a liar? What if he smell out falsely, bringing those to death who are innocent of evil? Is it then sacrilege to bring him to that end which he has given to many another? Say, O king!"

"Good words!" answered Chaka. "Now tell me, son of Makedama, how may this matter be put to proof?"

Then I leaned forward, whispering into the ear of the Black One, and he nodded heavily.

Thus I spoke then, because I, too, saw the evil of the Isanusis, I who knew their secrets. Also, I feared for my own life and for the lives of all those who were dear to me. For they hated me as one instructed in their magic, one who had the seeing eye and the hearing ear.

One morning thereafter a new thing came to pass in the royal kraal, for the king himself ran out, crying aloud to all people to come and see the evil that had been worked upon him by a wizard. They came together and saw this. On the doorposts of the gateway of the Intunkulu, the house of the king, were great smears of blood. The knees of men strong in the battle trembled when they saw it; women wailed aloud as they wail over the dead; they wailed because of the horror of the omen.

"Who has done this thing?" cried Chaka in a terrible voice. "Who has dared to bewitch the king and to strike blood upon his house?"

There was no answer, and Chaka spoke again. "This is no little matter," he said, "to be washed away with the blood of one or two and be forgotten. The man who wrought it shall not die alone or travel with a few to the world of spirits. All his tribe shall go with him, down to the baby in his hut and cattle in his kraal! Let messengers go out east and west, and north and south, and summon the witch-doctors from every quarter! Let them summon the captains from every regiment and the headmen from every kraal! On the tenth day from now the circle of the Ingomboco must be set, and there shall be such a smelling out of wizards and of witches as has not been known in Zululand!"

So the messengers went out to do the bidding of the king, taking the names of those who should be summoned from the lips of the *indunas*, and day by day people flocked up to the gates of the royal kraal, and, creeping on their knees before the majesty of the king, praised him aloud. But he vouchsafed an answer to none. One noble only he caused to be killed, because he carried in his hand a stick of the royal red wood, which Chaka himself had given him in bygone years.*

On the last night before the forming of the Ingomboco, the witch-doctors, male and female, entered the kraal. There were a hundred and a half of them, and they were made hideous and terrible with the white bones of men, with bladders of fish and of oxen, with fat of wizards, and with skins of snakes. They walked in silence till they came in front of the Intunkulu, the royal house; then they stopped and sang this song for the king to hear: —

We have come, O king, we have come from the caves and the rocks
    and the swamps,
  To wash in the blood of the slain;
We have gathered our host from the air as vultures are gathered in
    war.
  When they scent the blood of the slain.

We come not alone, O king: with each Wise One there passes a ghost,
  Who hisses the name of the doomed.
We come not alone, for we are the sons and *Indunas* of Death,
  And he guides our feet to the doomed.

Red rises the moon o'er the plain, red sinks the sun in the west,
  Look, wizards, and bid them farewell!
We count you by hundreds, you who cried for a curse on the king.
  Ha! soon shall we bid *you* farewell!

Then they were silent, and went in silence to the place appointed for them, there to pass the night in mutterings and magic. But those who were gathered together shivered with fear when they heard their words, for they knew well that many a man would be switched with the gnu's tail before the sun sank once more. And I, too, trembled, for my heart was full of fear. Ah! my father, those were evil days to live in when Chaka ruled, and death met us at every turn! Then no man might call his life

* This beautiful wood is known in Natal as "red ivory." — EDITOR

his own, or that of his wife or child, or anything. All were the king's, and what war spared that the witch-doctors took.

The morning dawned heavily, and before it was well light the heralds were out summoning all to the king's Ingomboco. Men came by hundreds, carrying short sticks only — for to be seen armed was death — and seated themselves in the great circle before the gates of the royal house. Oh! their looks were sad, and they had little stomach for eating that morning, they who were food for death. They seated themselves; then round them on the outside of the circle gathered knots of warriors, chosen men, great and fierce, armed with kerries only. These were the slayers.

When all was ready, the king came out, followed by his *indunas* and by me. As he appeared, wrapped in the *kaross* of tiger-skins and towering a head higher than any man there, all the multitude — and it was many as the game on the hills — cast themselves to earth, and from every lip sharp and sudden went up the royal salute of Bayéte. But Chaka took no note; his brow was cloudy as a mountaintop. He cast one glance at the people and one at the slayers, and wherever his eye fell men turned grey with fear. Then he stalked on, and sat himself upon a stool to the north of the great ring looking toward the open space.

For awhile there was silence; then from the gates of the women's quarters came a band of maidens arrayed in their beaded dancing-dresses, and carrying green branches in their hands. As they came, they clapped their hands and sang softly: —

We are the heralds of the king's feast. Ai! Ai!
Vultures shall eat it. Ah! Ah!
It is good — it is good to die for the king!

They ceased, and ranged themselves in a body behind us. Then Chaka held up his hand, and there was a patter of running feet. Presently from behind the royal huts appeared the great company of the Abangoma, the witch-doctors — men to the right and women to the left. In the left hand of each was the tail of a vilderbeeste, in the right a bundle of assegais and a little shield. They were awful to see, and the bones about them rattled as they ran, the bladders and the snake-skins floated in the air behind them, their faces shone with the fat of anointing, their eyes started like the eyes of fishes, and their lips twitched hungrily as they glared round the death-ring. Ha! ha! little did those evil children guess who should be the slayers and who should be the slain before that sun sank!

On they came, like a grey company of the dead. On they came in silence broken only by the patter of their feet and the dry rattling of their bony necklets, till they stood in long ranks before the Black One. Awhile they stood thus, then suddenly everyone of them thrust forward the little shield in his hand, and with a single voice they cried, "Hail, Father!"

"Hail, my children!" answered Chaka.

"What seekest thou, Father?" they cried again. "Blood?"

"The blood of the guilty," he answered.

They turned and spoke each to each; the company of the men spoke to the company of the women.

"The Lion of the Zulu seeks blood."

"He shall be fed!" screamed the women.

"The Lion of the Zulu smells blood."

"He shall see it!" screamed the women.

"His eyes search out the wizards."

"He shall count their dead!" screamed the women.

"Peace!" cried Chaka. "Waste not the hours in talk, but to the work. Hearken! Wizards have bewitched me! Wizards have dared to smite blood upon the gateways of the king. Dig in the burrows of the earth and find them, ye rats! Fly through the paths of the air and find them, ye vultures! Smell at the gates of the people and name them, ye jackals! ye hunters in the night! Drag them from the caves if they be hidden, from the distance if they be fled, from the graves if they be dead. To the work! to the work! Show them to me truly, and your gifts shall be great; and for them, if they be a nation, they shall be slain. Now begin. Begin by companies of ten, for you are many, and all must be finished ere the sun sink."

"It shall be finished, Father," they answered.

Then ten of the women stood forward, and at their head was the most famous witch-doctress of that day — an aged woman named Nobela, a woman to whose eyes the darkness was no evil, whose scent was keen as a dog's, who heard the voices of the dead as they cried in the night, and spoke truly of what she heard. All the other Isanusis, male and female, sat down in a half-moon facing the king, but this woman drew forward, and with her came nine of her sisterhood. They turned east and west, north and south, searching the heavens; they turned east and west, north and south, searching the earth; they turned east and west, north and south, searching the hears of men. Then they crept round and round the great ring like cats; then they threw themselves upon the earth and smelt it. And all the time there was silence, silence deep as midnight,

and in it men hearkened to the beating of their hearts; only now and
again the vultures shrieked in the trees.

At length Nobela spoke: —

"Do you smell him, sisters?"

"We smell him," they answered.

"Does he sit in the east, sisters?"

"He sits in the east," they answered.

"Is he the son of a stranger, sisters?"

"He is the son of a stranger."

Then they crept nearer, crept on their hands and knees, till they were
within ten paces of where I sat among the *indunas* near to the king. The
indunas looked on each other and grew grey with fear; and for me, my
father, my knees were loosened and my marrow turned to water in my
bones. For I knew well who was that son of a stranger of whom they
spoke. It was I, my father, I who was about to be smelt out; and if I was
smelt out I should be killed with all my house, for the king's oath would
scarcely avail me against the witch-doctors. I looked at the fierce faces
of the Isanusis before me, as they crept, crept like snakes. I glanced
behind and saw the slayers grasping their kerries for the deed of death,
and I say I felt like one for whom the bitterness is overpast. Then I
remembered the words which the king and I had whispered together of
the cause for which this Ingomboco was set, and hope crept back to me
like the first gleam of the dawn upon a stormy night. Still I did not
hope overmuch, for it well might happen that the king had but set a
trap to catch me.

Now they were quite near and halted.

"Have we dreamed falsely, sisters?" asked Nobela, the aged.

"What we dreamed in the night we see in the day," they answered.

"Shall I whisper his name in your ears, sisters?"

They lifted their heads from the ground like snakes and nodded, and
as they nodded the necklets of bones rattled on their skinny necks. Then
they drew their heads to a circle, and Nobela thrust hers into the center
of the circle and said a word.

"Ha! ha!" they laughed, "we hear you! His is the name. Let him be
named by it in the face of Heaven, him and all his house; then let him
hear no other name forever!"

And suddenly they sprang up and rushed towards me, Nobela, the
aged Isanusi, at their head. They leaped at me, pointing to me with the
tails of the vilderbeestes in their hands. Then Nobela switched me in
the face with the tail of the beast, and cried aloud: —

"Greeting, Mopo, son of Makedama! Thou art the man who smotest blood on the doorposts of the king to bewitch the king. Let thy house be stamped flat!"

I saw her come, I felt the blow on my face as a man feels in a dream. I heard the feet of the slayers as they bounded forward to hale me to the dreadful death, but my tongue clave to the roof of my mouth — I could not say a word. I glanced at the king, and, as I did so, I thought that I heard him mutter: "Near the mark, not in it."

Then he held up his spear, and all was silence. The slayers stopped in their stride, the witch-doctors stood with outstretched arms, the world of men was as though it had been frozen into sleep.

"Hold!" he said. "Stand aside, son of Makedama, who art named an evildoer! Stand aside, thou, Nobela, and those with thee who have named him evildoer! What? Shall I be satisfied with the life of one dog? Smell on, ye vultures, company by company, smell on! For the day the labor, at night the feast!"

I rose, astonished, and stood on one side. The witch-doctresses also stood on one side, wonderstruck, since no such smelling out as this had been seen in the land. For till this hour, when a man was swept with the gnu's tail of the Isanusi that was the instant of his death. Why, then, men asked in their hearts, was the death delayed? The witch-doctors asked it also, and looked to the king for light, as men look to a thundercloud for the flash. But from the Black One there came no word.

So we stood on one side, and a second party of the Isanusi women began their rites. As the others had done, so they did, and yet they worked otherwise, for this is the fashion of the Isanusis, that no two of them smell out in the same way. And this party swept the faces of certain of the king's councilors, naming them guilty of the witch-work.

"Stand ye on one side!" said the king to those who had been smelt out; "and ye who have hunted out their wickedness, stand ye with those who named Mopo, son of Makedama. It well may be that all are guilty."

So these stood on one side also, and a third party took up the tale. And they named certain of the great generals, and were in turn bidden to stand on one side together with those whom they had named.

So it went on through all the day. Company by company the women doomed their victims, till there were no more left in their number, and were commanded to stand aside together with those whom they had doomed. Then the male Isanusis began, and I could see well that by this time their hearts were fearful, for they smelt a snare. Yet the king's bidding must be done, and though their magic failed them here, victims must be found. So they smelt out this man and that man till we were a great company of the doomed, who sat in silence on the ground looking at each other with sad eyes and watching the sun, which we deemed our last, climb slowly down the sky. And ever as the day waned those who were left untried of the witch-doctors grew madder and more fierce. They leaped into the air, they ground their teeth, and rolled upon the ground. They drew forth snakes and devoured them alive, they shrieked out to the spirits and called upon the names of ancient kings.

At length it drew on to evening, and the last company of the witch-doctors did their work, smelling out some of the keepers of the Emposeni, the house of the women. But there was one man of their company, a young man and a tall, who held back and took no share in the work, but stood by himself in the center of the great circle, fixing his eyes on the heavens.

And when this company had been ordered to stand aside also together with those whom they had smelt out, the king called aloud to the last of the witch-doctors, asking him of his name and tribe, and why he alone did not do his office.

"My name is Indabazimbi, the son of Arpi, O king," he answered, "and I am of the tribe of the Maquilisini. Does the king bid me to smell out him of whom the spirits have spoken to me as the worker of this deed?"

"I bid thee," said the king.

Then the young man Indabazimbi stepped straight forward across the ring, making no cries or gestures, but as one who walks from his gate to the cattle kraal, and suddenly he struck the king in the face with the tail in his hand, saying, "I smell out the Heavens above me!"*

Now a great gasp of wonder went up from the multitude, and all looked to see this fool killed by torture. But Chaka rose and laughed aloud.

"Thou hast said it," he cried, "and thou alone! Listen, ye people! I did the deed! I smote blood upon the gateways of my kraal; with my own hand I smote it, that I might learn who were the true doctors and who were the false! Now it seems that in the land of the Zulu there is one true doctor — this young man — and of the false, look at them and count them, they are like the leaves. See! there they stand, and by them stand those whom they have doomed — the innocent whom, with their wives and children, they have doomed to the death of the dog. Now I ask you, my people, what reward shall be given to them?"

Then a great roar went up from all the multitude, "Let them die, O king!"

"Aye!" he answered. "Let them die as liars should!"

---

* A Zulu title for the king. — EDITOR

Now the Isanusis, men and women, screamed aloud in fear, and cried for mercy, tearing themselves with their nails, for least of all things did they desire to taste of their own medicine of death. But the king only laughed the more.

"Hearken ye!" he said, pointing to the crowd of us who had been smelt out. "Ye were doomed to death by these false prophets. Now glut yourselves upon them. Slay them, my children! slay them all! wipe them away! stamp them out! – all! all, save this young man!"

Then we bounded from the ground, for our hearts were fierce with hate and with longing to avenge the terrors we had borne. The doomed slew the doomers, while from the circle of the Ingomboco a great roar of laughter went up, for men rejoiced because the burden of the witch-doctors had fallen from them.

At last it was done, and we drew back from the heap of the dead. Nothing was heard there now – no more cries or prayers or curses. The witch-fingers traveled the path on which they had set the feet of many. The king drew near to look. He came alone, and all who had done his bidding bent their heads and crept past him, praising him as they went. Only I stood still, covered, as I was with mire and filth, for I did not fear to stand in the presence of the king. Chaka drew near, and looked at the piled-up heaps of the slain and the cloud of dust that yet hung over them.

"There they lie, Mopo," he said. "There lie those who dared to prophecy falsely to the king! That was a good word of thine, Mopo, which taught me to set the snare for them; yet methought I saw thee start when Nobela, queen of the witch-doctresses, switched death on thee. Well, they are dead, and the land breathes more freely; and for the evil which they have done, it is as yonder dust, that shall soon sink again to earth and there be lost."

Thus he spoke, then ceased – for lo! something moved beneath the cloud of dust, something broke a way through the heap of the dead. Slowly it forced its path, pushing the slain this way and that, till at length it stood upon its feet and tottered towards us – a thing dreadful to look on. The shape was the shape of an aged woman, and even through the blood and mire I knew her. It was Nobela, she who had doomed me, she whom but now I had smitten to earth, but who had come back from the dead to curse me!

On she tottered, her apparel hanging round her in red rags, a hundred wounds upon her face and form. I saw that she was dying, but life still flickered in her, and the fire of hate burned in her snaky eyes.

"Hail, king!" she screamed.

"Peace, liar!" he answered; "thou art dead!"

"Not yet, king. I heard thy voice and the voice of yonder dog, whom I would have given to the jackals, and I will not die till I have spoken. I smelt him out this morning when I was alive; now that I am as one already dead, I smell him out again. He shall bewitch thee with blood indeed, Chaka — he and Unandi, thy mother, and Baleka, thy wife. Think of my words when the assegai reddens before thee for the last time, king! Farewell!" And she uttered a great cry and rolled upon the ground dead.

"The witch lies hard and dies hard," said the king carelessly, and turned upon his heel. But those words of dead Nobela remained fixed in his memory, or so much of them as had been spoken of Unandi and Baleka. There they remained like seeds in the earth, there they grew to bring forth fruit in their season.

And thus ended the great Ingomboco of Chaka, the greatest Ingomboco that ever was held in Zululand.

Chapter IX
THE LOSS OF UMSLOPOGAAS

*N*ow, after the smelling out of the witch-doctors, Chaka caused a watch to be kept upon his mother Unandi, and his wife Baleka, my sister, and report was brought to him by those who watched, that the two women came to my huts by stealth, and there kissed and nursed a boy — one of my children. Then Chaka remembered the prophecy of Nobela, the dead Isanusi, and his heart grew dark with doubt. But to me he said nothing of the matter, for then, as always, his eyes looked over my head. He did not fear me or believe that I plotted against him, I who was his dog. Still, he did this, though whether by chance or design I do not know: he bade me go on a journey to a distant tribe that lived near the borders of the Amaswazi, there to take count of certain of the king's cattle which were in the charge of that tribe, and to bring him account of the tale of their increase. So I bowed before the king, and said that I would run like a dog to do his bidding, and he gave me men to go with me.

Then I returned to my huts to bid farewell to my wives and children, and there I found that my wife, Anadi, the mother of Moosa, my son, had fallen sick with a wandering sickness, for strange things came into her mind, and what came into her mind that she said, being, as I did not doubt, bewitched by some enemy of my house.

Still, I must go upon the king's business, and I told this to my wife Macropha, the mother of Nada, and, as it was thought, of Umslopogaas, the son of Chaka. But when I spoke to Macropha of the matter she burst into tears and clung to me. I asked her why she wept thus, and she answered that the shadow of evil lay upon her heart, for she was sure that if I left her at the king's kraal, when I returned again I should find neither her nor Nada, my child, nor Umslopogaas, who was named my son, and whom I loved as a son, still in the land of life. Then I tried to calm her; but the more I strove the more she wept, saying that she knew well that these things would be so.

Now I asked her what could be done, for I was stirred by her tears, and the dread of evil crept from her to me as shadows creep from the valley to the mountain.

She answered, "Take me with you, my husband, that I may leave this evil land, where the very skies rain blood, and let me rest awhile in the place of my own people till the terror of Chaka has gone by."

"How can I do this?" I said. "None may leave the king's kraal without the king's pass."

"A man may put away his wife," she replied. "The king does not stand between a man and his wife. Say, my husband, that you love me no longer, that I bear you no more children, and that therefore you send me back whence I came. By-and-bye we will come together again if we are left among the living."

"So be it," I answered. "Leave the kraal with Nada and Umslopogaas this night, and tomorrow morning meet me at the riverbank, and we shall go on together, and for the rest may the spirits of our fathers hold us safe."

So we kissed each other, and Macropha went on secretly with the children.

Now at the dawning on the morrow I summoned the men whom the king had given me, and we started upon our journey. When the sun was well up we came to the banks of the river, and there I found my wife Macropha, and with her the two children. They rose as I came, but I frowned at my wife and she gave me no greeting. Those with me looked at her askance.

"I have divorced this woman," I said to them. "She is a withered tree, a worn out old hag, and now I take her with me to send her to the country of the Swazis, whence she came. Cease weeping," I added to Macropha, "it is my last word."

"What says the king?" asked the men.

"I will answer to the king," I said. And we went on.

Now I must tell how we lost Umslopogaas, the son of Chaka, who was then a great lad drawing on to manhood, fierce in temper, well grown and broad for his years.

We had journeyed seven days, for the way was long, and on the night of the seventh day we came to a mountainous country in which there were few kraals, for Chaka had eaten them all up years before. Perhaps you know the place, my father. In it is a great and strange mountain. It is haunted also, and named the Ghost Mountain, and on the top of it is a grey peak rudely shaped like the head of an aged woman. Here in this wild place we must sleep, for darkness drew on. Now we soon learned that there were many lions in the rocks around, for we heard their roaring and were much afraid, all except Umslopogaas, who feared nothing. So we made a circle of thorn-bushes and sat in it, holding our assegais ready. Presently the moon came up — it was a full-grown moon and very bright, so bright that we could see everything for a long way round. Now some six spear-throws from where we sat was a cliff, and at the top of the cliff was a cave, and in this cave lived two lions and their young. When the moon grew bright we saw the lions come out and stand upon the edge of the cliff, and with them were two little ones that played about like kittens, so that had we not been frightened it would have been beautiful to see them.

"Oh! Umslopogaas," said Nada, "I wish that I had one of the little lions for a dog."

The boy laughed, saying, "Then, shall I fetch you one, sister?"

"Peace, boy," I said. "No man may take young lions from their lair and live."

"Such things have been done, my father," he answered, laughing. And no more was said of the matter.

Now when the cubs had played awhile, we saw the lioness take up the cubs in her mouth and carry them into the cave. Then she came out again, and went away with her mate to seek food, and soon we heard them roaring in the distance. Now we stacked up the fire and went to sleep in our enclosure of thorns without fear, for we knew that the lions were far away eating game. But Umslopogaas did not sleep, for he had determined that he would fetch the cub which Nada had desired, and, being young and foolhardy, he did not think of the danger which he would bring upon himself and all of us. He knew no fear, and now, as ever, if Nada spoke a word, nay, even if she thought of a thing to desire it, he would not rest till it was won for her. So while we slept Umslopogaas crept like a snake from the fence of thorns, and, taking an assegai in his hand, he slipped away to the foot of the cliff where the lions had their den. Then he climbed the cliff, and, coming to the cave, entered there and groped his way into it. The cubs heard him, and, thinking that it was their mother who returned, began to whine and purr for food. Guided by the light of their yellow eyes, he crept over the bones, of which there were many in the cave, and came to where they lay. Then he put out his hands and seized one of the cubs, killing the other with his assegai, because he could not carry both of them. Now he made haste thence before the lions returned, and came back to the thorn fence where we lay just as dawn as breaking.

I awoke at the coming of the dawn, and, standing up, I looked out. Lo! there, on the farther side of the thorn fence, looking large in the grey mist, stood the lad Umslopogaas, laughing. In his teeth he held the assegai, yet dripping with blood, and in his hands the lion cub that, despite its whines and struggles, he grasped by the skin of the neck and the hind legs.

"Awake, my sister!" he cried; "here is the dog you seek. Ah! he bites now, but he will soon grow tame."

Nada awoke, and rising, cried out with joy at the sight of the cub, but for a moment I stood astonished.

"Fool!" I cried at last, "let the cub go before the lions come to rend us!"

"I will not let it go, my father," he answered sullenly. "Are there not five of us with spears, and can we not fight two cats? I was not afraid to go alone into their den. Are you all afraid to meet them in the open?"

"You are mad," I said; "let the cub go!" And I ran towards Umslopogaas to take it from him. But he sprang aside and avoided me.

"I will never let that go of which I have got hold," he said, "at least not living!" And suddenly he seized the head of the cub and twisted its neck; then threw it on to the ground, and added, "See, now I have done your bidding, my father!"

As he spoke we heard a great sound of roaring from the cave in the cliff. The lions had returned and found one cub dead and the other gone.

"Into the fence! — back into the fence!" I cried, and we sprang over the thorn-bushes where those with us were making ready their spears, trembling as they handled them with fear and the cold of the morning. We looked up. There, down the side of the cliff, came the lions, bounding on the scent of him who had robbed them of their young. The lion ran first, and as he came he roared; then followed the lioness, but she did not roar, for in her mouth was the cub that Umslopogaas had assegaied in the cave. Now they drew near, mad with fury, their manes bristling, and lashing their flanks with their long tails.

"Curse you for a fool, son of Mopo," said one of the men with me to Umslopogaas; "presently I will beat you till the blood comes for this trick."

"First beat the lions, then beat me if you can," answered the lad, "and wait to curse till you have done both."

Now the lions were close to us; they came to the body of the second cub, that lay outside the fence of thorns. The lion stopped and sniffed it. Then he roared — ah! he roared till the earth shook. As for the lioness, she dropped the dead cub which she was carrying, and took the other into her mouth, for she could not carry both.

"Get behind me, Nada," cried Umslopogaas, brandishing his spear, "the lion is about to spring."

As the words left his mouth the great brute crouched to the ground. Then suddenly he sprang from it like a bird, and like a bird he traveled through the air towards us.

"Catch him on the spears!" cried Umslopogaas, and by nature, as it were, we did the boy's bidding; for huddling ourselves together, we held out the assegais so that the lion fell upon them as he sprang, and their blades sank far into him. But the weight of his charge carried us to the ground, and he fell on to us, striking at us and at the spears, and roaring with pain and fury as he struck. Presently he was on his legs biting at the spears in his breast. Then Umslopogaas, who alone did not wait his onslaught, but had stepped aside for his own ends, uttered a loud cry and drove his assegai into the lion behind the shoulder, so that with a groan the brute rolled over dead.

Meanwhile, the lioness stood without the fence, the second dead cub in her mouth, for she could not bring herself to leave either of them. But when she heard her mate's last groan she dropped the cub and gathered herself together to spring. Umslopogaas alone stood up to face her, for he only had withdrawn his assegai from the carcass of the lion. She swept on towards the lad, who stood like a stone to meet her. Now she met his spear, it sunk in, it snapped, and down fell Umslopogaas dead or senseless beneath the mass of the lioness. She sprang up, the broken spear standing in her breast, sniffed at Umslopogaas, then, as though she knew that it was he who had robbed her, she seized him by the loins and *moocha*, and sprang with him over the fence.

"Oh, save him!" cried the girl Nada in bitter woe. And we rushed after the lioness shouting.

For a moment she stood over her dead cubs, Umslopogaas hanging from her mouth, and looked at them as though she wondered; and we hoped that she might let him fall. Then, hearing our cries, she turned and bounded away towards the bush, bearing Umslopogaas in her mouth. We seized our spears and followed; but the ground grew stony, and, search as we would, we could find no trace of Umslopogaas or of the lioness. They had vanished like a cloud. So we came back, and, ah! my heart was sore, for I loved the lad as though he had indeed been my son. But I knew that he was dead, and there was an end.

"Where is my brother?" cried Nada when we came back.

"Lost," I answered. "Lost, never to be found again."

Then the girl gave a great and bitter cry, and fell to the earth saying, "I would that I were dead with my brother!"

"Let us be going," said Macropha, my wife.

"Have you no tears to weep for your son?" asked a man of our company.

"What is the use of weeping over the dead? Does it, then, bring them back?" she answered. "Let us be going!"

The man thought these words strange, but he did not know that Umslopogaas was not born of Macropha.

Still, we waited in that place a day, thinking that, perhaps, the lioness would return to her den and that, at least, we might kill her. But she came back no more. So on the next morning we rolled up our blankets and started forward on our journey, sad at heart. In truth, Nada was so weak from grief that she could hardly travel, but I never heard the name of Umslopogaas pass her lips again during that journey. She buried him in her heart and said nothing. And I too said nothing, but I wondered why it had been brought about that I should save the life of Umslopogaas from the jaws of the Lion of Zulu, that the lioness of the rocks might devour him.

And so the time went on till we reached the kraal where the king's business must be done, and where I and my wife should part.

On the morning after we came to the kraal, having kissed in secret, though in public we looked sullenly on one another, we parted as those part who meet no more, for it was in our thoughts, that we should never see each other's face again, nor, indeed, did we do so. And I drew Nada aside and spoke to her thus: "We part, my daughter; nor do I know when we shall meet again, for the times are troubled and it is for your safety and that of your mother that I rob my eyes of the sight of you. Nada, you will soon be a woman, and you will be fairer than any woman among our people, and it may come about that many great men will seek you in marriage, and, perhaps, that I, your father, shall not be there to choose for you whom you shall wed, according to the custom of our land. But I charge you, as far as may be possible for you to do so, take only a man whom you can love, and be faithful to him alone, for thus shall a woman find happiness."

Here I stopped, for the girl took hold of my hand and looked into my face. "Peace, my father," she said, "do not speak to me of marriage, for I will wed no man, now that Umslopogaas is dead because of my foolishness. I will live and die alone, and, oh! may I die quickly, that I may go to seek him whom I love only!"

"Nay, Nada," I said, "Umslopogaas was your brother, and it is not fitting that you should speak of him thus, even though he is dead."

"I know nothing of such matters, my father," she said. "I speak what my heart tells me, and it tells me that I loved Umslopogaas living, and, though he is dead, I shall love him alone to the end. Ah! you think me but a child, yet my heart is large, and it does not lie to me."

Now I upbraided the girl no more, because I knew that Umslopogaas was not her brother, but one whom she might have married. Only I marveled that the voice of nature should speak so truly in her, telling her that which was lawful, even when it seemed to be most unlawful.

"Speak no more of Umslopogaas," I said, "for surely he is dead, and though you cannot forget him, yet speak of him no more, and I pray of you, my daughter, that if we do not meet again, yet you should keep me in your memory, and the love I bear you, and the words which from time to time I have said to you. The world is a thorny wilderness, my daughter, and its thorns are watered with a rain of blood, and we wander in our wretchedness like lost travelers in a mist; nor do I know why our feet are set on this wandering. But at last there comes an end, and we die and go hence, none know where, but perhaps where we go the evil may change to the good, and those who were dear to each other on the earth may become yet dearer in the heavens; for I believe that man is not born to perish altogether, but is rather gathered again to the Umkulunkulu who sent him on his journeyings. Therefore keep hope, my daughter, for if these things are not so, at least sleep remains, and sleep is soft, and so farewell."

Then we kissed and parted, and I watched Macropha, my wife, and Nada, my daughter, till they melted into the sky, as they walked upon their journey to Swaziland, and was very sad, because, having lost

Umslopogaas, he who in after days was named the Slaughterer and the Woodpecker, I must lose them also.

Chapter X

THE TRIAL OF MOPO

*N*ow I sat four days in the huts of the tribe whither I had been sent, and did the king's business. And on the fifth morning I rose up, together with those with me, and we turned our faces towards the king's kraal. But when we had journeyed a little way we met a party of soldiers, who commanded us to stand.

"What is it, king's men?" I asked boldly.

"This, son of Makedama," answered their spokesman: "give over to us your wife Macropha and your children Umslopogaas and Nada, that we may do with them as the king commands."

"Umslopogaas," I answered, "has gone where the king's arm cannot stretch, for he is dead; and for my wife Macropha and my daughter Nada, they are by now in the caves of the Swazis, and the king must seek them there with an army if he will find them. To Macropha he is welcome, for I hate her, and have divorced her; and as for the girl, well, there are many girls, and it is no great matter if she lives or dies, yet I pray him to spare her."

Thus I spoke carelessly, for I knew well that my wife and child were beyond the reach of Chaka.

"You do well to ask the girl's life," said the soldier, laughing, "for all those born to you are dead, by order of the king."

"Is it indeed so?" I answered calmly, though my knees shook and my tongue clove to my lips. "The will of the king be done. A cut stick puts out new leaves; I can have more children."

"Aye, Mopo; but first you must get new wives, for yours are dead also, all five of them."

"Is it indeed so?" I answered. "The king's will be done. I wearied of those brawling women."

"So, Mopo," said the soldier; "but to get other wives and have more children born to you, you must live yourself, for no children are born to the dead, and I think that Chaka has an assegai which you shall kiss."

"Is it so?" I answered. "The king's will be done. The sun is hot, and I tire of the road. He who kisses the assegai sleeps sound."

Thus I spoke, my father, and, indeed, in that hour I desired to die. The world was empty for me. Macropha and Nada were gone, Umslopogaas was dead, and my other wives and children were murdered. I had no heart to begin to build up a new house, none were left for me to love, and it seemed well that I should die also.

The soldiers asked those with me if that tale was true which I told of the death of Umslopogaas and of the going of Macropha and Nada into Swaziland. They said, Yes, it was true. Then the soldiers said that they would lead me back to the king, and I wondered at this, for I thought that they would kill me where I stood. So we went on, and piece by piece I learned what had happened at the king's kraal.

On the day after I left, it came to the ears of Chaka, by the mouth of his spies, that my second wife — Anadi — was sick and spoke strange words in her sickness. Then, taking three soldiers with him, he went to my kraal at the death of the day. He left the three soldiers by the gates of the kraal, bidding them to suffer none to come in or go out, but Chaka himself entered the large hut where Anadi lay sick, having his toy assegai, with the shaft of the royal red wood, in his hand. Now, as it chanced, in the hut were Unandi, the mother of Chaka, and Baleka, my sister, the wife of Chaka, for, not knowing that I had taken away Umslopogaas, the son of Baleka, according to their custom, these two foolish women had come to kiss and fondle the lad. But when they entered the hut they found it full of my other wives and children. These they sent away, all except Moosa, the son of Anadi — that boy who was born eight days before Umslopogaas, the son of Chaka. But they kept Moosa in the hut, and kissed him, giving him *imphi** to eat, fearing lest it should seem strange to the women, my wives, if, Umslopogaas being gone, they refused to take notice of any other child.

Now as they sat this, presently the doorway was darkened, and, behold! the king himself crept through it, and saw them fondling the child Moosa. When they knew who it was that entered, the women flung themselves upon the ground before him and praised him. But he smiled grimly, and bade them be seated. Then he spoke to them, saying, "You

---

* A variety of sugar-cane. — Editor

wonder, Unandi, my mother, and Baleka, my wife, why it is that I am
come here into the hut of Mopo, son of Makedama. I will tell you: it
is because he is away upon my business, and I hear that his wife Anadi
is sick — it is she who lies there, is it not? Therefore, as the first doctor
in the land, I am come to cure her, Unandi, my mother, and Baleka,
my sister."

Thus he spoke, eyeing them as he did so, and taking snuff from the
blade of his little assegai, and though his words were gentle they shook
with fear, for when Chaka spoke thus gently he meant death to many.
But Unandi, Mother of the Heavens, answered, saying that it was well
that the king had come, since his medicine would bring rest and peace
to her who lay sick.

"Yes," he answered; "it is well. It is pleasant, moreover, my mother
and sister, to see you kissing yonder child. Surely, were he of your own
blood you could not love him more."

Now they trembled again, and prayed in their hearts that Anadi, the
sick woman, who lay asleep, might not wake and utter foolish words in
her wandering. But the prayer was answered from below and not from
above, for Anadi woke, and, hearing the voice of the king, her sick mind
flew to him whom she believed to be the king's child.

"Ah!" she said, sitting upon the ground and pointing to her own son,
Moosa, who squatted frightened against the wall of the hut. "Kiss him,
Mother of the Heavens, kiss him! Whom do they call him, the young
cub who brings ill-fortune to our doors? They call him the son of Mopo
and Macropha!" And she laughed wildly, stopped speaking, and sank
back upon the bed of skins.

"They call him the son of Mopo and Macropha," said the king in a
low voice. "Whose son is he, then, woman?"

"Oh, ask her not, O king," cried his mother and his wife, casting
themselves upon the ground before him, for they were mad with fear.
"Ask her not; she has strange fancies such as are not meet for your ears
to hear. She is bewitched, and has dreams and fancies."

"Peace!" he answered. "I will listen to this woman's wanderings.
Perhaps some star of truth shines in her darkness, and I would see light.
Who, then, is he, woman?"

"Who is he?" she answered. "Are you a fool that ask who he is? He
is — hush! — put your ear close — let me speak low lest the reeds of the
hut speak it to the king. He is — do you listen? He is — the son of Chaka
and Baleka, the sister of Mopo, the changeling whom Unandi, Mother
of the Heavens, palmed off upon this house to bring a curse on it, and
whom she would lead out before the people when the land is weary of
the wickedness of the king, her son, to take the place of the king."

"It is false, O king!" cried the two women. "Do not listen to her; it is false. The boy is her own son, Moosa, whom she does not know in her sickness."

But Chaka stood up in the hut and laughed terribly. "Truly, Nobela prophesied well," he cried, "and I did ill to slay her. So this is the trick thou hast played upon me, my mother. Thou wouldst give a son to me who will have no son: thou wouldst give me a son to kill me. Good! Mother of the Heavens, take thou the doom of the Heavens! Thou wouldst give me a son to slay me and rule in my place; now, in turn, I, thy son, will rob me of a mother. Die, Unandi! — die at the hand thou didst bring forth!" And he lifted the little assegai and smote it through her.

For a moment Unandi, Mother of the Heavens, wife of Senzangacona, stood uttering no cry. Then she put up her hand, and drew the assegai from her side.

"So shalt thou die also, Chaka the Evil!" she cried, and fell down dead there in the hut.

Thus, then, did Chaka murder his mother Unandi.

Now when Baleka saw what had been done, she turned and fled from the hut into the Emposeni, and so swiftly that the guards at the gates could not stop her. But when she reached her own hut Baleka's strength failed her, and she fell senseless on the ground. But the boy Moosa, my son, being overcome with terror, stayed where he was, and Chaka, believing him to be his son, murdered him also, and with his own hand.

Then he stalked out of the hut, and leaving the three guards at the gate, commanded a company of soldiers to surround the kraal and fire it. This they did, and as the people rushed out they killed them, and those who did not run out were burned in the fire. Thus, then, perished all my wives, my children, my servants, and those who were within the gates in their company. The tree was burned, and the bees in it, and I alone was left living — I and Macropha and Nada, who were far away.

Nor was Chaka yet satisfied with blood, for, as has been told, he sent messengers bidding them kill Macropha, my wife, and Nada, my daughter, and him who was named by son. But he commanded the messengers that they should not slay me, but bring me living before them.

Now when the soldiers did not kill me I took counsel with myself, for it was my belief that I was saved alive only that I might die later, and in a more cruel fashion. Therefore for awhile I thought that it would be well if I did that for myself which another purposed to do for me. Why should I, who was already doomed, wait to meet my doom? What had I left to keep me in the place of life, seeing that all whom I loved were dead or gone? To die would be easy, for I knew the ways of death.

In my girdle I carried a secret medicine; he who eats of it, my father, will see the sun's shadow move no more, and will never look upon the stars again. But I was minded to know the assegai or the kerrie; nor would I perish more slowly beneath the knives of the tormentors, nor be parched by the pangs of thirst, or wander eyeless to my end. Therefore it was that, since I had sat in the doom ring looking hour after hour into the face of death, I had borne this medicine with me by night and by day. Surely now was the time to use it.

So I thought as I sat through the watches of the night, aye! and drew out the bitter drug and laid it on my tongue. But as I did so I remembered my daughter Nada, who was left to me, though she so-journed in a far country, and my wife Macropha and my sister Baleka, who still lived, so said the soldiers, though how it came about that the king had not killed her I did not know then. Also another thought was born in my heart. While life remained to me, I might be revenged upon him who had wrought me this woe; but can the dead strike? Alas! the dead are strengthless, and if they still have hearts to suffer, they have no hands to give back blow for blow. Nay, I would live on. Time to die when death could no more be put away. Time to die when the voice of Chaka spoke my doom. Death chooses for himself and answers no questions; he is a guest to whom none need open the door of his hut, for when he wills he can pass through the thatch like air. Not yet would I taste of that medicine of mine.

So I lived on, my father, and the soldiers led me back to the kraal of Chaka. Now when we came to the kraal it was night, for the sun had sunk as we passed through the gates. Still, as he had been commanded, the captain of those who watched me went in before the king and told him that I lay without in bonds. And the king said, "Let him be brought before me, who was my physician, that I may tell him how I have doctored those of his house."

So they took me and led me to the royal house, and pushed me through the doorway of the great hut.

Now a fire burned in the hut, for the night was cold, and Chaka sat on the further side of the fire, looking towards the opening of the hut, and the smoke from the fire wreathed him round, and its light shone upon his face and flickered in his terrible eyes.

At the door of the hut certain councilors seized me by the arms and dragged me towards the fire. But I broke from them, and prostrating myself, for my arms were free, I praised the king and called him by his royal names. The councilors sprang towards me to seize me again, but Chaka said, "Let him be; I would talk with my servant." Then the councilors bowed themselves on either side, and laid their hands on their sticks, their foreheads touching the ground. But I sat down on the floor of the hut over against the king, and we talked through the fire.

"Tell me of the cattle that I sent thee to number, Mopo, son of Makedama," said Chaka. "Have my servants dealt honestly with my cattle?"

"They have dealt honestly, O king," I answered.

"Tell me, then, of the number of the cattle and of their markings, Mopo, forgetting none."

So I sat and told him, ox by ox, cow by cow, and heifer by heifer, forgetting none; and Chaka listened silently as one who is asleep. But I knew that he did not sleep, for all the while the firelight flickered in his fierce eyes. Also I knew that he did but torment me, or that, perhaps, he would learn of the cattle before he killed me. At length all the tale was told.

"So," said the king, "it goes well. There are yet honest men left in the land. Knowest thou, Mopo, that sorrow has come upon thy house while thou wast about my business."

"I have heard it, O king!" I answered, as one who speaks of a small matter.

"Yes, Mopo, sorrow has come upon thy house, the curse of Heaven has fallen upon thy kraal. They tell me, Mopo, that the fire from above ran briskly through they huts."

"I have heard it, I king!"

"They tell me, Mopo, that those within thy gates grew mad at the sight of the fire, and dreaming there was no escape, that they stabbed themselves with assegais or leaped into the flames."

"I have heard it, O king! What of it? Any river is deep enough to drown a fool!"

"Thou hast heard these things, Mopo, but thou hast not yet heard all. Knowest thou, Mopo, that among those who died in thy kraal was she who bore me, she who was named Mother of the Heavens?"

Then, my father, I, Mopo, acted wisely, because of the thought which my good spirit gave me, for I cast myself upon the ground, and wailed aloud as though in utter grief.

"Spare my ears, Black One!" I wailed. "Tell me not that she who bore thee is dead, O Lion of the Zulu. For the others, what is it? It is a breath of wind, it is a drop of water; but this trouble is as the gale or as the sea."

"Cease, my servant, cease!" said the mocking voice of Chaka; "but know this, thou hast done well to grieve aloud, because the Mother of the Heavens is no more, and ill wouldst thou have done to grieve because the fire from above has kissed thy gates. For hadst thou done this last thing or left the first undone, I should have known that thy heart was wicked, and by now thou wouldst have wept indeed — tears of blood, Mopo. It is well for thee, then, that thou hast read my riddle aright."

Now I saw the depths of the pit that Chaka had dug for me, and blessed my Ehlose who had put into my heart those words which I should answer. I hoped also that Chaka would now let me go; but it was not to be, for this was but the beginning of my trial.

"Knowest thou, Mopo," said the king, "that as my mother died yonder in the flames of thy kraal she cried out strange and terrible words which came to my ears through the singing of the fire. These were her words: that thou, Mopo, and thy sister Baleka, and thy wives, had conspired together to give a child to me who would be childless. These were her words, the words that came to me through the singing of the fire. Tell me now, Mopo, where are those children that thou leddest from thy kraal, the boy with the lion eyes who is named Umslopogaas, and the girl who is named Nada?"

"Umslopogaas is dead by the lion's mouth, O king!" I answered, "and Nada sits in the Swazi caves." And I told him of the death of Umslopogaas and of how I had divorced Macropha, my wife.

"The boy with the lion eyes to the lion's mouth!" said Chaka. "Enough of him; he is gone. Nada may yet be sought for with the assegai in the Swazi caves; enough of her. Let us speak of this song that my mother — who, alas! is dead, Mopo — this song she sang through the singing of the flames. Tell me, Mopo, tell me now, was it a true tale."

"Nay, O king! surely the Mother of the Heavens was maddened by the Heavens when she sang that song," I answered. "I know nothing of it, O king."

"Thou knowest naught of it, Mopo?" said the king. And again he looked at me terribly through the reek of the fire. "Thou knowest naught of it, Mopo? Surely thou art a-cold; thy hands shake with cold. Nay, man, fear not — warm them, warm them, Mopo. See, now, plunge that hand of thine into the heart of the flame!" And he pointed with his little assegai, the assegai handled with the royal wood, to where the fire glowed reddest — aye, he pointed and laughed.

Then, my father, I grew cold indeed — yes, I grew cold who soon should be hot, for I saw the purpose of Chaka. He would put me to the trial by fire.

For a moment I sat silent, thinking. Then the king spoke again in a great voice: "Nay, Mopo, be not so backward; shall I sit warm and see thee suffer cold? What, my councilors, rise, take the hand of Mopo, and hold it to the flame, that his heart may rejoice in the warmth of the flame while we speak together of this matter of the child that was, so my mother sang, born to Baleka, my wife, the sister of Mopo, my servant."

"There is little need for that, O king," I answered, being made bold by fear, for I saw that if I did nothing death would swiftly end my doubts. Once, indeed, I bethought me of the poison that I bore, and was minded to swallow it and make an end, but the desire to live is great, and keen is the thirst for vengeance, so I said to my heart, "Not yet awhile; I will endure this also; afterwards, if need be, I can die."

"I thank the king for his graciousness, and I will warm me at the fire. Speak on, O king, while I warm myself, and thou shalt hear true words," I said boldly.

Then, my father, I stretched out my left hand and plunged it into the fire — not into the hottest of the fire, but where the smoke leapt from the flame. Now my flesh was wet with the sweat of fear, and for a little moment the flames curled round it and did not burn me. But I knew that the torment was to come.

For a short while Chaka watched me, smiling. Then he spoke slowly, that the fire might find time to do its work.

"Say, then, Mopo, thou knowest nothing of this matter of the birth of a son to thy sister Baleka?"

"I know this only, O king!" I answered, "that a son was born in past years to thy wife Baleka, that I killed the child in obedience to thy word, and laid its body before thee."

Now, my father, the steam from my flesh had been drawn from my hand by the heat, and the flame got hold of me and ate into my flesh, and its torment was great. But of this I showed no sign upon my face, for I knew well that if I showed sign or uttered cry, then, having failed in the trial, death would be my portion.

Then the king spoke again, "Dost thou swear by my head, Mopo, that no son of mine was suckled in thy kraals?"

"I swear it, O king! I swear it by thy head," I answered.

And now, my father, the agony of the fire was such as may not be told. I felt my eyes start forward in their sockets, my blood seemed to boil within me, it rushed into my head, and down my face their ran two tears of blood. But yet I held my hand in the fire and made no sign, while the king and his councilors watched me curiously. Still, for a moment Chaka said nothing, and that moment seemed to me as all the years of my life.

"Ah!" he said at length, "I see that thou growest warm, Mopo! Withdraw thy hand from the flame. I am answered; thou hast passed the trial; thy heart is clean; for had there been lies in it the fire had given them tongue, and thou hadst cried aloud, making thy last music, Mopo!"

Now I took my hand from the flame, and for awhile the torment left me.

"It is well, O king," I said calmly. "Fire has no power of hurt on those whose heart is pure."

But as I spoke I looked at my left hand. It was black, my father — black as a charred stick, and the nails were gone from the twisted fingers. Look at it now, my father; you can see, though my eyes are blind. The hand is white, like yours — it is white and dead and shriveled. These are the marks of the fire in Chaka's hut — the fire that kissed me many, many years ago; I have had but little use of that hand since this night of torment. But my right arm yet remained to me, my father, and, ah! I used it.

"It seems that Nobela, the doctress, who is dead, lied when she prophesied evil on me from thee, Mopo," said Chaka again. "It seems that thou art innocent of this offence, and that Baleka, thy sister, is innocent, and that the song which the Mother of the Heavens sang through the singing flames was no true song. It is well for thee, Mopo, for in such a matter my oath had not helped thee. But my mother is dead — dead in the flames with thy wives and children, Mopo, and in this there is witchcraft. We will have a mourning, Mopo, thou and I, such a mourning as has not been seen in Zululand, for all the people on the earth shall weep at it. And there shall be a 'smelling out' at this mourning, Mopo. But we will summon no witch-doctors, thou and I will be witch-doctors, and ourselves shall smell out those who have brought these woes upon us. What! shall my mother die unavenged, she who bore me and has perished by witchcraft, and shall thy wives and children die unavenged — thou being innocent? Go forth, Mopo, my faithful servant, whom I have honored with the warmth of my fire, go forth!" And once again he stared at me through the reek of the flame, and pointed with his assegai to the door of the hut.

Chapter XI
THE COUNSEL OF BALEKA

I rose, I praised the king with a loud voice, and I went from the Intunkulu, the house of the king. I walked slowly through the gates, but when I was without the gates the anguish that took me because of my burned hand was more than I could bear. I ran to and fro groaning till I came to the hut of one whom I knew. There I found fat, and having plunged my hand in the fat, I wrapped it round with a skin and passed out again, for I could not stay still. I went to and fro, till at length I reached the spot where my huts had been. The outer fence of the huts still stood; the fire had not caught it. I passed through the fence; there within were the ashes of the burned huts — they lay ankle-deep. I walked in among the ashes; my feet struck upon things that were sharp. The moon was bright, and I looked; they were the blackened bones of my wives and children. I flung myself down in the ashes in bitterness of heart; I covered myself over with the ashes of my kraal and with the bones of my wives and children. Yes, my father, there I lay, and on me were the ashes, and among the ashes were the bones. Thus, then, did I lie for the last time in my kraal, and was sheltered from the frost of the night by the dust of those to whom I had given life. Such were the things that befell us in the days of Chaka, my father; yes, not to me alone, but to many another also.

I lay among the ashes and groaned with the pain of my burn, and groaned also from the desolation of my heart. Why had I not tasted the poison, there in the hut of Chaka, and before the eyes of Chaka? Why did I not taste it now and make an end? Nay, I had endured the agony; I would not give him this last triumph over me. Now, having passed the fire, once more I should be great in the land, and I would become great. Yes, I would bear my sorrows, and become great, that in a day to be I might wreak vengeance on the king. Ah! my father, there, as I rolled among the ashes, I prayed to the Amatongo, to the ghosts of my ancestors. I prayed to my Ehlose, to the spirit that watches me — aye, and I even dared to pray to the Umkulunkulu, the great soul of the world, who moves through the heavens and the earth unseen and unheard. And thus I prayed, that I might yet live to kill Chaka as he had killed those who were dear to me. And while I prayed I slept, or, if I did not sleep, the light of thought went out of me, and I became as one dead. Then there came a vision to me, a vision that was sent in answer to my prayer, or, perchance, it was a madness born of my sorrows. For, my father, it seemed to me that I stood upon the bank of a great and wide river. It was gloomy there, the light lay low upon the face of the river, but far away on the farther side was a glow like the glow of a stormy dawn, and in the glow I saw a mighty bed of reeds that swayed about in the breath of dawn, and out of the reeds came men and women and children, by hundreds and thousands, and plunged into the waters of the river and were buffeted about by them. Now, my father, all the people that I saw in the water were black people, and all those who were torn out of the reeds were black — they wee none of them white like your people, my father, for this vision was a vision of the Zulu race, who alone are "torn out of the reeds." Now, I saw that of those who swam in the river some passed over very quickly and some stood still, as it were, still in the water — as in life, my father, some die soon and some live for many years. And I saw the countless faces of those in the water, among them were many that I knew. There, my father, I saw the face of Chaka, and near him was my own face; there, too, I saw the face of Dingaan, the prince, his brother, and the face of the boy Umslopogaas and the face of Nada, my daughter, and then for the first time I knew that Umslopogaas was not dead, but only lost.

Now I turned in my vision, and looked at that bank of the river on which I stood. Then I saw that behind the bank was a cliff, mighty and black, and in the cliff were doors of ivory, and through them came light and the sound of laughter; there were other doors also, black as though fashioned of coal, and through them came darkness and the sounds of groans. I saw also that in front of the doors was set a seat, and on the seat was the figure of a glorious woman. She was tall, and she alone was white, and clad in robes of white, and her hair was like gold which is molten in the fire, and her face shone like the midday sun. Then I saw that those who came up out of the river stood before the woman, the water yet running from them, and cried aloud to her.

"Hail, Inkosazana-y-Zulu! Hail, Queen of the Heavens!"

Now the figure of the glorious woman held a rod in either hand, and the rod in her right hand was white and of ivory, and the rod in her left hand was black and of ebony. And as those who came up before her throne greeted her, so she pointed now with the wand of ivory in her right hand, and now with the wand of ebony in her left hand. And with the wand of ivory she pointed to the gates of ivory, through which came light and laughter, and with the wand of ebony she pointed to the gates of coal, through which came blackness and groans. And as she pointed, so those who greeted her turned, and went, some through the gates of light and some through the gates of blackness.

Presently, as I stood, a handful of people came up from the bank of the river. I looked on them and knew them. There was Unandi, the mother of Chaka, there was Anadi, my wife, and Moosa, my son, and all my other wives and children, and those who had perished with them.

They stood before the figure of the woman, the Princess of the Heavens, to whom the Umkulunkulu has given it to watch over the people of the Zulu, and cried aloud, "Hail, Inkosazana-y-Zulu! Hail!"

Then she, the Inkosazana, pointed with the rod of ivory to the gates of ivory; but still they stood before her, not moving. Now the woman spoke for the first time, in a low voice that was sad and awful to hear.

"Pass in, children of my people, pass in to the judgment. Why tarry ye? Pass in through the gates of light."

But still they tarried, and in my vision Unandi spoke: "We tarry, Queen of the Heavens — we tarry to pray for justice on him who murdered us. I, who on earth was named Mother of the Heavens, on behalf of all this company, pray to thee, Queen of the Heavens, for justice on him who murdered us."

"How is he named?" asked the voice that was low and awful.

"Chaka, king of the Zulus," answered the voice of Unandi. "Chaka, my son."

"Many have come to ask for vengeance on that head," said the voice of the Queen of the Heavens, "and many more shall come. Fear not, Unandi, it shall fall. Fear not, Anadi and ye wives and children of Mopo, it shall fall, I say. With the spear that pierced thy breast, Unandi, shall the breast of Chaka be also pierced, and, ye wives and children of Mopo, the hand that pierces shall be the hand of Mopo. As I guide him so shall he go. Aye, I will teach him to wreak my vengeance on the earth! Pass in, children of my people — pass in to the judgment, for the doom of Chaka is written."

Thus I dreamed, my father. Aye, this was the vision that was sent me as I lay in pain and misery among the bones of my dead in the ashes of my kraal. Thus it was given me to see the Inkosazana of the Heavens as she is in her own place. Twice more I saw her, as you shall hear, but that was on the earth and with my waking eyes. Yes, thrice has it been given to me in all to look upon that face that I shall now see no more till I am dead, for no man may look four times on the Inkosazana and live. Or am I mad, my father, and did I weave these visions from the woof of my madness? I do not know, but it is true that I seemed to see them.

I woke when the sky was grey with the morning light; it was the pain of my burned hand that aroused me from my sleep or from my stupor. I rose shaking the ashes from me, and went without the kraal to wash away their defilement. Then I returned, and sat outside the gates of the Emposeni, waiting till the king's women, whom he named his sisters, should come to draw water according to their custom. At last they came, and, sitting with my *kaross* thrown over my face to hide it, looked for the passing of Baleka. Presently I saw her; she was sad-faced, and walked slowly, her pitcher on her head. I whispered her name, and she drew aside behind an aloe bush, and, making pretence that her foot was pierced with a thorn, she lingered till the other women had gone by. Then she came up to me, and we greeted one another, gazing heavily into each other's eyes.

"In an ill day did I hearken to you, Baleka," I said, "to you and to the Mother of the Heavens, and save your child alive. See now what has sprung from this seed! Dead are all my house, dead is the Mother of the Heavens — all are dead — and I myself have been put to the torment by fire," and I held out my withered hand towards her.

"Aye, Mopo, my brother," she answered, "but flesh is nearest to flesh, and I should think little of it were not my son Umslopogaas also dead, as I have heard but now."

"You speak like a woman, Baleka. Is it, then, nothing to you that I, your brother, have lost — all I love?"

"Fresh seed can yet be raised up to you, my brother, but for me there is no hope, for the king looks on me no more. I grieve for you, but I had this one alone, and flesh is nearest to flesh. Think you that I shall escape? I tell you nay. I am but spared for a little, then I go where the others have gone. Chaka has marked me for the grave; for a little while I may be left, then I die: he does but play with me as a leopard plays with a wounded buck. I care not, I am weary, but I grieve for the boy; there was no such boy in the land. Would that I might die swiftly and go to seek him."

"And if the boy is not dead, Baleka, what then?"

"What is that you said?" she answered, turning on me with wild eyes. "Oh, say it again — again, Mopo! I would gladly die a hundred deaths to know that Umslopogaas still lives."

"Nay, Baleka, I know nothing. But last night I dreamed a dream," and I told her all my dream, and also of that which had gone before the dream.

She listened as one listens to the words of a king when he passes judgment for life or for death.

"I think that there is wisdom in your dreams, Mopo," she said at length. "You were ever a strange man, to whom the gates of distance are no bar. Now it is borne in upon my heart that Umslopogaas still lives, and now I shall die happy. Yes, gainsay me not; I shall die, I know it. I read it in the king's eyes. But what is it? It is nothing, if only the prince Umslopogaas yet lives."

"Your love is great, woman," I said; "and this love of yours has brought many woes upon us, and it may well happen that in the end it shall all be for nothing, for there is an evil fate upon us. Say now, what shall I do? Shall I fly, or shall I abide here, taking the chance of things?"

"You must stay here, Mopo. See, now! This is in the king's mind. He fears because of the death of his mother at his own hand — yes, even he; he is afraid lest the people should turn upon him who killed his own mother. Therefore he will give it out that he did not kill her, but that she perished in the fire which was called down upon your kraals by witchcraft; and, though all men know the lie, yet none shall dare to gainsay him. As he said to you, there will be a smelling out, but a smelling out of a new sort, for he and you shall be the witch-finders, and at that smelling out he will give to death all those whom he fears, all those whom he knows hate him for his wickedness and because with his own hand he slew his mother. For this cause, then, he will save you alive, Mopo — yes, and make you great in the land, for if, indeed, his mother Unandi died through witchcraft, as he shall say, are you not also wronged by him, and did not your wives and children also perish by witchcraft? Therefore, do not fly; abide here and become great — become great to the great end of vengeance, Mopo, my brother. You have much wrong to wreak; soon you will have more, for I, too, shall be gone, and my blood also shall cry for vengeance to you. Hearken, Mopo. Are there not other princes in the land? What of Dingaan, what of Umhlangana, what of Umpanda, brothers to the king? Do not these also desire to be kings? Do they not day by day rise from sleep feeling their limbs to know if they yet live, do they not night by night lie down to sleep not knowing if it shall be their wives that they shall kiss ere dawn or the red assegai of the king? Draw near to them, my brother; creep into their hearts and learn their counsel or teach them yours; so in the end shall Chaka be brought to that gate through which your wives have passed, and where I also am about to tread."

Thus Baleka spoke and she was gone, leaving me pondering, for her words were heavy with wisdom. I knew well that the brothers of the king went heavily and in fear of death, for his shadow was on them. With

Panda, indeed, little could be done, for he lived softly, speaking always as one whose wits are few. But Dingaan and Umhlangana were of another wood, and from them might be fashioned a kerrie that should scatter the brains of Chaka to the birds. But the time to speak was not now; not yet was the cup of Chaka full.

Then, having finished my thought, I rose, and, going to the kraal of my friend, I doctored my burned hand, that pained me, and as I was doctoring it there came a messenger to me summoning me before the king.

I went in before the king, and prostrated myself, calling him by his royal names; but he took me by the hand and raised me up, speaking softly.

"Rise, Mopo, my servant!" he said. "Thou hast suffered much woe because of the witchcraft of thine enemies. I, I have lost my mother, and thou, thou hast lost thy wives and children. Weep, my councilors, weep, because I have lost my mother, and Mopo, my servant, as lost his wives and children, by the witchcraft of our foes!"

Then all the councilors wept aloud, while Chaka glared at them.

"Hearken, Mopo!" said the king, when the weeping was done. "None can give me back my mother; but I can give thee more wives, and thou shalt find children. Go in among the damsels who are reserved to the king, and choose thee six; go in among the cattle of the king, and choose thee ten times ten of the best; call upon the servants of the king that they build up thy kraal greater and fairer than it was before! These things I give thee freely; but thou shalt have more, Mopo — yes! thou shalt have vengeance! On the first day of the new moon I summon a great meeting, a *bandhla* of all the Zulu people: yes, thine own tribe, the Langeni, shall be there also. Then we will mourn together over our woes; then, too, we will learn who brought these woes upon us. Go now, Mopo, go! And go ye also, my councilors, leaving me to weep alone because my mother is dead!"

Thus, then, my father, did the words of Baleka come true, and thus, because of the crafty policy of Chaka, I grew greater in the land than ever I had been before. I chose the cattle, they were fat; I chose the wives, they were fair; but I took no pleasure in them, nor were anymore children born to me. For my heart was like a withered stick; the sap and strength had gone from my heart — it was drawn out in the fire of Chaka's hut, and lost in my sorrow for those whom I had loved.

Chapter XII
THE TALE OF GALAZI THE WOLF

*N*ow, my father, I will go back a little, for my tale is long and winds in and out like a river in a plain, and tell of the fate of Umslopogaas when the lion had taken him, as he told it to me in the after years.

The lioness bounded away, and in her mouth was Umslopogaas. Once he struggled, but she bit him hard, so he lay quiet in her mouth, and looking back he saw the face of Nada as she ran from the fence of thorns, crying "Save him!" He saw her face, he heard her words, then he saw and heard little more, for the world grew dark to him and he passed, as it were, into a deep sleep. Presently Umslopogaas awoke again, feeling pain in his thigh, where the lioness had bitten him, and heard a sound of shouting. He looked up; near to him stood the lioness that had loosed him from her jaws. She was snorting with rage, and in front of her was a lad long and strong, with a grim face, and a wolf's hide, black and grey, bound about his shoulders in such fashion that the upper jar and teeth of the wolf rested on his head. He stood before the lioness, shouting, and in one hand he held a large war-shield, and in the other he grasped a heavy club shod with iron.

Now the lioness crouched herself to spring, growling terribly, but the lad with the club did not wait for her onset. He ran in upon her and struck her on the head with the club. He smote hard and well, but this did not kill her, for she reared herself upon her hind legs and struck at him heavily. He caught the blow upon his shield, but the shield was driven against his breast so strongly that he fell backwards beneath it, and lay there howling like a wolf in pain. Then the lioness sprang upon him and worried him. Still, because of the shield, as yet she could not come at him to slay him; but Umslopogaas saw that this might not endure, for presently the shield would be torn aside and the stranger must be killed. Now in the breast of the lioness still stood the half of Umslopogaas's broken spear, and its blade was a span deep in her breast.

Then this thought came into the mind of Umslopogaas, that he would drive the spear home or die. So he rose swiftly, for strength came back to him in his need, and ran to where the lioness worried at him who lay beneath the shield. She did not heed him, so he flung himself upon his knees before her, and, seizing the haft of the broken spear, drive it deep into her and wrenched it round. Now she saw Umslopogaas and turned roaring, and clawed at him, tearing his breast and arms. Then, as he lay, he heard a mighty howling, and, behold! grey wolves and black leaped upon the lioness and rent and worried her till she fell and was torn to pieces by them. After this the senses of Umslopogaas left him again, and the light went out of his eyes so that he was as one dead.

At length his mind came back to him, and with it his memory, and he remembered the lioness and looked up to find her. But he did not find her, and he saw that he lay in a cave upon a bed of grass, while all about him were the skins of beasts, and at his side was a pot filled with water. He put out his hand and, taking the pot, drank of the water, and then he saw that his arm was wasted as with sickness, and that his breast was thick with scars scarcely skinned over.

Now while he lay and wondered, the mouth of the cave was darkened, and through it entered that same lad who had done battle with the lioness and been overthrown by her, bearing a dead buck upon his shoulders. He put down the buck upon the ground, and, walking to where Umslopogaas lay, looked at him.

"*Ou!*" he said, "your eyes are open – do you, then, live, stranger?"

"I live," answered Umslopogaas, "and I am hungry."

"It is time," said the other, "since with toil I bore you here through the forest, for twelve days you have lain without sense, drinking water only. So deeply had the lion clawed you that I thought of you as dead. Twice I was near to killing you, that you might cease to suffer and I to be troubled; but I held my hand, because of a word which came to me from one who is dead. Now eat, that your strength may return to you. Afterwards, we will talk."

So Umslopogaas ate, and little by little his health returned to him – every day a little. And afterwards, as they sat at night by the fire in the cave they spoke together.

"How are you named?" asked Umslopogaas of the other.

"I am named Galazi the Wolf," he answered, "and I am of Zulu blood – aye, of the blood of Chaka the king; for the father of Senzangacona, the father of Chaka, was my great-grandfather."

"Whence came you, Galazi?"

"I came from Swaziland – from the tribe of the Halakazi, which I should rule. This is the story: Siguyana, my grandfather, was a younger brother of Senzangacona, the father of Chaka. But he quarreled with Senzangacona, and became a wanderer. With certain of the people of the Umtetwa he wandered into Swaziland, and sojourned with the Halakazi tribe in their great caves; and the end of it was that he killed the chief of the tribe and took his place. After he was dead, my father ruled in his place; but there was a great party in the tribe that hated his rule because he was of the Zulu race, and it would have set up a chief of the old Swazi blood in his place. Still, they could not do this, for my father's hand was heavy on the people. Now I was the only son of my father by his head wife, and born to be chief after him, and therefore those of the Swazi party, and they were many and great, hated me also. So matters stood till last year in the winter, and then my father set his heart on killing twenty of the headmen, with their wives and children, because he knew that they plotted against him. But the headmen learned what was to come, and they prevailed upon a wife of my father, a woman of their own blood, to poison him. So she poisoned him in the night and in the morning it was told me that my father lay sick and summoned me, and I went to him. In his hut I found him, and he was writhing with pain.

"'What is it, my father?' I said. 'Who has done this evil?'

"'It is this, my son,' he gasped, 'that I am poisoned, and she stands yonder who has done the deed.' And he pointed to the woman, who stood at the side of the hut near the door, her chin upon her breast, trembling as she looked upon the fruit of her wickedness.

"Now the girl was young and fair, and we had been friends, yet I say that I did not pause, for my heart was mad within me. I did not pause, but, seizing my spear, I ran at her, and, though she cried for mercy, I killed her with the spear.

"'That was well done, Galazi!' said my father. 'But when I am gone, look to yourself, my son, for these Swazi dogs will drive you out and rob you of your place! But if they drive you out and you still live, swear this to me — that you will not rest till you have avenged me.'

"'I swear it, my father,' I answered. 'I swear that I will stamp out the men of the tribe of Halakazi, every one of them, except those of my own blood, and bring their women to slavery and their children to bonds!'

"'Big words for a young mouth,' said my father. 'Yet shall you live to bring these things about, Galazi. This I know of you now in my hour of death: you shall be a wanderer for a few years of your life, child of Siguyana, and wandering in another land you shall die a man's death, and not such a death as yonder witch has given to me.' Then, having spoken thus, he lifted up his head, looked at me, and with a great groan he died.

"Now I passed out of the hut dragging the body of the dead girl after me. In front of the hut were gathered many headmen waiting for the end, and I saw that their looks were sullen.

"'The chief, my father, is dead!' I cried in a loud voice, 'and I, Galazi, who am the chief, have slain her who murdered him!' And I rolled the body of the girl over on to her back so that they might look upon her face.

"Now the father of the girl was among those who stood before me, he who had persuaded her to the deed, and he was maddened at the sight.

"'What, my brothers?' he cried. 'Shall we suffer that this young Zulu dog, this murderer of a girl, be chief over us? Never! The old lion is dead, now for the cub!' And he ran at me with spear aloft.

"'Never!' shouted the others, and they, too, ran towards me, shaking their spears.

"I waited, I did not hasten, for I knew well that I should not die then, I knew it from my father's last words. I waited till the man was near me; he thrust, I sprang aside and drove my spear through him, and on the daughter's body the father fell dead. Then I shouted aloud and rushed through them. None touched me; none could catch me; the man does not live who can overtake me when my feet are on the ground and I am away."

"Yet I might try," said Umslopogaas, smiling, for of all lads among the Zulus he was the swiftest of foot.

"First walk again, then run," answered Galazi.

"Take up the tale," quoth Umslopogaas; "it is a merry one."

"Something is left to tell, stranger. I fled from the country of the Halakazi, nor did I linger at all in the land of the Swazis, but came on swiftly into the Zulu. Now, it was in my mind to go to Chaka and tell him of my wrongs, asking that he would send an *impi* to make an end of the Halakazi. But while I journeyed, finding food and shelter as I might, I came one night to the kraal of an old man who knew Chaka, and had known Siguyana, my grandfather, and to him, when I had stayed there two days, I told my tale. But the old man counseled me against my plan, saying that Chaka, the king, did not love to welcome new shoots sprung from the royal stock, and would kill me; moreover, the man offered me a place in his kraal. Now, I held that there was wisdom in his words, and thought no more of standing before the king to cry for justice, for he who cries to kings for justice sometimes finds death. Still, I would not stay in the kraal of the old man, for he had sons to come after him who looked on me with no liking; moreover, I wished to be a chief myself, even if I lived alone. So I left the kraal by night and walked on, not knowing where I should go.

"Now, on the third night, I came to a little kraal that stands on the farther side of the river at the foot of the mountain. In front of the kraal sat a very old woman basking in the rays of the setting sun. She saw me, and spoke to me, saying, 'Young man, you are tall and strong and swift of foot. Would you earn a famous weapon, a club, that destroys all who stand before it?'

"I said that I wished to have such a club, and asked what I should do to win it.

"'You shall do this,' said the old woman: 'tomorrow morning, at the first light, you shall go up to yonder mountain,' and she pointed to the mountain where you are now, stranger, on which the stone Witch sits forever waiting for the world to die. 'Two-thirds of the way up the mountain you will come to a path that is difficult to climb. You shall climb the path and enter a gloomy forest. It is very dark in the forest, but you must push through it till you come to an open place with a wall of rock behind it. In the wall of rock is a cave, and in the cave you will find the bones of a man. Bring down the bones in a bag, and I will give you the club!'

"While she spoke thus people came out of the kraal and listened.

"'Do not heed her, young man,' they said, 'unless you are weary of life. Do not heed her: she is crazy. The mountain is haunted; it is a place of ghosts. Look at the stone Witch who sits upon it! Evil spirits live in that forest, and no man has walked there for many years. This woman's son was foolish: he went to wander in the forest, saying that he cared nothing for ghosts, and the Amatongo, the ghost-folk, killed him. That was many years ago, and none have dared to seek his bones. Ever she sits here and asks of the passers by that they should bring him to her, offering the great club for a reward; but they dare not!'

"'They lie!' said the old woman. 'There are no ghosts there. The ghosts live only in their cowardly hearts; there are but wolves. I know that the bones of my son lie in the cave, for I have seen them in a dream; but, alas! my old limbs are too weak to carry me up the mountain path, and all these are cowards; there is no man among them since the Zulus killed my husband, covering him with wounds!'

"Now, I listened, answering nothing; but when all had done, I asked to see the club which should be given to him who dared to face the Amatongo, the spirits who lived in the forest upon the Ghost Mountain. Then the old woman rose, and creeping on her hands went into the hut. Presently she returned again, dragging the great club after her.

"Look at it, stranger! look at it! Was there ever such a club?" And Galazi held it up before the eyes of Umslopogaas.

In truth, my father, that was a club, for I, Mopo, saw it in after days. It was great and knotty, black as iron that had been smoked in the fire, and shod with metal that was worn smooth with smiting.

"I looked at it," went on Galazi, "and I tell you, stranger, a great desire came into my heart to possess it.

"'How is this club named?' I asked of the old woman.

"'It is named Watcher of the Fords,' she answered, 'and it has not watched in vain. Five men have held that club in war and a hundred-and-seventy-three have given up their lives beneath its strokes. He who held it last slew twenty before he was slain himself, for this fortune goes with the club — that he who owns it shall die holding it, but in a noble fashion. There is but one other weapon to match with it in Zululand, and that is the great axe of Jikiza, the chief of the People of the Axe, who dwells in the kraal yonder; the ancient horn-hafted Imbubuzi, the Groan-Maker, that brings victory. Were axe, Groan-Maker, and club, Watcher of the Fords, side by side, there are no thirty men in Zululand who could stand before them. I have said. Choose!' And the aged woman watched me cunningly through her horny eyes.

"'She speaks truly now,' said one of those who stood near. 'Let the club be, young man: he who owns it smites great blows indeed, but in the end he dies by the assegai. None dare own the Watcher of the Fords.'

"'A good death and a swift!' I answered. And pondered a time, while still the old woman watched me through her horny eyes. At length she rose, 'La!, la!' she said, 'the Watcher is not for this one. This is but a child, I must seek me a man, I must seek me a man!'

"'Not so fast, old wife,' I said. 'Will you lend me this club to hold in my hand while I go to find the bones of your son and to snatch them from the people of the ghosts?'

"'Lend you the Watcher, boy? Nay, nay! I should see little of you again or of the good club either.'

"'I am no thief,' I answered. 'If the ghosts kill me, you will see me no more, or the club either; but if I live I will bring you back the bones, or, if I do not find them, I will render the Watcher into your hands again. At the least I say that if you will not lend me the club, then I will not go into the haunted place.'

"'Boy, your eyes are honest,' she said, still peering at me. 'Take the Watcher, go seek the bones. If you die, let the club be lost with you; if you fail, bring it back to me; but if you win the bones, then it is yours, and it shall bring you glory and you shall die a man's death at last holding him aloft among the dead.'

"So on the morrow at dawn I took the club Watcher in my hand and a little dancing shield, and made ready to start. The old woman blessed me and bade me farewell, but the other people of the kraal mocked, saying: 'A little man for so big a club! Beware, little man, lest the ghosts use the club on you!' So they spoke, but one girl in the kraal – she is a granddaughter of the old woman – led me aside, praying me not to go, for the forest on the Ghost Mountain had an evil name: none dared walk there, since it was certainly full of spirits, who howled like wolves. I thanked the girl, but to the others I said nothing, only I asked of the path to the Ghost Mountain.

"Now stranger, if you have strength, come to the mouth of the cave and look out, for the moon is bright."

So Umslopogaas rose and crept through the narrow mouth of the cave. There, above him, a great grey peak towered high into the air, shaped like a seated woman, her chin resting upon her breast, the place where the cave was being, as it were, on the lap of the woman. Below this place the rock sloped sharply, and was clothed with little bushes. Lower down yet was a forest, great and dense, that stretched to the top of a cliff, and at the foot of the cliff, beyond the waters of the river, lay the wide plains of Zululand.

"Yonder, stranger," said Galazi, pointing with the club Watcher of the Fords far away to the plain beneath; "yonder is the kraal where the aged woman dwelt. There is a cliff rising from the plain, up which I must climb; there is the forest where dwell the Amatongo, the people of the ghosts; there, on the hither side of the forest, runs the path to the cave, and here is the cave itself. See this stone lying at the mouth of the cave, it turns thus, shutting up the entrance hole – it turns gently; though it is so large, a child may move it, for it rests upon a sharp point of rock. Only mark this, the stone must be pushed too far; for, look! if it came to here," and he pointed to a mark in the mouth of the cave, "then that man need be strong who can draw it back again, though I have done it myself, who am not a man full grown. But if it pass beyond this mark, then, see, it will roll down the neck of the cave like a pebble down the neck of a gourd, and I think that two men, one striving from within and one dragging from without, scarcely could avail to push it clear. Look now, I close the stone, as is my custom of a night, so," – and he grasped the rock and swung it round upon its pivot, on which it turned as a door turns. "Thus I leave it, and though, except those to whom the secret is know, none would guess that a cave was here, yet it can be rolled back again with a push of the hand. But enough of the stone. Enter again, wanderer, and I will go forward with my tale, for it is long and strange.

"I started from the kraal of the old woman, and the people of the kraal followed me to the brink of the river. It was in flood, and few had dared to cross it.

"'Ha! ha!' they cried, 'now your journey is done, little man; watch by the ford you who would win the Watcher of the Ford! Beat the water with the club, perhaps so it shall grow gentle that your feet may pass it!'

"I answered nothing to their mocking, only I bound the shield upon my shoulders with a string, and the bag that I had brought I made fast about my middle, and I held the great club in my teeth by the thong. Then I plunged into the river and swam. Twice, stranger, the current bore me under, and those on the bank shouted that I was lost; but I rose again, and in the end I won the farther shore.

"Now those on the bank mocked no more; they stood still wondering, and I walked on till I came to the foot of the cliff. That cliff is hard to climb, stranger; when you are strong upon your feet, I will show you the path. Yet I found a way up it, and by midday I came to the forest. Here, on the edge of the forest, I rested awhile, and ate a little food that I had brought with me in the bag, for now I must gather up my strength to meet the ghosts, if ghosts there were. Then I rose and plunged into the forest. The trees were great that grow there, stranger, and their leaves are so think that in certain places the light is as that of night when the moon is young. Still, I wended on, often losing my path. But from time to time between the tops of the trees I saw the figure of the grey stone woman who sits on the top of Ghost Mountain, and shaped my course towards her knees. My heart beat as I traveled through the forest in dark and loneliness like that of the night, and ever I looked round searching for the eyes of the Amatongo. But I saw no spirits, though at times great spotted snakes crept from before my feet, and perhaps these were the Amatongo. At times, also, I caught glimpses of some grey wolf as he slunk from tree to tree watching me, and always high above my head the wind sighed in the great boughs with a sound like the sighing of women.

"Still, I went on, singing to myself as I went, that my heart might not be faint with fear, and at length, towards the end of the second hour, the trees grew fewer, the ground sloped upwards, and the light poured down from the heavens again. But, stranger, you are weary, and the night wears on; sleep now, and tomorrow I will end the tale. Say, first, how are you named?"

"I am named Umslopogaas, son of Mopo," he answered, "and my tale shall be told when yours is done; let us sleep!"

Now when Galazi heard this name he started and was troubled, but said nothing. So they laid them down to sleep, and Galazi wrapped Umslopogaas with the skins of bucks.

But Galazi the Wolf was so hardy that he lay on the bare ground and had no covering. So they slept, and without the door of the cave the wolves howled, scenting the blood of men.

Chapter XIII

GALAZI BECOMES KING OF THE WOLVES

On the morrow Umslopogaas awoke, and knew that strength was growing on him fast. Still, all that day he rested in the cave, while Galazi went out to hunt. In the evening he returned, bearing a buck upon his shoulders, and they skinned the buck and ate of it as they sat by the fire. And when the sun was down Galazi took up his tale.

"Now Umslopogaas, son of Mopo, hear! I had passed the forest, and had come, as it were, to the legs of the old stone Witch who sits up aloft there forever waiting for the world to die. Here the sun shone merrily, here lizards ran and birds flew to and fro, and though it grew towards the evening — for I had wandered long in the forest — I was afraid no more. So I climbed up the steep rock, where little bushes grow like hair on the arms of a man, till at last I came to the knees of the stone Witch, which are the space before the cave. I lifted by head over the brink of the rock and looked, and I tell you, Umslopogaas, my blood ran cold and my heart turned to water, for there, before the cave, rolled wolves, many and great. Some slept and growled in their sleep, some gnawed at the skulls of dead game, some sat up like dogs and their tongues hung from their grinning jaws. I looked, I saw, and beyond I discovered the mouth of the cave, where the bones of the boy should be. But I had no wish to come there, being afraid of the wolves, for now I knew that these were the ghosts who live upon the mountain. So I bethought me that I would fly, and turned to go. And, Umslopogaas, even as I turned, the great club Watcher of the Fords swung round and smote me on the back with such a blow as a man smites upon a coward. Now whether this was by chance or whether the Watcher would shame him who bore it, say you, for I do not know. At the least, shame entered into me. Should I go back to be mocked by the people of the kraal and by the old woman? And if I wished to go, should I not be killed by the ghosts at night in the forest? Nay, it was better to die in the jaws of the wolves, and at once.

"Thus I thought in my heart; then, tarrying not, lest fear should come upon me again, I swung up the Watcher, and crying aloud the war-cry of the Halakazi, I sprang over the brink of the rock and rushed upon the wolves. They, too, sprang up and stood howling, with bristling hides and fiery eyes, and the smell of them came into my nostrils. Yet when they saw it was a man that rushed upon them, they were seized with sudden fear and fled this way and that, leaping by great bounds from the place of rock, which is the knees of the stone Witch, so that presently I stood alone in front of the cave. Now, having conquered the wolf ghosts and no blow struck, my heart swelled within me, and I walked to the mouth of the cave proudly, as a cock walks upon a roof, and looked in through the opening. As it chanced, the sinking sun shone at this hour full into the cave, so that all its darkness was made red with light. Then, once more, Umslopogaas, I grew afraid indeed, for I could see the end of the cave.

"Look now! There is a hole in the wall of the cave, where the firelight falls below the shadow of the roof, twice the height of a man from the floor. It is a narrow hole and a high, is it not? — as though one had cut it with iron, and a man might sit in it, his legs hanging towards the floor of the cave. Aye, Umslopogaas, a man might sit in it, might he not? And there a man sat, or that which had been a man. There sat the bones of a man, and the black skin had withered on his bones, holding them together, and making him awful to see. His hands were open beside him, he leaned upon them, and in the right hand was a piece of hide from his *moocha*. It was half eaten, Umslopogaas; he had eaten it before he died. His eyes also were bound round with a band of leather, as though to hide something from their gaze, one foot was gone, one hung over the edge of the niche towards the floor, and beneath it on the floor, red with rust, lay the blade of a broken spear.

"Now come hither, Umslopogaas, place your hand upon the wall of the cave, just here; it is smooth, is it not? — smooth as the stones on which women grind their corn. 'What made it so smooth?' you ask. I will tell you.

"When I peered through the door of the cave I saw this: on the floor of the cave lay a she-wolf panting, as though she had galloped many a mile; she was great and fierce. Near to her was another wolf – he was a dog – old and black, bigger than any I have seen, a very father of wolves, and all his head and flanks were streaked with grey. But this wolf was on his feet. As I watched he drew back nearly to the mouth of the cave, then of a sudden he ran forward and bounded high into the air towards the withered foot of that which hung from the cleft of the rock. His pads struck upon the rock here where it is smooth, and there for a second he seemed to cling, while his great jaws closed with a clash but a spear's breadth beneath the dead man's foot. Then he fell back with a howl of rage, and drew slowly down the cave. Again he ran and leaped, again the great jaws closed, again he fell down howling. Then the she-wolf rose, and they sprang together, striving to pull down him who sat above. But it was all in vain; they could never come nearer than within a spear's breadth of the dead man's foot. And now, Umslopogaas, you know why the rock is smooth and shines. From month to month and year to year the wolves had ravened there, seeking to devour the bones of him who sat above. Night upon night they had leaped thus against the wall of the cave, but never might their clashing jaws close upon his foot. One foot they had, indeed, but the other they could not come by.

"Now as I watched, filled with fear and wonder, the she-wolf, her tongue lolling from her jaws, made so mighty a bound that she almost reached the hanging foot, and yet not quite. She fell back, and then I saw that the leap was her last for that time, for she had oversprung herself, and lay there howling, the black blood flowing from her mouth. The wolf saw also: he drew near, sniffed at her, then, knowing that she was hurt, seized her by the throat and worried her. Now all the place was filled with groans and choking howls, as the wolves rolled over and over beneath him who sat above, and in the blood-red light of the dying sun the sight and sounds were so horrid that I trembled like a child. The she-wolf grew faint, for the fangs of her mate were buried in her throat. Then I saw that now was the time to smite him, lest when he had killed her he should kill me also. So I lifted the Watcher and sprang into the cave, having it in my mind to slay the wolf before he lifted up his head. But he heard my footsteps, or perhaps my shadow fell upon him. Loosing his grip, he looked up, this father of wolves; then, making no sound, he sprang straight at my throat.

"I saw him, and whirling the Watcher aloft, I smote with all my strength. The blow met him in mid-air; it fell full on his chest and struck him backwards to the earth. But there he would not say, for, rising before I could smite again, once more he sprang at me. This time I leaped aside and struck downwards, and the blow fell upon his right leg and broke it, so that he could spring no more. Yet he ran at me on three feet, and, though the club fell on his side, he seized me with his teeth, biting through that leather bag, which was wound about my middle, into the flesh behind. Then I yelled with pain and rage, and lifting the Watcher endways, drove it down with both hands, as a man drives a stake into the earth, and that with so great a stroke that the skull of the wolf was shattered like a pot, and he fell dead, dragging me with him. Presently I sat up on the ground, and, placing the handle of the Watcher between his jaws, I forced them open, freeing my flesh from the grip of his teeth. Then I looked at my wounds; they were not deep, for the leather bag had saved me, yet I feel them to this hour, for there is poison in the mouth of a wolf. Presently I glanced up, and saw that the she-wolf had found her feet again, and stood as though unhurt; for this is the nature of these ghosts, Umslopogaas, that, though they fight continually, they cannot destroy each other. They may be killed by man alone, and that hardly. There she stood, and yet she did not look at me or on her dead mate, but at him who sat above. I saw, and crept softly behind her, then, lifting the Watcher, I dashed him down with all my strength. The blow fell on her neck and broke it, so that she rolled over and at once was dead.

"Now I rested awhile, then went to the mouth of the cave and looked out. The sun was sinking: all the depth of the forest was black, but the light still shone on the face of the stone woman who sits forever on the mountain. Here, then, I must bide this night, for, though the moon shone white and full in the sky, I dared not wend towards the plains alone with the wolves and the ghosts. And if I dared not go alone, how much less should I dare to go bearing with me him who sat in the cleft of the rock! Nay, here I must bide, so I went out of the cave to the spring which flows from the rock on the right yonder and washed my wounds and drank. Then I came back and sat in the mouth of the cave, and watched the light die away from the face of the world. While it was dying there was silence, but when it was dead the forest awoke. A wind sprang up and tossed it till the green of its boughs waved like troubled water on which the moon shines faintly. From the heart of it, too, came howlings of ghosts and wolves, that were answered by howls from the rocks above – hearken, Umslopogaas, such howlings as we hear tonight!

"It was awful here in the mouth of the cave, for I had not yet learned the secret of the stone, and if I had known it, should I have dared to close it, leaving myself alone with the dead wolves and him whom the wolves had struggled to tear down? I walked out yonder on to the platform and looked up. The moon shone full upon the face of the stone Witch who sits aloft forever. She seemed to grin at me, and, oh! I grew afraid, for now I knew that this was a place of dead men, a place where spirits perch like vultures in a tree, as they sweep round and round the world. I went back to the cave, and feeling that I must do something lest I should go mad, I drew to me the carcass of the great dog-wolf which I had killed, and, taking my knife of iron, I began to skin it by the light of the moon. For an hour or more I skinned, singing to myself as I worked, and striving to forget him who sat in the cleft above and the howlings which ran about the mountains. But ever the moonlight shone more clearly into the cave: now by it I could see his shape of bone and skin, aye, and even the bandage about his eyes. Why had he tied it there? I wondered — perhaps to hide the faces of the fierce wolves as they sprang upwards to grip him. And always the howlings drew nearer; now I could see grey forms creeping to and fro in the shadows of the rocky place before me. Ah! there before me glared two red eyes: a sharp snout sniffed at the carcass which I skinned. With a yell, I lifted the Watcher and smote. There came a scream of pain, and something galloped away into the shadows.

"Now the skin was off. I cast it behind me, and seizing the carcass dragged it to the edge of the rock and left it. Presently the sound of howlings drew near again, and I saw the grey shapes creep up one by one. Now they gathered round the carcass, now they fell upon it and rent it, fighting horribly till all was finished. Then, licking their red chops, they slunk back to the forest.

"Did I sleep or did I wake? Nay, I cannot tell. But I know this, that of a sudden I seemed to look up and see. I saw a light — perchance, Umslopogaas, it was the light of the moon, shining upon him that sat aloft at the end of the cave. It was a red light, and he glowed in it as glows a thing that is rotten. I looked, or seemed to look, and then I thought that the hanging jaw moved, and from it came a voice that was harsh and hollow as of one who speaks from an empty belly, through a withered throat.

"'Hail, Galazi, child of Siguyana!' said the voice, 'Galazi the Wolf! Say, what dost thou here in the Ghost Mountain, where the stone Witch sits forever, waiting for the world to die?'

"Then, Umslopogaas, I answered, or seemed to answer, and my voice, too, sounded strange and hollow: —

"'Hail, Dead One, who sittest like a vulture on a rock! I do this on the Ghost Mountain. I come to seek thy bones and bear them to thy mother for burial.'

"'Many and many a year have I sat aloft, Galazi,' answered the voice, 'watching the ghost-wolves leap and leap to drag me down, till the rock grew smooth beneath the wearing of their feet. So I sat seven days and nights, being yet alive, the hungry wolves below, and hunger gnawing at my heart. So I have sat many and many a year, being dead in the heart of the old stone Witch, watching the moon and the sun and the stars, hearkening to the howls of the ghost-wolves as they ravened beneath me, and learning the wisdom of the old witch who sits above in everlasting stone. Yet my mother was young and fair when I trod the haunted forest and climbed the knees of stone. How seems she now, Galazi?'

"'She is white and wrinkled and very aged,' I answered. 'They call her mad, yet at her bidding I came to seek thee, Dead One, bearing the Watcher that was thy father's and shall be mine.'

"'It shall be thine, Galazi,' said the voice, 'for thou alone hast dared the ghosts to me sleep and burial. Hearken, thine also shall be the wisdom of the old witch who sits aloft forever, frozen into everlasting stone — thine and one other's. These are not wolves that thou hast seen, that is no wolf which thou hast slain; nay, they are ghosts — evil ghosts of men who lived in ages gone, and who must now live till they be slain by men. And knowest thou how they lived, Galazi, and what was the food they ate? When the light comes again, Galazi, climb to the breasts of the stone Witch, and look in the cleft which is between her breasts. There shalt thou see how these men lived. And now this doom is on them: they must wander gaunt and hungry in the shape of wolves, haunting that Ghost Mountain where they once fed, till they are led forth to die at the hands of men. Because of their devouring hunger they have leapt from year to year, striving to reach my bones; and he whom thou hast slain was the king of them, and she at his side was their queen.

"'Now, Galazi the Wolf, this is the wisdom that I give thee: thou shalt be king of the ghost-wolves, thou and another, whom a lion shall bring thee. Gird the black skin upon thy shoulders, and the wolves shall follow thee; all the three hundred and sixty and three of them that are left, and let him who shall be brought to thee gird on the skin of grey. Where ye twain lead them, there shall they raven, bringing you victory till all are dead. But know this, that there only may they raven where in life they ravened, seeking for their food. Yet, that was an ill gift thou tookest from my mother — the gift of the Watcher, for though without the Watcher thou hadst never slain the king of the ghost-wolves, yet, bearing the Watcher, thou shalt thyself be slain. Now, on the morrow carry me back to my mother, so that I may sleep where the ghost-wolves leap no more. I have spoken, Galazi.'

"Now the Dead One's voice seemed to grow ever fainter and more hollow as he spoke, till at the last I could scarcely hear his words, yet I answered him, asking him this: —

"'Who is it, then, that the lion shall bring to me to rule with me over the ghost-wolves, and how is he named?'

"Then the Dead One spoke once more very faintly, yet in the silence of the place I heard his words: —

"'He is named Umslopogaas the Slaughterer, son of Chaka, Lion of the Zulu.'"

Now Umslopogaas started up from his place by the fire.

"I am named Umslopogaas," he said, "but the Slaughterer I am not named, and I am the son of Mopo, and not the son of Chaka, Lion of the Zulu; you have dreamed a dream, Galazi, or, if it was no dream, then the Dead One lied to you."

"Perchance this was so, Umslopogaas," answered Galazi the Wolf. "Perhaps I dreamed, of perhaps the Dead One lied; nevertheless, if he lied in this matter, in other matters he did not lie, as you shall hear.

"After I had heard these words, or had dreamed that I heard them, I slept indeed, and when I woke the forest beneath was like the clouds of mist, but the grey light glinted upon the face of her who sits in stone above. Now I remembered the dream that I had dreamed, and I would see if it were all a dream. So I rose, and leaving the cave, found a place where I might climb up to the breasts and head of the stone Witch. I climbed, and as I went the rays of the sun lit upon her face, and I rejoiced to see them. But, when I drew near, the likeness to the face of a woman faded away, and I saw nothing before me but rugged heaps of piled-up rock. For this, Umslopogaas, is the way of witches, be they of stone or flesh — when you draw near to them they change their shape.

"Now I was on the breast of the mountain, and wandered to and for awhile between the great heaps of stone. At length I found, as it were, a crack in the stone thrice as wide as a man can jump, and in length half a spear's throw, and near this crack stood great stones blackened by fire, and beneath them broken pots and a knife of flint. I looked down into the crack — it was very deep, and green with moss, and tall ferns grew about in it, for the damp gathered there. There was nothing else. I had dreamed a lying dream. I turned to go, then found another mind, and climbed down into the cleft, pushing aside the ferns. Beneath the ferns was moss; I scraped it away with the Watcher. Presently the iron of the club struck on something that was yellow and round like a stone, and from the yellow thing came a hollow sound. I lifted it, Umslopogaas; it was the skull of a child.

"I dug deeper and scraped away more moss, till presently I saw. Beneath the moss was nothing but the bones of men — old bones that had lain there many years; the little ones had rotted, the larger ones remained — some were yellow, some black, and others still white. They were not broken, as are those that hyenas and wolves have worried, yet on some of them I could see the marks of teeth. Then, Umslopogaas, I went back to the cave, never looking behind me.

"Now when I was come to the cave I did this: I skinned the she-wolf also. When I had finished the sun was up, and I knew that it was time to go. But I could not go alone — he who sat aloft in the cleft of the cave must go with me. I greatly feared to touch him — this Dead One, who had spoken to me in a dream; yet I must do it. So I brought stones and piled them up till I could reach him; then I lifted him down, for he was very light, being but skin and bones. When he was down, I bound the hides of the wolves about me, then leaving the leather bag, into which he could not enter, I took the Dead One and placed him on my shoulders as a man might carry a child, for his legs were fixed somewhat apart, and holding him by the foot which was left on him, I set out for the kraal. Down the slope I went as swiftly as I could, for now I knew the way, seeing and hearing nothing, except once, when there came a rush of wings, and a great eagle swept down at that which sat upon my shoulders. I shouted, and the eagle flew away, then I entered the dark of the forest. Here I must walk softly, lest the head of him I carried should strike against the boughs and be smitten from him.

"For awhile I went on thus, till I drew near to the heart of the forest. Then I heard a wolf howl on my right, and from the left came answering howls, and these, again, were answered by others in front of and behind me. I walked on boldly, for I dared not stay, guiding myself by the sun, which from time to time shone down on me redly through the boughs of the great trees. Now I could see forms grey and black slinking near my path, sniffing at the air as they went, and now I came to a little open place, and, behold! all the wolves in the world were gathered together there. My heart melted, my legs trembled beneath me. On every side were the brutes, great and hungry. And I stood still, with club aloft, and slowly they crept up, muttering and growling as they came, till they formed a deep circle round me. Yet they did not spring on me, only drew nearer and ever nearer. Presently one sprang, indeed, but not at me; he sprang at that which sat upon my shoulders. I moved aside, and he missed his aim, and, coming to the ground again, stood there growling and whining like a beast afraid. Then I remembered the words of my dream, if dream it were, how that the Dead One had given me wisdom that I should be king of the ghost-wolves — I and another whom a lion should bear to me. Was it not so? If it was not so, how came it that the wolves did not devour me?

"For a moment I stood thinking, then I lifted up my voice and howled like a wolf, and lo! Umslopogaas, all the wolves howled in answer with a mighty howling. I stretched out my hand and called to them. They ran to me, gathering round me as though to devour me. But they did not harm me; they licked my legs with their red tongues, and fighting to come near me, pressed themselves against me as does a cat. One, indeed, snatched at him who sat on my shoulder, but I struck him with the Watcher and he slunk back like a whipped hound; moreover, the others bit him so that he yelled. Now I knew that I had no more to fear, for I was king of the ghost-wolves, so I walked on, and with me came all the great pack of them. I walked on and on, and they trotted beside me silently, and the fallen leaves crackled beneath their feet, and the dust rose up about them, till at length I reached the edge of the forest.

"Now I remembered that I must not be seen thus by men, lest they should think me a wizard and kill me. Therefore, at the edge of the forest I halted and made signs to the wolves to go back. At this they howled piteously, as though in grief, but I called to them that I would come again and be their king, and it seemed as though their brute hearts understood my words. Then they all went, still howling, till presently I was alone.

"And now, Umslopogaas, it is time to sleep; tomorrow night I will end my tale."

Chapter XIV
THE WOLF-BRETHREN

*N*ow, my father, on the morrow night, once again Umslopogaas and Galazi the wolf sat by the fire in the mouth of their cave, as we sit tonight, my father, and Galazi took up his tale.

"I passed on till I came to the river; it was still full, but the water had run down a little, so that my feet found foothold. I waded into the river, using the Watcher as a staff, and the stream reached to my elbows, but no higher. Now one on the farther bank of the river saw that which sat upon my shoulders, and saw also the wolf's skin on my head, and ran to the kraal crying, 'Here comes one who walks the waters on the back of a wolf.'

"So it came about that when I drew towards the kraal all the people of the kraal were gathered together to meet me, except the old woman, who could not walk so far. But when they saw me coming up the slope of the hill, and when they knew what it was that sat upon my shoulders, they were smitten with fear. Yet they did not run, because of their great wonder, only they walked backward before me, clinging each to each and saying nothing. I too came on silently, till at length I reached the kraal, and before its gates sat the old woman basking in the sun of the afternoon. Presently she looked up and cried: —

"'What ails you, people of my house, that you walk backwards like men bewitched, and who is that tall and deathly man who comes toward you?'

"But still they drew on backward, saying no word, the little children clinging to the women, the women clinging to the men, till they had passed the old wife and ranged themselves behind her like a regiment of soldiers. Then they halted against the fence of the kraal. But I came on to the old woman, and lifted him who sat upon my shoulders, and placed him on the ground before her, saying, 'Woman, here is your son; I have snatched him with much toil from the jaws of the ghosts — and they are many up yonder — all save one foot, which I could not find. Take him now and bury him, for I weary of his fellowship.'

"She looked upon that which sat before her. She put out her withered hand and drew the bandage from his sunken eyes. Then she screamed aloud a shrill scream, and, flinging her arms about the neck of the Dead One, she cried: 'It is my son whom I bore — my very son, whom for twice ten years and half a ten I have not looked upon. Greeting, my son, greeting! Now shalt thou find burial, and I with three — aye, I with thee!'

"And once more she cried aloud, standing upon her feet with arms outstretched. Then of a sudden foam burst from her lips, and she fell forward upon the body of her son, and was dead.

"Now silence came upon the place again, for all were fearful. At last one cried: 'How is this man named who has won the body from the ghosts?'

"'I am named Galazi,' I answered.

"'Nay,' said he. 'The Wolf you are named. Look at the wolf's red hide upon his head!'

"'I am named Galazi, and the Wolf you have named me,' I said again. 'So be it: I am named Galazi the Wolf.'

"'Methinks he is a wolf,' said he. 'Look, now, at his teeth, how they grin! This is no man, my brothers, but a wolf.'

"'No wolf and no man,' said another, 'but a wizard. None but a wizard could have passed the forest and won the lap of her who sits in stone forever.'

"'Yes, yes! he is a wolf — he is a wizard!' they screamed. 'Kill him! Kill the wolf-wizard before he brings the ghosts upon us!' And they ran towards me with uplifted spears.

"'I am a wolf indeed,' I cried, 'and I am a wizard indeed, and I will bring wolves and ghosts upon you ere all is done.' And I turned and fled so swiftly that soon they were left behind me. Now as I ran I met a girl; a basket of mealies was on her head, and she bore a dead kid in her hand. I rushed at her howling like a wolf, and I snatched the mealies from her head and the kid from her hand. Then I fled on, and coming to the river, I crossed it, and for that night I hid myself in the rocks beyond, eating the mealies and the flesh of the kid.

"On the morrow at dawn I rose and shook the dew from the wolf-hide. Then I went on into the forest and howled like a wolf. They knew my voice, the ghost-wolves, and howled in answer from far and near. Then I heard the pattering of their feet, and they came round me by tens and by twenties, and fawned upon me. I counted their number; they numbered three hundred and sixty and three.

"Afterwards, I went on to the cave, and I have lived there in the cave, Umslopogaas, for nigh upon twelve moons, and I have become a wolf-man. For with the wolves I hunt and raven, and they know me, and what I bid them that they do. Stay, Umslopogaas, now you are strong again, and, if your courage does not fail you, you shall see this very night. Come now, have you the heart, Umslopogaas?"

Then Umslopogaas rose and laughed aloud. "I am young in years," he cried, "and scarcely come to the full strength of men; yet hitherto I have not turned my back on lion or witch, on wolf or man. Now let us see this *impi* of yours — this *impi* black and grey, that runs on four legs with fangs for spears!"

"You must first bind on the she-wolf's hide, Umslopogaas," quoth Galazi, "else, before a man could count his fingers twice there would be little enough left of you. Bind it about the neck and beneath the arms, and see that the fastenings do not burst, lest it be the worse for you."

So Umslopogaas took the grey wolf's hide and bound it on with thongs of leather, and its teeth gleamed upon his head, and he took a spear in his hand. Galazi also bound on the hide of the king of the wolves, and they went out on to the space before the cave. Galazi stood there awhile, and the moonlight fell upon him, and Umslopogaas saw that his face grew wild and beastlike, that his eyes shone, and his teeth grinned beneath his curling lips. He lifted up his head and howled out upon the night. Thrice Galazi lifted his head and thrice he howled loudly, and yet more loud. But before ever the echoes had died in the air, from the heights of the rocks above and the depths of the forest beneath, there came howlings in answer. Nearer they grew and nearer; now there was a sound of feet, and a wolf, great and grey, bounded towards them, and after him many another. They came to Galazi, they sprang upon him, fawning round him, but he beat them down with the Watcher. Then of a sudden they saw Umslopogaas, and rushed at him open-mouthed.

"Stand and do not move!" cried Galazi. "Be not afraid!"

"I have always fondled dogs," answered Umslopogaas, "shall I learn to fear them now?"

Yet though he spoke boldly, in his heart he was afraid, for this was the most terrible of all sights. The wolves rushed on him open-mouthed, from before and from behind, so that in a breath he was well-nigh hidden by their forms. Yet no fang pierced him, for as they leapt they smelt the smell of the skin upon him. Then Umslopogaas saw that the wolves leapt at him no more, but the she-wolves gathered round him who wore the she-wolf's skin. They were great and gaunt and hungry, all were full-grown, there were no little ones, and their number was so many that he could not count them in the moonlight. Umslopogaas, looking into their red eyes, felt his heart become as the heart of a wolf, and he, too, lifted up his head and howled, and the she-wolves howled in answer.

"The pack is gathered; now for the hunt!" cried Galazi. "Make your feet swift, my brother, for we shall journey far tonight. Ho, Blackfang! ho, Greysnout! Ho, my people black and grey, away! away!"

He spoke and bounded forward, and with him went Umslopogaas, and after him streamed the ghost-wolves. They fled down the mountain sides, leaping from boulder to boulder like bucks. Presently they stood by a kloof that was thick with trees. Galazi stopped, holding up the Watcher, and the wolves stopped with him.

"I smell a quarry," he cried; "in, my people, in!"

Then the wolves plunged silently into the great kloof, but Galazi and Umslopogaas drew to the foot of it and waited. Presently there came a sound of breaking boughs, and lo! before them stood a buffalo, a bull who lowed fiercely and sniffed the air.

"This one will give us a good chase, my brother; see, he is gaunt and thin! Ah! that meat is tender which my people have hunted to the death!"

As Galazi spoke, the first of the wolves drew from the covert and saw the buffalo; then, giving tongue, they sprang towards it. The bull saw also, and dashed down the hill, and after him came Galazi and Umslopogaas, and with them all their company, and the rocks shook with the music of their hunting. They rushed down the mountain side, and it came into the heart of Umslopogaas, that he, too, was a wolf. They rushed madly, yet his feet were swift as the swiftest; no wolf could outstrip him, and in him was but one desire — the desire of prey. Now they neared the borders of the forest, and Galazi shouted. He shouted to Greysnout and to Blackfang, to Blood and to Deathgrip, and these four leaped forward from the pack, running so swiftly that their bellies seemed to touch the ground. They passed about the bull, turning him from the forest and setting his head up the slope of the mountain. Then the chase wheeled, the bull leaped and bounded up the mountain side, and on one flank lay Greysnout and Deathgrip and on the other lay Blood and Blackfang, while behind came the Wolf-Brethren, and after them the wolves with lolling tongues. Up the hill they sped, but the feet of Umslopogaas never wearied, his breath did not fail him. Once more they drew near the lap of the Grey Witch where the cave was. On rushed the bull, mad with fear. He ran so swiftly that the wolves were left behind, since here for a space the ground was level to his feet. Galazi looked on Umslopogaas at his side, and grinned.

"You do not run so ill, my brother, who have been sick of late. See now if you can outrun me! Who shall touch the quarry first?"

Now the bull was ahead by two spear-throws. Umslopogaas looked and grinned back at Galazi. "Good!" he cried, "away!"

They sped forward with a bound, and for awhile it seemed to Umslopogaas as though they stood side by side, only the bull grew nearer and nearer. Then he put out his strength and the swiftness of his feet, and lo! when he looked again he was alone, and the bull was very near. Never were feet so swift as those of Umslopogaas. Now he reached the bull as he labored on. Umslopogaas placed his hands upon the back of the bull and leaped; he was on him, he sat him as you white men sit a horse. Then he lifted the spear in his hand, and drove it down between the shoulders to the spine, and of a sudden the great buffalo staggered, stopped, and fell dead.

Galazi came up. "Who now is the swiftest, Galazi?" cried Umslopogaas, "I, or you, or your wolf host?"

"You are the swiftest, Umslopogaas," said Galazi, gasping for his breath. "Never did a man run as you run, nor ever shall again."

Now the wolves streamed up, and would have torn the carcass, but Galazi beat them back, and they rested awhile. Then Galazi said, "Let us cut meat from the bull with a spear."

So they cut meat from the bull, and when they had finished Galazi motioned to the wolves, and they fell upon the carcass, fighting furiously. In a little while nothing was left except the larger bones, and yet each wolf had but a little.

Then they went back to the cave and slept.

Afterwards Umslopogaas told Galazi all his tale, and Galazi asked him if he would abide with him and be his brother, and rule with him over the wolf-kind, or seek his father Mopo at the kraal of Chaka.

Umslopogaas said that it was rather in his mind to seek his sister Nada, for he was weary of the kraal of Chaka, but he thought of Nada day and night.

"Where, then, is Nada, your sister?" asked Galazi.

"She sleeps in the caves of your people, Galazi; she tarries with the Halakazi."

"Stay awhile, Umslopogaas," cried Galazi; "stay till we are men indeed. Then we will seek this sister of yours and snatch her from the caves of the Halakazi."

Now the desire of this wolf-life had entered into the heart of Umslopogaas, and he said that it should be so, and on the morrow they made them blood-brethren, to be one till death, before all the company of ghost-wolves, and the wolves howled when they smelt the blood of men. In all things thenceforth these two were equal, and the ghost-wolves hearkened to the voice of both of them. And on many a moonlight night they and the wolves hunted together, winning their food. At times they crossed the river, hunting in the plains, for game was scarce on the mountain, and the people of the kraal would come out, hearing the mighty howling, and watch the pack sweep across the veldt, and with them a man or men. Then they would say that the ghosts were abroad and creep into their huts shivering with fear. But as yet the Wolf-Brethren and their pack killed no men, but game only, or, at times, elephants and lions.

Now when Umslopogaas had abode some moons in the Watch Mountain, on a night he dreamed of Nada, and awakening soft at heart, bethought himself that he would learn tidings concerning me, his father, Mopo, and what had befallen me and her whom he deemed his mother, and Nada, his sister, and his other brethren. So he clothed himself, hiding his nakedness, and, leaving Galazi, descended to that kraal where the old woman had dwelt, and there gave it out that he was a young man, a chief's son from a far place, who sought a wife. The people of the kraal listened to him, though they held that his look was fierce and wild, and one asked if this were Galazi the Wolf, Galazi the Wizard. But another answered that this was not Galazi, for their eyes had seen him. Umslopogaas said that he knew nothing of Galazi, and little of wolves, and lo! while he spoke there came an *impi* of fifty men and entered the kraal. Umslopogaas looked at the leaders of the *impi* and knew them for captains of Chaka. At first he would have spoken to them, but his Ehlose bade him hold his peace. So he sat in a corner of the big hut and listened. Presently the headman of the kraal, who trembled with fear, for he believed that the *impi* had been sent to destroy him and all that were his, asked the captain what was his will.

"A little matter, and a vain," said the captain. "We are sent by the king to search for a certain youth, Umslopogaas, the son of Mopo, the king's doctor. Mopo gave it out that the youth was killed by a lion near these mountains, and Chaka would learn if this is true."

"We know nothing of the youth," said the headman. "But what would ye with him?"

"Only this," answered the captain, "to kill him."

"That is yet to do," thought Umslopogaas.

"Who is this Mopo?" asked the headman.

"An evildoer, whose house the king has eaten up — man, woman, and child," answered the captain.

Chapter XV
THE DEATH OF THE KING'S SLAYERS

*W*hen Umslopogaas heard these words his heart was heavy, and a great anger burned in his breast, for he thought that I, Mopo, was dead with the rest of his house, and he loved me. But he said nothing; only, watching till none were looking, he slipped past the backs of the captains and won the door of the hut. Soon he was clear of the kraal, and, running swiftly, crossed the river and came to the Ghost Mountain. Meanwhile, the captain asked the headman of the kraal if he knew anything of such a youth as him for whom they sought. The headman told the captain of Galazi the Wolf, but the captain said that this could not be the lad, for Galazi had dwelt many moons upon the Ghost Mountain.

"There is another youth," said the headman; "a stranger, fierce, strong and tall, with eyes that shine like spears. He is in the hut now; he sits yonder in the shadow."

The captain rose and looked into the shadow, but Umslopogaas was gone.

"Now this youth is fled," said the headman, "and yet none saw him fly! Perhaps he also is a wizard! Indeed, I have heard that now there are two of them upon the Ghost Mountain, and that they hunt there at night with the ghost-wolves, but I do not know if it is true."

"Now I am minded to kill you," said the captain in wrath, "because you have suffered this youth to escape me. Without doubt it is Umslopogaas, son of Mopo."

"It is no fault of mine," said the headmen. "These young men are wizards, who can pass hither and thither at will. But I say this to you, captain of the king, if you will go on the Ghost Mountain, you must go there alone with your soldiers, for none in these parts dare to tread upon that mountain."

"Yet I shall dare tomorrow," said the captain. "We grow brave at the kraal of Chaka. There men do not fear spears or ghosts or wild beasts or magic, but they fear the king's word alone. The sun sets — give us food. Tomorrow we will search the mountain."

Thus, my father, did this captain speak in his folly, — he who should never see another sun.

Now Umslopogaas reached the mountain, and when he had passed the forest — of which he had learned every secret way — the darkness gathered, and the wolves awoke in the darkness and drew near howling. Umslopogaas howled in answer, and presently that great wolf Deathgrip came to him. Umslopogaas saw him and called him by his name; but, behold! the brute did not know him, and flew at him, growling. Then Umslopogaas remembered that the she-wolf's skin was not bound about his shoulders, and therefore it was that the wolf Deathgrip knew him not. For though in the daytime, when the wolves slept, he might pass to and fro without the skin, at night it was not so. He had not brought the skin, because he dared not wear it in the sight of the men of the kraal, lest they should know him for one of the Wolf-Brethren, and it had not been his plan to seek the mountain again that night, but rather on the morrow. Now Umslopogaas knew that his danger was great indeed. He beat back Deathgrip with his kerrie, but others were behind him, for the wolves gathered fast. Then he bounded away towards the cave, for he was so swift of foot that the wolves could not catch him, though they pressed him hard, and once the teeth of one of them tore his *moocha*. Never before did he run so fast, and in the end he reached the cave and rolled the rock to, and as he did so the wolves dashed themselves against it. Then he clad himself in the hide of the she-wolf, and, pushing aside the stone, came out. And, lo! the eyes of the wolves were opened, and they knew him for one of the brethren who ruled over them, and slunk away at his bidding.

Now Umslopogaas sat himself down at the mouth of the cave waiting for Galazi, and he thought. Presently Galazi came, and in few words Umslopogaas told him all his tale.

"You have run a great risk, my brother," said Galazi. "What now?"

"This," said Umslopogaas: "these people of ours are hungry for the flesh of men; let us feed them full on the soldiers of Chaka, who sit yonder at the kraal seeking my life. I would take vengeance for Mopo, my father, and all my brethren who are dead, and for my mothers, the wives of Mopo. What say you?"

Galazi laughed aloud. "That will be merry, my brother," he said. "I weary of hunting beasts, let us hunt men tonight."

"Aye, tonight," said Umslopogaas, nodding. "I long to look upon that captain as a maid longs for her lover's kiss. But first let us rest and eat, for the night is young; then, Galazi, summon our *impi.*"

So they rested and ate, and afterwards went out armed, and Galazi howled to the wolves, and they came in tens and twenties till all were gathered together. Galazi moved among them, shaking the Watcher, as they sat upon their haunches, and followed him with their fiery eyes.

"We do not hunt game tonight, little people," he cried, "but men, and you love the flesh of men."

Now all the wolves howled as though they understood. Then the pack divided itself as was its custom, the she-wolves following Umslopogaas, the dog-wolves following Galazi, and in silence they moved swiftly down towards the plain. They came to the river and swam it, and there, eight spear throws away, on the farther side of the river stood the kraal. Now the Wolf-Brethren took counsel together, and Galazi, with the dog-wolves, went to the north gate, and Umslopogaas with the she-wolves to the south gate. They reached them safely and in silence, for at the bidding of the brethren the wolves ceased from their howlings. The gates were stopped with thorns, but the brethren pulled out the thorns and made a passage. As they did this it chanced that certain dogs in the kraal heard the sound of the stirred boughs, and awakening, caught the smell of the wolves that were with Umslopogaas, for the wind blew from that quarter. These dogs ran out barking, and presently they came to the south gate of the kraal, and flew at Umslopogaas, who pulled away the thorns. Now when the wolves saw the dogs they could be restrained no longer, but sprang on them and tore them to fragments, and the sound of their worrying came to the ears of the soldiers of Chaka and of the dwellers in the kraal, so that they sprang from sleep, snatching their arms. And as they came out of the huts they saw in the moonlight a man wearing a wolf's hide rushing across the empty cattle kraal, for the grass was long and the cattle were out at graze, and with him countless wolves, black and grey. Then they cried aloud in terror, saying that the ghosts were on them, and turned to flee to the north gate of the kraal. But, behold! here also they met a man clad in a wolf's skin only, and with him countless wolves, black and grey.

Now, some flung themselves to earth screaming in their fear, and some strove to run away, but the greater part of the soldiers, and with them many of the men of the kraal, came together in knots, being minded to die like men at teeth of the ghosts, and that though they shook with fear. Then Umslopogaas howled aloud, and howled Galazi, and they flung themselves upon the soldiers and the people of the kraal, and with them came the wolves. Then a crying and a baying rose up to heaven as the grey wolves leaped and bit and tore. Little they heeded the spears and kerries of the soldiers. Some were killed, but the rest did not stay. Presently the knots of men broke up, and to each man wolves hung by twos and threes, dragging him to earth. Some few fled, indeed, but the wolves hunted them by gaze and scent, and pulled them down before they passed the gates of the kraal.

The Wolf-Brethren also ravened with the rest. Busy was the Watcher, and many bowed beneath him, and often the spear of Umslopogaas flashed in the moonlight. It was finished; none were left living in that kraal, and the wolves growled sullenly as they took their fill, they who had been hungry for many days. Now the brethren met, and laughed in their wolf joy, because they had slaughtered those who were sent out to slaughter. They called to the wolves, bidding them search the huts, and the wolves entered the huts as dogs enter a thicket, and killed those who lurked there, or drove them forth to be slain without. Presently a man, great and tall, sprang from the last of the huts, where he had hidden himself, and the wolves outside rushed on him to drag him down. But Umslopogaas beat them back, for he had seen the face of the man: it was that captain whom Chaka had sent out to kill him. He beat them back, and stalked up to the captain, saying: "Greeting to you, captain of the king! Now tell us what is your errand here, beneath the shadow of her who sits in stone?" And he pointed with his spear to the Grey Witch on the Ghost Mountain, on which the moon shone bright.

Now the captain had a great heart, though he had hidden from the wolves, and answered boldly: —

"What is that to you, wizard? Your ghost wolves had made an end of my errand. Let them make an end of me also."

"Be not in haste, captain," said Umslopogaas. "Say, did you not seek a certain youth, the son of Mopo?"

"That is so," answered the captain. "I sought one youth, and I have found many evil spirits." And he looked at the wolves tearing their prey, and shuddered.

"Say, captain," quoth Umslopogaas, drawing back his hood of wolf's hide so that the moonlight fell upon his face, "is this the face of that youth whom you sought?"

"It is the face," answered the captain, astonished.

"Aye," laughed Umslopogaas, "it is the face. Fool! I knew your errand and heard your words, and thus have I answered them." And he pointed to the dead. "Now choose, and swiftly. Will you run for your life against my wolves? Will you do battle for your life against these four?" And he pointed to Greysnout and to Blackfang, to Blood and to Deathgrip, who watched him with slavering lips; "or will you stand face to face

with me, and if I am slain, with him who bears the club, and with whom
I rule this people black and grey?"

"I fear ghosts, but of men I have no fear, though they be wizards,"
answered the captain.

"Good!" cried Umslopogaas, shaking his spear.

Then they rushed together, and that fray was fierce. For presently the
spear of Umslopogaas was broken in the shield of the captain and he
was left weaponless. Now Umslopogaas turned and fled swiftly, bounding over the dead and the wolves who preyed upon them, and the captain
followed with uplifted spear, and mocked him as he came. Galazi also
wondered that Umslopogaas should fly from a single man. Hither and
thither fled Umslopogaas, and always his eyes were on the earth. Of a
sudden, Galazi, who watched, saw him sweep forward like a bird and
stoop to the ground. Then he wheeled round, and lo! there was an axe
in his hand. The captain rushed at him, and Umslopogaas smote as he
rushed, and the blade of the great spear that was lifted to pierce him
fell to the ground hewn from its haft. Again Umslopogaas smote: the
moon-shaped axe sank through the stout shield deep into the breast
beyond. Then the captain threw up his arms and fell to the earth.

"Ah!" cried Umslopogaas, "you sought a youth to slay him, and have
found an axe to be slain by it! Sleep softly, captain of Chaka."

Then Umslopogaas spoke to Galazi, saying: "My brother, I will fight
no more with the spear, but with the axe alone; it was to seek an axe
that I ran to and fro like a coward. But this is a poor thing! See, the haft
is split because of the greatness of my stroke! Now this is my desire —
to win that great axe of Jikiza, which is called Groan-Maker, of which
we have heard tell, so that axe and club may stand together in the fray."

"That must be for another night," said Galazi. "We have not done so
ill for once. Now let us search for pots and corn, of which we stand in
need, and then to the mountain before dawn finds us."

Thus, then, did the Wolf-Brethren bring death on the *impi* of Chaka,
and this was but the first of many deaths that they wrought with the
help of the wolves. Forever they ravened through the land at night, and,
falling on those they hated, they ate them up, till their name and the
name of the ghost-wolves became terrible in the ears of men, and the
land was swept clean. But they found that the wolves would not go
abroad to worry everywhere. Thus, on a certain night, they set out to
fall upon the kraals of the People of the Axe, where dwelt the chief
Jikiza, who was named the Unconquered, and owned the axe Groan-
Maker, but when they neared the kraal the wolves turned back and fled.
Then Galazi remembered the dream that he had dreamed, in which the
Dead One in the cave had seemed to speak, telling him that there only

where the men-eaters had hunted in the past might the wolves hunt today. So they returned home, but Umslopogaas set himself to find a plan to win the axe.

Chapter XVI
UMSLOPOGAAS VENTURES OUT TO WIN THE AXE

*N*ow many moons had gone by since Umslopogaas became a king of the wolves, and he was a man full grown, a man fierce and tall and keen; a slayer of men, fleet of foot and of valor unequaled, seeing by night as well as by day. But he was not yet named the Slaughterer, and not yet did he hold that iron chieftainess, the axe Groan-Maker. Still, the desire to win the axe was foremost in his mind, for no woman had entered there, who when she enters drives out all other desire — aye, my father, even that of good weapons. At times, indeed, Umslopogaas would lurk in the reeds by the river looking at the kraal of Jikiza the Unconquered, and would watch the gates of his kraal, and once as he lurked he saw a man great, broad and hairy, who bore upon his shoulder a shining axe, hafted with the horn of a rhinoceros. After that his greed for this axe entered into Umslopogaas more and more, till at length he scarcely could sleep for thinking of it, and to Galazi he spoke of little else, wearying him much with his talk, for Galazi loved silence. But for all his longing he could find no means to win it.

Now it befell that as Umslopogaas hid one evening in the reeds, watching the kraal of Jikiza, he saw a maiden straight and fair, whose skin shone like the copper anklets on her limbs. She walked slowly towards the reeds where he lay hidden. Nor did she top at the brink of the reeds; she entered them and sat herself down within a spear's length of where Umslopogaas was seated, and at once began to weep, speaking to herself as she wept.

"Would that the ghost-wolves might fall on him and all that is his," she sobbed, "aye, and on Masilo also! I would hound them on, even if I myself must next know their fangs. Better to die by the teeth of the wolves than to be sold to this fat pig of a Masilo. Oh! if I must wed him, I will give him a knife for the bride's kiss. Oh! that I were a lady of the ghost-wolves, there should be a picking of bones in the kraal of Jikiza before the moon grows young again."

Umslopogaas heard, and of a sudden reared himself up before the maid, and he was great and wild to look on, and the she-wolf's fangs shone upon his brow.

"The ghost-wolves are at hand, damsel," he said. "They are ever at hand for those who need them."

Now the maid saw him and screamed faintly, then grew silent, wondering at the greatness and the fierce eyes of the man who spoke to her.

"Who are you?" she asked. "I fear you not, whoever you are."

"There you are wrong, damsel, for all men fear me, and they have cause to fear. I am one of the Wolf-Brethren, whose names have been told of; I am a wizard of the Ghost Mountain. Take heed, now, lest I kill you. It will be of little avail to call upon your people, for my feet are fleeter than theirs."

"I have no wish to call upon my people, Wolf-Man," she answered. "And for the rest, I am too young to kill."

"That is so, maiden," answered Umslopogaas, looking at her beauty. "What were the words upon your lips as to Jikiza and a certain Masilo? Were they not fierce words, such as my heart likes well?"

"It seems that you heard them," answered the girl. "What need to waste breath in speaking them again?"

"No need, maiden. Now tell me your story; perhaps I may find a way to help you."

"There is little to tell," she answered. "It is a small tale and a common. My name is Zinita, and Jikiza the Unconquered is my step-father. He married my mother, who is dead, but none of his blood is in me. Now he would give me in marriage to a certain Masilo, a fat man and an old, whom I hate, because Masilo offers many cattle for me."

"Is there, then, another whom you would wed, maiden?" asked Umslopogaas.

"There is none," answered Zinita, looking him in the eyes.

"And is there no path by which you may escape from Masilo?"

"There is only one path, Wolf-Man — by death. If I die, I shall escape; if Masilo dies, I shall escape; but to little end, for I shall be given to another; but if Jikiza dies, then it will be well. What of that wolf-people of yours, are they not hungry, Wolf-Man?"

"I cannot bring them here," answered Umslopogaas. "Is there no other way?"

"There is another way," said Zinita, "if one can be found to try it." And again she looked at him strangely, causing the blood to beat within him. "Hearken! do you not know how our people are governed? They are governed by him who holds the axe Groan-Maker. He that can win the axe in war from the hand of him who holds it, shall be our chief. But if he who holds the axe dies unconquered, then his son takes his place and with it the axe. It has been thus, indeed, for four generations, since he who held Groan-Maker has always been unconquerable. But I have heard that the great-grandfather of Jikiza won the axe from him who held it in his day; he won it by fraud. For when the axe had fallen on him but lightly, he fell over, feigning death. Then the owner of the axe laughed, and turned to walk away. But the forefather of Jikiza sprang up behind him and pierced him through with a spear, and thus he became chief of the People of the Axe. Therefore, it is the custom of Jikiza to hew off the heads of those whom he kills with the axe."

"Does he, then, slay many?" asked Umslopogaas.

"Of late years, few indeed," she said, "for none dare stand against him — no, not with all to win. For, holding the axe Groan-Maker, he is unconquerable, and to fight with him is sure death. Fifty-and-one have tried in all, and before the hut of Jikiza there are piled fifty-and-one white skulls. And know this, the axe must be won in fight; if it is stolen or found, it has no virtue — nay, it brings shame and death to him who holds it."

"How, then, may a man give battle to Jikiza?" he asked again.

"Thus: Once in every year, on the first day of the new moon of the summer season, Jikiza holds a meeting of the headmen. Then he must rise and challenge all or any to come forward and do battle with him to win the axe and become chief in his place. Now if one comes forward, they go into the cattle kraal, and there the matter is ended. Afterwards, when the head is hewn from his foe, Jikiza goes back to the meeting of the headmen, and they talk as before. All are free to come to the meeting, and Jikiza must fight with them if they wish it, whoever they be."

"Perhaps I shall be there," said Umslopogaas.

"After this meeting at the new moon, I am to be given in marriage to Masilo," said the maid. "But should one conquer Jikiza, then he will be chief, and can give me in marriage to whom he will."

Now Umslopogaas understood her meaning, and knew that he had found favor in her sight; and the thought moved him a little, for women were strange to him as yet.

"If perchance I should be there," he said, "and if perchance I should win the iron chieftainess, the axe Groan-Maker, and rule over the People of the Axe, you should not live far from the shadow of the axe thenceforward, maid Zinita."

"It is well, Wolf-Man, though some might not wish to dwell in that shadow; but first you must win the axe. Many have tried, and all have failed."

"Yet one must succeed at last," he said, "and so, farewell!" and he leaped into the torrent of the river, and swam it with great strokes.

Now the maid Zinita watched him till he was gone, and love of him entered into her heart — a love that was fierce and jealous and strong. But as he wended to the Ghost Mountain Umslopogaas thought rather of axe Groan-Maker than of Maid Zinita; forever, at the bottom, Umslopogaas loved war more than women, though this has been his fate, that women have brought sorrow on his head.

Fifteen days must pass before the day of the new moon, and during this time Umslopogaas thought much and said little. Still, he told Galazi something of the tale, and that he was determined to do battle with Jikiza the Unconquered for the axe Groan-Maker. Galazi said that he would do well to let it be, and that it was better to stay with the wolves than to go out seeking strange weapons. He said also that even if he won the axe, the matter might not stay there, for he must take the girl also, and his heart boded no good of women. It had been a girl who poisoned his father in the kraals of the Halakazi. To all of which Umslopogaas answered nothing, for his heart was set both on the axe and the girl, but more on the first than the last.

So the time wore on, and at length came the day of the new moon. At the dawn of that day Umslopogaas arose and clad himself in a *moocha*, binding the she-wolf's skin round his middle beneath the *moocha*. In his hand he took a stout fighting-shield, which he had made of buffalo hide, and that same light moon-shaped axe with which he had slain the captain of Chaka.

"A poor weapon with which to kill Jikiza the Unconquerable," said Galazi, eyeing it askance.

"It shall serve my turn," answered Umslopogaas.

Now Umslopogaas ate, and then they moved together slowly down the mountain and crossed the river by a ford, for he wished to save his strength. On the farther side of the river Galazi hid himself in the reeds, because his face was known, and there Umslopogaas bade him farewell, not knowing if he should look upon him again. Afterwards he walked up to the Great Place of Jikiza. Now when he reached the gates of the kraal, he saw that many people were streaming through them, and mingled with the people. Presently they came to the open space in front of the huts of Jikiza, and there the headmen were gathered together. In the center of them, and before a heap of the skulls of men which were piled up against his doorposts, sat Jikiza, a huge man, a hairy and a proud, who glared about him rolling his eyes. Fastened to his arm by a thong of leather was the great axe Groan-Maker, and each man as he came up saluted the axe, calling it "Inkosikaas," or chieftainess, but he did not salute Jikiza. Umslopogaas sat down with the people in front of the councilors, and few took any notice of him, except Zinita, who moved sullenly to and fro bearing gourds of beer to the councilors. Near to Jikiza, on his right hand, sat a fat man with small and twinkling eyes, who watched the maid Zinita greedily.

"Yon man," thought Umslopogaas, "is Masilo. The better for blood-letting will you be, Masilo."

Presently Jikiza spoke, rolling his eyes: "This is the matter before you, councilors. I have settled it in my mind to give my step-daughter Zinita in marriage to Masilo, but the marriage gift is not yet agreed on. I demand a hundred head of cattle from Masilo, for the maid is fair and straight, a proper maid, and, moreover, my daughter, though not of my blood. But Masilo offers fifty head only, therefore I ask you to settle it."

"We hear you, Lord of the Axe," answered one of the councilors, "but first, O Unconquered, you must on this day of the year, according to ancient custom, give public challenge to any man to fight you for the Groan-Maker and for your place as chief of the People of the Axe."

"This is a wearisome thing," grumbled Jikiza. "Can I never have done in it? Fifty-and-three have I slain in my youth without a wound, and now for many years I have challenged, like a cock on a dunghill, and none crow in answer."

"Ho, now! Is there any man who will come forward and do battle with me, Jikiza, for the great axe Groan-Maker? To him who can win it, it shall be, and with it the chieftainship of the People of the Axe."

Thus he spoke very fast, as a man gabbles a prayer to a spirit in whom he has little faith, then turned once more to talk of the cattle of Masilo and of the maid Zinita. But suddenly Umslopogaas stood up, looking at him over the top of his war shield, and crying, "Here is one, O Jikiza, who will do battle with you for the axe Groan-Maker and for the chieftainship that is to him who holds the axe."

Now, all the people laughed, and Jikiza glared at him.

"Come forth from behind that big shield of yours," he said. "Come out and tell me your name and lineage — you who would do battle with the Unconquered for the ancient axe."

Then Umslopogaas came forward, and he looked so fierce, though he was but young, that the people laughed no more.

"What is my name and lineage to you, Jikiza?" he said. "Let it be, and hasten to do me battle, as you must by the custom, for I am eager to handle the Groan-Maker and to sit in your seat and settle this matter of the cattle of Masilo the Pig. When I have killed you I will take a name who now have none."

Now once more the people laughed, but Jikiza grew mad with wrath, and sprang up gasping.

"What!" he said, "you dare to speak thus to me, you babe unweaned, to me the Unconquered, the holder of the axe! Never did I think to live to hear such talk from a long-legged pup. On to the cattle kraal, to the cattle kraal, People of the Axe, that I may hew this braggart's head from his shoulders. He would stand in my place, would he? — the place that I and my fathers have held for four generations by virtue of the axe. I tell you all, that presently I will stand upon his head, and then we will settle the matter of Masilo."

"Babble not so fast, man," quoth Umslopogaas, "or if you must babble, speak those words which you would say ere you bid the sun farewell."

Now, Jikiza choked with rage, and foam came from his lips so that he could not speak, but the people found this sport — all except Masilo, who looked askance at the stranger, tall and fierce, and Zinita, who looked at Masilo, and with no love. So they moved down to the cattle kraal, and Galazi, seeing it from afar, could keep away no longer, but drew near and mingled with the crowd.

Chapter XVII

UMSLOPOGAAS BECOMES CHIEF
OF THE PEOPLE OF THE AXE

*N*ow, when Umslopogaas and Jikiza the Unconquered had come to the cattle kraal, they were set in its center and there were ten paces between them. Umslopogaas was armed with the great shield and the light moon-shaped axe, Jikiza carried the Groan-Maker and a small dancing shield, and, looking at the weapons of the two, people thought that the stranger would furnish no sport to the holder of the axe.

"He is ill-armed," said an old man, "it should be otherwise — large axe, small shield. Jikiza is unconquerable, and the big shield will not help this long-legged stranger when Groan-Maker rattles on the buffalo hide." The old man spoke thus in the hearing of Galazi the Wolf, and Galazi thought that he spoke wisely, and sorrowed for the fate of his brother.

Now, the word was given, and Jikiza rushed on Umslopogaas, roaring, for his rage was great. But Umslopogaas did not stir till his foe was about to strike, then suddenly he leaped aside, and as Jikiza passed he smote him hard upon the back with the flat of his axe, making a great sound, for it was not his plan to try and kill Jikiza with this axe. Now, a shout of laughter went up from the hundreds of the people, and the laughter went up from the hundreds of the people, and the heart of Jikiza nearly burst with rage because of the shame of that blow. Round he came like a bull that is mad, and once more rushed at Umslopogaas, who lifted his shield to meet him. Then, of a sudden, just when the great axe leapt on high, Umslopogaas uttered a cry as of fear, and, turning, fled before the face of Jikiza. Now once more the shout of laughter went up, while Umslopogaas fled swiftly, and after him rushed Jikiza, blind with fury. Round and about the kraal sped Umslopogaas, scarcely a spear's length ahead of Jikiza, and he ran keeping his back to the sun as much as might be, that he might watch the shadow of Jikiza. A second time he sped round, while the people cheered the chase as hunters cheer a dog which pursues a buck. So cunningly did Umslopogaas run, that, though he seemed to reel with weakness in such fashion that men thought his breath was gone, yet he went ever faster and faster, drawing Jikiza after him.

Now, when Umslopogaas knew by the breathing of his foe and by the staggering of his shadow that his strength was spent, suddenly he made as though he were about to fall himself, and stumbled out of the path far to the right, and as he stumbled he let drop his great shield full in the way of Jikiza's feet. Then it came about that Jikiza, rushing on blindly, caught his feet in the shield and fell headlong to earth. Umslopogaas saw, and swooped on him like an eagle to a dove. Before men could so much as think, he had seized the axe Groan-Maker, and with a blow of the steel he held had severed the thong of leather which bound it to the wrist of Jikiza, and sprung back, holding the great axe aloft, and casting down his own weapon upon the ground. Now, the watchers saw all the cunning of his fight, and those of them who hated Jikiza shouted aloud. But others were silent.

Slowly Jikiza gathered himself from the ground, wondering if he were still alive, and as he rose he grasped the little axe of Umslopogaas, and, looking at it, he wept. But Umslopogaas held up the great Groan-Maker, the iron chieftainess, and examined its curved points of blue steel, the gouge that stands behind it, and the beauty of its haft, bound about with wire of brass, and ending in a knob like the knob of a stick, as a lover looks upon the beauty of his bride. Then before all men he kissed the broad blade and cried aloud: —

"Greeting to thee, my Chieftainess, greeting to thee, Wife of my youth, whom I have won in war. Never shall we part, thou and I, and together will we die, thou and I, for I am not minded that others should handle thee when I am gone."

Thus he cried in the hearing of men, then turned to Jikiza, who stood weeping, because he had lost all.

"Where now is your pride, O Unconquered?" laughed Umslopogaas. "Fight on. You are as well armed as I was a while ago, when I did not fear to stand before you."

Jikiza looked at him for a moment, then with a curse he hurled the little axe at him, and, turning, fled swiftly towards the gates of the cattle kraal.

Umslopogaas stooped, and the little axe sped over him. Then he stood for a while watching, and the people thought that he meant to let Jikiza go. But that was not his desire; he waited, indeed, until Jikiza had covered nearly half the space between him and the gate, then with a roar he leaped forward, as light leaps from a cloud, and so fast did his feet fly that the watchers could scarce see them move. Jikiza fled fast also, yet he seemed but as one who stands still. Now he reached the gate of the kraal, now there was rush, a light of downward falling steel, and something swept past him. Then, behold! Jikiza fell in the gateway of the cattle kraal, and all saw that he was dead, smitten to death by that mighty axe Groan-Maker, which he and his fathers had held for many years.

A great shout went up from the crowd of watchers when they knew that Jikiza the Unconquered was killed at last, and there were many who hailed Umslopogaas, naming him Chief and Lord of the People of the Axe. But the sons of Jikiza to the number of ten, great men and brave, rushed on Umslopogaas to kill him. Umslopogaas ran backwards, lifting up the Groan-Maker, when certain councilors of the people flung themselves in between them, crying, "Hold!"

"Is not this your law, ye councilors," said Umslopogaas, "that, having conquered the chief of the People of the Axe, I myself am chief?"

"That is our law indeed, stranger," answered an aged councilor, "but this also is our law: that now you must do battle, one by one, with all who come against you. So it was in my father's time, when the grandfather of him who now lies dead won the axe, and so it must be again today."

"I have nothing to say against the rule," said Umslopogaas. "Now who is there who will come up against me to do battle for the axe Groan-Maker and the chieftainship of the People of the Axe?"

Then all the ten sons of Jikiza stepped forward as one man, for their hearts were made with wrath because of the death of their father and because the chieftainship had gone from their race, so that in truth they cared little if they lived or died. But there were none besides these, for all men feared to stand before Umslopogaas and the Groan-Maker.

Umslopogaas counted them. "There are ten, by the head of Chaka!" he cried. "Now if I must fight all these one by one, no time will be left to me this day to talk of the matter of Masilo and of the maid Zinita. Hearken! What say you, sons of Jikiza the Conquered? If I find one other to stand beside me in the fray, and all of you come on at once against us twain, ten against two, to slay us or be slain, will that be to your minds?"

The brethren consulted together, and held that so they should be in better case than if they went up one by one.

"So be it," they said, and the councilors assented.

Now, as he fled round and round, Umslopogaas had seen the face of Galazi, his brother, in the throng, and knew that he hungered to share the fight. So he called aloud that he whom he should choose, and who would stand back to back with him in the fray, if victory were theirs, should be the first after him among the People of the Axe, and as he called, he walked slowly down the line scanning the faces of all, till he came to where Galazi stood leaning on the Watcher.

"Here is a great fellow who bears a great club," said Umslopogaas. "How are you named, fellow?"

"I am named Wolf," answered Galazi.

"Say, now, Wolf, are you willing to stand back to back with me in this fray of two against ten? If victory is ours, you shall be next to me amongst this people."

"Better I love the wild woods and the mountain's breast than the kraals of men and the kiss of wives, Axebearer," answered Galazi. "Yet, because you have shown yourself a warrior of might, and to taste again of the joy of battle, I will stand back to back with you, Axebearer, and see this matter ended."

"A bargain, Wolf!" cried Umslopogaas. And they walked side by side — a mighty pair! — till they came to the center of the cattle kraal. All there looked on them wondering, and it came into the thoughts of some of them that these were none other than the Wolf-Brethren who dwelt upon the Ghost Mountain.

"Now axe Groan-maker and club Watcher are come together, Galazi," said Umslopogaas as they walked, "and I think that few can stand before them."

"Some shall find it so," answered Galazi. "At the least, the fray will be merry, and what matter how frays end?"

"Ah," said Umslopogaas, "victory is good, but death ends all and is best of all."

Then they spoke of the fashion in which they would fight, and Umslopogaas looked curiously at the axe he carried, and at the point on its hammer, balancing it in his hand. When he had looked long, the pair took their stand back to back in the center of the kraal, and people saw that Umslopogaas held the axe in a new fashion, its curved blade being inwards towards his breast, and the hollow point turned towards the foe. The ten brethren gathered themselves together, shaking their assegais; five of them stood before Umslopogaas and five before Galazi the Wolf. They were all great men, made fierce with rage and shame.

"Now nothing except witchcraft can save these two," said a councilor to one who stood by him.

"Yet there is virtue in the axe," answered the other, "and for the club, it seems that I know it: I think it is named Watcher of the Fords, and woe to those who stand before the Watcher. I myself have seen him aloft when I was young; moreover, these are no cravens who hold the axe and the club. They are but lads, indeed, yet they have drunk wolf's milk."

Meanwhile, an aged man drew near to speak the word of onset; it was that same man who had set out the law to Umslopogaas. He must give the signal by throwing up a spear, and when it struck the ground, then the fight would begin. The old man took the spear and threw it, but his hand was weak, and he cast so clumsily that it fell among the sons of Jikiza, who stood before Umslopogaas, causing them to open up to let it pass between them, and drawing the eyes of all ten of them to it. but Umslopogaas watched for the touching of the spear only, being careless where it touched. As the point of it kissed the earth, he said a word, and lo! Umslopogaas and Galazi, not waiting for the onslaught of the ten, as men had thought they must, sprang forward, each at the line of foes who were before him. While the ten still stood confused, for it had been their plan to attack, the Wolf-Brethren were upon them. Groan-Maker was up, but as for no great stroke. He did but peck, as a bird pecks with his bill, and yet a man dropped dead. The Watcher also was up, but he fell like a falling tree, and was the death of one. Through the lines of the ten passed the Wolf-Brethren in the gaps that each had made. Then they turned swiftly and charged towards each other again; again Groan-Maker pecked, again the Watcher thundered, and lo! once more Umslopogaas stood back to back unhurt, but before them lay four men dead.

The onslaught and the return were so swift, that men scarcely understood what had been done; even those of the sons of Jikiza who were left stared at each other wondering. Then they knew that they were but six, for four of them were dead. With a shout of rage they rushed upon the pair from both sides, but in either case one was the most eager, and outstepped the other two, and thus it came about that time was given the Wolf-Brethren to strike at him alone, before his fellows were at his side. He who came at Umslopogaas drove at him with his spear, but he was not to be caught this, for he bent his middle sideways, so that the spear only cut his skin, and as he bent tapped with the point of the axe at the head of the smiter, dealing death on him.

"Yonder Woodpecker has a bill of steel, and he can use it well," said the councilor to him who stood by him.

"This is a Slaughterer indeed," the man answered, and the people heard the names. Thenceforth they knew Umslopogaas as the Woodpecker, and as Bulalio, or the Slaughterer, and by no other names. Now, he who came at Galazi the Wolf rushed on wildly, holding his spear short. But Galazi was cunning in war. He took one step forward to meet him, then, swinging the Watcher backward, he let him fall at the full length of arms and club. The child of Jikiza lifted his shield to catch the blow, but the shield was to the Watcher what a leaf is to the wind. Full on its hide the huge club fell, making a loud sound; the war-shield doubled up like a raw skin, and he who bore it fell crushed to the earth.

Now for a moment, the four who were left of the sons of Jikiza hovered round the pair, feinting at them from afar, but never coming within reach of axe or club. One threw a spear indeed, and though Umslopogaas leaped aside, and as it sped towards him smote the haft in two with the blade of Groan-Maker, yet its head flew on, wounding Galazi in the flank. Then he who had thrown the spear turned to fly, for his hands were empty, and the others followed swiftly, for the heart was out of them, and they dared to do battle with these two no more.

Thus the fight was ended, and from its beginning till the finish was not longer than the time in which men might count a hundred slowly.

"It seems that none are left for us to kill, Galazi," said Umslopogaas, laughing aloud. "Ah, that was a cunning fight! Ho! you sons of the Unconquered, who run so fast, stay your feet. I give you peace; you shall live to sweep my huts and to plow my fields with the other women of my kraal. Now, councilors, the fighting is done, so let us to the chief's hut, where Masilo waits us," and he turned and went with Galazi, and after him followed all the people, wondering and in silence.

When he reached the hut Umslopogaas sat himself down in the place where Jikiza had sat that morning, and the maid Zinita came to him with a wet cloth and washed the wound that the spear had made. He thanked her; then she would have washed Galazi's wound also, and this was deeper, but Galazi bade her to let him be roughly, as he would have no woman meddling with his wounds. For neither then nor at any other time did Galazi turn to women, but he hated Zinita most of them all.

Then Umslopogaas spoke to Masilo the Pig, who sat before him with a frightened face, saying, "It seems, O Masilo, that you have sought this maid Zinita in marriage, and against her will, persecuting her. Now I had intended to kill you as an offering to her anger, but there has been enough blood-letting today. Yet you shall have a marriage gift to this girl, whom I myself will take in marriage: you shall give a hundred head of cattle. Then get you gone from among the People of the Axe, lest a worse thing befall you, Masilo the Pig."

So Masilo rose up and went, and his face was green with fear, but he paid the hundred head of cattle and fled towards the kraal of Chaka. Zinita watched him go, and she was glad of it, and because the Slaughterer had named her for his wife.

"I am well rid of Masilo," she said aloud, in the hearing of Galazi, "but I had been better pleased to see him dead before me."

"This woman has a fierce heart," thought Galazi, "and she will bring no good to Umslopogaas, my brother."

Now the councilors and the captains of the People of the Axe *konzaed* to him whom they named the Slaughterer, doing homage to him as chief and holder of the axe, and also they did homage to the axe itself. So Umslopogaas became chief over this people, and their number was many, and he grew great and fat in cattle and wives, and none dared to gainsay him. From time to time, indeed, a man ventured to stand up before him in fight, but none could conquer him, and in a little while no one sought to face Groan-Maker when he lifted himself to peck.

Galazi also was great among the people, but dwelt with them little, for best he loved the wild woods and the mountain's breast, and often, as of old, he swept at night across the forest and the plains, and the howling of the ghost-wolves went with him.

But henceforth Umslopogaas the Slaughterer hunted very rarely with the wolves at night; he slept at the side of Zinita, and she loved him much and bore him children.

Chapter XVIII

THE CURSE OF BALEKA

*N*ow, my father, my story winds back again as the river bends towards its source, and I tell of those events which happened at the king's kraal of Gibamaxegu, which you white people name Gibbeclack, the kraal that is called "Pick-out-the-old-men," for it was there that Chaka murdered all the aged who were unfit for war.

After I, Mopo, had stood before the king, and he had given me new wives and fat cattle and a kraal to dwell in, the bones of Unandi, the Great Mother Elephant, Mother of the Heavens, were gathered together from the ashes of my huts, and because all could not be found, some of the bones of my wives were collected also to make up the number.

But Chaka never knew this. When all were brought together, a great pit was dug and the bones were set out in order in the pit and buried; but not alone, for round them were placed twelve maidens of the servants of Unandi, and these maidens were covered over with the earth, and left to die in the pit by the bones of Unandi, their mistress. Moreover, all those who were present at the burial were made into a regiment and commanded that they should dwell by the grave for the space of a year. They were many, my father, but I was not one of them. Also Chaka gave orders that no crops should be sown that year, that the milk of the cows should be spilled upon the ground, and that no woman should give birth to a child for a full year, and that if any should dare to bear children, then that they should be slain and their husbands with them. And for a space of some months these things were done, my father, and great sorrow came upon the land.

Then for a little while there was quiet, and Chaka went about heavily, and he wept often, and we who waited on him wept also as we walked, till at length it came about by use that we could weep without ceasing for many hours. No angry woman can weep as we wept in those days; it was an art, my father, for the teaching of which I received many cattle, for woe to him who had no tears in those days. Then it was also that Chaka sent out the captain and fifty soldiers to search for Umslopogaas, for, though he said nothing more to me of this matter, he did not believe all the tale that I had told him of the death of Umslopogaas in the jaws of a lion and the tale of those who were with me. How that company fared at the hands of Umslopogaas and of Galazi the Wolf, and at the fangs of the people black and grey, I have told you, my father. None of them ever came back again. In after days it was reported to the king that these soldiers were missing, never having returned, but he only laughed, saying that the lion which ate Umslopogaas, son of Mopo, was a fierce one, and had eaten them also.

At last came the night of the new moon, that dreadful night to be followed by a more dreadful morrow. I sat in the kraal of Chaka, and he put his arm about my neck and groaned and wept for his mother, whom he had murdered, and I groaned also, but I did not weep, because it was dark, and on the morrow I must weep much in the sight of king and men. Therefore, I spared my tears, lest they should fail me in my need.

All night long the people drew on from every side towards the kraal, and, as they came in thousands and tens of thousands, they filled the night with their cries, till it seemed as though the whole world were mourning, and loudly. None might cease their crying, and none dared to drink so much as a cup of water. The daylight came, and Chaka rose, saying, "Come, let us go forth, Mopo, and look on those who mourn with us." So we went out, and after us came men armed with clubs to do the bidding of the king.

Outside the kraal the people were gathered, and their number was countless as the leaves upon the trees. On every side the land was black with them, as at times the veldt is black with game. When they saw the king they ceased from their howling and sang the war-song, then once again they howled, and Chaka walked among them weeping. Now, my father, the sight became dreadful, for, as the sun rose higher the day grew hot, and utter weariness came upon the people, who were packed together like herds of cattle, and, though oxen slain in sacrifice lay around, they might neither eat nor drink. Some fell to the ground, and were trampled to death, others took too much snuff to make them weep, others stained their eyes with saliva, others walked to and fro, their tongues hanging from their jaws, while groans broke from their parched throats.

"Now, Mopo, we shall learn who are the wizards that have brought these ills upon us," said the king, "and who are the true-hearted men."

As we spoke we cam upon a man, a chief of renown. He was named Zwaumbana, chief of the Amabovus, and with him were his wives and followers. This man could weep no more; he gasped with thirst and heat. The king looked at him.

"See, Mopo," he said, "see that brute who has no tears for my mother who is dead! Oh, the monster without a heart! Shall such as he live to look upon the sun, while I and thou must weep, Mopo? Never! never! Take him away, and all those who are with him! Take them away, the people without hearts, who do not weep because my mother is dead by witchcraft!"

And Chaka walked on weeping, and I followed also weeping, but the chief Zwaumbana and those with him were all slain by those who do the bidding of the king, and the slayers also must weep as they slew. Presently we came upon another man, who, seeing the king, took snuff secretly to bring tears to his eyes. But the glance of Chaka was quick, and he noted it.

"Look at him, Mopo," he said, "look at the wizard who has no tears, though my mother is dead by witchcraft. See, he takes snuff to bring tears to his eyes that are dry with wickedness. Take him away, the heartless brute! Oh, take him away!"

So this one also was killed, and these were but the first of thousands, for presently Chaka grew mad with wickedness, with fury, and with the lust of blood. He walked to and fro, weeping, going now and again into his hut to drink beer, and I with him, for he said that we who sorrowed must have food. And ever as he walked he would wave his arm or his assegai, saying, "Take them away, the heartless brutes, who do not weep because my mother is dead," and those who chanced to stand before his arm were killed, till at length the slayers could slay no more, and themselves were slain, because their strength had failed them, and they had no more tears. And I also, I must slay, lest if I slew not I should myself be slain.

And now, at length, the people also went mad with their thirst and the fury of their fear. They fell upon each other, killing each other; every man who had a foe sought him out and killed him. None were spared, the place was but a shambles; there on that day died full seven thousand men, and still Chaka walked weeping among them, saying, "Take them away, the heartless brutes, take them away!" Yet, my father, there was cunning in his cruelty, for though he destroyed many for sport alone, also he slew on this day all those whom he hated or whom he feared.

At length the night came down, the sun sank red that day, all the sky was like blood, and blood was all the earth beneath. Then the killing ceased, because none had now the strength to kill, and the people lay panting in heaps upon the ground, the living and the dead together. I looked at them, and saw that if they were not allowed to eat and drink, before day dawned again the most of them would be dead, and I spoke to the king, for I cared little in that hour if I lived or died; even my hope of vengeance was forgotten in the sickness of my heart.

"A mourning indeed, O King," I said, "a merry mourning for true-hearted men, but for wizards a mourning such as they do not love. I think that thy sorrows are avenged, O King, thy sorrows and mine also."

"Not so, Mopo," answered the king, "this is but the beginning; our mourning was merry today, it shall be merrier tomorrow."

"Tomorrow, O King, few will be left to mourn; for the land will be swept of men."

"Why, Mopo, son of Makedama? But a few have perished of all the thousands who are gathered together. Number the people and they will not be missed."

"But a few have died beneath the assegai and the kerrie, O King. Yet hunger and thirst shall finish the spear's work. The people have neither eaten nor drunk for a day and a night, and for a day and a night they have wailed and moaned. Look without, Black One, there they lie in heaps with the dead. By tomorrow's light they also will be dead or dying."

Now, Chaka thought awhile, and he saw that the work would go too far, leaving him but a small people over whom to rule.

"It is hard, Mopo," he said, "that thou and I must mourn alone over our woes while these dogs feast and make merry. Yet, because of the gentleness of my heart, I will deal gently with them. Go out, son of Makedama, and bid my children eat and drink if they have the heart, for this mourning is ended. Scarcely will Unandi, my mother, sleep well, seeing that so little blood has been shed on her grave – surely her spirit will haunt my dreams. Yet, because of the gentleness of my heart, I declare this mourning ended. Let my children eat and drink, if, indeed, they have the heart."

"Happy are the people over whom such a king is set," I said in answer. Then I went out and told the words of Chaka to the chiefs and captains, and those of them who had the voice left to them praised the goodness of the king. But the most gave over sucking the dew from their sticks, and rushed to the water like cattle that have wandered five days in the desert, and drank their fill. Some of them were trampled to death in the water.

Afterwards I slept as I might best; it was not well, my father, for I knew that Chaka was not yet gutted with slaughter.

On the morrow many of the people went back to their homes, having sought leave from the king, others drew away the dead to the place of bones, and yet others were sent out in *impis* to kill such as had not come to the mourning of the king. When midday was past, Chaka said that he would walk, and ordered me and other of his *indunas* and servants to walk with him. We went on in silence, the king leaning on my shoulder as on a stick. "What of thy people, Mopo," he said at length, "what of the Langeni tribe? Were they at my mourning? I did not see them."

Then I answered that I did not know, they had been summoned, but the way was long and the time short for so many to march so far.

"Dogs should run swiftly when their master calls, Mopo, my servant," said Chaka, and the dreadful light came into his eyes that never shone in the eyes of any other man. Then I grew sick at heart, my father – aye, though I loved my people little, and they had driven me away, I grew sick at heart. Now we had come to a spot where there is a great rift of black rock, and the name of that rift is U'Donga-lu-ka-Tatiyana. On either side of this donga the ground slopes steeply down towards its yawning lips, and from its end a man may see the open country. Here Chaka sat down at the end of the rift, pondering. Presently he looked up and saw a vast multitude of men, women, and children, who wound like a snake across the plain beneath towards the kraal Gibamaxegu.

"I think, Mopo," said the king, "that by the color of their shields, yonder should be the Langeni tribe – thine own people, Mopo."

"It is my people, O King," I answered.

Then Chaka sent messengers, running swiftly, and bade them summon the Langeni people to him where he sat. Other messengers he sent also to the kraal, whispering in their ears, but what he said I did not know then.

Now, for a while, Chaka watched the long black snake of men winding towards him across the plain till the messengers met them and the snake began to climb the slope of the hill.

"How many are these people of thine, Mopo?" asked the king.

"I know not, O Elephant," I answered, "who have not seen them for many years. Perhaps they number three full regiments."

"Nay, more," said the king; "what thinkest thou, Mopo, would this people of thine fill the rift behind us?" and he nodded at the gulf of stone.

Now, my father, I trembled in all my flesh, seeing the purpose of Chaka; but I could find no words to say, for my tongue clave to the roof of my mouth.

"The people are many," said Chaka, "yet, Mopo, I bet thee fifty head of cattle that they will not fill the donga."

"The king is pleased to jest," I said.

"Yea, Mopo, I jest; yet as a jest take thou the bet."

"As the king wills," I murmured — who could not refuse. Now the people of my tribe drew near: at their head was an old man, with white hair and beard, and, looking at him, I knew him for my father, Makedama. When he came within earshot of the king, he gave him the royal salute of Bayéte, and fell upon his hands and knees, crawling towards him, and *konzaed* to the king, praising him as he came. All the thousands of the people also fell on their hands and knees, and praised the king aloud, and the sound of their praising was like the sound of a great thunder.

At length Makedama, my father, writhing on his breast like a snake, lay before the majesty of the king. Chaka bade him rise, and greeted him kindly; but all the thousands of the people yet lay upon their breasts beating the dust with their heads.

"Rise, Makedama, my child, father of the people of the Langeni," said Chaka, "and tell me why art thou late in coming to my mourning?"

"The way was far, O King," answered Makedama, my father, who did not know me. "The way was far and the time short. Moreover, the women and the children grew weary and footsore, and they are weary in this hour."

"Speak not of it, Makedama, my child," said the king. "Surely thy heart mourned and that of thy people, and soon they shall rest from their weariness. Say, are they here every one?"

"Every one, O Elephant! — none are wanting. My kraals are desolate, the cattle wander untended on the hills, birds pick at the unguarded crops."

"It is well, Makedama, thou faithful servant! Yet thou wouldst mourn with me an hour — is it not so? Now, hearken! Bid thy people pass to the right and to the left of me, and stand in all their numbers upon the slopes of the grass that run down to the lips of the rift."

So Makedama, my father, bade the people do the bidding of the king, for neither he nor the *indunas* saw his purpose, but I, who knew his wicked heart, I saw it. Then the people filed past to the right and to the left by hundreds and by thousands, and presently the grass of the slopes could be seen no more, because of their number. When all had passed, Chaka spoke again to Makedama, my father, bidding him climb down to the bottom of the donga, and thence lift up his voice in mourning. The old man obeyed the king. Slowly, and with much pain, he clambered to the bottom of the rift and stood there. It was so deep and narrow that the light scarcely seemed to reach to where he stood, for I could only see the white of his hair gleaming far down in the shadows.

Then, standing far beneath, he lifted up his voice, and it reached the thousands of those who clustered upon the slopes. It seemed still and small, yet it came to them faintly like the voice of one speaking from a mountaintop in a time of snow: —

"Mourn, children of Makedama!"

And all the thousands of the people — men, women, and children — echoed his words in a thunder of sound, crying: —

"Mourn, children of Makedama!"

Again he cried: —

"Mourn, people of the Langeni, mourn with the whole world!"

And the thousands answered: —

"Mourn, people of the Langeni, mourn with the whole world!"

A third time came his voice: —

"Mourn, children of Makedama, mourn, people of the Langeni, mourn with the whole world!

"Howl, ye warriors; weep, ye women; beat your breasts, ye maidens; sob, ye little children!

"Drink of the water of tears, cover yourselves with the dust of affliction.

"Mourn, O tribe of the Langeni, because the Mother of the Heavens is no more.

"Mourn, children of Makedama, because the Spirit of Fruitfulness is no more.

"Mourn, O ye people, because the Lion of the Zulu is left so desolate.

"Let your tears fall as the rain falls, let your cries be as the cries of women who bring forth.

"For sorrow is fallen like the rain, the world has conceived and brought forth death.

"Great darkness is upon us, darkness and the shadow of death.

"The Lion of the Zulu wanders and wanders in desolation, because the Mother of the Heavens is no more.

"Who shall bring him comfort? There is comfort in the crying of his children.

"Mourn, people of the Langeni; let the voice of your mourning beat against the skies and rend them.

"Ou-ai! Ou-ai! Ou-ai!"

Thus sang the old man, my father Makedama, far down in the deeps of the cleft. He sang it in a still, small voice, but, line after line, his song was caught up by the thousands who stood on the slopes above, and thundered to the heavens till the mountains shook with its sound. Moreover, the noise of their crying opened the bosom of a heavy rain-cloud that had gathered as they mourned, and the rain fell in great slow drops, as though the sky also wept, and with the rain came lightning and the roll of thunder.

Chaka listened, and large tears coursed down his cheeks, whose heart was easily stirred by the sound of song. Now the rain hissed fiercely, making as it were a curtain about the thousands of the people; but still their cry went up through the rain, and the roll of the thunder was lost in it. Presently there came a hush, and I looked to the right. There, above the heads of the people, coming over the brow of the hill, were the plumes of warriors, and in their hands gleamed a hedge of spears. I looked to the left; there also I saw the plumes of warriors dimly through the falling rain, and in their hands a hedge of spears. I looked before me, towards the end of the cleft; there also loomed the plumes of warriors, and in their hands was a hedge of spears.

Then, from all the people there arose another cry, a cry of terror and of agony.

"Ah! now they mourn indeed, Mopo," said Chaka in my ear; "now thy people mourn from the heart and not with the lips alone."

As he spoke the multitude of the people on either side of the rift surged forward like a wave, surged back again, once more surged forward, then, with a dreadful crying, driven on by the merciless spears of the soldiers, they began to fall in a torrent of men, women, and children, far into the black depths below.

M y father, forgive me the tears that fall from these blind eyes of mine; I am very aged, I am but as a little child, and as a little child I weep. I cannot tell it. At last it was done, and all grew still.

Thus was Makedama buried beneath the bodies of his people; thus was ended the tribe of the Langeni; as my mother had dreamed, so it came about; and thus did Chaka take vengeance for that cup of milk which was refused to him many a year before.

"Thou hast not won thy bet, Mopo," said the king presently. "See there is a little space where one more may find room to sleep. Full to the brim is this corn-chamber with the ears of death, in which no living grain is left. Yet there is one little space, and is there not one to fill it? Are all the tribe of the Langeni dead indeed?"

"There is one, O King!" I answered. "I am of the tribe of the Langeni, let my carcass fill the place."

"Nay, Mopo, nay! Who then should take the bet? Moreover, I slay thee not, for it is against my oath. Also, do we not mourn together, thou and I?"

"There is no other left living of the tribe of the Langeni, O King! The bet is lost; it shall be paid."

"I think that there is another," said Chaka. "There is a sister to thee and me, Mopo. Ah, see, she comes!"

I looked up, my father, and I saw this: I saw Baleka, my sister, walking towards us, and on her shoulders was a *kaross* of wildcat skins, and behind her were two soldiers. She walked proudly, holding her head high, and her step was like the step of a queen. Now she saw the sight of death, for the dead lay before her like black water in a sunless pool. A moment she stood shivering, having guessed all, then walked on and stood before Chaka.

"What is thy will with me, O King?" she said.

"Thou art come in a good hour, sister," said Chaka, turning his eyes from hers. "It is thus: Mopo, my servant and thy brother, made a bet with me, a bet of cattle. It was a little matter that we wagered on — as to whether the people of the Langeni tribe — thine own tribe, Baleka, my sister — would fill yonder place, U'Donga-lu-ka-Tatiyana. When they heard of the bet, my sister, the people of the Langeni hurled themselves into the rift by thousands, being eager to put the matter to the proof.

And now it seems that thy brother has lost the bet, for there is yet place for one yonder ere the donga is full. Then, my sister, thy brother Mopo brought it to my mind that there was still one of the Langeni tribe left upon the earth, who, should she sleep in that place, would turn the bet in his favor, and prayed me to send for her. So, my sister, as I would not take that which I have not won, I have done so, and now do thou go apart and talk with Mopo, thy brother, alone upon this matter, as once before thou didst talk when a child was born to thee, my sister!"

Now Baleka took no heed of the words of Chaka which he spoke of me, for she knew his meaning well. Only she looked him in the eyes and said: —

"Ill shalt thou sleep from this night forth, Chaka, till thou comest to a land where no sleep is. I have spoken."

Chaka saw and heard, and of a sudden he quailed, growing afraid in his heart, and turned his head away.

"Mopo, my brother," said Baleka, "let us speak together for the last time; it is the king's word."

So I drew apart with Baleka, my sister, and a spear was in my hand. We stood together alone by the people of the dead and Baleka threw the corner of the *kaross* about her brows and spoke to me swiftly from beneath its shadow.

"What did I say to you a while ago, Mopo? It has come to pass. Swear to me that you will live on and that this same hand of yours shall taken vengeance for me."

"I swear it, my sister."

"Swear to me that when the vengeance is done you will seek out my son Umslopogaas if he still lives, and bless him in my name."

"I swear it, my sister."

"Fare you well, Mopo! We have always loved each other much, and now all fades, and it seems to me that once more we are little children playing about the kraals of the Langeni. So may we play again in another land! Now, Mopo" — and she looked at me steadily, and with great eyes — "I am weary. I would join the spirits of my people. I hear them calling in my ears. It is finished."

*F*or the rest, I will not tell it to you, my father.

Chapter XIX

MASILO COMES TO THE KRAAL DUGUZA

*T*hat night the curse of Baleka fell upon Chaka, and he slept ill. So ill did he sleep that he summoned me to him, bidding me walk abroad with him. I went, and we walked alone and in silence, Chaka leading the way and I following after him. Now I saw that his feet led him towards the U'Donga-lu-ka-Tatiyana, that place where all my people lay dead, and with them Baleka, my sister. We climbed the slope of the hill slowly, and came to the mouth of the cleft, to that same spot where Chaka had stood when the people fell over the lips of the rock like water. Then there had been noise and crying, now there was silence, for the night was very still. The moon was full also, and lighted up the dead who lay near to us, so that I could see them all; yes, I could see even the face of Baleka, my sister — they had thrown her into the midst of the dead. Never had it looked so beautiful as in this hour, and yet as I gazed I grew afraid. Only the far end of the donga was hid in shadow.

"Thou wouldst not have won thy bet now, Mopo, my servant," said Chaka. "See, they have sunk together! The donga is not full by the length of a stabbing-spear."

I did not answer, but at the sound of the king's voice jackals stirred and slunk away.

Presently he spoke again, laughing loudly as he spoke: "Thou shouldst sleep well this night, my mother, for I have sent many to hush thee to rest. Ah, people of the Langeni tribe, you forgot, but I remembered! You forgot how a woman and a boy came to you seeking food and shelter, and you would give them none — no, not a gourd of milk. What did I promise you on that day, people of the Langeni tribe? Did I not promise you that for every drop the gourd I craved would hold I would take the life of a man? And have I not kept my promise? Do not men lie here more in number than the drops of water in a gourd, and with them

woman and children countless as the leaves? O people of the Langeni
tribe, who refused me milk when I was little, having grown great, I am
avenged upon you! Having grown great! Ah! who is there so great as I?
The earth shakes beneath my feet; when I speak the people tremble,
when I frown they die — they die in thousands. I have grown great, and
great I shall remain! The land is mine, far as the feet of man can travel
the land is mine, and mine are those who dwell in it. And I shall grow
greater yet — greater, ever greater. Is it thy face, Baleka, that stares upon
me from among the faces of the thousands whom I have slain? Thou
didst promise me that I should sleep ill henceforth. Baleka, I fear thee
not — at the least, thou sleepest sound. Tell me, Baleka — rise from thy
sleep and tell me whom there is that I should fear!" — and suddenly he
ceased the ravings of his pride.

Now, my father, while Chaka the king spoke thus, it came into my
mind to make an end of things and kill him, for my heart was made
with rage and the thirst of vengeance. Already I stood behind him,
already the stick in my hand was lifted to strike out his brains, when I
stopped also, for I saw something. There, in the midst of the dead, I saw
an arm stir. It stirred, it lifted itself, it beckoned towards the shadow
which hid the head of the cleft and the piled-up corpses that lay there,
and it seemed to me that the arm was the arm of Baleka. Perchance it
was not her arm, perchance it was but the arm of one who yet lived
among the thousands of the dead, say you, my father! At the least, the
arm rose at her side, and was ringed with such bracelets as Baleka wore,
and it beckoned from her side, though her cold face changed not at all.
Thrice the arm rose, thrice it stood awhile in air, thrice it beckoned with
crooked finger, as though it summoned something from the depths of
the shadow, and from the multitudes of the dead. Then it fell down,
and in the utter silence I heard its fall and a clank of brazen bracelets.
And as it fell there rose from the shadow a sound of singing, of singing
wild and sweet, such as I had never heard. The words of that song came
to me then, my father; but afterwards they passed from me, and I
remember them no more. Only I know this, that the song was of the
making of Things, and of the beginning and the end of Peoples. It told
of how the black folk grew, and of how the white folk should eat them
up, and wherefore they were and wherefore they should cease to be. It
told of Evil and of Good, of Woman and of Man, and of how these war
against each other, and why it is that they war, and what are the ends
of the struggle. It told also of the people of the Zulu, and it spoke of a
place of a Little Hand where they should conquer, and of a place where
a White Hand should prevail against them, and how they shall melt
away beneath the shadow of the White Hand and be forgotten, passing

to a land where things do not die, but live on forever, the Good with the Good, the Evil with the Evil. It told of Life and of Death, of Joy and of Sorrow, of Time and of that sea in which Time is but a floating leaf, and of why all these things are. Many names also came into the song, and I knew but a few of them, yet my own was there, and the name of Baleka and the name of Umslopogaas, and the name of Chaka the Lion. But a little while did the voice sing, yet all this was in the song — aye, and much more; but the meaning of the song is gone from me, though I knew it once, and shall know it again when all is done. The voice in the shadow sang on till the whole place was full of the sound of its singing, and even the dead seemed to listen. Chaka heard it and shook with fear, but his ears were deaf to its burden, though mine were open.

The voice came nearer, and now in the shadow there was a faint glow of light, like the glow that gathers on the six-days' dead. Slowly it drew nearer, through the shadow, and as it came I saw that the shape of the light was the shape of a woman. Now I could see it well, and I knew the face of glory. My father, it was the face of the Inkosazana-y-Zulu, the Queen of Heaven! She came towards us very slowly, gliding down the gulf that was full of dead, and the path she trod was paved with the dead; and as she came it seemed to me that shadows rose from the dead, following her, the Queen of the Dead — thousands upon thousands of them. And, ah! her glory, my father — the glory of her hair of molten gold — of her eyes, that were as the noonday sky — the flash of her arms and breast, that were like the driven snow, when it glows in the sunset. Her beauty was awful to look on, but I am glad to have lived to see it as it shone and changed in the shifting robe of light which was her garment.

Now she drew near to us, and Chaka sank upon the earth, huddled up in fear, hiding his face in his hands; but I was not afraid, my father — only the wicked need fear to look on the Queen of Heaven. Nay, I was not afraid: I stood upright and gazed upon her glory face to face. In her hand she held a little spear hafted with the royal wood: it was the shadow of the spear that Chaka held in his hand, the same with which he had slain his mother and wherewith he should himself be slain. Now she ceased her singing, and stood before the crouching king and before me, who was behind the king, so that the light of her glory shone upon us. She lifted the little spear, and with it touched Chaka, son of Senzangacona, on the brow, giving him to doom. Then she spoke; but, though Chaka felt the touch, he did not hear the words, that were for my ears alone.

"Mopo, son of Makedama," said the low voice, "stay thy hand, the cup of Chaka is not full. When, for the third time, thou seest me riding down the storm, then *smite*, Mopo, my child."

Thus she spoke, and a cloud swept over the face of the moon. When it passed she was gone, and once more I was alone with Chaka, with the night and the dead.

Chaka looked up, and his face was grey with the sweat of fear.

"Who was this, Mopo?" he said in a hollow voice.

"This was the Inkosazana of the Heavens, she who watches ever over the people of our race, O King, and who from time to time is seen of men ere great things shall befall."

"I have heard speak of this queen," said Chaka. "Wherefore came she now, what was the song she sang, and why did she touch me with a spear?"

"She came, O King, because the dead hand of Baleka summoned her, as thou sawest. The song she sang was of things too high for me; and why she touched thee on the forehead with the spear I do not know, O King! Perchance it was to crown thee chief of a yet greater realm."

"Yea, perchance to crown me chief of a realm of death."

"That thou art already, Black One," I answered, glancing at the silent multitude before us and the cold shape of Baleka.

Again Chaka shuddered. "Come, let us be going, Mopo," he said; "now I have learnt what it is to be afraid."

"Early or late, Fear is a guest that all must feast, even kings, O Earth-Shaker!" I answered; and we turned and went homewards in silence.

Now after this night Chaka gave it out that the kraal of Gibamaxegu was bewitched, and bewitched was the land of the Zulus, because he might sleep no more in peace, but woke ever crying out with fear, and muttering the name of Baleka. Therefore, in the end he moved his kraal far away, and built the great town of Duguza here in Natal.

Look now, my father! There on the plain far away is a place of the white men — it is called Stanger. There, where is the white man's town, stood the great kraal Duguza. I cannot see, for my eyes are dark; but you can see. Where the gate of the kraal was built there is a house; it is the place where the white man gives out justice; that is the place of the gate of the kraal, through which Justice never walked. Behind is another house, where the white men who have sinned against Him pray to the King of Heaven for forgiveness; there on that spot have I seen many a one who had done no wrong pray to a king of men for mercy, but I have never seen but one who found it. *Ou!* the words of Chaka have come true: I will tell them to you presently, my father. The white man holds the land, he goes to and fro about his business of peace where *impis* ran forth to kill; his children laugh and gather flowers where men died in blood by hundreds; they bathe in the waters of the Imbozamo, where once the crocodiles were fed daily with human flesh; his young men woo the maidens where other maids have kissed the assegai. It is changed, nothing is the same, and of Chaka are left only a grave yonder and a name of fear.

Now, after Chaka had come to the Duguza kraal, for a while he sat quiet, then the old thirst of blood came on him, and he sent his *impis* against the people of the Pondos, and they destroyed that people, and brought back their cattle. But the warriors might not rest; again they were doctored for war, and sent out by tens of thousands to conquer Sotyangana, chief of the people who live north of the Limpopo. They went singing, after the king had looked upon them and bidden them return victorious or not at all. Their number was so great that from the hour of dawn till the sun was high in the heavens they passed the gates of the kraal like countless herds of cattle — they the unconquered. Little did they know that victory smiled on them no more; that they must die by thousands of hunger and fever in the marshes of the Limpopo, and that those of them who returned should come with their shields in their bellies, having devoured their shields because of their ravenous hunger! But what of them? They were nothing. "Dust" was the name of one of the great regiments that went out against Sotyangana, and dust they were — dust to be driven to death by the breath of Chaka, Lion of the Zulu.

Now few men remained in the kraal Duguza, for nearly all had gone with the *impi*, and only women and aged people were left. Dingaan and Umhlangana, brothers of the king, were there, for Chaka would not suffer them to depart, fearing lest they should plot against him, and he looked on them always with an angry eye, so that they trembled for their lives, though they dared not show their fear lest fate should follow fear. But I guessed it, and like a snake I wound myself into their secrets, and we talked together darkly and in hints. But of that presently, my father, for I must tell of the coming of Masilo, he who would have wed Zinita, and whom Umslopogaas the Slaughterer had driven out from the kraals of the People of the Axe.

It was on the day after the *impi* had left that Masilo came to the kraal Duguza, craving leave to speak with the king. Chaka sat before his hut, and with him were Dingaan and Umhlangana, his royal brothers. I was there also, and certain of the *indunas*, councilors of the king. Chaka was weary that morning, for he had slept badly, as now he always did. Therefore, when one told him that a certain wanderer named Masilo would speak with him, he did not command that the man should be killed, but bade them bring him before him. Presently there was a sound of praising, and I saw a fat man, much worn with travel, who crawled through the dust towards us giving the sibonga, that is, naming the king by his royal names. Chaka bade him cease from praising and tell his business. Then the man sat up and told all that tale which you have heard, my father, of how a young man, great and strong, came to the place of the People of the Axe and conquered Jikiza, the holder of the axe, and become chief of that people, and of how he had taken the cattle of Masilo and driven him away. Now Chaka knew nothing of this People of the Axe, for the land was great in those days, my father, and there were many little tribes in it, living far away, of whom the king had not even heard; so he questioned Masilo about them, and of the number of their fighting-men, of their wealth in cattle, of the name of the young man who ruled them, and especially as to the tribute which they paid to the king.

Masilo answered, saying that the number of their fighting-men was perhaps the half of a full regiment, that their cattle were many, for they were rich, that they paid no tribute, and that the name of the young man was Bulalio the Slaughterer — at the least, he was known by that name, and he had heard no other.

Then the king grew wroth. "Arise, Masilo," he said, "and run to this people, and speak in the ear of the people, and of him who is named the Slaughterer, saying: 'There is another Slaughterer, who sits in a kraal that is named Duguza, and this is his word to you, O People of the Axe, and to thee, thou who holdest the axe. Rise up with all the people, and with all the cattle of your people, and come before him who sits in the kraal Duguza, and lay in his hands the great axe Groan-Maker. Rise up swiftly and do this bidding, lest ye sit down shortly and for the last time of all.'"*

Masilo heard, and said that it should be so, though the way was far, and he feared greatly to appear before him who was called the Slaughterer, and who sat twenty days' journey to the north, beneath the shadow of the Witch Mountain.

"Begone," said the king, "and stand before me on the thirtieth day from now with the answer of this boy with an axe! If thou standest not before me, then some shall come to seek thee and the boy with an axe also."

So Masilo turned and fled swiftly to do the bidding of the king, and Chaka spoke no more of that matter. But I wondered in my heart who this young man with an axe might be; for I thought that he had dealt with Jikiza and with the sons of Jikiza as Umslopogaas would have dealt

---

* The Zulu are buried sitting.

with them had he come to the years of his manhood. But I also said nothing of the matter.

Now on this day also there came to me news that my wife Macropha and my daughter Nada were dead among their people in Swaziland. It was said that the men of the chief of the Halakazi tribe had fallen on their kraal and put all in it to the assegai, and among them Macropha and Nada. I heard the news, but I wept no tear, for, my father, I was so lost in sorrows that nothing could move me anymore.

Chapter XX

MOPO BARGAINS WITH THE PRINCES

*E*ight-and-twenty days went by, my father, and on the nine-and-twentieth it befell that Chaka, having dreamed a dream in his troubled sleep, summoned before him certain women of the kraal, to the number of a hundred or more. Some of these were his women, whom he named his "sisters," and some were maidens not yet given in marriage; but all were young and fair. Now what this dream of Chaka may have been I do not know, or have forgotten, for in those days he dreamed many dreams, and all his dreams led to one end, the death of men. He sat in front of his hut scowling, and I was with him. To the left of him were gathered the girls and women, and their knees were weak with fear. One by one they were led before him, and stood before him with bowed heads. Then he would bid them be of good cheer, and speak softly to them, and in the end would ask them this question: "Hast thou, my sister, a cat in thy hut?"

Now, some would say that they had a cat, and some would say that they had none, and some would stand still and make no answer, being dumb with fear. But, whatever they said, the end was the same, for the king would sigh gently and say: "Fare thee well, my sister; it is unfortunate for thee that there is a cat in thy hut," or "that there is no cat in thy hut," or "that thou canst not tell me whether there be a cat in thy hut or no."

Then the woman would be taken by the slayers, dragged without the kraal, and their end was swift. So it went on for the most part of that day, till sixty-and-two women and girls had been slaughtered. But at last a maiden was brought before the king, and to this one her snake had given a ready wit; for when Chaka asked her whether or no there was a cat in her hut, she answered, saying that she did not know, "but that there was a half a cat upon her," and she pointed to a cat's-skin which was bound about her loins.

Then the king laughed, and clapped his hands, saying that at length his dream was answered; and he killed no more that day nor ever again – save once only.

That evening my heart was heavy within me, and I cried in my heart, "How long?" – nor might I rest. So I wandered out from the kraal that was named Duguza to the great cleft in the mountains yonder, and sat down upon a rock high up in the cleft, so that I could see the wide lands rolling to the north and the south, to my right and to my left. Now, the day was drawing towards the night, and the air was very still, for the heat was great and a tempest was gathering, as I, who am a Heaven-Herd, knew well. The sun sank redly, flooding the land with blood; it was as though all the blood that Chaka had shed flowed about the land which Chaka ruled. Then from the womb of the night great shapes of cloud rose up and stood before the sun, and he crowned them with his glory, and in their hearts the lightning quivered like a blood of fire. The shadow of their wings fell upon the mountain and the plains, and beneath their wings was silence. Slowly the sun sank, and the shapes of cloud gathered together like a host at the word of its captain, and the flicker of the lightning was as the flash of the spears of a host. I looked, and my heart grew afraid. The lightning died away, the silence deepened and deepened till I could hear it, no leaf moved, no bird called, the world seemed dead – I alone lived in the dead world.

Now, of a sudden, my father, a bright star fell from the height of heaven and lit upon the crest of the storm, and as it lit the storm burst. The grey air shivered, a moan ran about the rocks and died away, then an icy breath burst from the lips of the tempest and rushed across the earth. It caught the falling star and drove it on towards me, a rushing globe of fire, and as it came the star grew and took shape, and the shape it took was the shape of a woman. I knew her now, my father; while she was yet far off I knew her – the Inkosazana who came as she had promised, riding down the storm. On she swept, borne forward by the blast, and oh! she was terrible to see, for her garment was the lightning, lightnings shone from her wide eyes and lightnings were in her streaming hair, while in her hand was a spear of fire, and she shook it as she came. Now she was at the mouth of the pass; before her was stillness, behind her beat the wings of the storm, the thunder roared, the rain hissed like snakes; she rushed on past me, and as she passed she turned her awful eyes upon me, withering me. She was there! she was gone! but she spoke no word, only shook her flaming spear. Yet it seemed to me that the storm spoke, that the rocks cried aloud, that the rain hissed out a word in my ear, and the word was: —

"Smite, Mopo!"

I heard it in my heart, or with my ears, what does it matter? Then I turned to look; through the rush of the tempest and the reek of the rain, still I could see her sweeping forward high in air. Now the kraal Duguza was beneath her feet, and the flaming spear fell from her hand upon the kraal and fire leaped up in answer.

Then she passed on over the edge of the world, seeking her own place. Thus, my father, for the third and last time did my eyes see the Inkosazana-y-Zulu, or mayhap my heart dreamed that I saw her. Soon I shall see her again, but it will not be here.

For a while I sat there in the cleft, then I rose and fought my way through the fury of the storm back to the kraal Duguza. As I drew near the kraal I heard cries of fear coming through the roaring of the wind and the hiss of the rain. I entered and asked one of the matter, and it was told me that fire from above had fallen on the hut of the king as he lay sleeping, and all the roof of the hut was burned away, but that the rain had put out the fire.

Then I went on till I came to the front of the great hut, and I saw by the light of the moon, which now shone out in the heavens, that there before it stood Chaka, shaking with fear, and the water of the rain was running down him, while he stared at the great hut, of which all the thatch was burned.

I saluted the king, asking him what evil thing had happened. Seeing me, he seized me by the arm, and clung to me as, when the slayers are at hand, a child clings to his father, drawing me after him into a small hut that was near.

"What evil thing has befallen, O King?" I said again, when light had been made.

"Little have I known of fear, Mopo," said Chaka, "yet I am afraid now; aye, as much afraid as when once on a bygone night the dead hand of Baleka summoned something that walked upon the faces of the dead."

"And what fearest thou, O King, who art the lord of all the earth?"

Now Chaka leaned forward and whispered to me: "Hearken, Mopo, I have dreamed a dream. When the judgment of those witches was done with, I went and laid me down to sleep while it was yet light, for I can scarcely sleep at all when darkness has swallowed up the world. My sleep has gone from me — that sister of thine, Baleka, took my sleep with her to the place of death. I laid me down and I slept, but a dream arose and sat by me with a hooded face, and showed me a picture. It seemed to me that the wall of my hut fell down, and I saw an open place, and in the center of the place I lay dead, covered with many wounds, while round my corpse my brothers Dingaan and Umhlangana stalked in pride like lions. On the shoulders of Umhlangana was my royal *kaross*, and there was blood on the *kaross*; and in the hand of Dingaan was my royal spear, and there was blood upon the spear. Then, in the vision of my dream, Mopo, thou didst draw near, and, lifting thy hand, didst give the royal salute of Bayéte to these brothers of mine, and with thy foot didst spurn the carcass of me, thy king. Then the hooded Dream pointed upwards and was gone, and I awoke, and lo! fire burned in the roof of my hut. Thus I dreamed, Mopo, and now, my servant, say thou, wherefore should I not slay thee, thou who wouldst serve other kings than I, thou who wouldst give my royal salute to the princes, my brothers?" and he glared upon me fiercely.

"As thou wilt, O King!" I answered gently. "Doubtless thy dream was evil, and yet more evil was the omen of the fire that fell upon thy hut. And yet —" and I ceased.

"And yet — Mopo, thou faithless servant?"

"And yet, O King, it seems to me in my folly that it were well to strike the head of the snake and not its tail, for without the tail the head may live, but not the tail without the head."

"Thou wouldst say, Mopo, that if these princes die never canst thou or any other man give them the royal names. Do I hear aright, Mopo?"

"Who am I that I should lift up my voice asking for the blood of princes?" I answered. "Judge thou, O King!"

Now, Chaka brooded awhile, then he spoke: "Say, Mopo, can it be done this night?"

"There are but few men in the kraal, O King. All are gone out to war; and of those few many are the servants of the princes, and perhaps they might give blow for blow."

"How then, Mopo?"

"Nay, I know not, O King; yet at the great kraal beyond the river sits that regiment which is named the Slayers. By midday tomorrow they might be here, and then —"

"Thou speakest wisely, my child Mopo; it shall be for tomorrow. Go summon the regiment of the Slayers, and, Mopo, see that thou fail me not."

"If I fail thee, O King, then I fail myself, for it seems that my life hangs on this matter."

"If all the words that ever passed thy lips are lies, yet is that word true, Mopo," said Chaka: "moreover, know this, my servant: if aught miscarries thou shalt die no common death. Begone!"

"I hear the king," I answered, and went out.

Now, my father, I knew well that Chaka had doomed me to die, though first he would use me to destroy the princes. But I feared nothing, for I knew this also, that the hour of Chaka was come at last.

For a while I sat in my hut pondering, then when all men slept I arose and crept like a snake by many paths to the hut of Dingaan the prince, who awaited me on that night. Following the shadow of the hut, I came to the door and scratched upon it after a certain fashion. Presently it was opened, and I crawled in, and the door was shut again. Now there was a little light in the hut, and by its flame I saw the two princes sitting side by side, wrapped about with blankets which hung before their brows.

"Who is this that comes?" said the Prince Dingaan.

Then I lifted the blanket from my head so that they might see my face, and they also drew the blankets from their brows. I spoke, saying: "Hail to you, Princes, who tomorrow shall be dust! Hail to you, sons of Senzangacona, who tomorrow shall be spirits!" and I pointed towards them with my withered hand.

Now the princes were troubled, and shook with fear.

"What meanest thou, thou dog, that thou dost speak to us words of such ill-omen?" said the Prince Dingaan in a low voice.

"Where dost thou point at us with that white and withered hand of thine, Wizard?" hissed the Prince Umhlangana.

"Have I not told you, O ye Princes!" I whispered, "that ye must strike or die, and has not your heart failed you? Now hearken! Chaka has dreamed another dream; now it is Chaka who strikes, and ye are already dead, ye children of Senzangacona."

"If the slayers of the king be without the gates, at least thou shalt die first, thou who hast betrayed us!" quoth the Prince Dingaan, and drew an assegai from under his *kaross*.

"First hear the king's dream, O Prince," I said; "then, if thou wilt, kill me, and die. Chaka the king slept and dreamed that he lay dead, and that one of you, the princes, wore his royal *kaross*."

"Who wore the royal *kaross?*" asked Dingaan, eagerly; and both looked up, waiting on my words.

"The Prince Umhlangana wore it — in the dream of Chaka — O Dingaan, shoot of a royal stock!" I answered slowly, taking snuff as I spoke, and watching the two of them over the edge of my snuff-spoon.

Now Dingaan scowled heavily at Umhlangana; but the face of Umhlangana was as the morning sky.

"Chaka dreamed this also," I went on: "that one of you, the princes, held his royal spear."

"Who held the royal spear?" asked Umhlangana.

"The Prince Dingaan held it — in the dream of Chaka — O Umhlangana, sprung from the root of kings! — and it dripped blood."

Now the face of Umhlangana grew dark as night, but that of Dingaan brightened like the dawn.

"Chaka dreamed this also: that I, Mopo, your dog, who am not worthy to be mentioned with such names, came up and gave the royal salute, even the Bayéte."

"To whom didst thou give the Bayéte, O Mopo, son of Makedama?" asked both of the princes as with one breath, waiting on my words.

"I gave it to both of you, O twin stars of the morning, princes of the Zulu — in the dream of Chaka I gave it to both of you."

Now the princes looked this way and that, and were silent, not knowing what to say, for these princes hated each other, though adversity and fear had brought them to one bed.

"But what avails it to talk thus, ye lords of the land," I went on, "seeing that, both of you, ye are already as dead men, and that vultures which are hungry tonight tomorrow shall be filled with meat of the best? Chaka the king is now a Doctor of Dreams, and to clear away such a dream as this he has a purging medicine."

Now the brows of these brothers grew black indeed, for they saw that their fate was on them.

"These are the words of Chaka the king, O ye bulls who lead the herd! All are doomed, ye twain and I, and many another man who loves us. In the great kraal beyond the river there sits a regiment: it is summoned — and then — good-night! Have ye any words to say to those yet left upon the earth? Perhaps it will be given to me to live a little while after ye are gone, and I may bring them to their ears."

"Can we not rise up now and fall upon Chaka?" asked Dingaan.

"It is not possible," I said; "the king is guarded."

"Hast thou no plan, Mopo?" groaned Umhlangana. "Methinks thou hast a plan to save us."

"And if I have a plan, ye Princes, what shall be my reward? It must be great, for I am weary of life, and I will not use my wisdom for a little thing."

Now both the princes offered me good things, each of them promising more than the other, as two young men who are rivals promise to the father of a girl whom both would wed. I listened, saying always that it was not enough, till in the end both of them swore by their heads, and by the bones of Senzangacona, their father, and by many other things, that I should be the first man in the land, after them, its kings, and should command the *impis* of the land, if I would but show them a way to kill Chaka and become kings. Then, when they had done swearing, I spoke, weighing my words: —

"In the great kraal beyond the river, O ye Princes, there sit, not one regiment but two. One is named the Slayers and loves Chaka the king, who has done well by them, giving them cattle and wives. The other is named the Bees, and that regiment is hungry and longs for cattle and girls; moreover, of that regiment the Prince Umhlangana is the general, and it loves him. Now this is my plan — to summon the Bees in the name of Umhlangana, not the Slayers in the name of Chaka. Bend forward, O Princes, that I may whisper in your ears."

So they bent forward, and I whispered awhile of the death of a king, and the sons of Senzangacona nodded their heads as one man in answer. Then I rose up, and crept from the hut as I had entered it, and rousing certain trusty messengers, I dispatched them, running swiftly through the night.

Chapter XXI

THE DEATH OF CHAKA

Now, on the morrow, two hours before midday, Chaka came from the hut where he had sat through the night, and moved to a little kraal surrounded by a fence that was some fifty paces distant from the hut. For it was my duty, day by day, to choose that place where the king should sit to hear the counsel of his *indunas,* and give judgment on those whom he would kill, and today I had chosen this place. Chaka went alone from his hut to the kraal, and, for my own reasons, I accompanied him, walking after him. As we went the king glanced back at me over his shoulder, and said in a low voice: —

"Is all prepared, Mopo?"

"All is prepared, Black One," I answered. "The regiment of the Slayers will be here by noon."

"Where are the princes, Mopo?" asked the king again.

"The princes sit with their wives in the houses of their women, O King," I answered; "they drink beer and sleep in the laps of their wives."

Chaka smiled grimly, "For the last time, Mopo!"

"For the last time, O King."

We came to the kraal, and Chaka sat down in the shade of the reed fence, upon an ox-hide that was brayed soft. Near to him stood a girl holding a gourd of beer; there were also present the old chief Inguazonca, brother of Unandi, Mother of the Heavens, and the chief Umxamama, whom Chaka loved. When we had sat a little while in the kraal, certain men came in bearing cranes' feathers, which the king had sent them to gather a month's journey from the kraal Duguza, and they were admitted before the king. These men had been away long upon their errand, and Chaka was angry with them. Now the leader of the men was an old captain of Chaka's, who had fought under him in many battles, but whose service was done, because his right hand had been shorn away by the blow of an axe. He was a great man and very brave.

Chaka asked the man why he had been so long in finding the feathers, and he answered that the birds had flown from that part of the country whither he was sent, and he must wait there till they returned, that he might snare them.

"Thou shouldst have followed the cranes, yes, if they flew through the sunset, thou disobedient dog!" said the king. "Let him be taken away, and all those who were with him."

Now some of the men prayed a little for mercy, but the captain did but salute the king, calling him "Father," and craving a boon before he died.

"What wouldst thou?" asked Chaka.

"My father," said the man, "I would ask thee two things. I have fought many times at thy side in battle while we both were young; nor did I ever turn my back upon the foe. The blow that shore the hand from off this arm was aimed at thy head, O King; I stayed it with my naked arm.

It is nothing; at thy will I live, and at thy will I die. Who am I that I should question the word of the king? Yet I would ask this, that thou wilt withdraw the *kaross* from about thee, O King, that for the last time my eyes may feast themselves upon the body of him whom, above all men, I love."

"Thou art long-winded," said the king, "what more?"

"This, my father, that I may bid farewell to my son; he is a little child, so high, O King," and he held his hand above his knee.

"Thy first boon is granted," said the king, slipping the *kaross* from his shoulders and showing the great breast beneath. "For the second it shall be granted also, for I will not willingly divide the father and the son. Bring the boy here; thou shalt bid him farewell, then thou shalt slay him with thine own hand ere thou thyself art slain; it will be good sport to see."

Now the man turned grey beneath the blackness of his skin, and trembled a little as he murmured, "The king's will is the will of his servant; let the child be brought."

But I looked at Chaka and saw that the tears were running down his face, and that he only spoke thus to try the captain who loved him to the last.

"Let the man go," said the king, "him and those with him."

So they went glad at heart, and praising the king.

I have told you this, my father, though it has not to do with my story, because then, and then only, did I ever see Chaka show mercy to one whom he had doomed to die.

As the captain and his people left the gate of the kraal, it was spoken in the ear of the king that a man sought audience with him. He was admitted crawling on his knees. I looked and saw that this was that Masilo whom Chaka had charged with a message to him who was named Bulalio, or the Slaughterer, and who ruled over the People of the Axe. It was Masilo indeed, but he was no longer fat, for much travel had made him thin; moreover, on his back were the marks of rods, as yet scarcely healed over.

"Who art thou?" said Chaka.

"I am Masilo, of the People of the Axe, to whom command was given to run with a message to Bulalio the Slaughterer, their chief, and to return on the thirtieth day. Behold, O King, I have returned, though in a sorry plight!"

"It seems so!" said the king, laughing aloud. "I remember now: speak on, Masilo the Thin, who wast Masilo the Fat; what of this Slaughterer? Does he come with his people to lay the axe Groan-Maker in my hands?"

"Nay, O King, he comes not. He met me with scorn, and with scorn he drove me from his kraal. Moreover, as I went I was seized by the servants of Zinita, she whom I wooed, but who is now the wife of the Slaughterer, and laid on my face upon the ground and beaten cruelly while Zinita numbered the strokes."

"Hah!" said the king. "And what were the words of this puppy?"

"These were his words, O King: 'Bulalio the Slaughterer, who sits beneath the shadow of the Witch Mountain, to Bulalio the Slaughterer who sits in the kraal Duguza — To thee I pay no tribute; if thou wouldst have the axe Groan-Maker, come to the Ghost Mountain and take it. This I promise thee: thou shalt look on a face thou knowest, for there is one there who would be avenged for the blood of a certain Mopo.'"

Now, while Masilo told this tale I had seen two things — first, that a little piece of stick was thrust through the straw of the fence, and, secondly, that the regiment of the Bees was swarming on the slope opposite to the kraal in obedience to the summons I had sent them in the name of Umhlangana. The stick told me that the princes were hidden behind the fence waiting the signal, and the coming of the regiment that it was time to do the deed.

When Masilo had spoken Chaka sprang up in fury. His eyes rolled, his face worked, foam flew from his lips, for such words as these had never offended his ears since he was king, and Masilo knew him little, else he had not dared to utter them.

For a while he gasped, shaking his small spear, for at first he could not speak. At length he found words: —

"The dog," he hissed, "the dog who dares thus to spit in my face! Hearken all! As with my last breath I command that this Slaughterer be torn limb from limb, he and all his tribe! And thou, thou darest to bring me this talk from a skunk of the mountains. And thou, too, Mopo, thy name is named in it. Well, of thee presently. Ho! Umxamama, my servant, slay me this slave of a messenger, beat out his brains with thy stick. Swift! swift!"

Now, the old chief Umxamama sprang up to do the king's bidding, but he was feeble with age, and the end of it was that Masilo, being mad with fear, killed Umxamama, not Umxamama Masilo. Then Inguazonca, brother of Unandi, Mother of the Heavens, fell upon Masilo and ended him, but was hurt himself in so doing. Now I looked at Chaka, who stood shaking the little red spear, and thought swiftly, for the hour had come.

"Help!" I cried, "one is slaying the King!"

As I spoke the reed fence burst asunder, and through it plunged the princes Umhlangana and Dingaan, as bulls plunge through a brake.

Then I pointed to Chaka with my withered hand, saying, "Behold your king!"

Now, from beneath the shelter of his *kaross*, each Prince drew out a short stabbing spear, and plunged it into the body of Chaka the king. Umhlangana smote him on the left shoulder, Dingaan struck him in the right side. Chaka dropped the little spear handled with the red wood and looked round, and so royally that the princes, his brothers, grew afraid and shrank away from him.

Twice he looked on each; then he spoke, saying: "What! do you slay me, my brothers — dogs of mine own house, whom I have fed? Do you slay me, thinking to possess the land and to rule it? I tell you it shall not be for long. I hear a sound of running feet — the feet of a great white people. They shall stamp you flat, children of my father! They shall rule the land that I have won, and you and your people shall be their slaves!"

Thus Chaka spoke while the blood ran down him to the ground, and again he looked on them royally, like a buck at gaze.

"Make an end, O ye who would be kings!" I cried; but their hearts had turned to water and they could not. Then I, Mopo, sprang forward and picked from the ground that little assegai handled with the royal wood — the same assegai with which Chaka had murdered Unandi, his mother, and Moosa, my son, and lifted it on high, and while I lifted it, my father, once more, as when I was young, a red veil seemed to wave before my eyes.

"Wherefore wouldst thou kill me, Mopo?" said the king.

"For the sake of Baleka, my sister, to whom I swore the deed, and of all my kin," I cried, and plunged the spear through him. He sank down upon the tanned ox-hide, and lay there dying. Once more he spoke, and once only, saying: "Would now that I had hearkened to the voice of Nobela, who warned me against thee, thou dog!"

Then he was silent forever. But I knelt over him and called in his ear the names of all those of my blood who had died at his hands — the names of Makedama, my father, of my mother, of Anadi my wife, of Moosa my son, and all my other wives and children, and of Baleka my sister. His eyes and ears were open, and I think, my father, that he saw and understood; I think also that the hate upon my face as I shook my withered hand before him was more fearful to him that the pain of death. At the least, he turned his head aside, shut his eyes, and groaned. Presently they opened again, and he was dead.

Thus then, my father, did Chaka the King, the greatest man who has ever lived in Zululand, and the most evil, pass by my hand to those kraals of the Inkosazana where no sleep is. In blood he died as he had lived in blood, for the climber at last falls with the tree, and in the end the swimmer is borne away by the stream. Now he trod that path which had been beaten flat for him by the feet of people whom he had slaughtered, many as the blades of grass upon a mountainside; but it is a lie to say, as some do, that he died a coward, praying for mercy. Chaka died, as he had lived, a brave man. *Ou!* my father, I know it, for these eyes saw it and this hand let out his life.

Now he was dead and the regiment of the Bees drew near, nor could I know how they would take this matter, for, though the Prince Umhlangana was their general, yet all the soldiers loved the king, because he had no equal in battle, and when he gave he gave with an open hand. I looked round; the princes stood like men amazed; the girl had fled; the chief Umxamama was dead at the hands of dead Masilo; and the old chief Inguazonca, who had killed Masilo, stood by, hurt and wondering; there were no others in the kraal.

"Awake, ye kings," I cried to the brothers, "the *impi* is at the gates! Swift, now stab that man!" — and I pointed to the old chief — "and leave the matter to my wit."

Then Dingaan roused himself, and springing upon Inguazonca, the brother of Unandi, smote him a great blow with his spear, so that he sank down dead without a word. Then again the princes stood silent and amazed.

"This one will tell no tales," I cried, pointing at the fallen chief.

Now a rumor of the slaying had got abroad among the women, who had heard cries and seen the flashing of spears above the fence, and from the women it had come to the regiment of the Bees, who advanced to the gates of the kraal singing. Then of a sudden they ceased their singing and rushed towards the hut in front of which we stood.

Then I ran to meet them, uttering cries of woe, holding in my hand the little assegai of the king red with the king's blood, and spoke with the captain's in the gate, saying: —

"Lament, ye captains and ye soldiers, weep and lament, for your father is no more! He who nursed you is no more! The king is dead! now earth and heaven will come together, for the king is dead!"

"How so, Mopo?" cried the leader of the Bees. "How is our father dead?"

"He is dead by the hand of a wicked wanderer named Masilo, who, when he was doomed to die by the king, snatched this assegai from the king's hand and stabbed him; and afterwards, before he could be cut down himself by us three, the princes and myself, he killed the chiefs Inguazonca and Umxamama also. Draw near and look on him who was the king; it is the command of Dingaan and Umhlangana, the kings, that you draw near and look on him who was the king, that his death at the hand of Masilo may be told through all the land."

"You are better at making of kings, Mopo, than at the saving of one who was your king from the stroke of a wanderer," said the leader of the Bees, looking at me doubtfully.

But his words passed unheeded, for some of the captains went forward to look on the Great One who was dead, and some, together with most of the soldiers, ran this way and that, crying in their fear that now the heaven and earth would come together, and the race of man would cease to be, because Chaka, the king, was dead.

Now, my father, how shall I, whose days are few, tell you of all the matters that happened after the dead of Chaka? Were I to speak of them all they would fill many books of the white men, and, perhaps, some of them are written down there. For this reason it is, that I may be brief, I have only spoken of a few of those events which befell in the reign of Chaka; for my tale is not of the reign of Chaka, but of the lives of a handful of people who lived in those days, and of whom I and Umslopogaas alone are left alive — if, indeed, Umslopogaas, the son of Chaka, is still living on the earth. Therefore, in a few words I will pass over all that came about after the fall of Chaka and till I was sent down by Dingaan, the king, to summon him to surrender to the king who was called the Slaughterer and who ruled the People of the Axe. Ah! would that I had known for certain that this was none other than Umslopogaas, for then had Dingaan gone the way that Chaka went and which Umhlangana followed, and Umslopogaas ruled the people of the Zulus as their king. But, alas! my wisdom failed me. I paid no heed to the voice of my heart which told me that this was Umslopogaas who sent the message to Chaka threatening vengeance for one Mopo, and I knew nothing till too late; surely, I thought, the man spoke of some other Mopo. For thus, my father, does destiny make fools of us men. We think that we can shape our fate, but it is fate that shapes us, and nothing befalls except fate will it. All things are a great pattern, my father, drawn by the hand of the Umkulunkulu upon the cup whence he drinks the water of his wisdom; and our lives, and what we do, and what we do not do, are but a little bit of the pattern, which is so big that only the eyes of Him who is above, the Umkulunkulu, can see it all. Even Chaka, the slayer of men, and all those he slew, are but as a tiny grain of dust in the greatness of that pattern. How, then, can we be wise, my father, who are but the tools of wisdom? how can be build who are but pebbles in a wall? how can we give life who are babes in the womb of fate? or how can we slay who are but spears in the hands of the slayer?

This came about, my father. Matters were made straight in the land after the death of Chaka. At first people said that Masilo, the stranger, had stabbed the king; then it was known that Mopo, the wise man, the doctor and the body-servant of the king, had slain the king, and that the two great bulls, his brothers Umhlangana and Dingaan, children of Senzangacona, had also lifted spears against him. But he was dead, and earth and heaven had not come together, so what did it matter? Moreover, the two new kings promised to deal gently with the people, and to lighten the heavy yoke of Chaka, and men in a bad case are always ready to home for a better. So it came about that the only enemies the princes found were each other and Engwade, the son of Unandi, Chaka's half-brother. But I, Mopo, who was now the first man in the land after the kings, ceasing to be a doctor and becoming a general, went up against Engwade with the regiment of the Bees and the regiment of the Slayers and smote him in his kraals. It was a hard fight, but in the end I destroyed him and all his people: Engwade killed eight men with his own hand before I slew him. Then I came back to the kraal with the few that were left alive of the two regiments.

After that the two kings quarreled more and more, and I weighed them both in my balance, for I would know which was the most favorable to me. In the end I found that both feared me, but that Umhlangana would certainly put me to death if he gained the upper hand, whereas this was not yet in the mind of Dingaan. So I pressed down the balance of Umhlangana and raised that of Dingaan, sending the fears of Umhlangana to sleep till I could cause his hut to be surrounded. Then Umhlangana followed upon the road of Chaka his brother, the road of the assegai; and Dingaan ruled alone for awhile. Such are the things that befall princes of this earth, my father. See, I am but a little man, and my lot is humble at the last, yet I have brought about the death of three of them, and of these two died by my hand.

It was fourteen days after the passing away of the Prince Umhlangana that the great army came back in a sorry plight from the marshes of the Limpopo, for half of them were left dead of fever and the might of the foe, and the rest were starving. It was well for them who yet lived that Chaka was no more, else they had joined their brethren who were dead on the way; since never before for many years had a Zulu *impi* returned unvictorious and without a single head of cattle. Thus it came about that they were glad enough to welcome a king who spared their lives, and thenceforth, till his fate found him, Dingaan reigned unquestioned.

Now, Dingaan was a prince of the blood of Chaka indeed; for, like Chaka, he was great in presence and cruel at heart, but he had not the might and the mind of Chaka. Moreover, he was treacherous and a liar, and these Chaka was not. Also, he loved women much, and spent with them the time that he should have given to matters of the State. Yet he reigned awhile in the land. I must tell this also; that Dingaan would have killed Panda, his half-brother, so that the house of Senzangacona, his father, might be swept out clean. Now Panda was a man of gentle heart, who did not love war, and therefore it was thought that he was half-witted; and, because I loved Panda, when the question of his slaying came on, I and the chief Mapita spoke against it, and pleaded for him, saying that there was nothing to be feared at his hands who was a fool. So in the end Dingaan gave way, saying, "Well, you ask me to spare this dog, and I will spare him, but one day he will bite me."

So Panda was made governor of the king's cattle. Yet in the end the words of Dingaan came true, for it was the grip of Panda's teeth that pulled him from the throne; only, if Panda was the dog that bit, I, Mopo, was the man who set him on the hunt.

Chapter XXII

MOPO GOES TO SEEK THE SLAUGHTERER

*N*ow Dingaan, deserting the kraal Duguza, moved back to Zululand, and built a great kraal by the Mahlabatine, which he named "Umgugundhlovu" — that is, "the rumbling of the elephant." Also, he caused all the fairest girls in the land to be sought out as his wives, and though many were found yet he craved for more. And at this time a rumor came to the ears of the King Dingaan that there lived in Swaziland among the Halakazi tribe a girl of the most wonderful beauty, who was named the Lily, and whose skin was whiter than are the skins of our people, and he desired greatly to have this girl to wife. So Dingaan sent an embassy to the chief of the Halakazi, demanding that the girl should be given to him. At the end of a month the embassy returned again, and told the king that they had found nothing but hard words at the kraal of the Halakazi, and had been driven thence with scorn and blows.

This was the message of the chief of the Halakazi to Dingaan, king of the Zulus: That the maid who was named the Lily, was, indeed, the wonder of the earth, and as yet unwed; for she had found no man upon whom she looked with favor, and she was held in such love by this people that it was not their wish to force any husband on her. Moreover, the chief said that he and his people defied Dingaan and the Zulus, as their fathers had defied Chaka before him, and spat upon his name, and that no maid of theirs should go to be the wife of a Zulu dog.

Then the chief of the Halakazi caused the maid who was named the Lily to be led before the messengers of Dingaan, and they found her wonderfully fair, for so they said: she was tall as a reed, and her grace was the grace of a reed that is shaken in the wind. Moreover, her hair curled, and hung upon her shoulders, her eyes were large and brown, and soft as a buck's, her color was the color of rich cream, her smile was like a ripple on the waters, and when she spoke her voice was low and sweeter than the sound of an instrument of music. They said also that the girl wished to speak with them, but the chief forbade it, and caused her to be led thence with all honor.

Now, when Dingaan heard this message he grew mad as a lion in a net, for he desired this maid above everything, and yet he who had all things could not win the maid. This was his command, that a great *impi* should be gathered and sent to Swaziland against the Halakazi tribe, to destroy them and seize the maid. But when the matter came on to be discussed with the *indunas* in the presence of the king, at the Amapakati or council, I, as chief of the *indunas,* spoke against it, saying that the tribe of the Halakazi were great and strong, and that war with them would mean war with the Swazis also; moreover, they had their dwelling in caves which were had to win. Also, I said, that this was no time to send *impis* to seek a single girl, for few years had gone by since the Black One fell; and foes were many, and the soldiers of the land had waxed few with slaughter, half of them having perished in the marshes of the Limpopo. Now, time must be given them to grow up again, for today they were as a little child, or like a man wasted with hunger. Maids were many, let the king take them and satisfy his heart, but let him make no war for this one.

Thus I spoke boldly in the face of the king, as none had dared to speak before Chaka; and courage passed from me to the hearts of the other *indunas* and generals, and they echoed my words, for they knew that, of all follies, to begin a new war with the Swazi people would be the greatest.

Dingaan listened, and his brow grew dark, yet he was not so firmly seated on the throne that he dared put away our words, for still there were many in the land who loved the memory of Chaka, and remembered that Dingaan had murdered him and Umhlangana also. For now that Chaka was dead, people forgot how evilly he had dealt with them, and remembered only that he was a great man, who had made the Zulu people out of nothing, as a smith fashions a bright spear from a lump of iron. Also, though they had changed masters, yet their burden was not lessened, for, as Chaka slew, so Dingaan slew also, and as Chaka oppressed, so did Dingaan oppress. Therefore Dingaan yielded to the voice of his *indunas* and no *impi* was sent against the Halakazi to seek the maid that was named the Lily. But still he hankered for her in his heart, and from that hour he hated me because I had crossed his will and robbed him of his desire.

Now, my father, there is this to be told: though I did not know it then, the maid who was named the Lily was no other than my daughter Nada. The thought, indeed, came into my mind, that none but Nada could be so fair. Yet I knew for certain that Nada and her mother Macropha were dead, for he who brought me the news of their death had seen their bodies locked in each other's arms, killed, as it were, by the same spear. Yet, as it chanced, he was wrong; for though Macropha indeed was killed, it was another maid who lay in blood beside her; for the people whither I had sent Macropha and Nada were tributary to the Halakazi tribe, and that chief of the Halakazi who sat in the place of Galazi the Wolf had quarreled with them, and fallen on them by night and eaten them up.

As I learned afterwards, the cause of their destruction, as in later days it was the cause of the slaying of the Halakazi, was the beauty of Nada and nothing else, for the fame of her loveliness had gone about the land, and the old chief of the Halakazi had commanded that the girl should be sent to his kraal to live there, that her beauty might shine upon his place like the sun, and that, if so she willed, she should choose a husband from the great men of the Halakazi. But the headmen of the kraal refused, for none who had looked on her would suffer their eyes to lose sight of Nada the Lily, though there was this fate about the maid that none strove to wed her against her will. Many, indeed, asked her in marriage, both there and among the Halakazi people, but ever she shook her head and said, "Nay, I would wed no man," and it was enough.

For it was the saying among men, that it was better that she should remain unmarried, and all should look on her, than that she should pass from their sight into the house of a husband; since they held that her beauty was given to be a joy to all, like the beauty of the dawn and of the evening. Yet this beauty of Nada's was a dreadful thing, and the mother of much death, as shall be told; and because of her beauty and the great love she bore, she, the Lily herself, must wither, and the cup of my sorrows must be filled to overflowing, and the heart of Umslopogaas the Slaughterer, son of Chaka the king, must become desolate as the black plain when fire has swept it. So it was ordained, my father, and so it befell, seeing that thus all men, white and black, seek that which is beautiful, and when at last they find it, then it passes swiftly away, or, perchance, it is their death. For great joy and great beauty are winged, nor will they sojourn long upon the earth. They come down like eagles out of the sky, and into the sky they return again swiftly.

Thus then it came about, my father, that I, Mopo, believing my daughter Nada to be dead, little guessed that it was she who was named the Lily in the kraals of the Halakazi, and whom Dingaan the king desired for a wife.

Now after I had thwarted him in this matter of the sending of an *impi* to pluck the Lily from the gardens of the Halakazi, Dingaan learned to hate me. Also I was in his secrets, and with me he had killed his brother Chaka and his brother Umhlangana, and it was I who held him back from the slaying of his brother Panda also; and, therefore, he hated me, as is the fashion of small-hearted men with those who have lifted them up. Yet he did not dare to do away with me, for my voice was loud in the land, and when I spoke the people listened. Therefore, in the end, he cast about for some way to be rid of me for a while, till he should grow strong enough to kill me.

"Mopo," said the king to me one day as I sat before him in council with others of the *indunas* and generals, "mindest thou of the last words of the Great Elephant, who is dead?" This he said meaning Chaka his brother, only he did not name him, for now the name of Chaka was *blonipa* in the land, as is the custom with the names of dead kings — that is, my father, it was not lawful that it should pass the lips.

"I remember the words, O King," I answered. "They were ominous words, for this was their burden: that you and your house should not sit long in the throne of kings, but that the white men should take away your royalty and divide your territories. Such was the prophecy of the Lion of the Zulu, why speak of it? Once before I heard him prophecy, and his words were fulfilled. May the omen be an egg without meat; may it never become fledged; may that bird never perch upon your roof, O King!"

Now Dingaan trembled with fear, for the words of Chaka were in his mind by night and by day; then he grew angry and bit his lip, saying: —

"Thou fool, Mopo! canst thou not hear a raven croak at the gates of a kraal but thou must needs go tell those who dwell within that he waits to pick their eyes? Such criers of ill to come may well find ill at hand, Mopo." He ceased, looked on me threateningly awhile, and went on: "I did not speak of those words rolling by chance from a tongue half loosed by death, but of others that told of a certain Bulalio, of a Slaughterer who rules the People of the Axe and dwells beneath the shadow of the Ghost Mountain far away to the north yonder. Surely I heard them all as I sat beneath the shade of the reed-fence before ever I came to save him who was my brother from the spear of Masilo, the murderer, whose spear stole away the life of a king?"

"I remember those words also, O King!" I said. "Is it the will of the king that an *impi* should be gathered to eat up this upstart? Such was the command of the one who is gone, given, as it were, with his last breath."

"Nay, Mopo, that is not my will. If no *impi* can be found by thee to wipe away the Halakazi and bring one whom I desire to delight my eyes, then surely none can be found to eat up this Slaughterer and his people. Moreover, Bulalio, chief of the People of the Axe, has not offended against me, but against an elephant whose trumpetings are done. Now this is my will, Mopo, my servant: that thou shouldst take with thee a few men only and go gently to this Bulalio, and say to him: 'A greater Elephant stalks through the land than he who has gone to sleep, and it has come to his ears — that thou, Chief of the People of the Axe, dost pay no tribute, and hast said that, because of the death of a certain Mopo, thou wilt have nothing to do with him whose shadow lies upon the land. Now one Mopo is sent to thee, Slaughterer, to know if this tale is true, for, if it be true, then shalt thou learn the weight of the hoof of that Elephant who trumpets in the kraal of Umgugundhlovu. Think, then, and weigh thy words before thou dost answer, Slaughterer.'"

Now I, Mopo, heard the commands of the king and pondered them in my mind, for I knew well that it was the design of Dingaan to be rid of me for a space that he might find time to plot my overthrow, and that he cared little for this matter of a petty chief, who, living far away, had dared to defy Chaka. Yet I wished to go, for there had arisen in me a great desire to see this Bulalio, who spoke of vengeance to be taken for one Mopo, and whose deeds were such as the deeds of Umslopogaas would have been, had Umslopogaas lived to look upon the light. Therefore I answered: —

"I hear the king. The king's word shall be done, though, O King, thou sendest a big man upon a little errand."

"Not so, Mopo," answered Dingaan. "My heart tells me that this chicken of a Slaughterer will grow to a great cock if his comb is not cut presently; and thou, Mopo, art versed in cutting combs, even of the tallest."

"I hear the king," I answered again.

So, my father, it came about that on the morrow, taking with me but ten chosen men, I, Mopo, started on my journey towards the Ghost Mountain, and as I journeyed I thought much of how I had trod that path in bygone days. Then, Macropha, my wife, and Nada, my daughter, and Umslopogaas, the son of Chaka, who was thought to be my son, walked at my side. Now, as I imagined, all were dead and I walked alone; doubtless I also should soon be dead. Well, people lived few days and evil in those times, and what did it matter? At the least I had wreaked vengeance on Chaka and satisfied my heart.

At length I came one night to that lonely spot where we had camped in the evil hour when Umslopogaas was borne away by the lioness, and once more I looked upon the cave whence he had dragged the cub, and upon the awful face of the stone Witch who sits aloft upon the Ghost Mountain forever and forever. I could sleep little that night, because of the sorrow at my heart, but sat awake looking, in the brightness of the moon, upon the grey face of the stone Witch, and on the depths of the forest that grew about her knees, wondering the while if the bones of Umslopogaas lay broken in that forest. Now as I journeyed, many tales had been told to me of this Ghost Mountain, which all swore was haunted, so said some, by men in the shape of wolves; and so said some, by the Esemkofu — that is, by men who have died and who have been brought back again by magic. They have no tongues, the Esemkofu, for had they tongues they would cry aloud to mortals the awful secrets of the dead, therefore, they can but utter a wailing like that of a babe. Surely one may hear them in the forests at night as they wail "Ai! — ah! Ai — ah!" among the silent trees!

You laugh, my father, but I did not laugh as I thought of these tales; for, if men have spirits, where do the spirits go when the body is dead? They must go somewhere, and would it be strange that they should return to look upon the lands where they were born? Yet I never thought much of such matters, though I am a doctor, and know something of the ways of the Amatongo, the people of the ghosts. To speak truth, my father, I have had so much to do with the loosing of the spirits of men that I never troubled myself overmuch with them after they were loosed; there will be time to do this when I myself am of their number.

So I sat and gazed on the mountain and the forest that grew over it like hair on the head of a woman, and as I gazed I heard a sound that came from far away, out of the heart of the forest as it seemed. At first it was faint and far off, a distant thing like the cry of children in a kraal across a valley; then it grew louder, but still I could not say what it might be; now it swelled and swelled, and I knew it — it was the sound of wild beats at chase. Nearer came the music, the rocks rang with it, and its voice set the blood beating but to hearken to it. That pack was great which ran a-hunting through the silent night; and now it was night, on the other side of the slope only, and the sound swelled so loud that those who were with me awoke also and looked forth. Now of a sudden a great *koodoo* bull appeared for an instant standing out against the sky on the crest of the ridge, then vanished in the shadow. He was running towards us; presently we saw him again speeding on his path with great bounds. We saw this also — forms grey and gaunt and galloping, in number countless, that leaped along his path, appearing on the crest of the rise, disappearing into the shadow, seen again on the slope, lost in the valley; and with them two other shapes, the shapes of men.

Now the big buck bounded past us not half a spear's throw away, and behind him streamed the countless wolves, and from the throats of the wolves went up that awful music. And who were these two that came with the wolves, shapes of men great and strong? They ran silently and swift, wolves' teeth gleamed upon their heads, wolves' hides hung about their shoulders. In the hands of one was an axe — the moonlight shone upon it — in the hand of the other a heavy club. Neck and neck they ran; never before had we seen men travel so fast. See! they sped down the slope towards us; the wolves were left behind, all except four of them; we heard the beating of their feet; they came, they passed, they were gone, and with them their unnumbered company. The music grew faint, it died, it was dead; the hunt was far away, and the night was still again!

"Now, my brethren," I asked of those who were with me, "what is this that we have seen?"

Then one answered, "We have seen the Ghosts who live in the lap of the old Witch, and those men are the Wolf-Brethren, the wizards who are kings of the Ghosts."

Chapter XXIII

MOPO REVEALS HIMSELF TO THE SLAUGHTERER

*A*ll that night we watched, but we neither saw nor heard anymore of the wolves, nor of the men who hunted with them. On the morrow, at dawn, I sent a runner to Bulalio, chief of the People of the Axe, saying that a messenger came to him from Dingaan, the king, who desired to speak with him in peace within the gates of his kraal. I charged the messenger, however, that he should not tell my name, but should say only that it was "Mouth of Dingaan." Then I and those with me followed slowly on the path of the man whom I sent forward, for the way was still far, and I had bidden him return and meet me bearing the words of the Slaughterer, Holder of the Axe.

All that day till the sun grew low we talked round the base of the great Ghost Mountain, following the line of the river. We met no one, but once we came to the ruins of a kraal, and in it lay the broken bones of many men, and with the bones rusty assegais and the remains of ox-hide shields, black and white in color. Now I examined the shields, and knew from their color that they had been carried in the hands of those soldiers who, years ago, were sent out by Chaka to seek for Umslopogaas, but who had returned no more.

"Now," I said, "it has fared ill with those soldiers of the Black One who is gone, for I think that these are the shields they bore, and that their eyes once looked upon the world through the holes in yonder skulls."

"These are the shields they bore, and those are the skulls they wore," answered one. "See, Mopo, son of Makedama, this is no man's work that has brought them to their death. Men do not break the bones of their foes in pieces as these bones are broken. Wow! men do not break them, but wolves do, and last night we saw wolves a-hunting; nor did they hunt alone, Mopo. Wow! this is a haunted land!"

Then we went on in silence, and all the way the stone face of the
Witch who sits aloft forever stared down on us from the mountain top.
At length, an hour before sundown, we came to the open lands, and
there, on the crest of a rise beyond the river, we saw the kraal of the
People of the Axe. It was a great kraal and well built, and their cattle
were spread about the plains like to herds of game for number. We went
to the river and passed it by the ford, then sat down and waited, till
presently I saw the man whom I had sent forward returning towards us.
He came and saluted me, and I asked him for news.

"This is my news, Mopo," he said: "I have seen him who is named
Bulalio, and he is a great man — long and lean, with a fierce face, and
carrying a mighty axe, such an axe as he bore last night who hunted
with the wolves. When I had been led before the chief I saluted him and
spoke to him — the words you laid upon my tongue I told to him. He
listened, then laughed aloud, and said: 'Tell him who sent you that the
mouth of Dingaan shall be welcome, and shall speak the words of
Dingaan in peace; yet I would that it were the head of Dingaan that
came and not his mouth only, for then Axe Groan-Maker would join
in our talk — aye, because of one Mopo, whom his brother Chaka
murdered, it would also speak with Dingaan. Still, the mouth is not the
head, so the mouth may come in peace.'"

Now I started when for the second time I heard talk of one Mopo,
whose name had been on the lips of Bulalio the Slaughterer. Who was
there that would thus have loved Mopo except one who was long dead?
And yet, perhaps the chief spoke of some other Mopo, for the name
was not my own only — in truth, Chaka had killed a chief of that name
at the great mourning, because he said that two Mopos in the land were
one too many, and that though this Mopo wept sorely when the tears
of others were dry. So I said only that this Bulalio had a high stomach,
and we went on to the gates of the kraal.

There were none to meet us at the gates, and none stood by the doors
of the huts within them, but beyond, from the cattle kraal that was in
the center of the huts, rose a dust and a din as of men gathering for
war. Now some of those were with me were afraid, and would have
turned back, fearing treachery, and they were yet more afraid when, on
coming to the inner entrance of the cattle kraal, we saw some five
hundred soldiers being mustered there company by company, by two
great men, who ran up and down the ranks shouting.

But I cried, "Nay! nay! Turn not back! Bold looks melt the hearts of
foes. Moreover, if this Bulalio would have murdered us, there was no
need for him to call up so many of his warriors. He is a proud chief,

and would show his might, not knowing that the king we serve can muster a company for every man he has. Let us go on boldly."

So we walked forward towards the *impi* that was gathered on the further side of the kraal. Now the two great men who were marshaling the soldiers saw us, and came to meet us, one following the other. He who came first bore the axe upon his shoulder, and he who followed swung a huge club. I looked upon the foremost of them, and ah! my father, my heart grew faint with joy, for I knew him across the years. It was Umslopogaas! my fosterling, Umslopogaas! and none other, now grown into manhood — aye, into such a man as was not to be found beside him in Zululand. He was great and fierce, somewhat spare in frame, but wide shouldered and shallow flanked. His arms were long and not over big, but the muscles stood out on them like knots in a rope; his legs were long also, and very thick beneath the knee. His eye was like an eagle's, his nose somewhat hooked, and he held his head a little forward, as a man who searches continually for a hidden foe. He seemed to walk slowly, and yet he came swiftly, but with a gliding movement like that of a wolf or a lion, and always his fingers played round the horn handle of the axe Groan-Maker. As for him who followed, he was great also, shorter than Umslopogaas by the half of a head, but of a sturdier build. His eyes were small, and twinkled unceasingly like little stars, and his look was very wild, for now and again he grinned, showing his white teeth.

When I saw Umslopogaas, my father, my bowels melted within me, and I longed to run to him and throw myself upon his neck. Yet I took council with myself and did not — nay, I dropped the corner of the *kaross* I wrote over my eyes, hiding my face lest he should know me. Presently he stood before me, searching me out with his keen eyes, for I drew forward to greet him.

"Greeting, Mouth of Dingaan!" he said in a loud voice. "You are a little man to be the mouth of so big a chief."

"The mouth is a little member, even of the body of a great king, O Chief Bulalio, ruler of the People of the Axe, wizard of the wolves that are upon the Ghost Mountain, who aforetime was named Umslopogaas, son of Mopo, son of Makedama."

Now when Umslopogaas heard these words he started like a child at a rustling in the dark and stared hard at me.

"You are well instructed," he said.

"The ears of the king are large, if his mouth be small, O Chief Bulalio," I answered, "and I, who am but the mouth, speak what the ears have heard."

"How know you that I have dwelt with the wolves upon the Ghost Mountain, O Mouth?" he asked.

"The eyes of the king see far, O Chief Bulalio. Thus last night they saw a great chase and a merry. It seems that they saw a *koodoo* bull running at speed, and after him countless wolves making their music, and with the wolves two men clad in wolves' skins, such men as you, Bulalio, and he with the club who follows you."

Now Umslopogaas lifted the axe Groan-Maker as though he would cut me down, then let it fall again, while Galazi the Wolf glared at me with wide-opened eyes.

"How know you that once I was named Umslopogaas, who have lost that name these many days? Speak, O Mouth, lest I kill you."

"Slay if you will, Umslopogaas," I answered, "but know that when the brains are scattered the mouth is dumb. He who scatters brains loses wisdom."

"Answer!" he said.

"I answer not. Who are you that I should answer you? I know; it is enough. To my business."

Now Umslopogaas ground his teeth in anger. "I am not wont to be thwarted here in my own kraal," he said; "but do your business. Speak it, little Mouth."

"This is my business, little Chief. When the Black One who is gone yet lived, you sent him a message by one Masilo — such a message as his ears had never heard, and that had been your death, O fool puffed up with pride, but death came first upon the Black One, and his hand was stayed. Now Dingaan, whose shadow lies upon the land, the king whom I serve, and who sits in the place of the Black One who is gone, speaks to you by me, his mouth. He would know this: if it is true that you refuse to own his sovereignty, to pay tribute to him in men and maids and cattle, and to serve him in his wars? Answer, you little headman! — answer in few words and short!"

Now Umslopogaas gasped for breath in his rage, and again he fingered the great axe. "It is well for you, O Mouth," he said, "that I swore safe conduct to you, else you had not gone hence — else you had been served as I served certain soldiers who in bygone years were sent to search out one Umslopogaas. Yet I answer you in few words and short. Look on those spears — they are but a fourth part of the number I can muster: that is my answer. Look now on yonder mountain, the mountain of ghosts and wolves — unknown, impassable, save to me and one other: that is my answer. Spears and mountains shall come together — the mountain shall be alive with spears and with the fangs of beasts. Let Dingaan seek his tribute there! I have spoken!"

Now I laughed shrilly, desiring to try the heart of Umslopogaas, my fosterling, yet further.

"Fool!" I said. "Boy with the brain of a monkey, for every spear you have Dingaan, whom I serve, can send a hundred, and your mountain shall be stamped flat; and for your ghosts and wolves, see, with the mouth of Dingaan I spit upon them!" and I spat upon the ground.

Now Umslopogaas shook in his rage, and the great axe glimmered as he shook. He turned to the captain who was behind him, and said: "Say, Galazi the Wolf, shall we kill this man and those with him?"

"Nay," answered the Wolf, grinning, "do not kill them; you have given them safe conduct. Moreover, let them go back to their dog of a king, that he may send out his puppies to do battle with our wolves. It will be a pretty fight."

"Get you gone, O Mouth," said Umslopogaas; "get you gone swiftly, lest mischief befall you! Without my gates you shall find food to satisfy your hunger. Eat of it and begone, for if tomorrow at the noon you are found within a spear's throw of this kraal, you and those with you shall bide there forever, O Mouth of Dingaan the king!"

Now I made as though I would depart, then, turning suddenly, I spoke once more, saying: —

"There were words in your message to the Black One who is dead of a certain man — nay, how was he named? — of a certain Mopo."

Now Umslopogaas started as one starts who is wounded by a spear, and stared at me.

"Mopo! What of Mopo, O Mouth, whose eyes are veiled? Mopo is dead, whose son I was!"

"Ah!" I said, "yes, Mopo is dead — that is, the Black One who is gone killed a certain Mopo. How came it, O Bulalio, that you were his son?"

"Mopo is dead," quoth Umslopogaas again; "he is dead with all his house, his kraal is stamped flat, and that is why I hated the Black One, and therefore I hate Dingaan, his brother, and will be as are Mopo and the house of Mopo before I pay him tribute of a single ox."

All this while I had spoken to Umslopogaas in a feigned voice, my father, but now I spoke again and in my own voice, saying: —

"So! Now you speak from your heart, young man, and by digging I have reached the root of the matter. It is because of this dead dog of a Mopo that you defy the king."

Umslopogaas heard the voice, and trembled no more with anger, but rather with fear and wonder. He looked at me hard, answering nothing.

"Have you a hut near by, O Chief Bulalio, foe of Dingaan the king, where I, the mouth of the king, may speak with you a while apart, for I would learn your message word by word that I may deliver it without fault. Fear not, Slaughterer, to sit alone with me in an empty hut! I am unarmed and old, and there is that in your hand which I should fear," and I pointed to the axe.

Now Umslopogaas, still shaking in his limbs, answered "Follow me, O Mouth, and you, Galazi, stay with these men."

So I followed Umslopogaas, and presently we came to a large hut. He pointed to the doorway, and I crept through it and he followed after me. Now for a while it seemed dark in the hut, for the sun was sinking without and the place was full of shadow; so I waited while a man might count fifty, till our eyes could search the darkness. Then of a sudden I threw the blanket from my face and looked into the yes of Umslopogaas.

"Look on me now, O Chief Bulalio, O Slaughterer, who once was named Umslopogaas – look on me and say who am I?" Then he looked at me and his jaw fell.

"Either you are Mopo my father grown old – Mopo, who is dead, or the Ghost of Mopo," he answered in a low voice.

"I am Mopo, your father, Umslopogaas," I said. "You have been long in knowing me, who knew you from the first."

Then Umslopogaas cried aloud, but yet softly, and letting fall the axe Groan-Maker, he flung himself upon my breast and wept there. And I wept also.

"Oh! my father," he said, "I thought that you were dead with the others, and now you have come back to me, and I, I would have lifted the axe against you in my folly. Oh, it is well that I have lived, and not died, since once more I look upon your face – the face that I thought dead, but which yet lives, though it be sorely changed, as though by grief and years."

"Peace, Umslopogaas, my son," I said. "I also deemed you dead in the lion's mouth, though in truth it seemed strange to me that any other man than Umslopogaas could have wrought the deeds which I have heard of as done by Bulalio, Chief of the People of the Axe – aye, and thrown defiance in the teeth of Chaka. But you are not dead, and I, I am not dead. It was another Mopo whom Chaka killed; I slew Chaka, Chaka did not slay me."

"And of Nada, what of Nada, my sister?" he said.

"Macropha, your mother, and Nada, your sister, are dead, Umslopogaas. They are dead at the hands of the people of the Halakazi, who dwell in Swaziland."

"I have heard of that people," he answered presently, "and so has Galazi the Wolf, yonder. He has a hate to satisfy against them – they murdered his father; now I have two, for they have murdered my mother and my sister. Ah, Nada, my sister! Nada, my sister!" and the great man covered his face with his hands, and rocked himself to and fro in his grief.

Now, my father, it came into my thoughts to make the truth plain to Umslopogaas, and tell him that Nada was no sister of his, and that he was no son of mine, but rather of that Chaka whom my hand had finished. And yet I did not, though now I would that I had done so. For I saw well how great was the pride and how high was the heart of Umslopogaas, and I saw also that if once he should learn that the throne of Zululand was his by right, nothing could hold him back, for he would swiftly break into open rebellion against Dingaan the king, and in my judgment the time was not ripe for that. Had I known, indeed, but one short year before that Umslopogaas still lived, he had sat where Dingaan sat this day; but I did not know it, and the chance had gone by for a while. Now Dingaan was king and mustered many regiments about him, for I had held him back from war, as in the case of the raid that he wished to make upon the Swazis. The chance had gone by, but it would come again, and till it came I must say nothing. I would do this rather, I would bring Dingaan and Umslopogaas together, that Umslopogaas might become known in the land as a great chief and the first of warriors. Then I would cause him to be advanced to be an *induna,* and a general ready to lead the *impis* of the king, for he who leads the *impis* is already half a king.

So I held my peace upon this matter, but till the dawn was grey Umslopogaas and I sat together and talked, each telling the tale of those years that had gone since he was borne from me in the lion's mouth. I told him how all my wives and children had been killed, how I had been put to the torment, and showed him my white and withered hand. I told him also of the death of Baleka, my sister, and of all my people of the Langeni, and of how I had revenged my wrongs upon Chaka, and made Dingaan to be king in his place, and was now the first man in the land under the king, though the king feared me much and loved me little. But I did not tell him that Baleka, my sister, was his own mother.

When I had done my tale, Umslopogaas told me his: how Galazi had rescued him from the lioness; how he became one of the Wolf-Brethren; how he had conquered Jikiza and the sons of Jikiza, and become chief of the People of the Axe, and taken Zinita to wife, and grown great in the land.

I asked him how it came about that he still hunted with the wolves as he had done last night. He answered that now he was great and there was nothing more to win, and at times a weariness of life came upon him, and then he must up, and together with Galazi hunt and harry with the wolves, for thus only could he find rest.

I said that I would show him better game to hunt before all was done, and asked him further if he loved his wife, Zinita. Umslopogaas answered that he would love her better if she loved him not so much, for she was jealous and quick to anger, and that was a sorrow to him. Then, when he had slept awhile, he led me from the hut, and I and my people were feasted with the best, and I spoke with Zinita and with Galazi the Wolf. For the last, I liked him well. This was a good man to have at one's back in battle; but my heart spoke to me against Zinita. She was handsome and tall, but with fierce eyes which always watched Umslopogaas, my fosterling; and I noted that he who was fearless of all other things yet seemed to fear Zinita. Neither did she love me, for when she saw how the Slaughterer clung to me, as it wee, instantly she grew jealous — as already she was jealous of Galazi — and would have been rid of me if she might. Thus it came about that my heart spoke against Zinita; nor did it tell me worse things of her than those which she was to do.

Chapter XXIV
THE SLAYING OF THE BOERS

On the morrow I led Umslopogaas apart, and spoke to him thus: —
"My son, yesterday, when you did not know me except as the Mouth of Dingaan, you charged me with a certain message for Dingaan the king, that, had it been delivered into the ears of the king, had surely brought death upon you and all your people. The tree that stands by itself on a plain, Umslopogaas, thinks itself tall and that there is no shade to equal its shade. Yet are there other and bigger trees. You are such a solitary tree, Umslopogaas, but the topmost branches of him whom I serve are thicker than your trunk, and beneath his shadow live many woodcutters, who go out to lop those that would grow too high. You are no match for Dingaan, though, dwelling here alone in an empty

land, you have grown great in your own eyes and in the eyes of those about you. Moreover, Umslopogaas, know this: Dingaan already hates you because of the words which in bygone years you sent by Masilo the fool to the Black One who is dead, for he heard those words, and it is his will to eat you up. He has sent me hither for one reason only, to be rid of me awhile, and, whatever the words I bring back to him, the end will be the same — that night shall come when you will find an *impi* at your gates."

"Then what need to talk more of the matter, my father?" asked Umslopogaas. "That will come which must come. Let me wait here for the *impi* of Dingaan, and fight till I do."

"Not so, Umslopogaas, my son; there are more ways of killing a man than by the assegai, and a crooked stick can still be bent straight in the stream. It is my desire, Umslopogaas, that instead of hate Dingaan should give you love; instead of death, advancement; and that you shall grow great in his shadow. Listen! Dingaan is not what Chaka was, though, like Chaka, he is cruel. This Dingaan is a fool, and it may well come about that a man can be found who, growing up in his shadow, in the end shall overshadow him. I might do it — I myself; but I am old, and, being worn with sorrow, have no longing to rule. But you are young, Umslopogaas, and there is no man like you in the land. Moreover, there are other matters of which it is not well to speak, that shall serve you as a raft whereon to swim to power."

Now Umslopogaas glanced up sharply, for in those days he was ambitious, and desired to be first among the people. Indeed, having the blood of Chaka in his veins, how could it be otherwise?

"What is your plan, my father?" he asked. "Say how can this be brought about?"

"This and thus, Umslopogaas. Among the tribe of the Halakazi in Swaziland there dwells a maid who is named the Lily. She is a girl of the most wonderful beauty, and Dingaan is afire with longing to have her to wife. Now, awhile since Dingaan dispatched an embassy to the chief of the Halakazi asking the Lily in marriage, and the chief of the Halakazi sent back insolent words, saying that the Beauty of the Earth should be given to no Zulu dog as a wife. Then Dingaan was angry, and he would have gathered his *impis* and sent them against the Halakazi to destroy them, and bring him the maid, but I held him back from it, saying that now was no time to begin a new war; and it is for this cause that Dingaan hates me, he is so set upon the plucking of the Swazi Lily. Do you understand now, Umslopogaas?"

"Something," he answered. "But speak clearly."

"Wow, Umslopogaas! Half words are better than whole ones in this land of ours. Listen, then! This is my plan: that you should fall upon the Halakazi tribe, destroy it, and bring back the maid as a peace-offering to Dingaan."

"That is a good plan, my father," he answered. "At the least, maid or no maid, there will be fighting in it, and cattle to divide when the fighting is done."

"First conquer, then reckon up the spoils, Umslopogaas."

Now he thought awhile, then said, "Suffer that I summon Galazi the Wolf, my captain. Do not fear, he is trusty and a man of few words."

Presently Galazi came and sat down before us. Then I put the matter to him thus: that Umslopogaas would fall upon the Halakazi and bring to Dingaan the maid he longed for as a peace-offering, but that I wished to hold him back from the venture because the Halakazi people were great and strong. I spoke in this sense so that I might have a door to creep out should Galazi betray the plot; and Umslopogaas read my purpose, though my craft was needless, for Galazi was a true man.

Galazi the Wolf listened in silence till I had finished, then he answered quietly, but it seemed to me that a fire shone in his eyes as he spoke: —

"I am chief by right of the Halakazi, O Mouth of Dingaan, and know them well. They are a strong people, and can put two full regiments under arms, whereas Bulalio here can muster but one regiment, and that a small one. Moreover, they have watchmen out by night and day, and spies scattered through the land, so that it will be hard to take them unawares; also their stronghold is a vast cave open to the sky in the middle, and none have won that stronghold yet, nor could it be found except by those who know its secret. They are few, yet I am one of them, for my father showed it to me when I was a lad. Therefore, Mouth of Dingaan, you will know that this is no easy task which Bulalio would set himself and us — to conquer the Halakazi. That is the face of the matter so far as it concerns Bulalio, but for me, O Mouth, it has another face. Know that, long years ago, I swore to my father as he lay dying by the poison of a witch of this people that I would not rest till I had avenged him — aye, till I had stamped out the Halakazi, and slain their men, and brought their women to the houses of strangers, and their children to bonds! Year by year and month by month, and night by night, as I have lain alone upon the Ghost Mountain yonder, I have wondered how I might bring my oath to pass, and found no way. Now it seems that there is a way, and I am glad. Yet this is a great adventure, and perhaps before it is done with the People of the Axe will be no more." And he ceased and took snuff, watching our faces over the spoon.

"Galazi the Wolf," said Umslopogaas, "for me also the matter has another face. You have lost your father at the hands of these Halakazi dogs, and, though till last night I did not know it, I have lost my mother by their spears, and with her one whom I loved above all in the world, my sister Nada, who loved me also. Both are dead and the Halakazi have killed them. This man, the mouth of Dingaan," and he pointed to me, Mopo, "this man says that if I can stamp out the Halakazi and make captive of the Lily maid, I shall win the heart of Dingaan. Little do I care for Dingaan, I who would go my way alone, and live while I may live, and die when I must, by the hands of Dingaan as by those of another — what does it matter? Yet, for this reason, because of the death of Macropha, my mother, and Nada, the sister who was dear to me, I will make war upon these Halakazi and conquer them, or be conquered by them. Perhaps, O Mouth of Dingaan, you will see me soon at the king's kraal on the Mahlabatine, and with me the Lily maid and the cattle of the Halakazi; or perhaps you shall not see me, and then you will know that I am dead, and the Warriors of the Axe are no more."

So Umslopogaas spoke to me before Galazi the Wolf, but afterwards he embraced me and bade me farewell, for he had no great hope that we should meet again. And I also doubted it; for, as Galazi said, the adventure was great; yet, as I had seen many times, it is the bold thrower who oftenest wins. So we parted — I to return to Dingaan and tell him that Bulalio, Chief of the People of the Axe, had gone up against the Halakazi to win the Lily maid and bring her to him in atonement; while Umslopogaas remained to make ready his *impi* for war.

I went swiftly from the Ghost Mountain back to the kraal Umgugund-hlovu, and presented myself before Dingaan, who at first looked on me coldly. But when I told him my message, and how that the Chief Bulalio the Slaughterer had taken the war-path to win him the Lily, his manner changed. He took me by the hand and said that I had done well, and he had been foolish to doubt me when I lifted up my voice to persuade him from sending an *impi* against the Halakazi. Now he saw that it was my purpose to rake this Halakazi fire with another hand than his, and to save his hand from the burning, and he thanked me.

Moreover, he said, that if this Chief of the People of the Axe brought him the maid his heart desired, not only would he forgive him the words he had spoken by the mouth of Masilo to the Black One who was dead, but also all the cattle of the Halakazi should be his, and he would make him great in the land. I answered that all this was as the king willed. I had but done my duty by the king and worked so that, whatever befell, a proud chief should be weakened and a foe should be attacked at no cost to the king, in such fashion also that perhaps it might come about that the king would shortly have the Lily at his side.

Then I sat down to wait what might befall.

Now it is, my father, that the white men come into my story, whom we named the Amaboona, but you call the Boers. *Ou!* I think ill of those Amaboona, though it was I who gave them the victory over Dingaan — I and Umslopogaas.

Before this time, indeed, a few white men had come to and fro to the kraals of Chaka and Dingaan, but these came to pray and not to fight. Now the Boers both fight and pray, also they steal, or used to steal, which I do not understand, for the prayers of you white men say that these things should not be done.

Well, when I had been back from the Ghost Mountain something less than a moon, the Boers came, sixty of them commanded by a captain named Retief, a big man, and armed with roers — the long guns they had in those days — or, perhaps they numbered a hundred in all, counting their servants and after-riders. This was their purpose: to get a grant of the land in Natal that lies between the Tugela and the Umzimoubu rivers. But, by my council and that of other *indunas,* Dingaan, bargained with the Boers that first they should attack a certain chief named Sigomyela, who had stolen some of the king's cattle, and who lived near the Quathlamba Mountains, and bring back those cattle. This the Boers agreed to, and went to attack the chief, and in a little while they came back again, having destroyed the people of Sigomyela, and driving his cattle before them as well as those which had been stolen from the king.

The face of Dingaan shone when he saw the cattle, and that night he called us, the council of the Amapakati, together, and asked us as to the granting of the country. I spoke the first, and said that it mattered little if he granted it, seeing that the Black One who was dead had already given it to the English, the People of George, and the end of the matter would be that the Amaboona and the People of George would fight for the land. Yet the words of the Black One were coming to pass, for already it seemed we could hear the sound of the running of a white folk who should eat up the kingdom.

Now when I had spoken thus the heart of Dingaan grew heavy and his face dark, for my words stuck in his breast like a barbed spear. Still, he made no answer, but dismissed the council.

On the morrow the king promised to sign the paper giving the lands they asked for to the Boers, and all was smooth as water when there is no wind. Before the paper was signed the king gave a great dance, for there were many regiments gathered at the kraal, and for three days this dance went on, but on the third day he dismissed the regiments, all except one, an *impi* of lads, who were commanded to stay. Now all this while I wondered what was in the mind of Dingaan and was afraid for the Amaboona. But he was secret, and told nothing except to the captains of the regiment alone — no, not even to one of his council. Yet I knew that he planned evil, and was half inclined to warn the Captain Retief, but did not, fearing to make myself foolish. Ah! my father, if I had spoken, how many would have lived who were soon dead! But what does it matter? In any case most of them would have been dead by now.

On the fourth morning, early, Dingaan sent a messenger to the Boers, bidding them meet him in the cattle kraal, for there he would mark the paper. So they came, stacking their guns at the gate of the kraal, for it was death for any man, white or black, to come armed before the presence of the king. Now, my father, the kraal Umgugundhlovu was built in a great circle, after the fashion of royal kraals. First came the high outer fence, then the thousands of huts that ran three parts round between the great fence and the inner one. Within this inner fence was the large open space, big enough to hold five regiments, and at the top of it — opposite the entrance — stood the cattle kraal itself, that cut off a piece of the open space by another fence bent like a bow. Behind this again were the Emposeni, the place of the king's women, the guard-house, the labyrinth, and the Intunkulu, the house of the king. Dingaan came out on that day and sat on a stool in front of the cattle kraal, and by him stood a man holding a shield over his head to keep the sun from him. Also we of the Amapakati, the council, were there, and ranged round the fence of the space, armed with short sticks only — not with kerries, my father — was that regiment of young men which Dingaan had not sent away, the captain of the regiment being stationed near to the king, on the right.

Presently the Boers came in on foot and walked up to the king in a body, and Dingaan greeted them kindly and shook hands with Retief, their captain. Then Retief drew the paper from a leather pouch, which set out the boundaries of the grant of land, and it was translated to the king by an interpreter. Dingaan said that it was good, and put his mark upon it, and Retief and all the Boers were pleased, and smiled across their faces. Now they would have said farewell, but Dingaan forbade them, saying that they must not go yet: first they must eat and see the soldiers dance a little, and he commanded dishes of boiled flesh which had been made ready and bowls of milk to be brought to them. The Boers said that they had already eaten; still, they drank the milk, passing the bowls from hand to hand.

Now the regiment began to dance, singing the Ingomo, that is the war chant of us Zulus, my father, and the Boers drew back towards the center of the space to give the soldiers room to dance in. It was at this moment that I heard Dingaan give an order to a messenger to run swiftly to the white Doctor of Prayers, who was staying without the kraal, telling him not to be afraid, and I wondered what this might mean; for why should the Prayer Doctor fear a dance such as he had often seen before? Presently Dingaan rose, and, followed by all, walked through the press to where the Captain Retief stood, and bade him good-bye, shaking him by the hand and bidding him *hamba gachlé*, to go in peace. Then he turned and walked back again towards the gateway which led to his royal house, and I saw that near this entrance stood the captain of the regiments, as one stands by who waits for orders.

Now, of a sudden, my father, Dingaan stopped and cried with a loud voice, "Bulalani Abatakati!" (slay the wizards), and having cried it, he covered his face with the corner of his blanket, and passed behind the fence.

We, the councilors, stood astounded, like men who had become stone; but before we could speak or act the captain of the regiment had also cried aloud, "Bulalani Abatakati!" and the signal was caught up from every side. Then, my father, came a yell and a rush of thousands of feet, and through the clouds of dust we saw the soldiers hurl themselves upon the Amaboona, and above the shouting we heard the sound of falling sticks. The Amaboona drew their knives and fought bravely, but before a man could count a hundred twice it was done, and they were being dragged, some few dead, but the most yet living, towards the gates of the kraal and out on to the Hill of Slaughter, and there, on the Hill of Slaughter, they were massacred, every one of them. How? Ah! I will not tell you — they were massacred and piled in a heap, and that was the end of their story, my father.

Now I and the other councilors turned away and walked silently towards the house of the king. We found him standing before his great hut, and, lifting our hands, we saluted him silently, saying no word. It was Dingaan who spoke, laughing a little as he spoke, like a man who is uneasy in his mind.

"Ah, my captains," he said, "when the vultures plumed themselves this morning, and shrieked to the sky for blood, they did not look for such a feast as I have given them. And you, my captains, you little guessed how great a king the Heavens have set to rule over you, nor how deep is the mind of the king that watches ever over his people's welfare. Now the land is free from the White Wizards of whose footsteps the Black One croaked as he gave up his life, or soon shall be, for this is but a beginning. Ho! Messengers!" and he turned to some men who stood behind him, "away swiftly to the regiments that are gathered behind the mountains, away to them, bearing the king's words to the captains. This is the king's word: that the *impi* shall run to the land of Natal and slay the Boers there, wiping them out, man, woman, and child. Away!"

Now the messengers cried out the royal salute of Bayéte, and, leaping forward like spears from the hand of the thrower, were gone at once. But we, the councilors, the members of the Amapakati, still stood silent.

Then Dingaan spoke again, addressing me: —

"Is thy heart at rest now, Mopo, son of Makedama? Ever hast thou bleated in my ear of this white people and of the deeds that they shall do, and lo! I have blown upon them with my breath and they are gone. Say, Mopo, are the Amaboona wizards yonder all dead? If any be left alive, I desire to speak with one of them."

Then I looked Dingaan in the face and spoke.

"They are all dead, and thou, O King, thou also art dead."

"It were well for thee, thou dog," said Dingaan, "that thou shouldst make thy meaning plain."

"Let the king pardon me," I answered; "this is my meaning. Thou canst not kill this white men, for they are not of one race, but of many races, and the sea is their home; they rise out of the black water. Destroy those that are here, and others shall come to avenge them, more and more and more! Now thou hast smitten in thy hour; in theirs they shall smite in turn. Now *they* lie low in blood at thy hand; in a day to come, O King, *thou* shalt lie low in blood at theirs. Madness has taken hold of thee, O King, that thou hast done this thing, and the fruit of thy madness shall be thy death. I have spoken, I, who am the king's servant. Let the will of the king be done."

Then I stood still waiting to be killed, for, my father, in the fury of my heart at the wickedness which had been worked I could not hold back my words. Thrice Dingaan looked on me with a terrible face, and yet there was fear in his face striving with its rage, and I waited calmly to see which would conquer, the fear or the rage. When at last he spoke, it was one word, "Go!" not three words, "Take him away." So I went yet living, and with me the councilors, leaving the king alone.

I went with a heavy heart, my father, for of all the evil sights that I have seen it seemed to me that this was the most evil — that the Amaboona should be slaughtered thus treacherously, and that the *impis* should be sent out treacherously to murder those who were left of them, together with their women and children. Aye, and they slew — six hundred of them did they slay — yonder in Weenen, the land of weeping.

Say, my father, why does the Umkulunkulu who sits in the Heavens above allow such things to be done on the earth beneath? I have heard the preaching of the white men, and they say that they know all about Him — that His names are Power and Mercy and Love. Why, then, does He suffer these things to be done — why does He suffer such men as Chaka and Dingaan to torment the people of the earth, and in the end pay them but one death for all the thousands that they have given to others? Because of the wickedness of the peoples, you say; but no, no, that cannot be, for do not the guiltless go with the guilty — aye, do not the innocent children perish by the hundred? Perchance there is another answer, though who am I, my father, that I, in my folly, should strive to search out the way of the Unsearchable? Perchance it is but a part of the great plan, a little piece of that pattern of which I spoke — the pattern on the cup that holds the waters of His wisdom. Wow! I do not understand, who am but a wild man, nor have I found more knowledge in the hearts of you tamed white people. You know many things, but of these you do not know: you cannot tell us what we were an hour before birth, nor what we shall be an hour after death, nor why we were born, nor why we die. You can only hope and believe — that is all, and perhaps, my father, before many days are sped I shall be wiser than all of you. For I am very aged, the fire of my life sinks low — it burns in my brain alone; there it is still bright, but soon that will go out also, and then perhaps I shall understand.

Chapter XXV

THE WAR WITH THE HALAKAZI PEOPLE

Now, my father, I must tell of how Umslopogaas the Slaughterer and Galazi the Wolf fared in their war against the People of the Halakazi.

When I had gone from the shadow of the Ghost Mountain, Umslopogaas summoned a gathering of all his headmen, and told them it was his desire that the People of the Axe should no longer be a little people; that they should grow great and number their cattle by tens of thousands.

The headmen asked how this might be brought about — would he then make war on Dingaan the King? Umslopogaas answered no, he would win the favor of the king thus: and he told them of the Lily maid and of the Halakazi tribe in Swaziland, and of how he would go up against that tribe. Now some of the headmen said yea to this and some said nay, and the talk ran high and lasted till the evening. But when the evening was come Umslopogaas rose and said that he was chief under the Axe, and none other, and it was his will that they should go up against the Halakazi. If there was any man there who would gainsay his will, let him stand forward and do battle with him, and he who conquered should order all things. To this there was no answer, for there were few who cared to face the beak of Groan-Maker, and so it came about that it was agreed that the People of the Axe should make war upon the Halakazi, and Umslopogaas sent out messengers to summon every fighting-man to his side.

But when Zinita, his head wife, came to hear of the matter she was angry, and upbraided Umslopogaas, and heaped curses on me, Mopo, whom she knew only as the mouth of Dingaan, because, as she said truly, I had put this scheme into the mind of the Slaughterer. "What!" she went on, "do you not live here in peace and plenty, and must you go to make war on those who have not harmed you; there, perhaps, to perish or to come to other ill? You say you do this to win a girl for Dingaan and to find favor in his sight. Has not Dingaan girls more than he can count? It is more likely that, wearying of us, your wives, you go to get girls for yourself, Bulalio; and as for finding favor, rest quiet, so shall you find most favor. If the king sends his *impis* against you, then it will be time to fight, O fool with little wit!"

Thus Zinita spoke to him, very roughly — for she always blurted out what was in her mind, and Umslopogaas could not challenge her to battle. So he must bear her talk as best he might, for it is often thus, my father, that the greatest of men grow small enough in their own huts. Moreover, he knew that it was because Zinita loved him that she spoke so bitterly.

Now on the third day all the fighting-men were gathered, and there might have been two thousand of them, good men and brave. Then Umslopogaas went out and spoke to them, telling them of this adventure, and Galazi the Wolf was with him. They listened silently, and it was plain to see that, as in the case of the headmen, some of them thought one thing and some another. Then Galazi spoke to them briefly, telling them that he knew the roads and the caves and the number of the Halakazi cattle; but still they doubted. Thereon Umslopogaas added these words: —

"Tomorrow, at the dawn, I, Bulalio, Holder of the Axe, Chief of the People of the Axe, go up against the Halakazi, with Galazi the Wolf, my brother. If but ten men follow us, yet we will go. Now, choose, you soldiers! Let those come who will, and let those who will stop at home with the women and the little children."

Now a great shout rose from every throat.

"We will go with you, Bulalio, to victory or death!"

So on the morrow they marched, and there was wailing among the women of the People of the Axe. Only Zinita did not wail, but stood by in wrath, foreboding evil; nor would she bid her lord farewell, yet when he was gone she wept also.

Now Umslopogaas and his *impi* traveled fast and far, hungering and thirsting, till at length they came to the land of the Umswazi, and after a while entered the territory of the Halakazi by a high and narrow pass. The fear of Galazi the Wolf was that they should find this pass held, for though they had harmed none in the kraals as they went, and taken only enough cattle to feed themselves, yet he knew well that messengers had sped by day and night to warn the people of the Halakazi. But they found no man in the pass, and on the other side of it they rested, for the night was far spent. At dawn Umslopogaas looked out over the wide plains beyond, and Galazi showed him a long low hill, two hours' march away.

"There, my brother," he said, "lies the head kraal of the Halakazi, where I was born, and in that hill is the great cave."

Then they went on, and before the sun was high they came to the crest of a rise, and heard the sound of horns on its farther side. They stood upon the rise, and looked, and lo! yet far off, but running towards them, was the whole *impi* of the Halakazi, and it was a great *impi*.

"They have gathered their strength indeed," said Galazi. "For every man of ours there are three of these Swazis!"

The soldiers saw also, and the courage of some of them sank low. Then Umslopogaas spoke to them: —

"Yonder are the Swazi dogs, my children; they are many and we are few. Yet, shall it be told at home that we, men of the Zulu blood, were hunted by a pack of Swazi dogs? Shall our women and children sing *that* song in our ears, O Soldiers of the Axe?"

Now some cried "Never!" but some were silent; so Umslopogaas spoke again: —

"Turn back all who will: there is yet time. Turn back all who will, but ye who are men come forward with me. Or if ye will, go back all of you, and leave Axe Groan-Maker and Club Watcher to see this matter out alone."

Now there arose a mighty shout of "We will die together who have lived together!"

"Do you swear it?" cried Umslopogaas, holding Groan-Maker on high.

"We swear it by the Axe," they answered.

Then Umslopogaas and Galazi made ready for the battle. They posted all the young men in the broken ground above the bottom of the slope, for these could best be spared to the spear, and Galazi the Wolf took command of them; but the veterans stayed upon the hillside, and with them Umslopogaas.

Now the Halakazi came on, and there were four full regiments of them. The plain was black with them, the air was rent with their shoutings, and their spears flashed like lightnings. On the farther side of the slope they halted and sent a herald forward to demand what the People of the Axe would have from them. The Slaughterer answered that they would have three things: First, the head of their chief, whose place Galazi should fill henceforth; secondly, that fair maid whom men named the Lily; thirdly, a thousand head of cattle. If these demands were granted, then he would spare them, the Halakazi; if not, he would stamp them out and take all.

So the herald returned, and when he reached the ranks of the Halakazi he called aloud his answer. Then a great roar of laughter went up from the Halakazi regiments, a roar that shook the earth. The brow of Umslopogaas the Slaughterer burned red beneath the black when he heard it, and he shook Groan-Maker towards their host.

"Ye shall sing another song before this sun is set," he cried, and strode along the ranks speaking to this man and that by name, and lifting up their hearts with great words.

Now the Halakazi raised a shout, and charged to come at the young men led by Galazi the Wolf; but beyond the foot of the slope was peaty ground, and they came through it heavily, and as they came Galazi and the young men fell upon them and slew them; still, they could not hold them back for long, because of their great numbers, and presently the battle ranged all along the slope. But so well did Galazi handle the young men, and so fiercely did they fight beneath his eye, that before they could be killed or driven back all the force of the Halakazi was doing battle with them. Aye, and twice Galazi charged with such as he could gather, and twice he checked the Halakazi rush, throwing them into confusion, till at length company was mixed with company and regiment with regiment. But it might not endure, for now more than half the young men were down, and the rest were being pushed back up the hill, fighting madly.

But all this while Umslopogaas and the veterans sat in their ranks upon the brow of the slope and watched. "Those Swazi dogs have a fool for their general," quoth Umslopogaas. "He has no men left to fall back on, and Galazi has broken his array and mixed his regiments as milk and cream are mixed in a bowl. They are no longer an *impi*, they are a mob."

Now the veterans moved restlessly on their haunches, pushing their legs out and drawing them in again. They glanced at the fray, they looked into each other's eyes and spoke a word here, a word there, "Well smitten, Galazi! Wow! that one is down! A brave lad! Ho! a good club is the Watcher! The fight draws near, my brother!" And ever as they spoke their faces grew fiercer and their fingers played with their spears.

At length a captain called aloud to Umslopogaas: —

"Say, Slaughterer, is it not time to be up and doing? The grass is wet to sit on, and our limbs grow cramped."

"Wait awhile," answered Umslopogaas. "Let them weary of their play. Let them weary, I tell you."

As he spoke the Halakazi huddled themselves together, and with a rush drove back Galazi and those who were left of the young men. Yes, at last they were forced to flee, and after them came the Swazis, and in the forefront of the pursuit was their chief, ringed round with a circle of his bravest.

Umslopogaas saw it and bounded to his feet, roaring like a bull. "At them now, wolves!" he shouted.

Then the lines of warriors sprang up as a wave springs, and their crests were like foam upon the wave. As a wave that swells to break they rose suddenly, like a breaking wave they poured down the slope. In front of them was the Slaughterer, holding Groan-Maker aloft, and oh! his feet were swift. So swift were his feet that, strive as they would, he outran them by the quarter of a spear's throw. Galazi heard the thunder of their rush; he looked round, and as he looked, lo! the Slaughterer swept past him, running like a buck. Then Galazi, too, bounded forward, and the Wolf-Brethren sped down the hill, the length of four spears between them.

The Halakazi also saw and heard, and strove to gather themselves together to meet the rush. In front of Umslopogaas was their chief, a tall man hedged about with assegais. Straight at the shield-hedge drove Umslopogaas, and a score of spears were lifted to greet him, a score of shields heaved into the air — this was a fence that none might pass alive. Yet would the Slaughterer pass it — not alone! See! he steadies his pace, he gathers himself together, and now he leaps! High into the air he leaps; his feet knock the heads of the warriors and rattle against the crowns of their shields. They smite upwards with the spear, but he has swept over them like a swooping bird. He has cleared them — he has lit — and now the shield-hedge guards two chiefs. But not for long. *Ou!* Groan-Maker is aloft, he falls — and neither shield nor axe may stay his stroke, both are cleft through, and the Halakazi lack a leader.

The shield-ring wheels in upon itself. Fools! Galazi is upon you! What was that? Look, now! see how many bones are left unbroken in him whom the Watcher falls on full! What! — another down! Close up, shield-men — close up! Ai! are you fled?

Ah! the wave has fallen on the beach. Listen to its roaring — listen to the roaring of the shields! Stand, you men of the Halakazi — stand! Surely they are but a few. So! it is done! By the head of Chaka! they break — they are pushed back — now the wave of slaughter seethes along the sands — now the foe is swept like floating weed, and from all the line there comes a hissing like the hissing of thin waters. "S'gee!" says the hiss. "S'gee! S'gee!"

There, my father, I am old. What have I do with the battle anymore, with the battle and its joy? Yet it is better to die in such a fight as that than to live any other way. I have seen such — I have seen many such. Oh! we could fight when I was a man, my father, but none that I knew could ever fight like Umslopogaas the Slaughterer, son of Chaka, and his blood-brother Galazi the Wolf! So, so! they swept them away, those Halakazi; they swept them as a maid sweeps the dust of a hut, as the wind sweeps the withered leaves. It was soon done when once it was begun. Some were fled and some were dead, and this was the end of that fight. No, no, not of all the war. The Halakazi were worsted in the field, but many lived to win the great cave, and there the work must be finished. Thither, then, went the Slaughterer presently, with such of his *impi* as was left to him. Alas! many were killed; but how could they have died better than in that fight? Also those who were left were as good as all, for now they knew that they should not be overcome easily while Axe and Club still led the way.

Now they stood before a hill, measuring, perhaps, three thousand paces round its base. It was of no great height, and yet unclimbable, for, after a man had gone up a little way, the sides of it were sheer, offering no foothold except to the rock-rabbits and the lizards. No one was to be seen without this hill, nor in the great kraal of the Halakazi that lay to the east of it, and yet the ground about was trampled with the hoofs of oxen and the feet of men, and from within the mountain came a sound of lowing cattle.

"Here is the nest of Halakazi," quoth Galazi the Wolf.

"Here is the nest indeed," said Umslopogaas; "but how shall we come at the eggs to suck them? There are no branches on this tree."

"But there is a hole in the trunk," answered the Wolf.

Now he led them a little way till they came to a place where the soil was trampled as it is at the entrance to a cattle kraal, and they saw that there was a low cave which led into the cliff, like an archway such as you white men build. but this archway was filled up with great blocks of stone placed upon each other in such a fashion that it could not be forced from without. After the cattle were driven in it had been filled up.

"We cannot enter here," said Galazi. "Follow me."

So they followed him, and came to the north side of the mountain, and there, two spear-casts away, a soldier was standing. But when he saw them he vanished suddenly.

"There is the place," said Galazi, "and the fox has gone to earth in it."

Now they ran to the spot and saw a little hole in the rock, scarcely bigger than an ant-bear's burrow, and through the hole came sounds and some light.

"Now where is the hyena who will try a new burrow?" cried Umslopogaas. "A hundred head of cattle to the man who wins through and clears the way!"

Then two young men sprang forward who were flushed with victory and desired nothing more than to make a great name and win cattle, crying: —

"Here are hyenas, Bulalio."

"To earth, then!" said Umslopogaas, "and let him who wins through hold the path awhile till others follow."

The two young men sprang at the hole, and he who reached it first went down upon his hands and knees and crawled in, lying on his shield and holding his spear before him. For a little while the light in the burrow vanished, and they heard the sound of his crawling. Then came the noise of blows, and once more light crept through the hole. The man was dead.

"This one had a bad snake," said the second soldier; "his snake deserted him. Let me see if mine is better."

So down he went on his hands and knees, and crawled as the first had done, only he put his shield over his head. For awhile they heard him crawling, then once more came the sound of blows echoing on the ox-hide shield, and after the blows groans. He was dead also, yet it seemed that they had left his body in the hole, for now no light came through. This was the cause, my father: when they struck the man he had wriggled back a little way and died there, and none had entered from the farther side to drag him out.

Now the soldiers stared at the mouth of the passage and none seemed to love the look of it, for this was but a poor way to die. Umslopogaas and Galazi also looked at it, thinking.

"Now I am named Wolf," said Galazi, "and a wolf should not fear the dark; also, these are my people, and I must be the first to visit them," and he went down on his hands and knees without more ado. But Umslopogaas, having peered once more down the burrow, said: "Hold, Galazi; I will go first! I have a plan. Do you follow me. And you, my children, shout loudly, so that none may hear us move; and, if we win through, follow swiftly, for we cannot hold the mouth of that place for long. Hearken, also! this is my counsel to you: if I fall choose another chief – Galazi the Wolf, if he is still living."

"Nay, Slaughterer, do not name me," said the Wolf, "for together we live or die."

"So let it be, Galazi. Then choose you some other man and try this road no more, for if we cannot pass it none can, but seek food and sit down here till those jackals bolt; then be ready. Farewell, my children!"

"Farewell, father," they answered, "go warily, lest we be left like cattle without a herdsman, wandering and desolate."

Then Umslopogaas crept into the hole, taking no shield, but holding Groan-Maker before him, and at his heels crept Galazi. When he had covered the length of six spears he stretched out his hand, and, as he trusted to do, he found the feet of that man who had gone before and died in the place. Then Umslopogaas the way did this: he put his head beneath the dead man's legs and thrust himself onward till all the body was on his back, and there he held it with one hand, gripping its two wrists in his hand. Then he crawled forward a little space and saw that he was coming to the inner mouth of the burrow, but that the shadow was deep there because of a great mass of rock which lay before the burrow shutting out the light. "This is well for me," thought Umslopogaas, "for now they will not know the dead from the living. I may yet look upon the son again." Now he heard the Halakazi soldiers talking without.

"The Zulu rats do not love this run," said one, "they fear the rat-catcher's stick. This is good sport," and a man laughed.

Then Umslopogaas pushed himself forward as swiftly as he could, holding the dead man on his back, and suddenly came out of the hole into the open place in the dark shadow of the great rock.

"By the Lily," cried a soldier, "here's a third! Take this, Zulu rat!" And he struck the dead man heavily with a kerrie. "And that!" cried another, driving his spear through him so that it pricked Umslopogaas beneath. "And that! and this! and that!" said others, as they smote and stabbed.

Now Umslopogaas groaned heavily in the deep shadow and lay still. "No need to waste more blows," said the man who had struck first. "This one will never go back to Zululand, and I think that few will care to follow him. Let us make an end: run, some of you, and find stones to stop the burrow, for now the sport is done."

He turned as he spoke and so did the others, and this was what the Slaughter sought. With a swift movement, he freed himself from the dead man and sprang to his feet. They heard the sound and turned again, but as they turned Groan-Maker pecked softly, and that man who had sworn by the Lily was no more a man. Then Umslopogaas leaped forwards, and, bounding on to the great rock, stood there like a buck against the sky.

"A Zulu rat is not so easily slain, O ye weasels!" he cried, as they came at him from all sides at once with a roar. He smote to the right and the left, and so swiftly that men could scarcely see the blows fall, for he struck with Groan-Maker's beak. But though men scarcely saw the blows, yet, my father, men fell beneath them. Now foes were all around, leaping up at the Slaughterer as rushing water leaps to hide a rock — everywhere shone spears, thrusting at him from this side and from that. Those in front and to the side Groan-Maker served to stay, but one wounded Umslopogaas in the neck, and another was lifted to pierce his back when the strength of its holder was bowed to the dust — to the dust, to become of the dust.

For now the Wolf was through the hole also, and the Watcher grew very busy; he was so busy that soon the back of the Slaughterer had nothing to fear — yet those had much to fear who stood behind his back. The pair fought bravely, making a great slaughter, and presently, one by one, plumed heads of the People of the Axe showed through the burrow and strong arms mingled in the fray. Swiftly they came, leaping into battle as otters leap to the water — now there were ten of them, now there were twenty — and now the Halakazi broke and fled, since they did not bargain for this. Then the rest of the Men of the Axe came

through in peace, and the evening grew towards the dark before all had
passed the hole.

Chapter XXVI

THE FINDING OF NADA

*U*mslopogaas marshaled his companies.

"There is little light left," he said, "but it must serve us to start these
conies from their burrows. Come, my brother Galazi, you know where
the conies hide, take my place and lead us."

So Galazi led the *impi*. Turning a corner of the glen, he came with
them to a large open space that had a fountain in its midst, and this
place was full of thousands of cattle. Then he turned again to the left,
and brought them to the inner side of the mountain, where the cliff
hung over, and here was the mouth of a great cave. Now the cave was
dark, but by its door was stacked a pile of resinous wood to serve as
torches.

"Here is that which will give us light," said Galazi, and one man of
every two took a torch and lit it at a fire that burned near the mouth
of the cave. Then they rushed in, waving the flaring torches and with
assegais aloft. Here for the last time the Halakazi stood against them,
and the torches floated up and down upon the wave of war. But they
did not stand for very long, for all the heart was out of them. Wow! yes,
many were killed – I do not know how many. I know this only, that
the Halakazi are no more a tribe since Umslopogaas, who is named
Bulalio, stamped them with his feet – they are nothing but a name now.
The People of the Axe drove them out into the open and finished the
fight by starlight among the cattle.

In one corner of the cave Umslopogaas saw a knot of men clustering
round something as though to guard it. He rushed at the men, and with
him went Galazi and others. But when Umslopogaas was through, by

the light of his torch he perceived a tall and slender man, who leaned against the wall of the cave and held a shield before his face.

"You are a coward!" he cried, and smote with Groan-Maker. The great axe pierced the hide, but, missing the head behind, rang loudly against the rock, and as it struck a sweet voice said: —

"Ah! soldier, do not kill me! Why are you angry with me?"

Now the shield had come away from its holder's hands upon the blade of the axe, and there was something in the notes of the voice that caused Umslopogaas to smite no more: it was as though a memory of childhood had come to him in a dream. His torch was burning low, but he thrust it forward to look at him who crouched against the rock. The dress was the dress of a man, but this was no man's form — nay, rather that of a lovely woman, well-nigh white in color. She dropped her hands from before her face, and now he could see her well. He saw eyes that shone like stars, hair that curled and fell upon the shoulders, and such beauty as was not known among our people. And as the voice had spoken to him of something that was lost, so did the eyes seem to shine across the blackness of many years, and the beauty to bring back he knew not what.

He looked at the girl in all her loveliness, and she looked at him in his fierceness and his might, red with war and wounds. They both looked long, while the torchlight flared on them, on the walls of the cave, and the broad blade of Groan-Maker, and from around rose the sounds of the fray.

"How are you named, who are so fair to see?" he asked at length.

"I am named the Lily now: once I had another name. Nada, daughter of Mopo, I was once; but name and all else are dead, and I go to join them. Kill me and make an end. I will shut my eyes, that I may not see the great axe flash."

Now Umslopogaas gazed upon her again, and Groan-Maker fell from his hand.

"Look on me, Nada, daughter of Mopo," he said in a low voice; "look at me and say who am I."

She looked once more and yet again. Now her face was thrust forward as one who gazes over the edge of the world; it grew fixed and strange. "By my heart," she said, "by my heart, you are Umslopogaas, my brother who is dead, and whom dead as living I have loved ever and alone."

Then the torch flared out, but Umslopogaas took hold of her in the darkness and pressed her to him and kissed her, the sister whom he found after many years, and she kissed him.

"You kiss me now," she said, "yet not long ago that great axe shore my locks, missing me but by a finger's-breadth — and still the sound of

fighting rings in my ears! Ah! a boon of you, my brother — a boon: let
there be no more death since we are met once more. The people of the
Halakazi are conquered, and it is their just doom, for thus, in this same
way, they killed those with whom I lived before. Yet they have treated
me well, not forcing me into wedlock, and protecting me from Dingaan;
so spare them, my brother, if you may."

Then Umslopogaas lifted up his voice, commanding that the killing
should cease, and sent messengers running swiftly with these words:
"This is the command of Bulalio: that he should lifts hand against one
more of the people of the Halakazi shall be killed himself"; and the
soldiers obeyed him, though the order came somewhat late, and no more
of the Halakazi were brought to doom. They were suffered to escape,
except those of the women and children who were kept to be led away
as captives. And they ran far that night. Nor did they come together
again to be a people, for they feared Galazi the Wolf, who would be
chief over them, but they were scattered wide in the world, to sojourn
among strangers.

Now when the soldiers had eaten abundantly of the store of the
Halakazi, and guards had been sent to ward the cattle and watch against
surprise, Umslopogaas spoke long with Nada the Lily, taking her apart,
and he told her all his story. She told him also the tale which you know,
my father, of how she had lived with the little people that were subject
to the Halakazi, she and her mother Macropha, and how the fame of
her beauty had spread about the land. Then she told him how the
Halakazi had claimed her, and of how, in the end, they had taken her
by force of arms, killing the people of that kraal, and among them her
own mother. Thereafter, she had dwelt among the Halakazi, who named
her anew, calling her the Lily, and they had treated her kindly, giving
her reverence because of her sweetness and beauty, and not forcing her
into marriage.

"And why would you not wed, Nada, my sister?" asked Umslopogaas,
"you who are far past the age of marriage?"

"I cannot tell you," she answered, hanging her head; "but I have no
heart that way. I only seek to be left alone."

Now Umslopogaas thought awhile and spoke. "Do you not know
then, Nada, why it is that I have made this war, and why the people of
the Halakazi are dead and scattered and their cattle the prize of my arm?
I will tell you: I am come here to win you, whom I knew only by report
as the Lily maid, the fairest of women, to be a wife to Dingaan. The
reason that I began this war was to win you and make my peace with
Dingaan, and now I have carried it through to the end."

Now when she heard these words, Nada the Lily trembled and wept, and, sinking to the earth, she clasped the knees of Umslopogaas in supplication: "Oh, do not this cruel thing by me, your sister," she prayed; "take rather that great axe and make an end of me, and of the beauty which has wrought so much woe, and most of all to me who wear it! Would that I had not moved my head behind the shield, but had suffered the axe to fall upon it. To this end I was dressed as a man, that I might meet the fate of a man. Ah! a curse be on my woman's weakness that snatched me from death to give me up to shame!"

Thus she prayed to Umslopogaas in her low sweet voice, and his heart was shaken in him, though, indeed, he did not now purpose to give Nada to Dingaan, as Baleka was given to Chaka, perhaps in the end to meet the fate of Baleka.

"There are many, Nada," he said, "who would think it no misfortune that they should be given as a wife to the first of chiefs."

"Then I am not of their number," she answered; "nay, I will die first, by my own hand if need be."

Now Umslopogaas wondered how it came about that Nada looked upon marriage thus, but he did not speak of the matter; he said only, "Tell me then, Nada, how I can deliver myself of this charge. I must go to Dingaan as I promised our father Mopo, and what shall I say to Dingaan when he asks for the Lily whom I went out to pluck and whom his heart desires? What shall I say to save myself alive from the wrath of Dingaan?"

Then Nada thought and answered, "You shall say this, my brother. You shall tell him that the Lily, being clothed in the war-dress of a warrior, fell by chance in the fray. See, now, none of your people know that you have found me; they are thinking of other things than maids in the hour of their victory. This, then, is my plan: we will search now by the starlight till we find the body of a fair maid, for, doubtless, some were killed by hazard in the fight, and on her we will set a warrior's dress, and lay by her the corpse of one of your own men. Tomorrow, at the light, you shall take the captains of your soldiers and, having laid the body of the girl in the dark of the cave, you shall show it to them hurriedly, and tell them that this was the Lily, slain by one of your own people, whom in your wrath you slew also. They will not look long on so common a sight, and if by hazard they see the maid, and think her not so very fair, they will deem that it is death which has robbed her of her comeliness. So the tale which you must tell to Dingaan shall be built up firmly, and Dingaan shall believe it to be true."

"And how shall this be, Nada?" asked Umslopogaas. "How shall this be when men see you among the captives and know you by your beauty? Are there, then, two such Lilies in the land?"

"I shall not be known, for I shall not be seen, Umslopogaas. You must set me free tonight. I will wander hence disguised as a youth and covered with a blanket, and if any meet me, who shall say that I am the Lily?"

"And where will you wander, Nada? to your death? Must we, then, meet after so many years to part again forever?"

"Where was it that you said you lived, my brother? Beneath the shade of a Ghost Mountain, that men may know by a shape of stone which is fashioned like an old woman frozen into stone, was it not? Tell me of the road thither."

So Umslopogaas told her the road, and she listened silently.

"Good," she said. "I am strong and my feet are swift; perhaps they may serve to bring me so far, and perhaps, if I win the shadow of that mountain, you will find me a hut to hide in, Umslopogaas, my brother."

"Surely it shall be so, my sister," answered Umslopogaas, "and yet the way is long and many dangers lie in the path of a maid journeying alone, without food or shelter," and as he spoke Umslopogaas thought of Zinita his wife, for he guessed that she would not love Nada, although she was only his sister.

"Still, it must be traveled, and the dangers must be braved," she answered, smiling. "Alas! there is no other way."

Then Umslopogaas summoned Galazi the Wolf and told him all this story, for Galazi was the only man whom he could trust. The Wolf listened in silence, marveling the while at the beauty of Nada, as the starlight showed it. When everything was told, he said only that he no longer wondered that the people of the Halakazi had defied Dingaan and brought death upon themselves for the sake of this maid. Still, to be plain, his heart thought ill of the matter, for death was not done with yet: there before them shone the Star of Death, and he pointed to the Lily.

Now Nada trembled at his words of evil omen, and the Slaughterer grew angry, but Galazi would neither add to them nor take away from them. "I have spoken that which my heart hears," he answered.

Then they rose and went to search among the dead for a girl who would suit their purpose; soon they found one, a tall and fair maiden, and Galazi bore her in his arms to the great cave. Here in the cave were none but the dead, and, tossed hither and thither in their last sleep, they looked awful in the glare of the torches.

"They sleep sound," said the Lily, gazing on them; "rest is sweet."

"We shall soon win it, maiden," answered Galazi, and again Nada trembled.

Then, having arrayed her in the dress of a warrior, and put a shield and spear by her, they laid down the body of the girl in a dark place in the cave, and, finding a dead warrior of the People of the Axe, placed him beside her. Now they left the cave, and, pretending that they visited the sentries, Umslopogaas and Galazi passed from spot to spot, while the Lily walked after them like a guard, hiding her face with a shield, holding a spear in her hand, and having with her a bag of corn and dried flesh.

So they passed on, till at length they came to the entrance in the mountain side. The stones that had blocked it were pulled down so as to allow those of the Halakazi to fly who had been spared at the entreaty of Nada, but there were guards by the entrance to watch that none came back. Umslopogaas challenged them, and they saluted him, but he saw that they were worn out with battle and journeying, and knew little of what they saw or said. Then he, Galazi, and Nada and passed through the opening on to the plain beyond.

Here the Slaughterer and the Lily bade each other farewell, while Galazi watched, and presently the Wolf saw Umslopogaas return as one who is heavy at heart, and caught sight of the Lily skimming across the plain lightly like a swallow.

"I do not know when we two shall meet again," said Umslopogaas so soon as she had melted into the shadows of the night.

"May you never meet," answered Galazi, "for I am sure that if you meet that sister of yours will bring death on many more than those who now lie low because of her loveliness. She is a Star of Death, and when she sets the sky shall be blood red."

Umslopogaas did not answer, but walked slowly through the archway in the mountain side.

"How is this, chief?" said he who was captain of the guard. "Three went out, but only two return."

"Fool!" answered Umslopogaas. "Are you drunk with Halakazi beer, or blind with sleep? Two went out, and two return. I sent him who was with us back to the camp."

"So be it, father," said the captain. "Two went out, and two return. All is well!"

Chapter XXVII

THE STAMPING OF THE FIRE

On the morrow the *impi* awoke refreshed with sleep, and, after they had eaten, Umslopogaas mustered them. Alas! nearly half of those who had seen the sun of yesterday would wake no more forever. The Slaughterer mustered them and thanked them for that which they had done, winning fame and cattle. They were merry, recking little of those who were dead, and sang his praises and the praises of Galazi in a loud song. When the song was ended Umslopogaas spoke to them again, saying that the victory was great, and the cattle they had won were countless. Yet something was lacking – she was lacking whom he came to seek to be a gift to Dingaan the king, and for whose sake this war was made. Where now was the Lily? Yesterday she had been here, clad in a *moocha* like a man and bearing a shield; this he knew from the captives. Where, then, was she now?

Then all the soldiers said that they had seen nothing of her. When they had done, Galazi spoke a word, as was agreed between him and Umslopogaas. He said that when they stormed the cave he had seen a man run at a warrior in the cave to kill him. Then as he came, he who was about to be slain threw down the shield and cried for mercy, and Galazi knew that this was no warrior of the Halakazi, but a very beautiful girl. So he called to the man to let her alone and not to touch her, for the order was that no women should be killed. But the soldier, being made with the lust of fight, shouted that maid or man she should die, and slew her. Thereon, he – Galazi – in his wrath ran up and smote the man with the Watcher and killed him also, and he prayed that he had done no wrong.

"You have done well, my brother," said Umslopogaas. "Come now, some of you, and let us look at this dead girl. Perhaps it is the Lily, and if so that is unlucky for us, for I do not know what tale we shall tell to Dingaan of the matter."

So the captains went with Umslopogaas and Galazi, and came to the spot where the girl had been laid, and by her the man of the People of the Axe.

"All is as the Wolf, my brother, has told," said Umslopogaas, waving the torch in his hand over the two who lay dead. "Here, without a doubt, lies she who was named the Lily, whom we came to win, and by her that fool who slew her, slain himself by the blow of the Watcher. An ill sight to see, and an ill tale for me to tell at the kraal of Dingaan. Still, what is is, and cannot be altered; and this maid who was the fairest of the fair is now none to lovely to look on. Let us away!" And he turned swiftly, then spoke again, saying: —

"Bind up this dead girl in ox hides, cover her with salt, and let her be brought with us." And they did so.

Then the captains said: "Surely it is so, my father; now it cannot be altered, and Dingaan must miss his bride." So said they all except that man who had been captain of the guard when Umslopogaas and Galazi and another passed through the archway. This man, indeed, said nothing, yet he was not without his thoughts. For it seemed to him that he had seen three pass through the archway, and not two. It seemed to him, moreover, that the *kaross* which the third wore had slipped aside as she pressed past him, and that beneath it he had seen the shape of a beautiful woman, and above it had caught the glint of a woman's eye — an eye full and dark, like a buck's.

Also, this captain noted that Bulalio called none of the captives to swear to the body of the Lily maid, and that he shook the torch to and fro as he held it over her — he whose hand was of the steadiest. All of this he kept in his mind, forgetting nothing.

Now it chanced afterwards, on the homeward march, my father, that Umslopogaas had cause to speak angrily to this man, because he tried to rob another of his share of the spoil of the Halakazi. He spoke sharply to him, degrading him from his rank, and setting another over him. Also he took cattle from the man, and gave them to him whom he would have robbed.

And thereafter, though he was justly served, this man thought more and more of the third who had passed through the arch of the cave and had not returned, and who seemed to him to have a fair woman's shape, and eyes which gleamed like those of a woman.

On that day, then, Umslopogaas began his march to the kraal Umgugundhlovu, where Dingaan sat. But before he set his face homewards, in the presence of the soldiers, he asked Galazi the Wolf if he would come back with him, or if he desired to stay to be chief of the Halakazi, as he was by right of birth and war. Then the Wolf laughed, and answered that he had come out to seek for vengeance, and not for the place of a chief, also that there were few of the Halakazi people left over whom he might rule if he wished. Moreover, he added this: that, like twin trees, they two blood-brethren had grown up side by side till their roots were matted together, and that, were one of them dug up and planted in Swazi soil, he feared lest both should wither, or, at the last, that he, Galazi, would wither, who loved but one man and certain wolves.

So Umslopogaas said no more of the chieftainship, but began his journey. With him he brought a great number of cattle, to be a gift for Dingaan, and a multitude of captives, young women and children, for he would appease the heart of Dingaan, because he did not bring her whom he sought — the Lily, flower of flowers. Yet, because he was cautious and put little faith in the kindness of kings, Umslopogaas, so soon as he reached the borders of Zululand, sent the best of the cattle and the fairest of the maids and children on to the kraal of the People of the Axe by the Ghost Mountain. And he who had been captain of the guard but now was a common soldier noticed this also.

Now it chanced that on a certain morning I, Mopo, sat in the kraal Umgugundhlovu in attendance on Dingaan. For still I waited on the king, though he had spoken no word to me, good or bad, since the yesterday, when I foretold to him that in the blood of the white men whom he had betrayed grew the flower of his own death. For, my father, it was on the morrow of the slaying of the Amaboona that Umslopogaas came to the kraal Umgugundhlovu.

Now the mind of Dingaan was heavy, and he sought something to lighten it. Presently he bethought himself of the white praying man, who had come to the kraal seeking to teach us people of the Zulu to worship other gods than the assegai and the king. Now this was a good man, but no luck went with his teaching, which was hard to understand; and, moreover, the *indunas* did not like it, because it seemed to set a master over the master, and a king over the king, and to preach of peace to those whose trade was war. Still, Dingaan sent for the white man that he might dispute with him, for Dingaan thought that he himself was the cleverest of all men.

Now the white man came, but his face was pale, because of that which he had seen befall the Boers, for he was gentle and hated such sights. The king bade him be seated and spoke to him saying: —

"The other day, O White Man, thou toldest me of a place of fire whither those go after death who have done wickedly in life. Tell me now of thy wisdom, do my fathers lie in that place?"

"How can I know, King," answered the prayer-doctor, "who may not judge of the deeds of men? This I say only: that those who murder and rob and oppress the innocent and bear false witness shall lie in that place of fire."

"It seems that my fathers have done all these things, and if they are in this place I would go there also, for I am minded to be with my fathers at the last. Yet I think that I should find a way to escape if ever I came there."

"How, King?"

Now Dingaan had set this trap for the prayer-doctor. In the center of that open space where he had caused the Boers to be fallen upon he had built up a great pyre of wood — brushwood beneath, and on top of the brushwood logs, and even whole trees. Perhaps, my father, there were sixty full wagonloads of dry wood piled together there in the center of the place.

"Thou shalt see with thine eyes, White Man," he answered, and bidding attendants set fire to the pile all round, he summoned that regiment of young men which was left in the kraal. Maybe there were a thousand and half a thousand of them — not more — the same that had slain the Boers.

Now the fire began to burn fiercely, and the regiment filed in and took its place in ranks. By the time that all had come, the pyre was everywhere a sheet of raging flame, and, though we sat a hundred paces from it, its heat was great when the wind turned our way.

"Now, Doctor of Prayers, is thy hot place hotter than yonder fire?" said the king.

He answered that he did not know, but the fire was certainly hot.

"Then I will show thee how I will come out of it if ever I go to lie in such a fire — aye, though it be ten times as big and fierce. Ho! my children!" he cried to the soldiers, and, springing up, "You see yonder fire. Run swiftly and stamp it flat with your feet. Where there was fire let there be blackness and ashes."

Now the White Man lifted his hands and prayed Dingaan not to do this thing that should be the death of many, but the king bade him be silent. Then he turned his eyes upward and prayed to his gods. For a moment also the soldiers looked on each other in doubt, for the fire raged furiously, and spouts of flame shot high toward the heaven, and above it and about it the hot air danced. But their captain called to them loudly: "Great is the king! Hear the words of the king, who honors you! Yesterday we ate up the Amaboona — it was nothing, they were unarmed. There is a foe more worthy of our valor. Come, my children, let us wash in the fire — we who are fiercer than the fire! Great is the king who honors us!"

Thus he spoke and ran forward, and, with a roar, after him sprang the soldiers, rank by rank. They were brave men indeed; moreover, they knew that if death lay before them death also awaited him who lagged behind, and it is far better to die with honor than ashamed. On they went, as to the joy of battle, their captain leading them, and as they went they sang the Ingomo, the war-chant of the Zulu. Now the captain neared the raging fire; we saw him lift his shield to keep off its heat. Then he was gone — he had sprung into the heart of the furnace, and but little of him was ever found again. After him went the first company. In they went, beating at the flames with their ox-hide shields, stamping them out with their naked feet, tearing down the burning logs and casting them aside. Not one man of that company lived, my father; they fell down like moths which flutter through a candle, and where they fell they perished. But after them came other companies, and it was well for those in this fight who were last to grapple with the foe. Now a great smoke was mixed with the flame, now the flame grew less and less, and the smoke more and more; and now blackened men, hairless, naked, and blistered, white with the scorching of the fire, staggered out on the farther side of the flames, falling to earth here and there. After them came others; now there was no flame, only a great smoke in which men moved dimly; and presently, my father, it was done: they had conquered the fire, and that with but very little hurt to the last seven companies, though every man had trodden it. How many perished? — nay, I know not, they were never counted; but what between the dead and the injured that regiment was at half strength till the king drafted more men into it.

"See, Doctor of Prayers," said Dingaan, with a laugh, "thus shall I escape the fires of that land of which thou tellest, if such there be indeed: I will bid my *impis* stamp them out."

Then the praying man went from the kraal saying that he would teach no more among the Zulus, and afterwards he left the land. When he had gone the burned wood and the dead were cleared away, the injured were doctored or killed according to their hurts, and those who had little harm came before the king and praised him.

"New shields and headdresses must be found for you, my children," said Dingaan, for the shields were black and shriveled, and of heads of hair and plumes there were but few left among that regiment.

"Wow!" said Dingaan again, looking at the soldiers who still lived: "shaving will be easy and cheap in that place of fire of which the white man speaks."

Then he ordered bear to be brought to the men, for the heat had made them thirsty.

Now though you may not guess it, my father, I have told you this tale because it has something to do with my story; for scarcely had the matter been ended when messengers came, saying that Bulalio, chief of the People of the Axe, and his *impi* were without, having returned with much spoil from the slaying of the Halakazi in Swaziland. Now when I heard this my heart leapt for joy, seeing that I had feared greatly for the fate of Umslopogaas, my fosterling. Dingaan also was very glad, and, springing up, danced to and fro like a child.

"Now at last we have good tidings," he said, at once forgetting the stamping of the fire, "and now shall my eyes behold that Lily whom my hand has longed to pluck. Let Bulalio and his people enter swiftly."

For awhile there was silence; then from far away, without the high fence of the great place, there came a sound of singing, and through the gates of the kraal rushed two great men, wearing black plumes upon their heads, having black shields in their left hands, and in their right, one an axe and one a club; while about their shoulders were bound wolf-skins. They ran low, neck and neck, with outstretched shields and heads held forward, as a buck runs when he is hard pressed by dogs, and no such running had been seen in the kraal Umgugundhlovu as the running of the Wolf-Brethren. Half across the space they ran, and halted suddenly, and, as they halted, the dead ashes of the fire flew up before their feet in a little cloud.

"By my head! look, these come armed before me!" said Dingaan, frowning, "and to do this is death. Now say who is that man, great and fierce, who bears an axe aloft? Did I not know him dead I should say it was the Black One, my brother, as he was in the days of the smiting of Zwide: so was his head set on his shoulders and so he was wont to look round, like a lion."

"I think that is Bulalio the Slaughterer, chief of the People of the Axe, O King," I answered.

"And who is the other with him? He is a great man also. Never have I seen such a pair!"

"I think that is Galazi the Wolf, he who is blood-brother to the Slaughterer, and his general," I said again.

Now after these two came the soldiers of the People of the Axe, armed with short sticks alone. Four by four they came, all holding their heads low, and with black shields outstretched, and formed themselves into companies behind the Wolf-Brethren, till all were there. Then, after them, the crowd of the Halakazi slaves were driven in, — women, boys, and maids, a great number — and they stood behind the ranks huddled together like frightened calves.

"A gallant sight, truly!" said Dingaan, as he looked upon the companies of black-plumed and shielded warriors. "I have no better soldiers in my *impis*, and yet my eyes behold these for the first time," and again he frowned.

Now suddenly Umslopogaas lifted his axe and started forward at full speed, and after him thundered the companies. On they rushed, and their plumes lay back upon the wind, till it seemed as though they must stamp us flat. But when he was within ten paces of the king Umslopogaas lifted Groan-Maker again, and Galazi held the Watcher on high, and every man halted where he was, while once more the dust flew up in clouds. They halted in long, unbroken lines, with outstretched shields and heads held low; no man's head rose more than the length of a dance kerrie from the earth. So they stood one minute, then, for the third time, Umslopogaas lifted Groan-Maker, and in an instant every man straightened himself, each shield was tossed on high, and from every throat was roared the royal salute, "Bayéte!"

"A pretty sight forsooth," quoth Dingaan; "but these soldiers are too well drilled who have never done me service nor the Black One who was before me, and this Slaughterer is too good a captain, I say. Come hither, ye twain!" he cried aloud.

Then the Wolf-Brethren strode forward and stood before the king, and for awhile they looked upon each other.

Chapter XXVIII
THE LILY IS BROUGHT TO DINGAAN

"*H*ow are you named?" said Dingaan.

"We are named Bulalio the Slaughterer and Galazi the Wolf, O King," answered Umslopogaas.

"Was it thou who didst send a certain message to the Black One who is dead, Bulalio?"

"Yea, O King, I sent a message, but from all I have heard, Masilo, my messenger, gave more than the message, for he stabbed the Black One. Masilo had an evil heart."

Now Dingaan winced, for he knew well that he himself and one Mopo had stabbed the Black One, but he thought that this outland chief had not heard the tale, so he said no more of the message.

"How is it that ye dare to come before me armed? Know ye not the rule that he who appears armed before the king dies?"

"We have not heard that law, O King," said Umslopogaas. "Moreover, there is this to be told: my virtue of the axe I bear I rule alone. If I am seen without the axe, then any man may take my place who can, for the axe is chieftainess of the People of the Axe, and he who holds it is its servant."

"A strange custom," said Dingaan, "but let it pass. And thou, Wolf, what hast thou to say of that great club of thine?"

"There is this to be told of the club, O King," answered Galazi: "by virtue of the club I guard my life. If I am seen without the club, then may any man take my life who can, for the club is my Watcher, not I Watcher of the club."

"Never wast thou nearer to the losing of both club and life," said Dingaan, angrily.

"It may be so, O King," answered the Wolf. "When the hour is, then, without a doubt, the Watcher shall cease from his watching."

"Ye are a strange pair," quoth Dingaan. "Where have you been now, and what is your business at the Place of the Elephant?"

"We have been in a far country, O King!" answered Umslopogaas. "We have wandered in a distant land to search for a Flower to be a gift to a king, and in our searching we have trampled down a Swazi garden, and yonder are some of those who tended it" — and he pointed to the captives — "and without are the cattle that plowed it."

"Good, Slaughterer! I see the gardeners, and I hear the lowing of the cattle, but what of the Flower? Where is this Flower ye went so far to dig in Swazi soil? Was it a Lily-bloom, perchance?"

"It was a Lily-bloom, O King! and yet, alas! the Lily has withered. Nothing is left but the stalk, white and withered as are the bones of men."

"What meanest thou?" said Dingaan, starting to his feet.

"That the king shall learn," answered Umslopogaas; and, turning, he spoke a word to the captains who were behind him. Presently the ranks opened up, and four men ran forward from the rear of the companies. On their shoulders they bore a stretcher, and upon the stretcher lay something wrapped about with raw ox-hides, and bound round with *rimpis.* The men saluted, and laid their burden down before the king.

"Open!" said the Slaughterer; and they opened, and there within the hides, packed in salt, lay the body of a girl who once was tall and fair.

"Here lies the Lily's stalk, O King!" said Umslopogaas, pointing with the axe, "but if her flower blooms on any air, it is not here."

Now Dingaan stared at the sight of death, and bitterness of heart took hold of him, since he desired above all things to win the beauty of the Lily for himself.

"Bear away this carrion and cast it to the dogs!" he cried, for thus he could speak of her whom he would have taken to wife, when once he deemed her dead. "Take it away, and thou, Slaughterer, tell me how it came about that the maid was slain. It will be well for thee if thou hast a good answer, for know thy life hangs on the words."

So Umslopogaas told the king all that tale which had been made ready against the wrath of Dingaan. And when he had finished Galazi told his story, of how he had seen the soldier kill the maid, and in his wrath had killed the soldier. Then certain of the captains who had seen the soldier and the maid lying in one death came forward and spoke to it.

Now Dingaan was very angry, and yet there was nothing to be done. The Lily was dead, and by no fault of any except of one, who was also dead and beyond his reach.

"Get you hence, you and your people," he said to the Wolf-Brethren. "I take the cattle and the captives. Be thankful that I do not take all your lives also — first, because ye have dared to make war without my word, and secondly, because, having made war, ye have so brought it about that, though ye bring me the body of her I sought, ye do not bring the life."

Now when the king spoke of taking the lives of all the People of the Axe, Umslopogaas smiled grimly and glanced at his companies. Then saluting the king, he turned to go. But as he turned a man sprang forwards from the ranks and called to Dingaan, saying: —

"Is it granted that I may speak truth before the king, and afterwards sleep in the king's shadow?"

Now this was that man who had been captain of the guard on the night when three passed out through the archway and two returned, that same man whom Umslopogaas had degraded from his rank.

"Speak on, thou art safe," answered Dingaan.

"O King, thy ears have been filled with lies," said the soldier. "Hearken, O King! I was captain of the guard of the gate on that night of the slaying of the Halakazi. Three came to the gate of the mountain — they were Bulalio, the Wolf Galazi, and another. That other was tall and slim, bearing a shield high — so. As the third passed the gate, the *kaross* he wore brushed against me and slipped aside. Beneath that *kaross* was no man's breast, O King, but the shape of a woman, almost white in color, and very fair. In drawing back the *kaross* this third one moved the shield. Behind that shield was no man's face, O King, but the face of a girl, lovelier than the moon, and having eyes brighter than the stars. Three went out at the mountain gate, O King, only two returned, and, peeping after them, it seemed that I saw the third running swiftly across the plains, as a young maid runs, O King. This also, Elephant, Bulalio yonder denied me when, as captain of the guard, I asked for the third who had passed the gate, saying that only two had passed. Further, none of the captives were called to swear to the body of the maid, and now it is too late, and that man who lay beside her was not killed by Galazi in the cave. He was killed outside the cave by a blow of a Halakazi kerrie. I saw him fall with my own eyes, and slew the man who smote him. One thing more, King of the World, the best of the captives and the cattle are not here for a gift to thee — they are at the kraal of Bulalio, Chief of the People of the Axe. I have spoken, O King, yes, because my heart loves not lies. I have spoken the truth, and now do thou protect me from these Wolf-Brethren, O King, for they are very fierce."

Now all this while that the traitor told his tale Umslopogaas, inch by inch, was edging near to him and yet nearer, till at length he might have touched him with an outstretched spear. None noted him except I, Mopo, alone, and perhaps Galazi, for all were watching the face of Dingaan as men watch a storm that is about to burst.

"Fear thou not the Wolf-Brethren, soldier," gasped Dingaan, rolling his red eyes; "the paw of the Lion guards thee, my servant."

Ere the words had left the king's lips the Slaughterer leapt. He leaped full on to the traitor, speaking never a word, and oh! his eyes were awful. He leaped upon him, he seized him with his hands, lifting no weapon, and in his terrible might he broke him as a child breaks a stick — nay, I know not how, it was too swift to see. He broke him, and, hurling him on high, cast him dead at the feet of Dingaan, crying in a great voice: —

"Take thy servant, King! Surely he 'sleeps in thy shadow'!"

Then there was silence, only through the silence was heard a gasp of fear and wonder, for no such deed as this had been wrought in the presence of the king — no, not since the day of Senzangacona the Root.

Now Dingaan spoke, and his voice came thick with rage, and his limbs trembled.

"Slay him!" he hissed. "Slay the dog and all those with him!"

"Now we come to a game which I can play," answered Umslopogaas. "Ho, People of the Axe! Will you stand to be slaughtered by these singed rats?" and he pointed with Groan-Maker at those warriors who had escaped without hurt in the fire, but whose faces the fire had scorched.

Then for answer a great shout went up, a shout and a roar of laughter. And this was the shout: —

"No, Slaughterer, not so are we minded!" and right and left they faced to meet the foe, while from all along the companies came the crackling of the shaken shields.

Back sprang Umslopogaas to head his men; forward leaped the soldiers of the king to work the king's will, if so they might. And Galazi the Wolf also sprang forward, towards Dingaan, and, as he sprang, swung up the Watcher, crying in a great voice: —

"Hold!"

Again there was silence, for men saw that the shadow of the Watcher lay dark upon the head of Dingaan.

"It is a pity that many should die when one will suffice," cried the Wolf again. "Let a blow be struck, and where his shadow lies there shall the Watcher be, and lo! the world will lack a king. A word, King!"

Now Dingaan looked up at the great man who stood above him, and felt the shadow of the shining club lie cold upon his brow, and again he shook — this time it was with fear.

"Begone in peace!" he said.

"A good word for thee, King," said the Wolf, grinning, and slowly he drew himself backwards towards the companies, saying, "Praise the king! The king bids his children go in peace."

But when Dingaan felt that his brow was no longer cold with the shadow of death his rage came back to him, and he would have called to the soldiers to fall upon the People of the Axe, only I stayed him, saying: —

"Thy death is in it, O King; the Slaughterer will grind such men as thou hast here beneath his feet, and then once more shall the Watcher look upon thee."

Now Dingaan saw that this was true, and gave no command, for he had only those men with him whom the fire had left. All the rest were gone to slaughter the Boers in Natal. Still, he must have blood, so he turned on me.

"Thou art a traitor, Mopo, as I have known for long, and I will serve thee as yonder dog served his faithless servant!" and he thrust at me with the assegai in his hand.

But I saw the stroke, and, springing high into the air, avoided it. Then I turned and fled very swiftly, and after me came certain of the soldiers. The way was not far to the last company of the People of the Axe; moreover, it saw me coming, and, headed by Umslopogaas, who walked behind them all, ran to meet me. Then the soldiers who followed to kill me hung back out of reach of the axe.

"Here with the king is no place for me anymore, my son," I said to Umslopogaas.

"Fear not, my father, I will find you a place," he answered.

Then I called a message to the soldiers who followed me, saying: —

"Tell this to the king: that he has done ill to drive me from him, for I, Mopo, set him on the throne and I alone can hold him there. Tell him this also, that he will do yet worse to seek me where I am, for that day when we are once more face to face shall be his day of death. Thus speaks Mopo the *inyanga*, Mopo the doctor, who never yet prophesied that which should not be."

Then we marched from the kraal Umgugundhlovu, and when next I saw that kraal it was to burn all of it which Dingaan had left unburned, and when next I saw Dingaan — ah! that is to be told of, my father.

We marched from the kraal, none hindering us, for there were none to hinder, and after we had gone a little way Umslopogaas halted and said: —

"Now it is in my mind to return whence we came and slay this Dingaan, ere he slay me."

"Yet it is well to leave a frightened lion in his thicket, my son, for a lion at bay is hard to handle. Doubt not that every man, young and old, in Umgugundhlovu now stands armed about the gates, lest such a thought should take you, my son; and though just now he was afraid, yet Dingaan will strike for his life. When you might have killed you did not kill; now the hour has gone."

"Wise words!" said Galazi. "I would that the Watcher had fallen where his shadow fell."

"What is your counsel now, father?" asked Umslopogaas.

"This, then: that you two should abide no more beneath the shadow of the Ghost Mountain, but should gather your people and your cattle, and pass to the north on the track of Mosilikatze the Lion, who broke away from Chaka. There you may rule apart or together, and never dream of Dingaan."

"I will not do that, father," he answered. "I will dwell beneath the shadow of the Ghost Mountain while I may."

"And so will I," said Galazi, "or rather among its rocks. What! shall my wolves lack a master when they would go a-hunting? Shall Greysnout and Blackfang, Blood and Deathgrip, and their company black and grey, howl for me in vain?"

"So be it, children. Ye are young and will not listen to the counsel of the old. Let it befall as it chances."

I spoke thus, for I did not know then why Umslopogaas would not leave his kraals. It was for this reason: because he had bidden Nada to meet him there.

Afterwards, when he found her he would have gone, but then the sky was clear, the danger-clouds had melted for awhile.

Oh! that Umslopogaas my fosterling had listened to me! Now he would have reigned as a king, not wandered an outcast in strange lands I know not where; and Nada should have lived, not died, nor would the People of the Axe have ceased to be a people.

This of Dingaan. When he heard my message he grew afraid once more, for he knew me to be no liar.

Therefore he held his hand for awhile, sending no *impi* to smite Umslopogaas, lest it might come about that I should bring him his death as I had promised. And before the fear had worn away, it happened that Dingaan's hands were full with the war against the Amaboona, because of his slaughter of the white people, and he had no soldiers to spare with whom to wreak vengeance on a petty chief living far away.

Yet his rage was great because of what had chanced, and, after his custom, he murdered many innocent people to satisfy it.

Chapter XXIX
MOPO TELLS HIS TALE

*N*ow afterwards, as we went upon our road, Umslopogaas told me all there was to tell of the slaying of the Halakazi and of the finding of Nada.

When I heard that Nada, my daughter, still lived, I wept for joy, though like Umslopogaas I was torn by doubt and fear, for it is far for an unaided maid to travel from Swaziland to the Ghost Mountain. Yet all this while I said nothing to Umslopogaas of the truth as to his birth, because on the journey there were many around us, and the very trees have ears, and the same wind to which we whispered might whisper to the king. Still I knew that the hour had come now when I must speak, for it was in my mind to bring it about that Umslopogaas should be proclaimed the son of Chaka, and be made king of the Zulus in the place of Dingaan, his uncle. Yet all these things had gone cross for us, because it was fated so, my father. Had I known that Umslopogaas still lived when I slew Chaka, then I think that I could have brought it about that he should be king. Or had things fallen out as I planned, and the Lily maid been brought to Dingaan, and Umslopogaas grew great in his sight, then, perhaps, I could have brought it about. But all things had gone wrong. The Lily was none other than Nada; and how could Umslopogaas give Nada, whom he thought his sister, and who was my daughter, to Dingaan against her will? Also, because of Nada, Dingaan and Umslopogaas were now at bitter enmity, and for this same cause I was disgraced and a fugitive, and my counsels would no longer be heard in the ear of the king.

So everything must be begun afresh: and as I walked with the *impi* towards the Ghost Mountain, I thought much and often of the manner in which this might be done. But as yet I said nothing.

Now at last we were beneath the Ghost Mountain, and looked upon the face of the old Witch who sits there aloft forever waiting for the

world to die; and that same night we came to the kraal of the People of
the Axe, and entered it with a great singing. But Galazi did not enter at
that time; he was away to the mountain to call his flock of wolves, and
as we passed its foot we heard the welcome that the wolves howled in
greeting to him.

Now as we drew near the kraal, all the women and children came out
to meet us, headed by Zinita, the head wife of Umslopogaas. They came
joyfully, but when they found how many were wanting who a moon
before had gone thence to fight, their joy was turned to mourning, and
the voice of their weeping went up to heaven.

Umslopogaas greeted Zinita kindly; and yet I thought that there was
something lacking. At first she spoke to him softly, but when she learned
all that had come to pass, her words were not soft, for she reviled me
and sang a loud song at Umslopogaas.

"See now, Slaughterer," she said, "see now what has came about
because you listened to this aged fool!" — that was I, my father — "this
fool who calls himself 'Mouth'! Aye, a mouth he is, a mouth out of
which proceed folly and lies! What did he counsel you to do? — to go
up against these Halakazi and win a girl for Dingaan! And what have
you done? — you have fallen upon the Halakazi, and doubtless have
killed many innocent people with that great axe of yours, also you have
left nearly half of the soldiers of the Axe to whiten in the Swazi caves,
and in exchange have brought back certain cattle of a small breed, and
girls and children whom we must nourish!

"Nor does the matter end here. You went, it seems, to win a girl whom
Dingaan desired, yet when you find that girl you let her go, because,
indeed, you say she was your sister and would not wed Dingaan.
Forsooth, is not the king good enough for this sister of yours? Now
what is the end of the tale? You try to play tricks on the king, because
of your sister, and are found out. Then you kill a man before Dingaan
and escape, bringing this fool of an aged Mouth with you, that he may
teach you his own folly. So you have lost half of your men, and you
have gained the king for a foe who shall bring about the death of all of
us, and a fool for a councilor. Wow! Slaughterer, keep to your trade and
let others find you wit."

Thus she spoke without ceasing, and there was some truth in her
words. Zinita had a bitter tongue. I sat silent till she had finished, and
Umslopogaas also remained silent, though his anger was great, because
there was no crack in her talk through which a man might thrust a word.

"Peace, woman!" I said at length, "do not speak ill of those who are
wise and who had seen much before you were born."

"Speak no ill of him who is my father," growled Umslopogaas. "Aye! though you do not know it, this Mouth whom you revile is Mopo, my father."

"Then there is a man among the People of the Axe who has a fool for a father. Of all tidings this is the worst."

"There is a man among the People of the Axe who has a jade and a scold for a wife," said Umslopogaas, springing up. "Begone, Zinita! — and know this, that if I hear you snarl such words of him who is my father, you shall go further than your own hut, for I will put you away and drive you from my kraal. I have suffered you too long."

"I go," said Zinita. "Oh! I am well served! I made you chief, and now you threaten to put me away."

"My own hands made me chief," said Umslopogaas, and, springing up, he thrust her from the hut.

"It is a poor thing to be wedded to such a woman, my father," he said presently.

"Yes, a poor thing, Umslopogaas, yet these are the burdens that men must bear. Learn wisdom from it, Umslopogaas, and have as little to do with women as may be; at the least, do not love them overmuch, so shall you find the more peace." Thus I spoke, smiling, and would that he had listened to my counsel, for it is the love of women which has brought ruin on Umslopogaas!

All this was many years ago, and but lately I have heard that Umslopogaas is fled into the North, and become a wanderer to his death because of the matter of a woman who had betrayed him, making it seem that he had murdered one Loustra, who was his blood brother, just as Galazi had been. I do not know how it came about, but he who was so fierce and strong had that weakness like his uncle Dingaan, and it has destroyed him at the last, and for this cause I shall behold him no more.

Now, my father, for awhile we were silent and alone in the hut, and as we sat I thought I heard a rat stir in the thatch.

Then I spoke. "Umslopogaas, at length the hour has come that I should whisper something into your ear, a word which I have held secret ever since you were born."

"Speak on, my father," he said, wondering.

I crept to the door of the hut and looked out. The night was dark and I could see none about, and could hear no one move, yet, being cautious, I walked round the hut. Ah, my father, when you have a secret to tell, be not so easily deceived. It is not enough to look forth and to peer round. Dig beneath the floor, and search the roof also; then, having done all this, go elsewhere and tell your tale. The woman was right: I

was but a fool, for all my wisdom and my white hairs. Had I not been
a fool I would have smoked out that rat in the thatch before ever I
opened my lips. For the rat was Zinita, my father — Zinita, who had
climbed the hut, and now lay there in the dark, her ear upon the
smoke-hole, listening to every word that passed. It was a wicked thing
to do, and, moreover, the worst of omens, but there is little honor among
women when they learn that which others wish to hide away from them,
nor, indeed, do they then weight omens.

So having searched and found nothing, I spoke to Umslopogaas, my
fosterling, not knowing that death in a woman's shape lay on the hut
above us. "Hearken," I said, "you are no son of mine, Umslopogaas,
though you have called me father from a babe. You spring from a loftier
stock, Slaughterer."

"Yet I was well pleased with my fathering, old man," said
Umslopogaas. "The breed is good enough for me. Say, then, whose son
am I?"

Now I bent forward and whispered to him, yet, alas! not low enough.
"You are the son of the Black One who is dead, yea, sprung from the
blood of Chaka and of Baleka, my sister."

"I still have some kinship with you then, Mopo, and that I am glad
of. Wow! who would have guessed that I was the son of the Silwana, of
that hyena man? Perhaps it is for this reason that, like Galazi, I love the
company of the wolves, though no love grows in my heart for my father
or any of his house."

"You have little cause to love him, Umslopogaas, for he murdered
your mother, Baleka, and would have slain you also. But you are the
son of Chaka and of no other man."

"Well, his eyes must be keen indeed, my uncle, who can pick his own
father out of a crowd. And yet I once heard this tale before, though I
had long forgotten it."

"From whom did you hear it, Umslopogaas? An hour since, it was
known to one alone, the others are dead who knew it. Now it is known
to two" — ah! my father, I did not guess of the third; — "from whom,
then, did you hear it?"

"It was from the dead; at least, Galazi the Wolf heard it from the dead
One who sat in the cave on Ghost Mountain, for the dead One told
him that a man would come to be his brother who should be named
Umslopogaas Bulalio, son of Chaka, and Galazi repeated it to me, but
I had long forgotten it."

"It seems that there is wisdom among the dead," I answered, "for lo!
today you are named Umslopogaas Bulalio, and today I declare you the
son of Chaka. But listen to my tale."

Then I told him all the story from the hour of his birth onwards, and when I spoke of the words of his mother, Baleka, after I had told my dream to her, and of the manner of her death by the command of Chaka, and of the great fashion in which she had died, then, I say, Umslopogaas wept, who, I think, seldom wept before or after. But as my tale drew it its end I saw that he listened ill, as a man listens who has a weightier matter pressing on his heart, and before it was well done he broke in: —

"So, Mopo, my uncle, if I am the son of Chaka and Baleka, Nada the Lily is no sister to me."

"Nay, Umslopogaas, she is only your cousin."

"Over near of blood," he said; "yet that shall not stand between us," and his face grew glad.

I looked at him in question.

"You grow dull, my uncle. This is my meaning: that I will marry Nada if she still lives, for it comes upon me now that I have never loved any woman as I love Nada the Lily," and while he spoke, I heard the rat stir in the thatch of the hut.

"Wed her if you will, Umslopogaas," I answered, "yet I think that one Zinita, your Inkosikasi, will find words to say in the matter."

"Zinita is my head wife indeed, but shall she hold me back from taking other wives, after the lawful custom of our people?" he asked angrily, and his anger showed that he feared the wrath of Zinita.

"The custom is lawful and good," I said, "but it has bred trouble at times. Zinita can have little to say if she continues in her place and you still love her as of old. But enough of her. Nada is not yet at your gates, and perhaps she will never find them. See, Umslopogaas, it is my desire that you should rule in Zululand by right of blood, and, though things point otherwise, yet I think a way can be found to bring it about."

"How so?" he asked.

"Thus: Many of the great chiefs who are friends to me hate Dingaan and fear him, and did they know that a son of Chaka lived, and that son the Slaughterer, he well might climb to the throne upon their shoulders. Also the soldiers love the name of Chaka, though he dealt cruelly with them, because at least he was brave and generous. But they do not love Dingaan, for his burdens are the burdens of Chaka but his gifts are the gifts of Dingaan; therefore they would welcome Chaka's son if once they knew him for certain. But it is here that the necklet chafes, for there is but my word to prove it. Yet I will try."

"Perhaps it is worth trying and perhaps it is not, my uncle," answered Umslopogaas. "One thing I know: I had rather see Nada at my gates tonight than hear all the chiefs in the land crying 'Hail, O King!'"

"You will live to think otherwise, Umslopogaas; and now spies must be set at the kraal Umgugundhlovu to give us warning of the mind of the king, lest he should send an *impi* suddenly to eat you up. Perhaps his hands may be too full for that ere long, for those white Amaboona will answer his assegais with bullets. And one more word: let nothing be said of this matter of your birth, least of all to Zinita your wife, or to any other woman."

"Fear not, uncle," he answered; "I know how to be silent."

Now after awhile Umslopogaas left me and went to the hut of Zinita, his Inkosikasi, where she lay wrapped in her blankets, and, as it seemed, asleep.

"Greeting, my husband," she said slowly, like one who wakens. "I have dreamed a strange dream of you. I dreamed that you were called a king, and that all the regiments of the Zulus filed past giving you the royal salute, Bayéte."

Umslopogaas looked at her wondering, for he did not know if she had learned something or if this was an omen. "Such dreams are dangerous," he said, "and he who dreams them does well to lock them fast till they be forgotten."

"Or fulfilled," said Zinita, and again Umslopogaas looked at her wondering.

Now after this night I began my work, for I established spies at the kraal of Dingaan, and from them I learned all that passed with the king.

At first he gave orders that an *impi* should be summoned to eat up the People of the Axe, but afterwards came tidings that the Boers, to the number of five hundred mounted men, were marching on the kraal Umgugundhlovu. So Dingaan had no *impi* to spare to send to the Ghost Mountain, and we who were beneath its shadow dwelt there in peace.

This time for Boers were beaten, for Bogoza, the spy, led them into an ambush; still few were killed, and they did but draw back that they might jump the further, and Dingaan knew this. At this time also the English white men of Natal, the people of George, who attacked Dingaan by the Lower Tugela, were slain by our soldiers, and those with them.

Also, by the help of certain witch-doctors, I filled the land with rumors, prophecies, and dark sayings, and I worked cunningly on the minds of many chiefs that were known to me, sending them messages hardly to be understood, such as should prepare their thoughts for the coming of one who should be declared to them. They listened, but the task was long, for the men dwelt far apart, and some of them were away with the regiments.

So the time went by, till many days had passed since we reached the Ghost Mountain. Umslopogaas had no more words with Zinita, but she always watched him, and he went heavily. For he awaited Nada, and Nada did not come.

But at length Nada came.

Chapter XXX

THE COMING OF NADA

One night – it was a night of full moon – I sat alone with Umslopogaas in my hut, and we spoke of the matter of our plots; then, when we had finished that talk, we spoke of Nada the Lily.

"Alas! my uncle," said Umslopogaas sadly, "we shall never look more on Nada; she is surely dead or in bonds, otherwise she had been here long ago. I have sought far and wide, and can hear no tidings and find nothing."

"All that is hidden is not lost," I answered, yet I myself believed that there was an end of Nada.

Then we were silent awhile, and presently, in the silence, a dog barked. We rose, and crept out of the hut to see what it might be that stirred, for the night drew on, and it was needful to be wary, since a dog might bark at the stirring of a leaf, or perhaps it might be the distant footfall of an *impi* that it heard.

We had not far to look, for standing gazing at the huts, like one who is afraid to call, was a tall slim man, holding an assegai in one hand and a little shield in the other. We could not see the face of the man, because the light was behind him, and a ragged blanket hung about his shoulders. Also, he was footsore, for he rested on one leg. Now we were peering round the hut, and its shadow hid us, so that the man saw nothing. For awhile he stood still, then he spoke to himself, and his voice was strangely soft.

"Here are many huts," said the voice, "now how may I know which is the house of my brother? Perhaps if I call I shall bring soldiers to me, and be forced to play the man before them, and I am weary of that. Well, I will lie here under the fence till morning; it is a softer bed than some I have found, and I am word out with travel – sleep I must," and the figure sighed and turned so that the light of the moon fell full upon its face.

My father, it was the face of Nada, my daughter, whom I had not seen for so many years, yet across the years I knew it at once; yes, though the bud had become a flower I knew it. The face was weary and worn, but ah! it was beautiful, never before nor since have I seen such beauty, for there was this about the loveliness of my daughter, the Lily: it seemed to flow from within – yes, as light will flow through the thin rind of a gourd, and in that she differed from the other women of our people, who, when they are fair are fair with the flesh alone.

Now my heart went out to Nada as she stood in the moonlight, one forsaken, not having where to lay her head, Nada, who alone was left alive of all my children. I motioned to Umslopogaas to hide himself in the shadow, and stepped forward.

"Ho!" I said roughly, "who are you, wanderer, and what do you here?"

Now Nada started like a frightened bird, but quickly gathered up her thoughts, and turned upon me in a lordly way.

"Who are you that ask me?" she said, feigning a man's voice.

"One who can use a stick upon thieves and night-prowlers, boy. Come, show your business or be moving. You are not of this people; surely that *moocha* is of a Swazi make, and here we do not love Swazis."

"Were you not old, I would beat you for your insolence," said Nada, striving to look brave and all the while searching a way to escape. "Also, I have no stick, only a spear, and that is for warriors, not for an old *umfagozan* like you." Aye, my father, I lived to hear my daughter name me an *umfagozan* – a low fellow!

Now making pretence to be angry, I leaped at her with my kerrie up, and, forgetting her courage, she dropped her spear, and uttered a little scream. But she still held the shield before her face. I seized her by the arm, and struck a blow upon the shield with my kerrie – it would scarcely have crushed a fly, but this brave warrior trembled sorely.

"Where now is your valor, you who name my *umfagozan?*" I said: "you who cry like a maid and whose arm is soft as a maid's."

She made no answer, but hugged her tattered blanket round her, and shifting my grip from her arm, I seized it and rent it, showing her breast and shoulder; then I let her go, laughing, and said: –

"Lo! here is the warrior that would beat an old *umfagozan* for his insolence, a warrior well shaped for war! Now, my pretty maid who wander at night in the garment of a man, what tale have you to tell? Swift with it, lest I drag you to the chief as his prize! The old man seeks a new wife, they tell me?"

Now when Nada saw that I had discovered her she threw down the shield after the spear, as a thing that was of no more use, and hung her head sullenly. But when I spoke of dragging her to the chief then she flung herself upon the ground, and clasped my knees, for since I called him old, she thought that this chief could not be Umslopogaas.

"Oh, my father," said the Lily, "oh, my father, have pity on me! Yes, yes! I am a girl, a maid — no wife — and you who are old, you, perchance have daughters such as I, and in their name I ask for pity. My father, I have journeyed far, I have endured many things, to find my way to a kraal where my brother rules, and now it seems I have come to the wrong kraal. Forgive me that I spoke to you so, my father; it was but a woman's feint, and I was hard pressed to hide my sex, for my father, you know it is ill to be a lonely girl among strange men."

Now I said nothing in answer, for this reason only: that when I heard Nada call me father, not knowing me, and saw her clasp my knees and pray to me in my daughter's name, I, who was childless save for her, went nigh to weeping. But she thought that I did not answer her because I was angry, and about to drag her to this unknown chief, and implored me the more even with tears.

"My father," she said, "do not this wicked thing by me. Let me go and show me the path that I shall ask: you who are old, you know that I am too fair to be dragged before this chief of yours. Hearken! All I knew are dead, I am alone except for this brother I seek. Oh! if you betray me may such a fate fall upon your own daughter also! May she also know the day of slavery, and the love that she wills not!" and she ceased, sobbing.

Now I turned my head and spoke towards the hut, "Chief," I said, "your Ehlose is kind to you tonight, for he has given you a maid fair as the Lily of the Halakazi" — here Nada glanced up wildly. "Come, then, and take the girl."

Now Nada turned to snatch up the assegai from the ground, but whether to kill me, or the chief she feared so much, or herself, I do not know, and as she turned, in her woe she called upon the name of Umslopogaas. She found the assegai, and straightened herself again. And lo! there before her stood a tall chief leaning on an axe; but the old man who threatened her was gone — not very far, in truth, but round the corner of the hut.

Now Nada the Lily looked, then rubbed her eyes, and looked again.

"Surely I dream?" she said at last. "But now I spoke to an old man, and in his place there stands before me the shape of one whom I desire to see."

"I thought, Maiden, that the voice of a certain Nada called upon one Umslopogaas," said he who leaned upon the axe.

"Aye, I called: but where is the old man who treated me so scurvily? Nay, what does it matter? — where he is, there let him stop. At least, you are Umslopogaas, my brother, or should be by your greatness and the axe. To the man I cannot altogether swear in this light; but to the axe I can swear, for once it passed so very near my eyes."

Thus she spoke on, gaining time, and all the while she watched Umslopogaas till she was sure that it was he and no other. Then she ceased talking, and, flinging herself on him, she kissed him.

"Now I trust that Zinita sleeps sound," murmured Umslopogaas, for suddenly he remembered that Nada was no sister of his, as she thought.

Nevertheless, he took her by the hand and said, "Enter, sister. Of all maidens in the world you are the most welcome here, for know I believed you dead."

But I, Mopo, ran into the hut before her, and when she entered she found me sitting by the fire.

"Now, here, my brother," said Nada, pointing at me with her finger, "here is that old *umfagozan,* that low fellow, who, unless I dream, but a very little while ago brought shame upon me — aye, my brother, he struck me, a maid, with his kerrie, and that only because I said that I would stab him for his insolence, and he did worse: he swore that he would drag me to some old chief of his to be a gift to him, and this he was about to do, had you not come. Will you suffer these things to go unpunished, my brother?"

Now Umslopogaas smiled grimly, and I answered: —

"What was it that you called me just now, Nada, when you prayed me to protect you? Father, was it not?" and I turned my face towards the blaze of the fire, so that the full light fell upon it.

"Yes, I called you father, old man. It is not strange, for a homeless wanderer must find fathers where she can — and yet! no, it cannot be — so changed — and that white hand? And yet, oh! who are you? Once there was a man named Mopo, and he had a little daughter, and she was called Nada — Oh! my father, my father, I know you now!"

"Aye, Nada, and I knew you from the first; through all your man's wrappings I knew you after these many years."

So the Lily fell upon my neck and sobbed there, and I remember that I also wept.

Now when she had sobbed her fill of joy, Umslopogaas brought Nada the Lily mass to eat and mealie porridge. She ate the curdled milk, but the porridge she would not eat, saying that she was too weary.

Then she told us all the tale of her wanderings since she had fled away from the side of Umslopogaas at the stronghold of the Halakazi, and it was long, so long that I will not repeat it, for it is a story by itself. This I will say only: that Nada was captured by robbers, and for awhile passed herself off among them as a youth. But, in the end, they found her out and would have given her as a wife to their chief, only she persuaded them to kill the chief and make her their ruler. They did this because of that medicine of the eyes which Nada had only among women, for as she ruled the Halakazi so she ruled the robbers. But, at the last, they all loved her, and she gave it out that she would wed the strongest. Then some of them fell to fighting, and while they killed each other — for it came about that Nada brought death upon the robbers as on all others — she escaped, for she said that she did not wish to look upon their struggle but would await the upshot in a place apart.

After that she had many further adventures, but at length she met an old woman who guided her on her way to the Ghost Mountain. And who this old woman was none could discover, but Galazi swore afterwards that she was the Stone Witch of the mountain, who put on the shape of an aged woman to guide Nada to Umslopogaas, to be the sorrow and the joy of the People of the Axe. I do not know, my father, yet it seems to me that the old witch would scarcely have put off her stone for so small a matter.

Now, when Nada had made an end of her tale, Umslopogaas told his, of how things had gone with Dingaan. When he told her how he had given the body of the girl to the king, saying that it was the Lily's stalk, she said it had been well done; and when he spoke of the slaying of the traitor she clapped her hands, though Nada, whose heart was gentle, did not love to hear of deeds of death. At last he finished, and she was somewhat sad, and said it seemed that her fate followed her, and that now the People of the Axe were in danger at the hands of Dingaan because of her.

"Ah! my brother," she cried, taking Umslopogaas by the hand, "it were better I should die than that I should bring evil upon you also."

"That would not mend matters, Nada," he answered. "For whether you be dead or alive, the hate of Dingaan. Also, Nada, know this: I am not your brother."

When the Lily heard these words she uttered a little cry, and, letting fall the hand of Umslopogaas, clasped mine, shrinking up against me.

"What is this tale, father?" she asked. "He who was my twin, he with whom I have been bred up, says that he has deceived me these many years, that he is not my brother; who, then, is he, father?"

"He is your cousin, Nada."

"Ah," she answered, "I am glad. It would have grieved me had he whom I loved been shown to be but a stranger in whom I have no part," and she smiled a little in the eyes and at the corners of her mouth. "But tell me this tale also."

So I told her the tale of the birth of Umslopogaas, for I trusted her.

"Ah," she said, when I had finished, "ah! you come of a bad stock, Umslopogaas, though it is a kingly one. I shall love you little henceforth, child of the hyena man."

"Then that is bad news," said Umslopogaas, "for know, Nada, I desire now that you should love me more than ever — that you should be my wife and love me as your husband!"

Now the Lily's face grew sad and sweet, and all the hidden mockery went out of her talk — for Nada loved to mock.

"Did you not speak to me on that night in the Halakazi caves, Umslopogaas, of one Zinita, who is your wife, and Inkosikaas of the People of the Axe?"

Then the brow of Umslopogaas darkened: "What of Zinita?" he said. "It is true she is my chieftainess; is it not allowed a man to take more than one wife?"

"So I trust," answered Nada, smiling, "else men would go unwed for long, for few maids would marry them who then must labor alone all their days. But, Umslopogaas, if there are twenty wives, yet one must be first. Now this has come about hitherto: that wherever I have been it has been thrust upon me to be first, and perhaps it might be thus once more — what then, Umslopogaas?"

"Let the fruit ripen before you pluck it, Nada," he answered. "If you love me and will wed me, it is enough."

"I pray that it may not be more than enough," she said, stretching out her hand to him. "Listen, Umslopogaas: ask my father here what were the words I spoke to him many years ago, before I was a woman, when, with my mother, Macropha, I left him to go among the Swazi people. It was after you had been borne away by the lion, Umslopogaas, I told my father that I would marry no man all my life, because I loved only you, who were dead. My father reproached me, saying that I must not speak thus of my brother, but it was my heart which spoke, and it spoke truly; for see, Umslopogaas, you are no brother to me! I have kept that vow. How many men have sort me in wedlock since I became a woman, Umslopogaas? I tell you that they are as the leaves upon a tree.

Yet I have given myself to none, and this has been my fortune: that none have sought to constrain me to marriage. Now I have my reward, for he whom I lost is found again, and to him alone I give my love. Yet, Umslopogaas, beware! Little luck has come to those who have loved me in the past; no, not even to those who have but sought to look on me."

"I will bear the risk, Nada," the Slaughterer answered, and gathering her to his great breast he kissed her.

Presently she slipped from his arms and bade him begone, for she was weary and would rest.

So he went.

Chapter XXXI

THE WAR OF THE WOMEN

*N*ow on the morrow at daybreak, leaving his wolves, Galazi came down from the Ghost Mountain and passed through the gates of the kraal.

In front of my hut he saw Nada the Lily and saluted her, for each remembered the other. Then he walked on to the place of assembly and spoke to me.

"So the Star of Death has risen on the People of the Axe, Mopo," he said. "Was it because of her coming that my grey people howled so strangely last night? I cannot tell, but I know this, the Star shone first on me this morning, and that is my doom. Well, she is fair enough to be the doom of many, Mopo," and he laughed and passed on, swinging the Watcher. But his words troubled me, though they were foolish; for I could not but remember that wherever the beauty of Nada had pleased the sight of men, there men had been given to death.

Then I went to lead Nada to the place of assembly and found her awaiting me. She was dressed now in some woman's garments that I had brought her; her curling hair fell upon her shoulders; on her wrist and neck and knee were bracelets of ivory, and in her hand she bore a lily bloom which she had gathered as she went to bathe in the river. Perhaps she did this, my father, because she wished here, as elsewhere, to be known as the Lily, and it is the Zulu fashion to name people from some such trifle. But who can know a woman's reason, or whether a thing is by chance alone, my father? Also she had begged me of a cape I had; it was cunningly made by Basutus, of the whitest feathers of the ostrich; this she put about her shoulders, and it hung down to her middle. It had been a custom with Nada from childhood not to go about as do other girls, naked except for their girdles, for she would always find some rag or skin to lie upon her breast. Perhaps it was because her skin was fairer than that of other women, or perhaps because she knew that she who hides her beauty often seems the loveliest, or because there was truth in the tale of her white blood and the fashion came to her with the blood. I do not know, my father; at the least she did so.

Now I took Nada by the hand and led her through the morning air to the place of assembly, and ah! she was sweeter than the air and fairer than the dawn.

There were many people in the place of assembly, for it was the day of the monthly meeting of the council of the headmen, and there also were all the women of the kraal, and at their head stood Zinita. Now it had got about that the girl whom the Slaughterer went to seek in the caves of the Halakazi had come to the kraal of the People of the Axe, and all eyes watched for her.

"Wow!" said the men as she passed smiling, looking neither to the right nor to the left, yet seeing all — "Wow! but this flower is fair! Little wonder that the Halakazi died for her!"

The women looked also, but they said nothing of the beauty of Nada; they scarcely seemed to see it.

"That is she for whose sake so many of our people lie unburied," said one.

"Where, then, does she find her fine clothes?" quoth another, "she who came here last night a footsore wanderer?"

"Feathers are not enough for her: look! she must bear flowers also. Surely they are fitter to her hands than the handle of a hoe," said a third.

"Now I think that the chief of the People of the Axe will find one to worship above the axe, and that some will be left mourning," put in a fourth, glancing at Zinita and the other women of the household of the Slaughterer.

Thus they spoke, throwing words like assegais, and Nada heard them all, and knew their meaning, but she never ceased from smiling. Only Zinita said nothing, but stood looking at Nada from beneath her bent brows, while by one hand she held the little daughter of Umslopogaas, her child, and with the other played with the beads about her neck. Presently, we passed her, and Nada, knowing well who this must be, turned her eyes full upon the angry eyes of Zinita, and held them there awhile. Now what there was in the glance of Nada I cannot say, but I know that Zinita, who was afraid of few things, found something to fear in it. At the least, it was she who turned her head away, and the Lily passed on smiling, and greeted Umslopogaas with a little nod.

"Hail, Nada!" said the Slaughterer. Then he turned to his headmen and spoke: "This is she whom we went to the caves of the Halakazi to seek for Dingaan. *Ou!* the story is known now; one told it up at the kraal Umgugundhlovu who shall tell it no more. She prayed me to save her from Dingaan, and so I did, and all would have gone well had it not been for a certain traitor who is done with, for I took another to Dingaan. Look on her now, my friends, and say if I did not well to win her — the Lily flower, such as there is no other in the world, to be the joy of the People of the Axe and a wife to me."

With one accord the headmen answered: "Indeed you did well, Slaughterer," for the glamour of Nada was upon them and they would cherish her as others had cherished her. Only Galazi the Wolf shook his head. But he said nothing, for words do not avail against fate. Now as I found afterwards, since Zinita, the head wife of Umslopogaas, had learned of what stock he was, she had known that Nada was no sister to him. Yet when she heard him declare that he was about to take the Lily to wife she turned upon him, saying: —

"How can this be, Lord?"

"Why do you ask, Zinita?" he answered. "Is it not allowed to a man to take another wife if he will?"

"Surely, Lord," she said; "but men do not wed their sisters, and I have heard that it was because this Nada was your sister that you saved her from Dingaan, and brought the wrath of Dingaan upon the People of the Axe, the wrath that shall destroy them."

"So I thought then, Zinita," he answered; "now I know otherwise. Nada is daughter to Mopo yonder indeed, but he is no father to me, though he has been named so, nor was the mother of Nada my mother. That is so, Councilors."

Then Zinita looked at me and muttered, "O fool of a Mouth, not for nothing did I fear evil at your hands."

I heard the words and took no note, and she poke again to Umslopogaas, saying: "Here is a mystery, O Lord Bulalio. Will it then please you to declare to us who is your father?"

"I have no father," he answered, waxing wroth; "the heavens above are my father. I am born of Blood and Fire, and she, the Lily, is born of Beauty to be my mate. Now, woman, be silent." He thought awhile, and added, "Nay, if you will know, my father was Indabazimbi the Witch-finder, the smeller-out of the king, the son of Arpi." This Umslopogaas said at a hazard, since, having denied me, he must declare a father, and dared not name the Black One who was gone. But in after years the saying was taken up in the land, and it was told that Umslopogaas was the son of Indabazimbi the Witch-finder, who had long ago fled the land; nor did he deny it. For when all this game had been played out he would not have it known that he was the son of Chaka, he who no longer sought to be a king, lest he should bring down the wrath of Panda upon him.

When the people heard this they thought that Umslopogaas mocked Zinita, and yet in his anger he spoke truth when he said first that he was born of the "heavens above," for so we Zulus name the king, and so the witch-doctor Indabazimbi named Chaka on the day of the great smelling out. But they did not take it in this sense. They held that he spoke truly when he gave it out that he was born of Indabazimbi the Witch-doctor, who had fled the land, whither I do not know.

Then Nada turned to Zinita and spoke to her in a sweet and gentle voice: "If I am not sister to Bulalio, yet I shall soon be sister to you who are the Chief's Inkosikaas, Zinita. Shall that not satisfy you, and will you not greet me kindly and with a kiss of peace, who have come from far to be your sister, Zinita?" and Nada held out her hands towards her, though whether she did this from the heart or because she would put herself in the right before the people I do not know. But Zinita scowled, and jerked at her necklace of beads, breaking the string on which they were threaded, so that the beads rolled upon the black earthen floor this way and that.

"Keep your kisses for our lord, girl," Zinita said roughly. "As my beads are scattered so shall you scatter this People of the Axe."

Now Nada turned away with a little sigh, and the people murmured, for they thought that Zinita had treated her badly. Then she stretched out her hand again, and gave the lily in it to Umslopogaas, saying: —

"Here is a token of our betrothal, Lord, for never a head of cattle have my father and I to send — we who are outcasts; and, indeed, the bridegroom must pay the cattle. May I bring you peace and love, my Lord!"

Umslopogaas took the flower, and looked somewhat foolish with it — he who was wont to carry the axe, and not a flower; and so that talk was ended.

Now as it chanced, this was that day of the year when, according to ancient custom, the Holder of the Axe must challenge all and sundry to come up against him to fight in single combat for Groan-Maker and the chieftainship of the people. Therefore, when the talk was done, Umslopogaas rose and went through the challenge, not thinking that any would answer him, since for some years none had dared to stand before his might. Yet three men stepped forward, and of these two were captains, and men whom the Slaughterer loved. With all the people, he looked at them astonished.

"How is this?" he said in a low voice to that captain who was nearest and who would do battle with him.

For answer the man pointed to the Lily, who stood by. Then Umslopogaas understood that because of the medicine of Nada's beauty all men desired to win her, and, since he who could win the axe would take her also, he must look to fight with many. Well, fight he must or be shamed.

Of the fray there is little to tell. Umslopogaas killed first one man and then the other, and swiftly, for, growing fearful, the third did not come up against him.

"Ah!" said Galazi, who watched, "what did I tell you, Mopo? The curse begins to work. Death walks ever with that daughter of yours, old man."

"I fear so," I answered, "and yet the maiden is fair and good and sweet."

"That will not mend matters," said Galazi.

Now on that day Umslopogaas took Nada the Lily to wife, and for awhile there was peace and quiet. But this evil thing came upon Umslopogaas, that, from the day when he wedded Nada, he hated even to look upon Zinita, and not at her alone, but on all his other wives also. Galazi said it was because Nada had bewitched him, but I know well that the only witcheries she used were the medicine of her eyes, her beauty, and her love. Still, it came to pass that henceforward, and until she had long been dead, the Slaughterer loved her, and her alone, and that is a strange sickness to come upon a man.

As may be guessed, my father, Zinita and the other women took this ill. They waited awhile, indeed, thinking that it would wear away, then they began to murmur, both to their husband and in the ears of other people, till at length there were two parties in the town, the party of Zinita and the party of Nada.

The party of Zinita was made up of women and of certain men who loved and feared their wives, but that of Nada was the greatest, and it was all of men, with Umslopogaas at the head of them, and from this division came much bitterness abroad, and quarreling in the huts. Yet neither the Lily nor Umslopogaas heeded it greatly, nor indeed, anything, so lost and well content were they in each other's love.

Now on a certain morning, after they had been married three full moons, Nada came from her husband's hut when the sun was already high, and went down through the rock gully to the river to bathe. On the right of the path to the river lay the mealie-fields of the chief, and in them labored Zinita and the other women of Umslopogaas, weeding the mealie-plants. They looked up and saw Nada pass, then worked on sullenly. After awhile they saw her come again fresh from the bath, very fair to see, and having flowers twined among her hair, and as she walked she sang a song of love. Now Zinita cast down her hoe.

"Is this to be borne, my sisters?" she said.

"No," answered another, "it is not to be borne. What shall we do — shall we fall upon her and kill her now?"

"It would be more just to kill Bulalio, our lord," answered Zinita. "Nada is but a woman, and, after the fashion of us women, takes all that she can gather. But he is a man and a chief, and should know wisdom and justice."

"She has bewitched him with her beauty. Let us kill her," said the other women.

"Nay," answered Zinita, "I will speak with her," and she went and stood in the path along which the Lily walked singing, her arms folded across her breast.

Now Nada saw her and, ceasing her song, stretched out her hand to welcome her, saying, "Greeting, sister." But Zinita did not take it. "It is not fitting, sister," she said, "that my hand, stained with toil, should defile yours, fresh with the scent of flowers. But I am charged with a message, on my own behalf and the behalf of the other wives of our Lord Bulalio; the weeds grow thick in yonder corn, and we women are few; now that your love days are over, will not you come and help us? If you brought no hoe from your Swazi home, surely we will buy you one."

Now Nada saw what was meant, and the blood poured to her head. Yet she answered calmly: —

"I would willingly do this, my sister, though I have never labored in the fields, for wherever I have dwelt the men have kept me back from all work, save such as the weaving of flowers or the stringing of beads. But there is this against it — Umslopogaas, my husband, charged me that I should not toil with my hands, and I may not disobey my husband."

"Our husband charged you so, Nada? Nay, then it is strange. See, now, I am his head wife, his Inkosikaas — it was I who taught him how to win the axe. Yet he has laid no command on me that I should not labor in the fields after the fashion of women, I who have borne him children; nor, indeed, has he laid such a command upon any of our sisters, his other wives. Can it then be that Bulalio loves you better than us, Nada?"

Now the Lily was in a trap, and she knew it. So she grew bold.

"One must be most loved, Zinita," she said, "as one must be most fair. You have had your hour, leave me mine; perhaps it will be short. Moreover this: Umslopogaas and I loved each other much long years before you or any of his wives saw him, and we love each other to the end. There is no more to say."

"Nay, Nada, there is still something to say; there is this to say: Choose one of two things. Go and leave us to be happy with our lord, or stay and bring death on all."

Now Nada thought awhile, and answered: "Did I believe that my love would bring death on him I love, it might well chance that I would go and leave him, though to do so would be to die. But, Zinita, I do not believe it. Death chiefly loves the weak, and if he falls it will be on the Flower, not on the Slayer of Men," and she slipped past Zinita and went on, singing no more.

Zinita watched her till she was over the ridge, and her face grew evil as she watched. Then she returned to the women.

"The Lily flouts us all, my sisters," she said. "Now listen: my counsel is that we declare a feast of women to be held at the new moon in a secret place far away. All the women and the children shall come to it except Nada, who will not leave her lover, and if there be any man whom a woman loves, perhaps, my sisters, that man would do well to go on a journey about the time of the new moon, for evil things may happen at the town of the People of the Axe while we are away celebrating our feast."

"What, then, shall befall, my sister?" asked one.

"Nay, how can I tell?" she answered. "I only know that we are minded to be rid of Nada, and thus to be avenged on a man who has scorned our love — aye, and on those men who follow after the beauty of Nada. Is it not so, my sisters?"

"It is so," they answered.

"Then be silent on the matter, and let us give out our feast."

Now Nada told Umslopogaas of those words which she had bandied with Zinita, and the Slaughterer was troubled. Yet, because of his foolishness and of the medicine of Nada's eyes, he would not turn from his way, and was ever at her side, thinking of little else except of her. Thus, when Zinita came to him, and asked leave to declare a feast of women that should be held far away, he consented, and gladly, for, above all things, he desired to be free from Zinita and her angry looks for awhile; nor did he suspect a plot. Only he told her that Nada should not go to the feast; and in a breath both Zinita and Nada answered that is word was their will, as indeed it was, in this matter.

Now I, Mopo, saw the glamour that had fallen upon my fosterling, and spoke of it with Galazi, saying that a means must be found to wake him. Then I took Galazi fully into my mind, and told him all that he did not know of Umslopogaas, and that was little. Also, I told him of my plans to bring the Slaughterer to the throne, and of what I had done to that end, and of what I proposed to do, and this was to go in person on a journey to certain of the great chiefs and win them over.

Galazi listened, and said that it was well or ill, as the chance might be. For his part, he believed that the daughter would pull down faster than I, the father, could build up, and he pointed to Nada, who walked past us, following Umslopogaas.

Yet I determined to go, and that was on the day before Zinita won leave to celebrate the feast of women. So I sought Umslopogaas and told him, and he listened indifferently, for he would be going after Nada, and wearied of my talk of policy. I bade him farewell and left him; to Nada also I bade farewell. She kissed me, yet the name of her husband was mingled with her good-bye.

"Now madness has come upon these two," I said to myself. "Well, it will wear off, they will be changed before I come again."

I guessed little, my father, how changed they would be.

Chapter XXXII
ZINITA COMES TO THE KING

Dingaan the king sat upon a day in the kraal Umgugundhlovu, waiting till his *impis* should return from the Income that is now named the Blood River. He had sent them thither to destroy the laager of the Boers, and thence, as he thought, they would presently return with victory. Idly he sat in the kraal, watching the vultures wheel above the Hill of Slaughter, and round him stood a regiment.

"My birds are hungry," he said to a councilor.

"Doubtless there shall soon be meat to feed them, O King!" the councilor answered.

As he spoke one came near, saying that a woman sought leave to speak to the king upon some great matter.

"Let her come," he answered; "I am sick for tidings, perhaps she can tell of the *impi.*"

Presently the woman was led in. She was tall and fair, and she held two children by the hand.

"What is thine errand?" asked Dingaan.

"Justice, O King," she answered.

"Ask for blood, it shall be easier to find."

"I ask blood, O King."

"The blood of whom?"

"The blood of Bulalio the Slaughterer, Chief of the People of the Axe, the blood of Nada the Lily, and of all those who cling to her."

Now Dingaan sprang up and swore an oath by the head of the Black One who was gone.

"What?" he cried, "does the Lily, then, live as the soldier thought?"

"She lives, O King. She is wife to the Slaughterer, and because of her witchcraft he has put me, his first wife, away against all law and honor. Therefore I ask vengeance on the witch and vengeance also on him who was my husband."

"Thou art a good wife," said the king. "May my watching spirit save me from such a one. Hearken! I would gladly grant thy desire, for I, too, hate this Slaughterer, and I, too, would crush this Lily. Yet, woman, thou comest in a bad hour. Here I have but one regiment, and I think that the Slaughterer may take some killing. Wait till my *impis* return from wiping out the white Amaboona, and it shall be as thou dost desire. Whose are those children?"

"They are my children and the children of Bulalio, who was my husband."

"The children of him whom thou wouldst cause to be slain."

"Yea, King."

"Surely, woman, thou art as good a mother as wife!" said Dingaan. "Now I have spoken — begone!"

But the heart of Zinita was hungry for vengeance, vengeance swift and terrible, on the Lily, who lay in her place, and on her husband, who had thrust her aside for the Lily's sake. She did not desire to wait — no, not even for an hour.

"Hearken, O King!" she cried, "the tale is not yet all told. This man, Bulalio, plots against thy throne with Mopo, son of Makedama, who was thy councilor."

"He plots against my throne, woman? The lizard plots against the cliff on which it suns itself? Then let him plot; and as for Mopo, I will catch him yet!"

"Yes, O King! but that is not all the tale. This man has another name — he is named Umslopogaas, son of Mopo. But he is no son of Mopo: he is son to the Black One who is dead, the mighty king who was thy brother, by Baleka, sister to Mopo. Yes, I know it from the lips of Mopo. I know all the tale. He is heir to thy throne by blood, O King, and thou sittest in his place."

For a little while Dingaan sat astounded. Then he commanded Zinita to draw near and tell him that tale.

Now behind the stool on which he sat stood two councilors, nobles whom Dingaan loved, and these alone had heard the last words of Zinita. He bade these nobles stand in front of him, out of earshot and away from every other man. Then Zinita drew near, and told Dingaan the tale of the birth of Umslopogaas and all that followed, and, by many a token and many a deed of Chaka's which he remembered, Dingaan the king knew that it was a true story.

When at length she had done, he summoned the captain of the regiment that stood around: he was a great man named Faku, and he also summoned certain men who do the king's bidding. To the captain of the *impi* he spoke sharply, saying: —

"Take three companies and guides, and come by night to the town of the People of the Axe, that is by Ghost Mountain, and burn it, and slay all the wizards who sleep therein. Most of all, slay the Chief of the People, who is named Bulalio the Slaughterer or Umslopogaas. Kill him by torture if you may, but kill him and bring his head to me. Take that wife of his, who is known as Nada the Lily, alive if ye can, and bring her to me, for I would cause her to be slain here. Bring the cattle also. Now go, and go swiftly, this hour. If ye return having failed in one jot of my command, ye die, every one of you — ye die, and slowly. Begone!"

The captain saluted, and, running to his regiment, issued a command. Three full companies leapt forward at his word, and ran after him through the gates of the kraal Umgugundhlovu, heading for the Ghost Mountain.

Then Dingaan called to those who do the king's bidding, and, pointing to the two nobles, his councilors, who had heard the words of Zinita, commanded that they should be killed.

The nobles heard, and, having saluted the king, covered their faces, knowing that they must die because they had learned too much. So they were killed. Now it was one of these councilors who had said that doubtless meat would soon be found to feed the king's birds.

Then the king commanded those who do his bidding that they should take the children of Zinita and make away with them.

But when Zinita heard this she cried aloud, for she loved her children. Then Dingaan mocked her.

"What?" he said, "art thou a fool as well as wicked? Thou sayest that thy husband, whom thou hast given to death, is born of one who is dead, and is heir to my throne. Thou sayest also that these children are born of him; therefore, when he is dead, they will be heirs to my throne. Am I then mad that I should suffer them to live? Woman, thou hast fallen into thine own trap. Take them away!"

Now Zinita tasted of the cup which she had brewed for other lips, and grew distraught in her misery, and wrung her hands, crying that she repented her of the evil and would warn Umslopogaas and the Lily of that which awaited them. And she turned to run towards the gates. But the king laughed and nodded, and they brought her back, and presently she was dead also.

Thus, then, my father, prospered the wickedness of Zinita, the head wife of Umslopogaas, my fosterling.

Now these were the last slayings that were wrought at the kraal Umgugundhlovu, for just as Dingaan had made an end of them and once more grew weary, he lifted his eyes and saw the hillsides black with men, who by their dress were of his own *impi* — men whom he had sent out against the Boers.

And yet where was the proud array, where the plumes and shields, where the song of victory? Here, indeed, were soldiers, but they walked in groups like women and hung their heads like chidden children.

Then he learned the truth. The *impi* had been defeated by the banks of the Income; thousands had perished at the laager, mowed down by the guns of the Boers, thousands more had been drowned in the Income, till the waters were red and the bodies of the slain pushed each other under, and those who still lived walked upon them.

Dingaan heard, and was seized with fear, for it was said that the Amaboona followed fast on the track of the conquered.

That day he fled to the bush on the Black Umfolozi river, and that night the sky was crimson with the burning of the kraal Umgugund-hlovu, where the Elephant should trumpet no more, and the vultures were scared from the Hill of Slaughter by the roaring of the flames.

Galazi sat on the lap of the stone Witch, gazing towards the wide plains below, that were yet white with the moon, though the night grew towards the morning. Greysnout whined at his side, and Deathgrip thrust his muzzle into his hand; but Galazi took no heed, for he was brooding on the fall of Umslopogaas from the man that he had been to the level of a woman's slave, and on the breaking up of the People of the Axe, because of the coming of Nada. For all the women and the children were gone to this Feast of Women, and would not return for long, and it seemed to Galazi that many of the men had slipped away also, as though they smelt some danger from afar.

"Ah, Deathgrip," said Galazi aloud to the wild brute at his side, "changed is the Wolf King my brother, all changed because of a woman's kiss. Now he hunts no more, no more shall Groan-Maker be aloft; it is a woman's kiss he craves, not the touch of your rough tongue, it is a woman's hand he holds, not the smooth haft of horn, he, who of all men, was the fiercest and the first; for this last shame has overtaken him. Surely Chaka was a great king though an evil, and he showed his greatness when he forbade marriage to the warriors, marriage that makes the heart soft and turns blood to water."

Now Galazi ceased, and gazed idly towards the kraal of the People of the Axe, and as he looked his eyes caught a gleam of light that seemed to travel in and out of the edge of the shadow of Ghost Mountain as a woman's needle travels through a skin, now seen and now lost in the skin.

He started and watched. Ah! there the light came out from the shadow. Now, by Chaka's head, it was the light of spears!

One moment more Galazi watched. It was a little *impi*, perhaps they numbered two hundred men, running silently, but not to battle, for they wore no plumes. Yet they went out to kill, for they ran in companies, and each man carried assegais and a shield.

Now Galazi had heard tell of such *impis* that hunt by night, and he knew well that these were the king's dogs, and their game was men, a big kraal of sleeping men, otherwise there had been fewer dogs. Is a whole pack sent out to catch an antelope on its form? Galazi wondered whom they sought. Ah! now they turned to the ford, and he knew. It was his brother Umslopogaas and Nada the Lily and the People of the Axe. These were the king's dogs, and Zinita had let them slip. For this reason she had called a feast of women, and taken the children with her; for this reason so many had been summoned from the kraal by one means or another: it was that they might escape the slaughter.

Galazi bounded to his feet. For one moment he thought. Might not these hunters be hunted? Could he not destroy them by the jaws of the wolves as once before they had destroyed a certain *impi* of the king's? Aye, if he had seen them but one hour before, then scarcely a man of them should have lived to reach the stream, for he would have waylaid them with his wolves. But now it might not be; the soldiers neared the ford, and Galazi knew well that his grey people would not hunt on the further plain, though for this he had heard one reason only, that which was given him by the lips of the dead in a dream.

What, then, might be done? One thing alone: warn Umslopogaas. Yet how? For him who could swim a rushing river, there was, indeed, a swifter way to the place of the People of the Axe — a way that was to the path of the *impi* as is the bow-string to the strung bow. And yet they had traveled well-nigh half the length of the bow. Still, he might do it, he whose feet were the swiftest in the land, except those of Umslopogaas. At the least, he would try. Mayhap, the *impi* would tarry to drink at the ford.

So Galazi thought in his heart, and his thought was swift as the light. Then with a bound he was away down the mountain side. From boulder to boulder he leapt like a buck, he crashed through the brake like a bull, he skimmed the level like a swallow. The mountain was traveled now; there in front of him lay the yellow river foaming in its flood, so he had swum it before when he went to see the dead. Ah! a good leap far out into the torrent; it was strong, but he breasted it. He was through, he stood upon the bank shaking the water from him like a dog, and now he was away up the narrow gorge of stones to the long slope, running low as his wolves ran.

Before him lay the town — one side shone silver with the sinking moon, one was grey with the breaking dawn. Ah! they were there, he saw them moving through the grass by the eastern gate; he saw the long lines of slayers creep to the left and the right.

How could he pass them before the circle of death was drawn? Six spear-throws to run, and they had but such a little way! The mealie-plants were tall, and at a spot they almost touched the fence. Up the path! Could Umslopogaas, his brother, move more fast, he wondered, than the Wolf who sped to save him? He was there, hidden by the mealie stalks, and there, along the fence to the right and to the left, the slayers crept!

"Wow! What was that?" said one soldier of the king to another man as they joined their guard completing the death circle. "Wow! something great and black crashed through the fence before me."

"I heard it, brother," answered the other man. "I heard it, but I saw nothing. It must have been a dog: no man could leap so high."

"More like a wolf," said the first; "at the least, let us pray that it was not an *Esedowan** who will put us into the hole in its back. Is your fire ready, brother? Wow! these wizards shall wake warm; the signal should be soon."

Then arose the sound of a great voice crying, "Awake, ye sleepers, the foe is at your gates!"

---

* A fabulous animal, reported by the Zulus to carry off human beings in a hole in its back.

Chapter XXXIII
THE END OF THE PEOPLE, BLACK AND GREY

Galazi rushed through the town crying aloud, and behind him rose a stir of men. All slept and no sentinels were set, for Umslopogaas was so lost in his love for Lily that he forgot his wisdom, and thought no more of war or death or of the hate of Dingaan. Presently the Wolf came to the large new hut which Umslopogaas had caused to be built for Nada the Lily, and entered it, for there he knew that he should find his brother Bulalio. On the far side of the hut the two lay sleeping, and the head of Umslopogaas rested on the Lily's breast, and by his side gleamed the great axe Groan-Maker.

"Awake!" cried the Wolf.

Now Umslopogaas sprang to his feet grasping at his axe, but Nada threw her arms wide, murmuring; "Let me sleep on, sweet is sleep."

"Sound shall ye sleep, anon!" gasped Galazi. "Swift, brother, bind on the wolf's hide, take shield! Swift, I say – for the Slayers of the king are at your gates!"

Now Nada sprang up also, and they did his bidding like people in a dream; and, while they found their garments and a shield, Galazi took beer and drank it, and got his breath again. They stood without the hut. Now the heaven was grey, and east and west and north and south tongues of flame shot up against the sky, for the town had been fired by the Slayers.

Umslopogaas looked and his sense came back to him: he understood. "Which way, brother?" he said.

"Through the fire and the *impi* to our Grey People on the mountain," said Galazi. "There, if we can win it, we shall find succor."

"What of my people in the kraal," asked Umslopogaas.

"They are not many, brother; the women and the children are gone. I have roused the men – most will escape. Hence, ere we burn!"

Now they ran towards the fence, and as they went men joined them to the number of ten, half awakened, fear-stricken, armed — some with spears, some with clubs — and for the most part naked. They sped on together towards the fence of the town that was now but a ring of fire, Umslopogaas and Galazi in front, each holding the Lily by a hand. They neared the fence — from without came the shouts of the Slayers — lo! it was afire. Nada shrank back in fear, but Umslopogaas and Galazi dragged her on. They rushed at the blazing fence, smiting with axe and club. It broke before them, they were through but little harmed. Without were a knot of the Slayers, standing back a small space because of the heat of the flames. The Slayers saw them, and crying, "This is Bulalio, kill the wizard!" sprang towards them with uplifted spears. Now the People of the Axe made a ring round Nada, and in the front of it were Umslopogaas and Galazi. Then they rushed on and met those of the Slayers who stood before them, and the men of Dingaan were swept away and scattered by Groan-Maker and the Watcher, as dust is swept of a wind, as grass is swept by a sickle.

They were through with only one man slain, but the cry went up that the chief of the wizards and the Lily, his wife, had fled. Then, as it was these whom he was chiefly charged to kill, the captain called off the *impi* from watching for the dwellers in the town, and started in pursuit of Umslopogaas. Now, at this time nearly a hundred men of the People of the Axe had been killed and of the Slayers some fifty men, for, having been awakened by the crying of Galazi, the soldiers of the axe fought bravely, though none saw where his brother stood, and none knew whither their chief had fled except those ten who went with the brethren.

Meanwhile, the Wolf-Brethren and those with them were well away, and it had been easy for them to escape, who were the swiftest-footed of any in the land. But the pace of a regiment is the pace of its slowest-footed soldier, and Nada could not run with the Wolf-Brethren. Yet they made good speed, and were halfway down the gorge that led to the river before the companies of Dingaan poured into it. Now they came to the end of it, and the foe was near — this end of the gorge is narrow, my father, like the neck of a gourd — then Galazi stopped and spoke: —

"Halt! ye People of the Axe," he said, "and let us talk awhile with these who follow till we get our breath again. But you, my brother, pass the river with the Lily in your hand. We will join you in the forest; but if perchance we cannot find you, you know what must be done: set the Lily in the cave, then return and call up the grey *impi*. Wow! my brother, I must find you if I may, for if these men of Dingaan have a mind for sport there shall be such a hunting on the Ghost Mountain as the old Witch has not seen. Go now, my brother!"

"It is not my way to turn and run while others stand and fight," growled Umslopogaas; "yet, because of Nada, it seems that I must."

"Oh! heed me not, my love," said Nada, "I have brought thee sorrow — I am weary, let me die; kill me and save yourselves!"

For answer, Umslopogaas took her by the hand and fled towards the river; but before he reached it he heard the sounds of the fray, the war-cry of the Slayers as they poured upon the People of the Axe, the howl of his brother, the Wolf, when the battle joined — aye, and the crash of the Watcher as the blow went home.

"Well bitten, Wolf!" he said, stopping; "that one shall need no more; oh! that I might" — but again he looked at Nada, and sped on.

Now they had leaped into the foaming river, and here it was well that the Lily could swim, else both had been lost. But they won through and passed forward to the mountain's flank. Here they walked on among the trees till the forest was almost passed, and at length Umslopogaas heard the howling of a wolf.

Then he must set Nada on his shoulders and carry her as once Galazi had carried another, for it was death for any except the Wolf-Brethren to walk on the Ghost Mountain when the wolves were awake.

Presently the wolves flocked around him, and leaped upon him in joy, glaring with fierce eyes at her who sat upon his shoulders. Nada saw them, and almost fell from her seat, fainting with fear, for they were many and dreadful, and when they howled her blood turned to ice.

But Umslopogaas cheered her, telling her that these were his dogs with whom he went out hunting, and with whom he should hunt presently. At length they came to the knees of the Old Witch and the entrance to the cave. It was empty except for a wolf or two, for Galazi abode here seldom now; but when he was on the mountain would sleep in the forest, which was nearer the kraal of his brother the Slaughterer.

"Here you must stay, sweet," said Umslopogaas when he had driven out the wolves. "Here you must rest till this little matter of the Slayers is finished. Would that we had brought food, but we had little time to seek it! See, now I will show you the secret of the stone; thus far I will push it, no farther. Now a touch only is needed to send it over the socket and home; but then they must be two strong men who can pull it back again. Therefore push it no farther except in the utmost need, lest it remain where it fall, whether you will it or not. Have no fear, you are safe here; none know of this place except Galazi, myself and the wolves, and none shall find it. Now I must be going to find Galazi, if he still lives; if not, to make what play I can against the Slayers, alone with the wolves."

Now Nada wept, saying that she feared to be left, and that she should never see him more, and her grief rung his heart. Nevertheless, Umslopogaas kissed her and went, closing the stone after him in that fashion of which he had spoken. When the stone was shut the cave was almost dark, except for a ray of light that entered by a hole little larger than a man's hand, that, looked at from within, was on the right of the stone. Nada sat herself so that this ray struck full on her, for she loved light, and without it she would pine as flowers do. There she sat and thought in the darksome cave, and was filled with fear and sorrow. And while she brooded thus, suddenly the ray went out, and she heard a noise as of some beast that smells at prey. She looked, and in the gloom she saw the sharp nose and grinning fangs of a wolf that were thrust towards her through the little hole.

Nada cried aloud in fear, and the fangs were snatched back, but presently she heard a scratching without the cave, and saw the stone shake. Then she thought in her foolishness that the wolf knew how to open the stone, and that he would do this, and devour her, for she had heard the tale that all these wolves were the ghosts of evil men, having the understanding of men. So, in her fear and folly, she seized the rock and dragged on it as Umslopogaas had shown her how to do. It shook, it slipped over the socket ledge, and rolled home like a pebble down the mouth of a gourd.

"Now I am safe from the wolves," said Nada. "See, I cannot so much as stir the stone from within." And she laughed a little, then ceased from laughing and spoke again. "Yet it would be ill if Umslopogaas came back no more to roll away that rock, for then I should be like one in a grave — as one who is placed in a grave being yet strong and quick." She shuddered as she thought of it, but presently started up and set her ear to the hole to listen, for from far down the mountain there rose a mighty howling and a din of men.

When Umslopogaas had shut the cave, he moved swiftly down the mountain, and with him went certain of the wolves; not all, for he had not summoned them. His heart was heavy, for he feared that Galazi was no more. Also he was mad with rage, and plotted in himself to destroy the Slayers of the king, every man of them; but first he must learn what they would do. Presently, as he wended, he heard a long, low howl far away in the forest; then he rejoiced, for he knew the call — it was the call of Galazi, who had escaped the spears of the Slayers.

Swiftly he ran, calling in answer. He won the place. There, seated on a stone, resting himself, was Galazi, and round him surged the numbers of the Grey People. Umslopogaas came to him and looked at him, for he seemed somewhat weary. There were flesh wounds on his great breast and arms, the little shield was well-nigh hewn to strips, and the Watcher showed signs of war.

"How went it, brother?" asked Umslopogaas.

"Not so ill, but all those who stood with me in the way are dead, and with them a few of the foe. I alone am fled like a coward. They came on us thrice, but we held them back till the Lily was safe; then, all our men being down, I ran, Umslopogaas, and swam the torrent, for I was minded to die here in my own place."

Now, though he said little of it, I must tell you, my father, that Galazi had made a great slaughter there in the neck of the donga. Afterwards I counted the slain, and they were many; the nine men of the People of the Axe were hidden in them.

"Perhaps it shall be the Slayers who die, brother."

"Perhaps, at least, there shall be death for some. Still it is in my mind, Slaughterer, that our brotherhood draws to an end, for the fate of him who bears the Watcher, and which my father foretold, is upon me. If so, farewell. While it lasted our friendship has been good, and its ending shall be good. Moreover, it would have endured for many a year to come had you not sought, Slaughterer, to make good better, and to complete our joy of fellowship and war with the love of women. From that source flow these ills, as a river from a spring; but so it was fated. If I fall in this fray may you yet live on to fight in many another, and at the last to die gloriously with axe aloft; and may you find a brisker man and a better Watcher to serve you in your need. Should you fall and I live on, I promise this: I will avenge you to the last and guard the Lily whom you love, offering her comfort, but no more. Now the foe draws on, they have traveled round about by the ford, for they dared not face the torrent, and they cried to me that they are sworn to slay us or be slain, as Dingaan, the king, commanded. So the fighting will be of the best, if, indeed, they do not run before the fangs of the Grey People. Now, Chief, speak your word that I may obey it."

Thus Galazi spoke in the circle of the wolves, while Umslopogaas leaned upon his Axe Groan-Maker, and listened to him, aye, and wept as he listened, for after the Lily and me, Mopo, he loved Galazi most dearly of all who lived. Then he answered: —

"Were it not for one in the cave above, who is helpless and tender, I would swear to you, Wolf, that if you fall, on your carcass I will die; and I do swear that, should you fall, while I live Groan-Maker shall be busy from year to year till every man of yonder *impi* is as you are. Perchance I did ill, Galazi, when first I hearkened to the words of Zinita and

suffered women to come between us. May we one day find a land where
there are no women, and war only, for in that land we shall grow great.
But now, at the least, we will make a good end to this fellowship, and
the Grey People shall fight their fill, and the old Witch who sits aloft
waiting for the world to die shall smile to see that fight, if she never
smiled before. This is my word: that we fall upon the men of Dingaan
twice, once in the glade of the forest whither they will come presently,
and, if we are beaten back, then we must stand for the last time on the
knees of the Witch in front of the cave where Nada is. Say, Wolf, will
the Grey Folk fight?"

"To the last, brother, so long as one is left to lead them, after that I
do not know! Still they have only fangs to set against spears. Slaughterer,
your plan is good. Come, I am rested."

So they rose and numbered their flock, and all were there, though it
was not as it had been years ago when first the Wolf-Brethren hunted
on Ghost Mountain; for many of the wolves had died by men's spears
when they harried the kraals of men, and no young were born to them.
Then, as once before, the pack was halved, and half, the she-wolves, went
with Umslopogaas, and half, the dog-wolves, went with Galazi.

Now they passed down the forest paths and hid in the tangle of the
thickets at the head of the darksome glen, one on each side of the glen.
Here they waited till they heard the footfall of the *impi* of the king's
Slayers, as it came slowly along seeking them. In front of the *impi* went
two soldiers watching for an ambush, and these two men were the same
who had talked together that dawn when Galazi sprang between them.
Now also they spoke as they peered this way and that; then, seeing
nothing, stood awhile in the mouth of the glen waiting the coming of
their company; and their words came to the ears of Umslopogaas.

"An awful place this, my brother," said one. "A place full of ghosts
and strange sounds, of hands that seem to press us back, and whinings
as of invisible wolves. It is named Ghost Mountain, and well named.
Would that the king had found other business for us than the slaying
of these sorcerers — for they are sorcerers indeed, and this is the home
of their sorceries. Tell me, brother, what was that which leaped between
us this morning in the dark! I say it was a wizard. Wow! they are all
wizards. Could any who was but a man have done the deeds which he
who is named the Wolf wrought down by the river yonder, and then
have escaped? Had the Axe but stayed with the Club they would have
eaten up our *impi*."

"The Axe had a woman to watch," laughed the other. "Yes, it is true
this is a place of wizards and evil things. Methinks I see the red eyes of
the *Esedowana* glaring at us through the dark of the trees and smell their

smell. Yet these wizards must be caught, for know this, my brother: if we return to Umgugundhlovu with the king's command undone, then there are stakes hardening in the fire of which we shall taste the point. If we are all killed in the catching, and some, it seems, are missing already, yet they must be caught. Say, my brother, shall we draw on? The *impi* is nigh. Would that Faku, our captain yonder, might find two others to take our place, for in this thicket I had rather run last than first. Well, here leads the spoor — a wondrous mass of wolf-spoor mixed with the footprints of men; perhaps they are sometimes the one and sometimes the other — who knows, my brother? It is a land of ghosts and wizards. Let us on! Let us on!"

Now all this while the Wolf-Brethren had much ado to keep their people quiet, for their mouths watered and their eyes shone at the sight of the men, and at length it could be done no more, for with a howl a single she-wolf rushed from her laid and leapt at the throat of the man who spoke, nor did she miss her grip. Down went wolf and man, rolling together on the ground, and there they killed each other.

"The *Esedowana!* the *Esedowana* are upon us!" cried the other scout, and, turning, fled towards the *impi*. But he never reached it, for with fearful howlings the ghost-wolves broke their cover and rushed on him from the right and the left, and lo! there was nothing of him left except his spear alone.

Now a low cry of fear rose from the *impi*, and some turned to fly, but Faku, the captain, a great and brave man, shouted to them, "Stand firm, children of the king, stand firm, these are no *Esedowana*, these are but the Wolf-Brethren and their pack. What! will ye run from dogs, ye who have laughed at the spears of men? Ring round! Stand fast!"

The soldiers heard the voice of their captain, and they obeyed his voice, forming a double circle, a ring within a ring. They looked to the right, there, Groan-Maker aloft, the wolf fangs on his brow, the worn wolf-hide streaming on the wind, Bulalio rushed upon them like a storm, and with him came his red-eyed company. They looked to the left — ah, well they know that mighty Watcher! Have they not heard his strokes down by the river, and well they know the giant who wields it like a wand, the Wolf King, with the strength of ten! Wow! They are here! See the people black and grey, hear them howl their war-chant! Look how they leap like water — leap in a foam of fangs against the hedge of spears! The circle is broken; Groan-Maker has broken it! Ha! Galazi also is through the double ring; now must men stand back to back or perish!

How long did it last? Who can say? Time flies fast when blows fall thick. At length the brethren are beaten back; they break out as they broke in, and are gone, with such of their wolf-folk as were left alive.

Yet that *impi* was somewhat the worse, but one-third of those lived who
looked on the sun without the forest; the rest lay smitten, torn, mangled,
dead, hidden under the heaps of bodies of wild beasts.

"Now this is a battle of evil spirits that live in the shapes of wolves,
and as for the Wolf-Brethren, they are sorcerers of the rarest," said Faku
the captain, "and such sorcerers I love, for they fight furiously. Yet I will
slay them or be slain. At the least, if there be few of us left, the most of
the wolves are dead also, and the arms of the wizards grow weary."

So he moved forward up the mountain with those of the soldiers
who remained, and all the way the wolves harried them, pulling down
a man here and a man there; but though they heard and saw them
cheering on their pack the Wolf-Brethren attacked them no more, for
they saved their strength for the last fight of all.

The road was long up the mountain, and the soldiers knew little of
the path, and ever the ghost-wolves harried on their flanks. So it was
evening before they came to the feet of the stone Witch, and began to
climb to the platform of her knees. There, on her knees as it were, they
saw the Wolf-Brethren standing side by side, such a pair as were not
elsewhere in the world, and they seemed afire, for the sunset beat upon
them, and the wolves crept round their feet, red with blood and fire.

"A glorious pair!" quoth great Faku; "would that I fought with them
rather than against them! Yet, they must die!" Then he began to climb
to the knees of the Witch.

Now Umslopogaas glanced up at the stone face of her who sat aloft,
and it was alight with the sunset.

"Said I not that the old Witch should smile at this fray?" he cried.
"Lo! she smiles! Up, Galazi, let us spend the remnant of our people on
the foe, and fight this fight out, man to man, with no beast to spoil it!
Ho! Blood and Greysnout! ho! Deathgrip! ho! wood-dwellers grey and
black, at them, my children!"

The wolves heard; they were few and they were sorry to see, with
weariness and wounds, but still they were fierce. With a howl, for the
last time they leaped down upon the foe, tearing, harrying, and killing
till they themselves were dead by the spear, every one of them except
Deathgrip, who crept back sorely wounded to die with Galazi.

"Now I am a chief without a people," cried Galazi. "Well, it has been
my lot in life. So it was in the Halakazi kraals, so it is on Ghost
Mountain at the last, and so also shall it be even for the greatest kings
when they come to their ends, seeing that they, too, must die alone. Say,
Slaughterer, choose where you will stand, to the left or to the right."

Now, my father, the track below separated, because of a boulder, and
there were two little paths which led to the platform of the Witch's knees

with, perhaps, ten paces between them. Umslopogaas guarded the left-hand path and Galazi took the right. Then they waited, having spears in their hands. Presently the soldiers came round the rock and rushed up against them, some on one path and some on the other.

Then the brethren hurled their spears at them and killed three men. Now the assegais were done, and the foe was on them. Umslopogaas bends forward, his long arm shoots out, the axe gleams, and a man who came on falls back.

"One!" cries Umslopogaas.

"One, my brother!" answers Galazi, as he draws back the Watcher from his blow.

A soldier rushes forward, singing. To and fro he moves in front of Umslopogaas, his spear poised to strike. Groan-Maker swoops down, but the man leaps back, the blow misses, and the Slaughterer's guard is down.

"A poor stroke, Sorcerer!" cries the man as he rushes in to stab him. Lo! the axe wheels in the air, it circles swiftly low down by the ground; it smites upward. Before the spearman can strike the horn of Groan-Maker has sped from chin to brain.

"But a good return, fool!" says Umslopogaas.

"Two!" cries Galazi, from the right.

"Two! my brother," answers Umslopogaas.

Again two men come on, one against each, to find no better luck. The cry of "Three!" passes from brother to brother, and after it rises the cry of "Four!"

Now Faku bids the men who are left to hold their shields together and push the two from the mouths of the paths, and this they do, losing four more men at the hands of the brethren before it is done.

"Now we are on the open! Ring them round and down with them!" cries Faku.

But who shall ring round Groan-Maker that shines on all sides at once, Groan-Maker who falls heavily no more, but pecks and pecks and pecks like a wood-bird on a tree, and never pecks in vain? Who shall ring round those feet swifter than the Sassaby of the plains? Wow! He is here! He is there! He is a sorcerer! Death is in his hand, and death looks out of his eyes!

Galazi lives yet, for still there comes the sound of the Watcher as it thunders on the shields, and the Wolf's hoarse cry of the number of the slain. He has a score of wounds, yet he fights on! his leg is almost hewn from him with an axe, yet he fights on! His back is pierced again and again, yet he fights on! But two are left alive before him, one twists round and spears him from behind. He heeds it not, but smites down the foe in front. Then he turns and, whirling the Watcher on high, brings him down for the last time, and so mightily that the man before him is crushed like an egg.

Galazi brushes the blood from his eyes and glares round on the dead. "All! Slaughterer," he cries.

"All save two, my brother," comes the answer, sounding above the clash of steel and the sound of smitten shields.

Now the Wolf would come to him, but cannot, for his life ebbs.

"Fare you well, my brother! Death is good! Thus, indeed, I would die, for I have made me a mat of men to lie on," he cried with a great voice.

"Fare you well! Sleep softly, Wolf!" came the answer. "All save one!"

Now Galazi fell dying on the dead, but he was not altogether gone, for he still spoke. "All save one! Ha! ha! ill for that one then when Groan-Maker yet is up. It is well to have lived so to die. Victory! Victory!"

And Galazi the Wolf struggled to his knees and for the last time shook the Watcher about his head, then fell again and died.

Umslopogaas, the son of Chaka, and Faku, the captain of Dingaan, gazed on each other. They alone were left standing upon the mountain, for the rest were all down. Umslopogaas had many wounds. Faku was unhurt; he was a strong man, also armed with an axe.

Faku laughed aloud. "So it has come to this, Slaughterer," he said, "that you and I must settle whether the king's word be done or no. Well, I will say that however it should fall out, I count it a great fortune to have seen this fight, and the highest of honors to have had to do with two such warriors. Rest you a little, Slaughterer, before we close. That wolf-brother of yours died well, and if it is given me to conquer in this bout, I will tell the tale of his end from kraal to kraal throughout the land, and it shall be a tale forever."

Chapter XXXIV

THE LILY'S FAREWELL

*U*mslopogaas listened, but he made no answer to the words of Faku the captain, though he liked them well, for he would not waste his breath in talking, and the light grew low.

"I am ready, Man of Dingaan," he said, and lifted his axe.

Now for awhile the two circled round and round, each waiting for a chance to strike. Presently Faku smote at the head of Umslopogaas, but the Slaughterer lifted Groan-Maker to ward the blow. Faku crooked his arm and let the axe curl downwards, so that its keen edge smote Umslopogaas upon the head, severing his man's ring and the scalp beneath.

Made mad with the pain, the Slaughterer awoke, as it were. He grasped Groan-maker with both hands and struck thrice. The first blow hewed away the plumes and shield of Faku, and drive him back a spear's length, the second missed its aim, the third and mightiest twisted in his wet hands, so that the axe smote sideways. Nevertheless, it fell full on the breast of the captain Faku, shattering his bones, and sweeping him from the ledge of rock on to the slope beneath, where he lay still.

"It is finished with the daylight," said Umslopogaas, smiling grimly. "Now, Dingaan, send more Slayers to seek your slain," and he turned to find Nada in the cave.

But Faku the captain was not yet dead, though he was hurt to death. He sat up, and with his last strength he hurled the axe in his hand at him whose might had prevailed against him. The axe sped true, and Umslopogaas did not see it fly. It sped true, and its point struck him on the left temple, driving in the bone and making a great hole. Then Faku fell back dying, and Umslopogaas threw up his arms and dropped like an ox drops beneath the blow of the butcher, and lay as one dead, under the shadow of a stone.

All day long Nada crouched in the cave listening to the sounds of
war that crept faintly up the mountain side; howling of wolves, shouting
of men, and the clamor of iron on iron. All day long she sat, and now
evening came apace, and the noise of battle drew near, swelled, and sank,
and died away. She heard the voices of the Wolf-Brethren as they called
to each other like bucks, naming the number of the slain. She heard
Galazi's cry of "Victory!" and her heart leapt to it, though she knew that
there was death in the cry. Then for the last time she heard the faint
ringing of iron on iron, and the light went out and all grew still.

All grew still as the night. There came no more shouting of men and
no more clash of arms, no howlings of wolves, no cries of pain or
triumph — all was quiet as death, for death had taken all.

For awhile Nada the Lily sat in the dark of the cave, saying to herself,
"Presently he will come, my husband, he will surely come; the Slayers
are slain — he does not but tarry to bind his wounds; a scratch, perchance,
here and there. Yes, he will come, and it is well, for I am weary of my
loneliness, and this place is grim and evil."

Thus she spoke to herself in hope, but nothing came except the
silence. Then she spoke again, and her voice echoed in the hollow cave.
"Now I will be bold, I will fear nothing, I will push aside the stone and
go out to find him. I know well he does but linger to tend some who
are wounded, perhaps Galazi. Doubtless Galazi is wounded. I must go
and nurse him, though he never loved me, and I do not love him
overmuch who would stand between me and my husband. This wild
wolf-man is a foe to women, and, most of all, a foe to me; yet I will be
kind to him. Come, I will go at once," and she rose and pushed at the
rock.

Why, what was this? It did not stir. Then she remembered that she
had pulled it beyond the socket because of her fear of the wolf, and that
the rock had slipped a little way down the neck of the cave. Umslopogaas
had told her that she must not do this, and she had forgotten his words
in her foolishness. Perhaps she could move the stone; no, not by the
breadth of a grain of corn. She was shut in, without food or water, and
here she must bide till Umslopogaas came. And if he did not come?
Then she must surely die.

Now she shrieked aloud in her fear, calling on the name of
Umslopogaas. The walls of the cave answered "Umslopogaas!
Umslopogaas!" and that was all.

Afterwards madness fell upon Nada, my daughter, and she lay in the
cave for days and nights, nor knew ever how long she lay. And with her
madness came visions, for she dreamed that the dead One whom Galazi

had told her of sat once more aloft in his niche at the end of the cave and spoke to her, saying: —

"Galazi is dead! The fate of him who bears the Watcher has fallen on him. Dead are the ghost-wolves; I also am of hunger in this cave, and as I died so shall you die, Nada the Lily! Nada, Star of Death! because of whose beauty and foolishness all this death has come about."

This is seemed to Nada, in her madness, that the shadow of him who had sat in the niche spoke to her from hour to hour.

It seemed to Nada, in her madness, that twice the light shone through the hole by the rock, and that was day, and twice it went out, and that was night. A third time the ray shone and died away, and lo! her madness left her, and she awoke to know that she was dying, and that a voice she loved spoke without the hole, saying in hollow accents: —

"Nada? Do you still live, Nada?"

"Yea," she answered hoarsely. "Water! give me water!"

Next she heard a sound as of a great snake dragging itself along painfully. A while passed, then a trembling hand thrust a little gourd of water through the hole. She drank, and now she could speak, though the water seemed to flow through her veins like fire.

"Is it indeed you, Umslopogaas?" she said, "or are you dead, and do I dream of you?"

"It is I, Nada," said the voice. "Hearken! have you drawn the rock home?"

"Alas! yes," she answered. "Perhaps, if the two of us strive at it, it will move."

"Aye, if our strength were what it was — but now! Still, let us try."

So they strove with a rock, but the two of them together had not the strength of a girl, and it would not stir.

"Give over, Umslopogaas," said Nada; "we do but waste the time that is left to me. Let us talk!"

For awhile there was no answer, for Umslopogaas had fainted, and Nada beat her breast, thinking that he was dead.

Presently he spoke, however, saying, "It may not be; we must perish here, one on each side of the stone, not seeing the other's face, for my might is as water; nor can I stand upon my feet to go and seek for food."

"Are you wounded, Umslopogaas?" asked Nada.

"Aye, Nada, I am pierced to the brain with the point of an axe; no fair stroke, the captain of Dingaan hurled it at me when I thought him dead, and I fell. I do not know how long I have lain yonder under the shadow of the rock, but it must be long, for my limbs are wasted, and those who fell in the fray are picked clean by the vultures, all except Galazi, for the old wolf Deathgrip lies on his breast dying, but not dead, licking my brother's wounds, and scares the fowls away. It was the beak of a vulture, who had smelt me out at last, that woke me from my sleep beneath the stone, Nada, and I crept hither. Would that he had not awakened me, would that I had died as I lay, rather than lived a little while till you perish thus, like a trapped fox, Nada, and presently I follow you."

"It is hard to die so, Umslopogaas," she answered, "I who am yet young and fair, who love you, and hoped to give you children; but so it has come about, and it may not be put away. I am well-nigh sped, husband; horror and fear have conquered me, my strength fails, but I suffer little. Let us talk no more of death, let us rather speak of our childhood, when we wandered hand in hand; let us talk also of our love, and of the happy hours that we have spent since your great axe rang upon the rock in the Halakazi caves, and my fear told you the secret of my womanhood. See, I thrust my hand through the hole; can you not kiss it, Umslopogaas?"

Now Umslopogaas stooped his shattered head, and kissed the Lily's little hand, then he held it in his own, and so they sat till the end – he without, resting his back against the rock, she within, lying on her side, her arm stretched through the little hole. They spoke of their love, and tried to forget their sorrow in it; he told her also of the fray which had been and how it went.

"Ah!" she said, "that was Zinita's work, Zinita who hated me, and justly. Doubtless she set Dingaan on this path."

"A little while gone," quoth Umslopogaas; "and I hoped that your last breath and mine might pass together, Nada, and that we might go together to seek great Galazi, my brother, where he is. Now I hope that help will find me, and that I may live a little while, because of a certain vengeance which I would wreak."

"Speak not of vengeance, husband," she answered, "I, too, am near to that land where the Slayer and the Slain, the Shedder of Blood and the Avenger of Blood are lost in the same darkness. I would die with love, and love only, in my heart, and your name, and yours only, on my lips, so that if anywhere we live again it shall be ready to spring forth to greet you. Yet, husband, it is in my heart that you will not go with me, but that you shall live on to die the greatest of deaths far away from here, and because of another woman. It seems that, as I lay in the dark of this cave, I saw you, Umslopogaas, a great man, gaunt and grey, stricken to the death, and the axe Groan-maker wavering aloft, and many a man dead upon a white and shimmering way, and about you the fair faces of white women; and you had a hole in your forehead, husband, on the left side."

"That is like to be true, if I live," he answered, "for the bone of my temple is shattered."

Now Nada ceased speaking, and for a long while was silent; Umslopogaas was also silent and torn with pain and sorrow because he must lose the Lily thus, and she must die so wretchedly, for one reason only, that the cast of Faku had robbed him of his strength. Alas! he who had done many deeds might not save her now; he could scarcely hold himself upright against the rock. He thought of it, and the tears flowed down his face and fell on to the hand of the Lily. She felt them fall and spoke.

"Weep not, my husband," she said, "I have been all too ill a wife to you. Do not mourn for me, yet remember that I loved you well." And again she was silent for a long space.

Then she spoke and for the last time of all, and her voice came in a gasping whisper through the hole in the rock: —

"Farewell, Umslopogaas, my husband and my brother, I thank you for your love, Umslopogaas. Ah! I die!"

Umslopogaas could make no answer, only he watched the little hand he held. Twice it opened, twice it closed upon his own, then it opened for the third time, turned grey, quivered, and was still forever!

Now it was at the hour of dawn that Nada died.

Chapter XXXV
THE VENGEANCE OF MOPO AND HIS FOSTERLING

It chanced that on this day of Nada's death and at that same hour of dawn I, Mopo, came from my mission back to the kraal of the People of the Axe, having succeeded in my end, for that great chief whom I had gone out to visit had hearkened to my words. As the light broke I reached the town, and lo! it was a blackness and a desolation.

"Here is the footmark of Dingaan," I said to myself, and walked to and fro, groaning heavily. Presently I found a knot of men who were of the people that had escaped the slaughter, hiding in the mealie-fields lest the Slayers should return, and from them I drew the story. I listened in silence, for, my father, I was grown old in misfortune; then I asked where were the Slayers of the king? They replied that they did not know; the soldiers had gone up the Ghost Mountain after the Wolf-Brethren and Nada the Lily, and from the forest had come a howling of beasts and sounds of war; then there was silence, and none had been seen to return from the mountain, only all day long the vultures hung over it.

"Let us go up the mountain," I said.

At first they feared, because of the evil name of the place; but in the end they came with me, and we followed on the path of the *impi* of the Slayers and guessed all that had befallen it. At length we reached the knees of stone, and saw the place of the great fight of the Wolf-Brethren. All those who had taken part in that fight were now but bones, because the vultures had picked them every one, except Galazi, for on the breast of Galazi lay the old wolf Deathgrip, that was yet alive. I drew near the body, and the great wolf struggled to his feet and ran at me with bristling hair and open jaws, from which no sound came. Then, being spent, he rolled over dead.

Now I looked round seeking the axe Groan-Maker among the bones of the slain, and did not find it and the hope came into my heart that Umslopogaas had escaped the slaughter. Then we went on in silence to where I knew the cave must be, and there by its mouth lay the body of a man. I ran to it — it was Umslopogaas, wasted with hunger, and in his temple was a great wound and on his breast and limbs were many other wounds. Moreover, in his hand he held another hand — a dead hand, that was thrust through a hole in the rock. I knew its shape well — it was the little hand of my child, Nada the Lily.

Now I understood, and, bending down, I felt the heart of Umslopogaas, and laid the down of an eagle upon his lips. His heart still stirred and the down was lifted gently.

I bade those with me drag the stone, and they did so with toil. Now the light flowed into the cave, and by it we saw the shape of Nada my daughter. She was somewhat wasted, but still very beautiful in her death. I felt her heart also: it was still, and her breast grew cold.

Then I spoke: "The dead to the dead. Let us tend the living."

So we bore in Umslopogaas, and I caused broth to be made and poured it down his throat; also I cleansed his great wound and bound healing herbs upon it, plying all my skill. Well I knew the arts of healing, my father; I who was the first of the *izinyanga* of medicine, and, had it not been for my craft, Umslopogaas had never lived, for he was very near his end. Still, there where he had once been nursed by Galazi the Wolf, I brought him back to life. It was three days till he spoke, and, before his sense returned to him, I caused a great hole to be dug in the floor of the cave. And there, in the hole, I buried Nada my daughter, and we heaped lily blooms upon her to keep the earth from her, and then closed in her grave, for I was not minded that Umslopogaas should look upon her dead, lest he also should die from the sight, and because of his desire to follow her. Also I buried Galazi the Wolf in the cave, and set the Watcher in his hand, and there they both sleep who are friends at last, the Lily and the Wolf together. Ah! when shall there be such another man and such another maid?

At length on the third day Umslopogaas spoke, asking for Nada. I pointed to the earth, and he remembered and understood. Thereafter the strength of Umslopogaas gathered on him slowly, and the hole in his skull skinned over. But now his hair was grizzled, and he scarcely smiled again, but grew even more grim and stern than he had been before.

Soon we learned all the truth about Zinita, for the women and children came back to the town of the People of the Axe, only Zinita and the children of Umslopogaas did not come back. Also a spy reached me from the Mahlabatine and told me of the end of Zinita and of the flight of Dingaan before the Boers.

Now when Umslopogaas had recovered, I asked him what he would do, and whether or not I should pursue my plots to make him king of the land.

But Umslopogaas shook his head, saying that he had no heart that way. He would destroy a king indeed, but now he no longer desired to be a king. He sought revenge alone. I said that it was well, I also sought vengeance, and seeking together we would find it.

Now, my father, there is much more to tell, but shall I tell it? The snow has melted, your cattle have been found where I told you they should be, and you wish to be gone. And I also, I would be gone upon a longer journey.

Listen, my father, I will be short. This came into my mind: to play off Panda against Dingaan; it was for such an hour of need that I had saved Panda alive. After the battle of the Blood River, Dingaan summoned Panda to a hunt. Then it was that I journeyed to the kraal of Panda on the Lower Tugela, and with me Umslopogaas. I warned Panda that he should not go to this hunt, for he was the game himself, but that he should rather fly into Natal with all his people. He did so, and then I opened talk with the Boers, and more especially with that Boer who was named Ungalunkulu, or Great Arm. I showed the Boer that Dingaan was wicked and not to be believed, but Panda was faithful and good. The end of it was that the Boers and Panda made war together on Dingaan. Yes, I made that war that we might be revenged on Dingaan. Thus, my father, do little things lead to great.

Were we at the big fight, the battle of Magongo? Yes, my father; we were there. When Dingaan's people drove us back, and all seemed lost, it was I who put into the mind of Nongalaza, the general, to pretend to direct the Boers where to attack, for the Amaboona stood out of that fight, leaving it to us black people. It was Umslopogaas who cut his way with Groan-Maker through a wing of one of Dingaan's regiments till he came to the Boer captain Ungalunkulu, and shouted to him to turn the flank of Dingaan. That finished it, my father, for they feared to stand against us both, the white and the black together. They fled, and we followed and slew, and Dingaan ceased to be a king.

He ceased to be a king, but he still lived, and while he lived our vengeance was hungry. So we went to the Boer captain and to Panda, and spoke to them nicely, saying, "We have served you well, we have fought for you, and so ordered things that victory is yours. Now grant us this request, that we may follow Dingaan, who has fled into hiding, and kill him wherever we find him, for he has worked us wrong, and we would avenge it."

Then the white captain and Panda smiled and said, "Go children, and prosper in your search. No one thing shall please us more than to know that Dingaan is dead." And they gave us men to go with us.

Then we hunted that king week by week as men hunt a wounded buffalo. We hunted him to the jungles of the Umfalozi and through them. But he fled ever, for he knew that the avengers of blood were on his spoor. After that for awhile we lost him. Then we heard that he had crossed the Pongolo with some of the people who still clung to him. We followed him to the place Kwa Myawo, and there we lay hid in the bush watching. At last our chance came. Dingaan walked in the bush and with him two men only. We stabbed the men and seized him.

Dingaan looked at us and knew us, and his knees trembled with fear. Then I spoke: —

"What was that message which I sent thee, O Dingaan, who art no more a king — that thou didst evil to drive me away, was it not? because I set thee on thy throne and I alone could hold thee there?"

He made no answer, and I went on: —

"I, Mopo, son of Makedama, set thee on thy throne, O Dingaan, who wast a king, and I, Mopo, have pulled thee down from thy throne. But my message did not end there. It said that, ill as thou hadst done to drive me away, yet worse shouldst thou do to look upon my face again, for that day should be thy day of doom."

Still he made no answer. Then Umslopogaas spoke: —

"I am that Slaughterer, O Dingaan, no more a king, whom thou didst send Slayers many and fierce to eat up at the kraal of the People of the Axe. Where are thy Slayers now, O Dingaan? Before all is done thou shalt look upon them."

"Kill me and make an end; it is your hour," said Dingaan.

"Not yet awhile, O son of Senzangacona," answered Umslopogaas, "and not here. There lived a certain woman and she was named Nada the Lily. I was her husband, O Dingaan, and Mopo here, he was her father. But, alas! she died, and sadly — she lingered three days and nights before she died. Thou shalt see the spot and hear the tale, O Dingaan. It will wring thy heart, which was ever tender. There lived certain children, born of another woman named Zinita, little children, sweet and loving. I was their father, O Elephant in a pit, and one Dingaan slew them. Of them thou shalt hear also. Now away, for the path is far!"

Two days went by, my father, and Dingaan sat bound and alone in the cave on Ghost Mountain. We had dragged him slowly up the mountain, for he was heavy as an ox. Three men pushing at him and three others pulling on a cord about his middle, we dragged him up, staying now and again to show him the bones of those whom he had sent out to kill us, and telling him the tale of that fight.

Now at length we were in the cave, and I sent away those who were with us, for we wished to be alone with Dingaan at the last. He sat down on the floor of the cave, and I told him that beneath the earth on which he sat lay the bones of that Nada whom he had murdered and the bones of Galazi the Wolf.

On the third day before the dawn we came again and looked upon him.

"Slay me," he said, "for the Ghosts torment me!"

"No longer art thou great, O shadow of a king," I said, "who now dost tremble before two Ghosts out of all the thousands that thou hast made. Say, then, how shall it fare with thee presently when thou art of their number?"

Now Dingaan prayed for mercy.

"Mercy, thou hyena!" I answered, "thou prayest for mercy who showed none to any! Give me back my daughter. Give this man back his wife and children; then we will talk of mercy. Come forth, coward, and die the death of cowards."

So, my father, we dragged him out, groaning, to the cleft that is above in the breast of the old Stone Witch, that same cleft where Galazi had found the bones. There we stood, waiting for the moment of the dawn, that hour when Nada had died. Then we cried her name into his ears and the names of the children of Umslopogaas, and cast him into the cleft.

This was the end of Dingaan, my father — Dingaan, who had the fierce heart of Chaka without its greatness.

Chapter XXXVI
MOPO ENDS HIS TALE

*T*hat is the tale of Nada the Lily, my father, and of how we avenged her. A sad tale — yes, a sad tale; but all was sad in those days. It was otherwise afterwards, when Panda reigned, for Panda was a man of peace.

There is little more to tell. I left the land where I could stay no longer who had brought about the deaths of two kings, and came here to Natal to live near where the kraal Duguza once had stood.

The bones of Dingaan as they lay in the cleft were the last things my eyes beheld, for after that I became blind, and saw the sun no more, nor any light — why I do not know, perhaps from too much weeping, my father. So I changed my name, lest a spear might reach the heart that had planned the death of two kings and a prince — Chaka, Dingaan, and Umhlangana of the blood royal. Silently and by night Umslopogaas, my fosterling, led me across the border, and brought me here to Stanger; and here as an old witch-doctor I have lived for many, many years. I am rich. Umslopogaas craved back from Panda the cattle of which Dingaan had robbed me, and drove them hither. But none were here who had lived in the kraal Duguza, none knew, in Zweete the

blind old witch-doctor, that Mopo who stabbed Chaka, the Lion of the
Zulu. None know it now. You have heard the tale, and you alone, my
father. Do not tell it again till I am dead.

Umslopogaas? Yes, he went back to the People of the Axe and ruled
them, but they were never so strong again as they had been before they
smote the Halakazi in their caves, and Dingaan ate them up. Panda let
him be and liked him well, for Panda did not know that the Slaughterer
was son to Chaka his brother, and Umslopogaas let that dog lie, for
when Nada died he lost his desire to be great. Yet he became captain of
the Nkomabakosi regiment, and fought in many battles, doing mighty
deeds, and stood by Umbulazi, son of Panda, in the great fray on the
Tugela, when Cetywayo slew his brother Umbulazi.

After that also he plotted against Cetywayo, whom he hated, and had
it not been for a certain white man, a hunter named Macumazahn,
Umslopogaas would have been killed. But the white man saved him by
his wit. Yes, and at times he came to visit me, for he still loved me as of
old; but now he has fled north, and I shall hear his voice no more. Nay,
I do not know all the tale; there was a woman in it. Women were ever
the bane of Umslopogaas, my fostering. I forget the story of that woman,
for I remember only these things that happened long ago, before I grew
very old.

Look on this right hand of mine, my father! I cannot see it now; and
yet I, Mopo, son of Makedama, seem to see it as once I saw, red with
the blood of two kings. Look on —

Suddenly the old man ceased, his head fell forward upon his withered
breast. When the White Man to whom he told this story lifted it and
looked at him, he was dead!

Lightning Source UK Ltd.
Milton Keynes UK
UKOW04f0626050118

315595UK00001B/78/P

9 781598 185508